Frankie slipped the
wall system. Whatever was on it, the sound quality
would be terrific.

The tape kicked in, and the killer's voice cut
through the room like shrapnel. 'Mr Chapelle?'

'Yes?'

'Listen to me now. I won't be repeatin' and I won't
be on long, neither.' You could hear him breathing;
he was frightened. I thought he sounded like a dangerous man, over and above the evidence of his having
shot Freddo three times at point-blank range.

'We're holdin' your brother and we want a hundred
million for him . . .' You could hear a collective
inhalation in the room and Glen swearing under
his breath on the tape. '. . . New bills, none over
a hundred. We'll watch the news for your answer
before we contact you again. If you don't give us
the money we'll kill him.'

Palm Monday

James David Buchanan

NEW ENGLISH LIBRARY
Hodder and Stoughton

First published in Great Britain in 1995
by Hodder and Stoughton
A division of Hodder Headline PLC
This New English Library paperback edition 1995

10 9 8 7 6 5 4 3 2 1

British Library Cataloguing in Publication Data

Buchanan, James David
Palm Monday
I. Title
823 [F]

ISBN 0 340 62898 7

Typeset by Hewer Text Composition Services, Edinburgh
Printed and bound in Great Britain by
Cox & Wyman, Reading, Berks.

Hodder and Stoughton
A division of Hodder Headline PLC
338 Euston Road
London NW1 3BH

To Irwin Bloom
For his work in Nighttown . . .

'They were careless people, Tom and Daisy – they smashed up things and creatures and then retreated back into their money or their vast carelessness, or whatever it was that kept them together, and let other people clean up the mess they had made . . .'

– Gatsby

I

SEAN

I wasn't there but I'd been there before, and knew them better than they knew themselves. Which I guess is a way of saying I didn't know them at all. What we all understood were interests. They also had manners of a sort. I have no doubt I can call up that night and march it before you with considerable accuracy.

Dinner over, the guests would have begun to chew on each other. Or what was usually safer, the less effulgent world beyond the neighborhood.

'. . . driving a Silver Cloud, for God sakes. Right on the Avenue near Donald Bruce . . .'

Imagine the speaker, a middle-aged woman with the darkest overall tan in a company marked by complexions burnt mahogany through ebony. She would have meant 'Worth Avenue' – there was no other.

Tapping blood-red fingernails as relentlessly as tribal drums against the stem of her wine glass: '. . . and when he got out he's wearing all this incredible truly tacky jewelry. Enough to stock an Arab bazaar, honestly.'

Herself wearing earrings, a necklace, pin, Rolex, two bracelets and three rings, but the right sort. And the pink Chanel suit compensatorily understated.

'He had a long fingernail on each hand – the pinkie, I think – like a Chinese person.'

Her husband leans close, pretending to confide. 'That's for measuring the "blow," darling.'

But a young woman with spectacular breasts is contemptuous. 'Measure, hell – shovel.' Someone across the table laughs knowingly. She turns to her escort, a young man wearing jeans and three earrings in one ear, whispering, 'Where has this person been?'

'I don't care. It was so hideous it made me shudder.'

'Quell' apparition!' exclaims a native of Detroit.

'Maybe he was in show business,' her husband suggests.

'No, he was dark, like a Colombian. I'm sure it was something like that. They have all the money in the world now, those people.'

The clash of silver and Spode as dinner is removed from the table. Smoke from the many candles melds with that of cigarettes and Havanas. These people still smoke a lot; probably it's some kind of statement. Port and Napoleon on the way now. The conversation continues in that tone which suggests great importance given to trivial matters.

James Chapelle, the host, is accepting of but indifferent to what has characterized his meals since he was first allowed to leave the servants and sit at table with his parents. He finds himself idly staring at the painting of a severe Spanish duke (as if there was any other kind) over the marble fireplace. Sixteenth or seventeenth century? He can't remember, can't even remember how it came to be where it is. Mother's family?

Tonight, thought drifting, the figure seems particularly judgmental with its uplifted aquiline features and contemptuous mouth. Come to think of it, it looks like Mother. Does the duke/mother particularly disapprove of this society, or just James? He peers down the long table through the smoke for a greater miscreant than himself among the guests, and decides there are many.

Despite the ancient formality of the room – the dark paneled walls, heavy Spanish furniture, chandeliers and Austrian drapes – the diners are mostly in resort wear, two duck-rows of flowered prints and blazers and Sperry

Topsiders confronting over a three-hundred-year-old lace cloth. Make a good whiskey ad, James thinks.

'If only we could build a wall like the Great Wall of China,' says a plump woman at the other end of the table, flapping a jeweled fan in rebuke of the lack of air-conditioning, 'between here and Miami.'

Her escort, a young man with an accent of Middle European origin, says in a stage whisper, 'Some Jew would only come along and sell it brick by brick, like the Berlin Wall.'

She turns on him and smiles oversweetly. 'No wonder you lost your little country, dear.' Then whispers, 'There's one here!' Petty bourgeois despite his silly title; she should have come with her ex-husband.

James wipes his mouth with a linen napkin, puts it down definitively and seeks his wife's attention. He had seen a *National Geographic* special about leopards and imagines that he had looked into her eyes then. Splendid, lustrous, at-rest-from-killing eyes in a face all slopes, angles and thrusts. Sylvia as a beautiful leopard – perfect. I know, because he once said those things to me in darker circumstances. He adores her despite everything, and always had.

'Sorry, dear. It's time.'

His wife is aware that he is speaking to her but gives nothing back. Staring, just as a great cat would. She notes his smile, the same one he wears when losing at roulette or baccarat. She had told a friend that he was as beautiful as Dorian Gray 'before the paint hardened.' The friend was puzzled.

Thirteen years older than she at fifty-two, he also appeared either younger or maybe just weaker. Or as his mother would have said, 'attentuated.' 'Leached,' he would joke, or 'overbred.' He could always joke about himself and always people liked him. Sylvia thought of herself as either loved or hated, but never liked; she preferred it that way.

Finally she asks, 'The cake?'

'Can't.' Still smiling, he stands.

At the other end of the table, 'Thank God my children aren't in the public schools these days.'

An Italian race-car driver calls out, 'Darling, your children haven't been in the public schools for two hundred years,' and everyone laughs whether they're amused or not, because it represents group solidarity.

James breaks in, announcing, 'Sorry, you'll have to forgive me. I'm off, as advertised.'

'Do you have to, lover?'

'Oh, James, you can't!'

'To hell with it, c'mon and stay . . .'

He's already moving along the table, kissing hands and cheeks, clapping shoulders. 'Six a.m. meeting at the airport in Miami . . . Company president laying over . . . On to Caracas . . . Only chance to talk . . .'

As he passes, the wife of a world-class yachtsman bobs close to her husband. 'I love his lies, they're so elaborate. Most of you don't even try.'

The husband belches softly, unimpressed.

Sylvia watches her husband's progress along the table, the only one in the room without some form of smile, and is watched in turn by the small, precise man beside her. His face is too alert to belong. And he's dressed too well. Parvenu.

'You'd think the CEO would know about that meeting, wouldn't you? If I had, I could have taken it.'

She turns to see if he is being ironic, prepared to tear off a piece, but he manages to look simply charitable. No one has ever been able to read Michael Duchow's face since the obstetrician who witnessed it first emerging. Probably a mixed blessing in society but a definite asset in business, and his was running the Chapelle family corporation. Running it well for a change.

Sylvia, I happen to know, called him 'the ferret' when

he first came aboard, detesting him, perhaps because they were both born poor. James had insisted she be agreeable, the man was important to them. Later, after she discovered what a proper and cunning bastard Duchow could be, I believe she felt more positive.

At the door James stops and turns to wave goodbyè and promises to return the next day. He won't. Sylvia calls perfunctorily to him to be careful. Then he's gone.

The plump woman calls down, 'Syl, you're an absolute saint to let him go on your anniversary.'

Someone else says, 'She'll get her reward in heaven.'

Sylvia smiles at no one in particular and murmurs, 'Or hell.'

Freddo drives the Mercedes SL up the extended white driveway to the front portico. He gets out and waits, sweating in the autumn heat, rolling his buffalo shoulders to loosen them. His uniform is limited to a dark jacket and tie, but even that much formality seems alien to his bent face with its layers of scar tissue and ears that dangle like something chewed.

Bored easily, he glances at his watch, reads ten-thirty, grunts, lights a cigarette and jams it in his mouth to stay. As other men seek unconsciously for their wallets, he gives his jacket a quick press to confirm the presence of the 9mm in its shoulder holster.

The estate has been in the possession of the Chapelles for most of this century, an archetypal 'Addison Mizner' or 'Mediterranean Revival,' that peculiar breed which distinguishes Palm Beach from the other kraals of the old rich on the slick pages of up-scale magazines. Managing to be both respectable and flamboyant with enough show-off plumage to please a Medici, they sit confronting a sea that seems always sun-washed or moon-lit with battalions of royal palms standing sentinel over huge aprons of the lushest and yet best manicured lawns in the world.

Freddo is unimpressed; he thinks it's funny-looking and

would prefer to live in closer proximity to cabstands and kiosks, delis and cooking tar, and certainly a different climate. He wipes his New York face and waits as muffled voices drift down from the doorway on the moist tropical air, James saying something to one of the servants as he departs.

Freddo flips his cigarette out on to the perfect grass and goes around to open the passenger door. James trots towards him in his boyish way, greets him with a simple, 'Good evening, Freddo.'

'Mr Chapelle.'

There was never much conversation between them but the bodyguard had told me that James was okay as bosses go. Just strange, he had never figured him out. The man seemed to have everything and nothing. Instructions are unnecessary; Freddo knows where they're going. The rest of the world would have to wonder.

They cross to the mainland on the Royal Palm Bridge, continue across Clear Lake on Okeechobee Boulevard, headed due west. They turn south finally on a familiar but little-used country road. After a while it is very dark with few buildings and mainly scrub on both sides of the road. There are swamps marginal to the Everglades close on the right. Freddo thinks the route absurdly cautious and can't understand why they can't use the expressway or turnpike, but it's always been like this.

In back of Boca Raton they turn west again on an unfinished macadam road. James is sleeping with his head against the side window. He grunts unhappily at the bouncing. Freddo, hoping not to wake him, mutters, 'Sorry, sir.'

They round a sharp curve and suddenly an accident scene appears to rocket into their headlights. Directly in front of them an old Cadillac is slanted across the road. The body of a man is sprawled face down in front of it. If all this were not revealed in microseconds, the fact that the body is placed in the geometric center of the pavement rather than in logical proximity to the only agape door would send a signal to a man practiced in violence.

Freddo hits the brake pedal with all two hundred and twenty pounds, simultaneously shooting out his right hand to separate his employer from the windshield. He has little faith in seat belts; an invention of the wussy class. James's eyes snap open.

They bellow, 'Shit!' like brothers, as the Merc fishtails and finally jerks to a stop, askew like the Cadillac.

'I'm sorry, Mr Chapelle. The curve back there . . .'

James strains to look ahead, his voice still thick with sleep and fear. 'My, God, look . . .!'

Freddo, the old soldier of so many disreputable wars, is already unwisely climbing out. James recovers quickly and follows.

As the chauffeur approaches, already hunching towards the prone figure, the man's head pops up wearing a stocking mask. His left hand snakes out from beneath his body and hefts a pistol until the bore looms huge on a line with Freddo's eyes.

'Happy anniversary, motherfucker,' he says cheerfully to James with a trace of an Irish accent.

The two moving figures freeze momentarily, and it must have seemed as if everything that constitutes a Florida night in the vicinity of the Everglades – birds, insects, savage cries and whimpers, distant traffic – had somehow gone silent. The whole world stopped; the tableau before the tragedy.

I have reason to think it went something like that.

The next morning I awoke at nine under protest. I don't know to whom; someone. Mine's a nocturnal soul and fortunately I have the kind of job where schedule is less important than some other things. In the back of my mind was the neighbor's dog as the disturber. Or maybe it was simply garbage morning.

I tried to sneak out for the *Herald* in shorts and a t-shirt, but she was laying for me at the top of the driveway. I live on the frayed edge of Coral Gables, a suburb of Miami. Not many single men want to come home to a little yellow stucco bungalow in a neighborhood as dull as decaf, but I embrace its quietude, it gives me a measure of stability. Also, it has opulent, forgiving flora and even a brown-thumb like me can bury his nerves in casual gardening without laying waste the landscape.

'You're late.'

'I've got time, Mrs Cardoza . . . give him a good workout.' No day should start without coffee and the sports page.

'You better. Ees bowels no been too good lately.' She emitted this amazingly loud, shrill whistle – the woman was seventy-five years old – and as always it was answered by a ratty hysterical mutt. It careened out from the house and raced all around us in frantic circles, dragging a leash. I regarded it through half-closed, glumphy eyes, then looked longingly at the house. She saw me and brought out the heavy stuff.

'Eet ees my arthritis.' She looked down, as if at a ravaged body, although it looked horse-healthy to me for one her age. 'You sure no ees big problemo, Mr Dunn?' As if she cared.

'No, no, I love the little fella.' I scooped up the leash and wrestled the dog to my Jeep. Dog and Jeep were a pair – old, unwashed, disreputable. 'Exercise is good for me. Gets the blood going, washes out the vitamins and minerals and other impurities.'

I heard her considered laugh as I got in the car; what a naughty man! When I drove off I noticed the mutt looking at me smugly. 'Your bowels better not improve in here, numbnuts, or I'll turn you into horsefood.' He grinned.

I usually took him out of town to a relatively deserted

road so I could stay in the car and trail the leash out the window. Here you could drive at less than five miles an hour and steer with your knees while balancing a styrofoam cup of coffee and a donut. Occasionally the dog would try to confound me by speeding up or slowing down.

'C'mon, Fidel, move it or lose it!' Señora Cardoza had the eccentric habit of constantly changing the dog's name, which might go a ways towards explaining its personality. I did my part to reduce alienation by consistently calling it after the flaky caudillo to the south.

The phone buzzed and in grabbing for it I spilled the coffee all over my shorts and running shoes. 'Dunn! Where the hell are you?'

'You made me spill my goddamned coffee.' Fortunately, the caller was a man tolerant of bad behavior before breakfast.

He was, however, sputtering. 'I need you. This is the biggest account we got, for Christ's sake. New York's goin' nuts.'

'What are you talking about?'

'Don't you watch TV? James Chapelle's been kidnapped.'

'No shit?' I hated to let him think that anything could shake me, but this did.

'Along with the driver, Freddo. Up in back of Boca Raton somewhere.'

'Why me?'

'Because they asked for you, why do you think? Now quit whackin' off and get your ass up to Palm Beach. Don't even come into the office.'

'I'm walking my neighbor's dog.'

'Kill it, and get going!'

'I don't want it, Emmett. Honest to Christ, give me— '

He had hung up. He always did. Suddenly the sweaty seat, the coffee stains, the coming rains and scrubby landscape, everything depressed me. I began to count the things I loved about my life, and when they depressed me too I knew I was depressed. Chapelles . . .

I braked and opened the passenger door. 'At your convenience. I'd like to go to work. Please.' At last he approved my tone, jumped in and sat up straight, looking ahead like any other passenger as we took off. At that moment I envied him his life.

FRANKIE

I looked at the beefy naked torso of this guy I'd known for three months and hardly knew, sprawled on the rumpled bed, heavy-bearded in the morning. The kind of man born to snore. It made me crazy. His cheeks bellowed when he breathed and one almost came up to meet the barrel of my police special.

'Wake up, sweetheart.' I said it sweetly, enticing him up to hell. My head ached, my eye hurt, I hadn't slept and I was getting my period. Very ragged and not a nice person.

He stiffened and fluttered his lips without opening his eyes. There was sweat on the upper one. He belched demurely, and I pulled away in revulsion. Jesus, Frankie, how could you? I knew how I could, but decided to take it out on him. I brought the gun back to nuzzle his temple.

'I wonder what color your brains are, you sonofabitch?' Again, it was softly said, toying with the moment, deciding, but it got through. Especially when I pulled back the hammer and it made that ominous click.

First his eyes snapped open like a terrified horse, then a volcanic realization brought him to a strangled cry. He started bolt upright but banged his head on that point of cold steel and flattened out. Good instincts for a drunk.

'Don't! It'll go off.' His eyes were vast now and pale with fear. 'Holy shit, Frankie, what are you doing? Don't joke.'

'What joke, sweetheart? I was awake all night trying to figure out whether I should kill you.'

He gasped, pleading, 'Why, for Christ's sake?! Why? C'mon, baby . . . shit . . .' The constricted, shrill voice in such a large man was ludicrous; his lack of dignity increased my disgust. For both of us.

I pointed to my bruised right eye. Not badly bruised, I've had worse, but poison for the soul. I lied shamelessly. 'Nobody's done that to me since my old man, and I almost got him.'

Breathing narrowly to control the panic, he was contrite. 'I was ripped. But you were too.'

'I didn't hit anybody.'

I don't know why, but the rage eased and I pulled the gun back a few inches. His breathing came closer to normal.

'You'd go to prison, lose your career. Is it worth it, for God's sakes?'

'Maybe not, but I got my standards. Piss-poor as they are.'

I had humiliated him; that seemed almost as satisfying as blood and a hell of a lot less dangerous. That thought enabled me to move a few feet back and lean against the arm of a chair. It always worked like that; so far, never over the edge. I admit I felt relieved.

He sat up, pulling the sheet over his wonderfuls, more out of vulnerability than modesty. I realized he was staring at me. I was naked under the robe and it had fallen open while I exercised this other kind of passion. Not happy with the idea that he had even touched my naked body, I wasn't going to let him drool over it now, so I closed the robe quickly. That was weak, like I should care?

He sat up on the edge of the bed, seemingly conflicted, but finally asked, 'Does this mean it's over?'

I laughed, I couldn't help myself, although the last thing I wanted was to appear good-natured. 'I'll tell you, a question that dumb makes the whole thing a lot easier.'

He wasn't amused. 'I ought to take that goddamned gun away from you.'

'In your dreams.' I waggled it, giving it life. 'Just get your pants on and get the hell out of here.'

He had made his gesture but now the heart leaked out of him and he began slamming himself into his clothes. 'You bitch. You can't threaten me. I'm a lawyer.'

'That was the main reason I was gonna shoot you.'

The phone rang. I backed up carefully, but finally lowered the gun – what was he going to do? 'Bodo.'

It was the Sheriff himself and, never having spoken directly to him before, I was paralyzed with nerves and excitement. 'Yessir.' I seemed to say that a lot in the next few minutes, but what he said in any detail eludes me still. I got the thrust though. 'It's my case?'

My lover, if that's what he was, three stupid months in my stupid life, hobbled out of the bedroom half dressed, only pausing in the doorway long enough to pass me a digital salute. Mr Class. At the moment I was too excited to have any feelings about it but after I had told the Sheriff I wouldn't let him down and was on my way, I began to think. The door slammed. I sat back and sighed, pressing my fingers to my temples.

'God, I do pick 'em.'

II

Of course, I had to go into the station, right into the Sheriff's office with all this brass, or lead might be more accurate, and hear what a wonderful thing it was they were doing in giving me this chance at a really big case, how it was their asses on the line – sure it was – and how much confidence they had in me. Chapelles were hot spit, they left no doubt.

My jerky captain, the Captain of Detectives, had never forgiven me for having two breasts and a vagina, but at least he's honest about it and you put up with a lot in police work. It was obvious he had been overruled in this instance, and later I found myself wondering why the hell they did want me on it? There was a preliminary briefing but I confess the adrenalin was taking my heart and mind out where the action was. Impetuosity has always been a weakness.

By the time I did get out to the crime scene somebody local had already given the order to haul the Mercedes out of the drainage ditch where the kidnappers had dumped it. It groaned like an old man coming, draped in kudzu, dripping muddy water. I stood in the middle of the road watching, scowling behind my shades, legs spread as wide as a female can to achieve authority, as spit and polish as a modest-length tailored summer suit in a neutral color allowed.

Maybe it had the right effect. A Boca Raton cop sounded a little worried when he called to me, 'Where you want it taken, Sergeant? Up to your place?'

13

JAMES DAVID BUCHANAN

'What I wanted was nothing should be touched till I got here.' Of course the fault really lay with all those politics and attitudes back at the station. They say women talk but men, especially when you put uniforms on them, can talk something to death where a woman would just get the hell on with it. But if you're going to serve in a town this rich, shit happens. At least they had decided I was the one to shovel it.

He shrugged in that special way, like every member of a force in the world; not my doing!

'Yeah, take it up to West Palm.'

Why did they even bother to dump it after the kidnapping, since the top had shown above the level of the roadbed? Some primitive idea of how to eliminate forensic stuff? Is that what we were dealing with here?

I heard a shout from down the road behind me. I looked and the Medical Examiner was waving at me. Somebody must have thought they spotted something or he wouldn't even have been out here. Behind him, a cluster of men were using a rope to drag a heavy object up the embankment from the same drainage canal fifty yards along.

You could feel if you couldn't hear the buzz of excitement, so I began to trot, never easy in heels, even the stumpy ones the Sheriff approves for female officers. Before I got there I could see they had an officer in a wet-suit and mask pushing it up from behind. 'Mud Man.' I don't know how he saw anything under there.

When they got it to the shoulder they flopped it over like a gaffed fish. A couple of the technicians put on rubber gloves, just like the big city, and one sensitive soul a mask. They began brushing away the weeds and dirt.

'Not bad for a floater,' the ME decided.

I stooped to get a closer look; one of the guys. It was green, bloated, half the face was shot away, another bleeder in the thorax. 'You boys get pretty relative, don't you.'

14

'Well, he's been under only twelve hours about and there's nothin' feedin' in there.'

One of the others said, 'We know what Chapelle had for dinner.'

'That's not him. Not with that face and wardrobe.'

A voice behind me said, 'That's Freddo, the chauffeur.' Then to the ME, 'Hi, Neddy . . . fellas . . .'

The ME grinned at him. They all grinned at him, and when I glanced over my shoulder Dunn was grinning. He always had that effect on people; it was irritating as hell.

Grinning, I decided, was what his face did best. He was maybe forty with a hard but not necessarily athletic body – that was okay, that could be said of me – but his face looked run-over. Later I found he liked to think he resembled Humphrey Bogart. Although I have to admit he wasn't any narcissist, wasn't in the least vain. Mostly he just looked run-over, used. For some reason people were made cheerful by that. He was wearing jeans, sneakers and a t-shirt that said: BIX LIVES! A message that eluded me at the time. I didn't like this at a murder scene.

'Who are you?'

'Sean Dunn.' He indicated the corpse. 'He's Freddo "Bad Eyes" Carfagno. Great name for a chauffeur, isn't it? I suppose it had another connotation.'

'*Who are you?!*'

'Ah. I work for Intersec Systems.' He could see that I disliked the sound of that – something in my chromosomes. 'Hey, it's a living. We handle corporate and family security for the Chapelles.'

I glanced at the car, looking like something the 'Glades had vomited, then at the corpse, who looked worse. 'Did a great job.'

He ignored that. 'They asked me to come up from Miami and investigate.'

'"Investigate"? Thank you, but the Sheriff's Department will do that, Mr Dunn. You've got no business here. Get

15

behind the barriers.' I pointed to one up the road, which set off a pack of shouting, gesticulating journalists. Preview of the mess to come. As much to avoid them, I started away quickly.

'Sergeant!'

I turned back very slowly, so he would get the idea.

'Chapelles want me here. They called the Sheriff. He thought it was a wonderful idea.'

He managed not to sound smug; I'll give him credit for that, he was never smug. I shook my head. 'Christ, you're all I need. What makes you so hot?'

He shrugged and grinned again. 'They like me. And I was a copper.'

This insane reasonableness was going to drive me nuts. As far as his history, I thought I remembered something hinky about him being on the Miami PD but to discuss it would suggest I cared. 'Where were you last night, Mr Dunn?'

'What do you mean? I was home. In Miami.'

'Alone?' At least I'd stopped his indiscriminate smiling.

He wiped his face with his hand; warm, humid morning. 'No, Madonna was over and brought some of her friends and we played "Battleship".'

'Let me show you.' I was on my own solid turf now. I walked him down the road. 'Look around. The actors just happened to be jammin' along down this godforsaken road in the middle of the night, and they just happen to see one of the richest dudes in the country cruising by and they say, "Boy, it's a good thing we got our guns with us, let's grab him"? Get real. An obvious set-up and who better than somebody who's supposed to be in charge of his security? Mr Dunn?'

'Sean. First of all, I'm not in charge of their security, the company is. I haven't even seen them in a couple years. But how do you know somebody wasn't tagging him? Forced him over?'

I took him over to some dark streaks on the pavement. Might as well get some fun out of this. 'Only one set of skid marks, the Merc's.' Pointing to where they stopped, I moved on. 'Chauffeur's shot here.' Obviously, the stain was the size of a small pond.

'Maybe that's Chapelle's blood.'

'We only got one shot-to-hell corpse, Mr Dunn, and one stain. Now what do you figure?' He gave up easily. I tracked the heel marks where the perpetrators dragged the body over to the ditch and dumped it in. 'Current carried it down there.'

'Doesn't seem to be much flow.'

'No, but when we enquire, and I will enquire, we will find out some truck farm or development or state agency to the north released some water into here during the night. You look a lot smarter than your questions, Mr Dunn, or do you get some kind of twisted thrill out of irritating me?'

SEAN

She was right; I was being a bit more dense than usual by way of holding her in conversation. I just hadn't been aware until called on it. She was a good-looking woman of about thirty, maybe early thirties since she was a sergeant. Not quite beautiful but striking. I liked watching her, seeing her move. What I think the French call a 'gamine,' unless those have to be short, because she wasn't. But with a real American edge to her – I liked that, too.

Her hair was black and worn in kind of bangs – not my area of expertise – and seemed to go well with brown eyes that were almost too large for her face. The skin was fair and there were a few freckles south of the eyes on either side of the nose. She did have a short person's impatience and enough energy to light Cleveland. The latter was obviously going to be a mixed blessing. Even

17

through the shades you could see trouble forming in the big eyes, for her and others.

I waved off her jab by way of submission and she went on, too pleased with herself to stop.

She showed with a gesture where the driver's door would have been. 'Bloodstains are placed consistent with the victim being the driver. Got out . . . came over . . . here. Chapelle must have got out too . . .'

'How do you know?'

She knelt to touch some shards marked by chalk circles on the pavement, two little spreads with a clear area running straight between. 'Stray bullet probably intended for the chauffeur if the shooter was over there. The passenger door had to be open, and I doubt they wanted to kill their meal ticket right off.'

'So you figure it was something on the road. Freddo came around the corner, hit the brakes— '

'Who hired him?'

She had taken off her Ray-Bans the better to give me the enforcer's stare, as if I hadn't been one myself. 'I did,' I told her cheerfully.

'He have a sheet?'

'Oh, hell, yes. Why don't we call him what he was; he wasn't a chauffeur just because he drove a car. And he had only one virtue, but it was loyalty. Didn't matter if you were a Mafia don or the President, he'd die for you.' I couldn't help glancing at the corpse. 'Which he seems to have done.'

'Frankie!'

She turned to look. It was her partner, Owen Metcalf, a black man of fifty or so with that certain gravity that goes with being a southerner, a veteran detective and a Baptist. I had met him, liked him; he didn't like me, I suspect, probably because he was a Baptist. Owen was the only one out here wearing a coat and tie in defiance of a sun near its zenith. He was actually frowning at me, or at me with her.

She waved in recognition, turned back. 'Try to stay out of the way, okay?'

'You sure it's a kidnapping for ransom?'

'Of course not, but it sure as hell looks like it, wouldn't you say?' When I didn't answer, she pushed. 'Well, what do you think it is?'

I was thinking, distracted. I shook my head. 'It's just that with people like this nothing's ever the way it looks.'

'"People like this?"'

'Remember something. The rich are pricks. Pricks who win.'

'What are you, a philosopher? And you're always smiling. I hate that in people. Especially in the morning.'

This time she did walk away from me. I watched her for a while, nice straight-ahead walk that carried a certain dignity without being masculine. I watched them until I satisfied myself that they were talking about me, and went about my business.

FRANKIE

When I'm walking back to join Owen, pulling off my gloves, I know Dunn's watching me. Not because I'm gorgeous, I'm not bad but I'm not gorgeous, but guys will watch a female moose if she's walking away from them. Here I was, with a life somewhere between fucked-up and zip, and I get my first big shot, my chance to make a world for myself I can live in, and I get stuck with this dumb bastard who's got a dubious past and is going to be reading my buns like an encyclopedia every time I turn my back on him. By the time I reached my partner I wished I'd shot the lawyer.

Owen was still frowning when I got there. 'I'd avoid him if I was you.'

'Chapelle family wants him. Talked to our leader. What's wrong with him?'

'He doesn't care. And you do.'

'If you mean as a boyfriend, forget it. I'm not having those any more.'

His tolerant look did everything except pat me on the head and say, 'There, there, young lady.' It wasn't sexism but I guess it was paternalism. So what? I tried to convince him. 'No, I mean it, Owen. It's the one part of my life where I have no goddamned sense.'

'I believe you,' he said, when he didn't. He held up a spent cartridge. There was something strange but unidentifiable about it, so I said what I always say when I punt. 'Looks funny. Foreign?'

And he responded the way they do about ninety-eight per cent of the time. 'Could be.' He twisted it in the light the way the natives do in our restaurants when they examine a glass of wine. 'Thirty-two. Got three in him. His was a 9mm. Missing.'

While he was studying the casing I was studying him. 'Owen, were you assigned to watch my ass?' We don't usually work in pairs; department's too small.

If a black could blush, he did. They ought to be happy about that – I hate blushing. 'Bein' a gentleman, I wouldn't 'xactly put it that way. More like alla you. Sorry.'

'Don't be. It's okay. I'm glad.' And I was.

'Maybe you better get on over to the house, don't you think?'

'Yeah, politics before investigation, right?'

'You got it now.'

I took a moment to look out over the crime scene. I wanted it held in my mind for a good long time. Beyond the people working was a whole flat, sunburned landscape of scrub, frayed palmettos, an occasional palm or pine tree. In the distance some new, already fading apartments. Or maybe they were unfinished. We would have to get to them.

PALM MONDAY

Above the 'Glades huge black rolling clouds came tumbling towards us over the sawgrass, spitting out lightning. It was starting out a hot September; a bad sign.

Half to Owen, I said, 'Mean season's here.'

'Amen.'

We knew.

III

I went up US 1 and over the Intercoastal Waterway on the Southern Boulevard Bridge to Palm Beach proper. We don't have tracks, as in 'other side of,' we have the Intercoastal, but if you grew up in West Palm you always felt a reflexive dip in your biorhythms, or somewhere, crossing it. I hated that, but it was there, demeaning as hell, making me want to punch somebody.

I'm good with mechanical things. I drive a Celica that I keep in terrific shape, neater, shinier than my apartment. A Marine colonel could tamp his cowlick in one of the fenders. A respectable car, which of course is the problem when you take it to Palm Beach and float it on a sea of Porsches, Mercs and 'Dinos.'

It made me wish I had kept my old 'Brat' pickup, but I had disposed of that when I made detective. Somebody said a detective had to have 'probity.' I didn't know what they meant at the time but I've improved my vocabulary since. I read a book a week. For now, no one was looking and I slipped a U2 tape into the deck and cranked up the volume. The car lifted a couple of feet off the road and flew the rest of the way.

The road where the Chapelles lived was wide, curving and so white it hurt your eyes. Every estate was walled and the walls themselves were blotted out by massive dense foliage. The flowers over there always struck me as something out of a weird painting, unnaturally brilliant somehow. I knew there would be a media death-watch at the mansion and there was, with a drooling band of reporters at the foot of the driveway, gossiping, pacing, chain smoking, as incapable of quiet as ants. Fortunately, the department had a public relations guy and I didn't have to talk to them. Which is just as well, because they do not have my respect. No way.

Before I got to the main gate I pulled over near to one of those vans that every force in the world uses as if nobody knew. A 'buggie' named Al popped out of the back and trotted over to my open window. No reason for clandestine ways in this neighborhood. Lurkers would stand out like a fly in buttermilk. Which was something to remember.

'Tell me you got something. Please.'

'Not from the doers. A zillion sympathy calls. These people whine a lot. And Chapelles got four different lines to do it on.'

'Who answers?'

'Servants mostly. The missus, she never picks up her private line. Just lets it record. We're gonna fill a warehouse with the tapes.'

'Need anything?' He shook his head; buggies are resourceful scavengers. 'Catch you later.'

He started away but remembered. 'One "friend" told Mrs Chapelle this wouldn't have happened if her old man kept it in his pants.'

'And they put it just like that?'

'You know, kind of. If he'd "behaved himself" or some shit like that.'

I asked him to pull that one for me and went on. It wasn't much but it made me feel like I had a little edge going into the castle.

At the gate I held up my shield and the private guard, from Dunn's company no doubt, swung the big iron gates open. There was a media surge in my direction but I kept the windows closed and ignored all the shooting and shouting and gunned it through.

There were a lot of cars up near the house, but not as

many as suggested by the mob inside; I think a lot of them could walk or bicycle over or were dropped off. Mine looked like a shiny cold-sore on Robert Redford but I stuck it right in there with the rest parked along the driveway and went up to the front door.

A Cuban maid opened it; she looked tired and was sullen. I put the buzzer in her face but it didn't seem to have any effect.

'Wha' you want?'

What did she think? 'Mrs Chapelle. I'm Sergeant Bodo.'

She thought that over. 'Jus' a minute. I tell her . . .' And she disappeared inside, shutting the door in my face.

I was irritated with myself for being irritated. Big deal, a snobby maid, when cops wade through hostility from academy to retirement. It would get a lot worse than this. After pacing around, taking out a cigarette and jamming it back in the pack, I decided to put things on another footing and pushed my way in.

The entranceway was probably intended to intimidate the working class, which was everyone except millionaires. It had a vaulted ceiling like a church, a table with two silver candlesticks that would have paid my salary for a year on either side of a giant floral display. Fresh flowers as tall as I was. There was a huge ornate mirror behind them. I glanced into it and started brushing a few hairs into line, checking the lipstick. The place had that effect on you; did you measure up?

I could hear a lot of voices and music further in, and followed it. Whatever the foyer promised, the living room delivered. It was castle-size with large Spanish or French or cathedral or whatever windows all the way around. You could see clear out across the lawn in back all the way to the ocean. In here there were people everywhere, a maid passing hors d'oeuvres, a houseman with a tray of drinks. I don't know where the music came from. The husband in this house has been kidnapped, one of the servants murdered, and here were people in tennis clothes sipping margueritas, chattering away at each other like any cocktail party.

What I hated the most was that they were all gorgeous – male, female, young, old, even the ugly ones were gorgeous – and I couldn't, have never been able to figure out, how do they do that? I looked down at my gray suit, a sparrow among flamingos. I'm standing next to two women who can't see me for the camouflage.

'Tourist season's coming. I think I'll kill myself.'

'Yes, but so's party season.'

'Maybe I'll wait.'

And they laughed. They talked like that. I set my jaw – fuck 'em, I was the law!

'You wanted to see me, Officer?'

The lady herself, taller than I am at five-eight and a half, wearing sandaled heels, white pants, a blue and white flowered blouse, very large shades and possessor of a body any woman would die for. She was extraordinary-looking, no way around it. On first meeting there was no telling if that beautiful face could smile. I introduced myself, told her I was in charge of the investigation; that seemed to throw her a little.

'You're very young.'

'I'm getting older.' It wasn't deliberately smartass, it was just the only way I could think of at the moment to hold my own. She didn't seem to notice; she never did.

'And a woman, too.'

'Yes, ma'am. All the way. Could we— ?'

'You know, there were police tramping through here all morning asking questions.' It struck me that she was seldom interested in what she was saying. A lot of what she did and said was programmed somewhere else by processes I could only imagine.

'I was out at the crime scene. I need to ask some more. By the way, the phone team out there, they're a little conspicuous and it's not too comfortable. Could you see your way to having them in the house?'

'I'd rather not.' She glanced at her Cartier watch. 'Let's go in the conservatory.'

She led the way with a languorous stride. 'Having all these people here, it isn't a very good idea, Mrs Chapelle.'

'Is for me. Cheers me up.' She asked if I wanted a drink. I said no and she called out to the maid in passing for a Bloody Mary.

I don't spend a lot of time in conservatories but I've seen pictures and this one didn't seem to exactly go with the architecture, but maybe it did. It was all covered with tinted glass that let in a peculiar light. The furniture was rattan with flowered pillows and there were big palms, ferns, flowers, even trees. The air felt thick, like before a hurricane. Outside I could see sailboats and a zoomie lolling beyond the surf with sunbathers atop it. There was even a couple in swimsuits down by the shoreline of the estate. It was so normal it hurt; we were talking about people dead or about to be in here, enclosed in what felt like a space capsule.

I looked down to find two men sitting la-de-da like they owned the goddamn plantation . . .

'This is Michael Duchow, Sergeant Bodo. He's CEO of Chapel Corp., our family's firm. And this is— '

. . . Dunn! Sunk deep in an oversized chair, drinking a beer out of a bottle and, of course, grinning benignly.

'I've met Mr Dunn.' There wasn't anybody there who missed the tone. 'If you don't mind, Mrs Chapelle, I'd like to interview you alone, then Mr Duchow.'

Duchow was quick to grab the opening. 'I'll be outside.' The way he slipped out of the room suggested to me how he ran the corporation and probably his life – quiet, seamless, eye on the prize. His knife never went in the front.

'I do mind. I want Sean here.'

Sean, huh. 'You're also entitled to have an attorney present, Mrs Chapelle. If you feel you need one.'

She sat down in a big high-backed planter's chair next to Dunn, very regal, like Bette Davis in those old movies. 'I don't. Not right now. I've talked to ours this morning and, anyway, Michael's an attorney.'

'Not a criminal attorney.'

'"Criminal?"'

'This is a criminal investigation, ma'am. Why don't you let us do our job. I can't question you in front of an employee who might or might not be involved in some way.'

'What on earth are you implying?' She leaned forward and took off her sunglasses. That was with one hand; the other was used to brush Dunn's leg with her fingernails.

If my implication bothered him you'd never know it; he seemed to be enjoying my awful start. 'Just that this kidnapping was obviously set up by somebody who knew Mr Chapelle's habits.'

'That's ridiculous.'

'No,' Dunn said, 'she's probably right.' We both looked at him in surprise, but hers was absorbed by the arrival of the Bloody Mary.

'Look,' I told her, risking the Sheriff's undying hatred, 'maybe you should ask for the FBI to come in. It wouldn't be hard to make the case— '

She cut me off. 'We don't want that unless we have to. There's too much attention already.'

SEAN

I stood up. The new kid – I thought of her that way at the time, no matter how unfairly – was stepping in it with every exchange. The ubiquitous FBI – her department would kill her. And Sylvia was a war all unto herself. I at least knew this disdainful lassitude was not all of her. 'Sergeant, maybe if we could have a few words in private this would go a little smoother.'

I saw the spark in her eyes and the fuse start running; I didn't blame her, it was hugely presumptuous. Her lips were forming 'no' and the few other involving words that might go with it, but I touched her arm gently and something happened, she let it happen.

Behind us as we went Sylvia sipped at her drink and, sounding a little flip, murmured, 'Be my guest.' I was lucky it didn't send Bodo snarling back into the room.

I took her down a long, windowless, cabinet-filled hallway that led to the kitchen and served as a pantry.

I thought I'd try sweet reason. 'She's a little unglued, and I know that she looks bitchy and callous to you, but around here they don't show how they feel. Which can lead to a lot of misunderstanding.' We stopped midway with our backs to opposite walls.

'I guess you're the expert. You get on with them pretty good.'

'They pay me, so they trust me.'

'To do what?'

'Protect their interests.'

'And what are those?'

'They'll know 'em when they see 'em.' Mistake – she wasn't in any mood for irony. 'What I'm trying to get across, I'm not here to cause you any more grief than you already got.'

Another mistake. Her voice rose querulously. 'What are you talking about? I haven't even got started yet.'

'Your first solo, right? As primary.' I kept my voice very low, laid-back, in order to try to settle her. Asking myself all the time why I cared.

'What business is that of yours?'

'It's just that I know suits, and they do this all the time to us.' I stressed 'us.' 'The kidnapping of somebody famous, suits know that's going to be a pisser, right? They always come home in a bag. Nobody gets fat except the media jackals. But at least they gave a woman a chance.'

It's an understatement to say that she lacked a good detective's ability to dissimulate. When she was angry the room knew it. She reminded me of my old man; if you poked him, he hit you twice and twice as hard before you ever took another breath, without thinking, without caring to think. Watching the fire come up out of her belly into her eyes, I thought when she was a kid she must have been the terror of every playground in town. I never cared much for it in my old man but I kind of liked it in her.

'Thanks a lot, you patronizing sonofabitch! I didn't earn it, I'm the token scapegoat. Well, let me tell you something. I've got a helluva good record in the Department, and they know it.'

She started back and I grabbed her arm. She yanked it away – strong. I grabbed again and held. She rounded on me, but I started talking fast. 'Goddammit, I'm trying to help you. Can't you see that?' She hesitated, as though it might be true. 'I don't care you're the badass cop who's gotta try harder than anybody else, stick it to everybody, and if I or anyone else tries to roll with it they're corrupt or wussy. Okay, that's your game, play it. But the way you're starting out, these people are going to squash you like a beetle.'

Like I said, I was keeping my voice down, but she yelled back, and that's pretty much the way it would be as long as we rubbed against each other. Right now neither of us cared who heard.

'How do you expect me to start out? I haven't had cooperation for shit. And that zoo out there? They're trampling all over potential evidence while they're dancing on this poor bastard's grave. But what the hell, he's only a servant, right?'

She had to swallow some air after that. I jumped in

with my calm voice and measured ways, which I suspect she hated by now, all the more so because they had an effect on her. 'I didn't say you were wrong. But just let me suggest something for now. I'll question her and give you my notes. If I don't ask the questions you would have asked, you go back at her. But first you question Duchow. I think a woman's got a better chance there.' I tried to leaven it. 'He's short and I'm not. But all I'll be is your assistant, the point man. You're still the boss.'

She glared at me for a moment, but then in the mercurial way she had it vanished. 'Okay. We'll give it a try.' She started back, saying over her shoulder, 'But raise your hand if you want to ask a question or go to the bathroom.'

Promising.

I sat very close in front of Sylvia because I knew her. It was necessary to have her confident, and to give her what she needed to work the magic she had for men. Some people like to interrogate the frightened; not my style. She sat straight up with the Bloody Mary in her hand and that enigmatic smile that was all slits and lines and those glowing green eyes from afar. With my leaning well forward and her head against the back of the throne chair, we were the same height, so why did it feel like she was looking down from a mountain?

She liked blunt speech and I've always given it to her. 'The cops tried all the airport hotels and he didn't have a reservation at any of them.'

'I'm not surprised.'

'How come?'

She picked up some cigarettes and handed me the lighter. 'Isn't it obvious? Where the car was found, behind Boca Raton, wasn't it? Practically back in the Everglades? That sure as hell isn't the way to the Miami Airport.'

'You have any idea what he was doing there?'

'No. Do you?'

'I thought maybe you knew of someone. Some friend of his in the area.'

Her look was almost pitying. 'Now what do you think? My God, Sean, why are we going through this charade?'

I might work for these people but I owed something to the sergeant and even to Freddo, so I stayed in the role and made my notes. 'I guess that's a "no." I'll put it down that way. How have you two been getting along?'

She groaned. 'You sound like a detective on television. If all there was to life was getting along we'd be great. I mean, you can't not get along with Jim, can you? Everyone in the world does. That's why . . .' She surprised me with the emotion, eyes suddenly glistening. I looked hard, trying to see what it meant. In the end, I believed in the moment. '. . . It's so hard to understand.'

'We'll get him back, Sylvia.'

'God, they murdered that poor chauffeur or whatever he was. When I think how I told Jim it was silly to have a bodyguard like some rock star. I know a lot of people who have money do, but I've always hated the idea of living that way.' She leaned forward with an intensity that was all the more unsettling in that it came out of a seemingly impenetrable calm, and laid her long red-nailed hand on the inside of my knee. Not the first time, but I never got used to it. 'Sean, do something, whatever it takes. Bring him home, please.'

'Bodo might surprise you. Give her a chance.'

She didn't believe it for a New York minute.

FRANKIE

The library was English with a heavy old oak desk, brass fixtures and prints of men in hunting clothes on horseback surrounded by dogs. The house, of course, was Spanish or Italian, and I don't think wealthy people should mix these things up, so it kind of set my teeth on edge. Or something did. There was a computer on the desk and a stacked sound system against one wall; that made me feel more comfortable. Duchow was sitting on a red leather settee, wearing a coat and tie and crossing his legs in order to put the Gucci loafers out front. It would have been easy, and dumb, to underestimate him.

'. . . Dunn's just an employee. We asked ISS for someone and they sent him. He's competent. More than competent.'

I like being taller or at least above the interrogatee if I can swing it, so I drifted, examining the contents of the office, picking up this, putting down that. His first answer and it was a lie.

'Any disgruntled employees in the family firm? What is it, "Chapel Corporation"?'

'None that I know of. And if there were they'd be more apt to want to take me?'

'You richer than the Chapelles?'

'Far from it, but it's harder to get money out of the really rich than anyone. They don't even pay their bills. *Noblesse oblige*. Besides, I'm not likable.' He took out a pocket computer and worked it with one hand like an old Greek with his worry-beads. I tried to ignore it.

'You're the CEO?'

'I keep it running but James is the major stockholder. He has control on those rare occasions he chooses to exercise it.'

'So he's kind of a playboy?'

'He has a variety of interests.'

'How'd they make all their money?'

'It's interesting. They'll tell you they're aristocracy, but an ancestor was a nanny for John D. Rockefeller. She took her Christmas bonuses in Standard Oil stocks, then worth a few cents. Eventually she retired and married a widower with two children, a common working man but with a bent for tinkering. He invented a tiny component that made escalators work, or work better. This small . . .'

He made a distance of about a half-inch between his thumb and forefinger. Usually when guys do that they're describing somebody's cock who beat them out of a job or a babe.

'Anyway, she backed him with her small fortune and they made a considerably bigger one. When prohibition came along, bootlegging by one of their descendants made it even larger. And with repeal, they had a whiskey empire. During the Second World War they bribed a lot of people and expanded into industrial areas with military contracts, parts for trucks, ships, planes. That was the high point, the post-war boom. Been downhill ever since, although it's a long way to the bottom and this generation doesn't have to worry.'

'Sounds like a family of crooks for people supposed to be so respectable.'

'Like most corporations, the tradition of illegality's been a constant thread running parallel to service to the nation. That is, until I came around, of course.'

He struck this attitude of bogus modesty, doing everything but bat his eyes at me. I guess he was being witty. You could see how nobody in this was going to be a walkover.

'How did James get to be the major stockholder?'

'A wonderful thing called inheritance. His younger brother, Glen, is vice-president with limited responsibilities.'

'Definitely second banana?'

He nodded. 'A way to put it.'

'How does he feel about that?'

'Ask Ted Kennedy.' He smiled to indicate that he had said something clever. About time.

'Is that an answer, Mr Duchow?' I sat opposite him on a hard-backed chair. I could have lazed and crossed my legs, which are pretty good, but what with the Department's skirt length it would have required something pretty obvious on my part, and this was a subtle man. Anyway, I'd rather be taller, more to the point, than sexy.

He frowned, not liking the challenge. 'Ability seeks its own level. Glen seems to be a rather unhappy person, but I don't think that's it. I believe he knows his limitations.'

'How come Mr Chapelle didn't tell you about this meeting at the airport?'

He thought about that for a moment. I guess he was wondering how much he ought to take me into their world. He didn't have to worry. I couldn't hurt him – yet – but he had a weakness and I knew now what Dunn had meant.

He sat back like he was going to tell an Uncle Remus story, the first person in history to do so with a crease in his pants. 'You've got to understand about Jim. He's a very nice man, which isn't true of most people with his money. You'll find that out in spades before this is over.'

'I've got a leg up on it.'

He laughed, knowing who I meant. 'Anyway, I think he must have had a pretty strange upbringing. I wouldn't know myself, but a lot of wealthy people seem to have these Byzantine childhoods where they learn to be secretive. I guess to survive. Funny, you'd think all they had to do was be happy.'

'If you had to speculate on where he was going?'

'I wouldn't.'

'Then just tell me. Because I think you know.'

'Wrong.' He hesitated, but he couldn't stop. 'I sup-pose most people would tell you a girlfriend. Jim's been a world-class womanizer since he got out of diapers. Or so they tell me, and he doesn't seem anxious to deny it . . .'

Bitchy, but it worked for me.

'. . . He was a father for the first time when he was only nineteen and home from school. And yet . . . he's a hopeless romantic. That's the saving grace. He could just have them, but he insists on courtship. He loves women. What can I say?'

I tipped my head in the general direction of the conservatory and tried to sound buddy-buddy. 'She know?'

He shrugged. 'She's very bright. Just because she's beautiful . . .'

'Yes?'

'I suppose she does, but that's another unusual thing. Most of the men and a lot of the women around here brag about their affairs. Even to their mates. But Jim's very decorous. And he obviously adores her.'

These people! He 'adores her' but he's ready to fuck anybody who can have a period, and for all I know everyone who doesn't. 'He "adores her." Okay. How much does she adore him?'

'It's the same kind of thing. This is Palm Beach.'

Their explanation for everything. 'Most of the people I meet have more than one weakness, Mr Duchow.'

'Maybe our worlds aren't that different, then.'

'I bet. Did he hang with any rough types? Like did he gamble, for instance? Vegas, Atlantic City . . .?'

'Chapelles don't go to Vegas, they go to Biarritz.'

'Where's that?'

'Europe. Monte Carlo, Venice, places like that. But no, he didn't gamble much.'

'How about Mrs Chapelle, does she have any close male friends?'

He was very quick to answer. 'I wouldn't know.'

SEAN

'You must be kidding. No. I don't have any lovers, and if I did it sure as hell wouldn't be that smarmy little man down there.' She glanced in the general direction of the library. 'I didn't even want to hire him but Jim said the company was rocky and he was capable of setting it right. I told him the French made that mistake with another seriously short man.'

'And he laughed.'

'Well, of course. You know him.'

'I get the idea you and Duchow aren't exactly enemies now.'

'We have interests in common.' My look demanded something more; she might have expected that. 'I admit I find his energy attractive. Come to think of it, that's what the women who should have known better said about Napoleon. Maybe it's the times, but all the males I know are so goddamned lethargic. Soigné. Ennui.' She enjoyed being self-satirizing, it was an indulgence that set her off.

'You know how bad it gets? Yesterday was my anniversary and my husband was kidnapped and I don't even know what day it was.'

'Monday.'

'Yes, but wasn't it something special, like a holiday, Palm Monday or something like that?'

'That's Palm Sunday, and it's in the spring.'

'You're right. Weekdays, weekends, same damn thing. Most people dread Mondays – I envy them. At least it's a feeling. Don't you ever get bored, Sean?'

'No.'

'God, how do you manage it?'

'Poverty.'

She laughed generously; the Pope would have succumbed to her in those moments. The only trouble was, her husband was missing and perhaps dead, and the man assigned to protect him known dead. 'It's a good thing,' I told her after the laugh, 'that I'm the one questioning you.'

'I don't trim my sails for anyone, you know that.'

'Any financial problems?'

'If there are, someone should have told me. Because I

went up to New York last week for my haircut at Clive Summers and spent sixty thousand on clothes alone.'

'James care?'

'He was a little irritated, but not enough for you to write it down. You know, Sean, I'm amazed you'd dare to ask some of this.'

'I've dared a lot more than that with you, Sylvia.'

That seemed to catch her up; I can't imagine what she expected. The only way to deal with her is straight in the eyes and she knows it. For a moment she looked away, and sighed. 'Yes, you have.'

There was a knock on the door jamb, causing a startled Sylvia to spin and look. Owen was leaning into the room with the wise expression of someone who knows they've interrupted a private moment.

''Scuse me. Would you all come into the library. Mr Chapelle's brother's brought a tape with a ransom call on it.'

Sylvia said, 'Oh, God, Sean,' and reached over to squeeze my hand.

I searched for the emotion, but all I saw was indecipherable fear. Leopards surely knew fear, but could they for a mate? Then, conscious of our holding hands, I remembered Owen. He was gone. No telling if he'd seen.

IV

Frankie slipped the cassette into a slot in the elaborate wall system. Whatever was on it, the sound quality would be terrific.

The brother – we always thought of him that way – was going on in the aggrieved yet somehow apologetic tone he used for every occasion. 'I was working in my office, trying to keep busy, trying to keep my mind off of Jim, when it came in on my private line. I didn't— '

The tape kicked in, and the killer's voice cut through the room like shrapnel. 'Mr Chapelle?'

'Yes?'

'Glen Chapelle, is it? The brother?'

I looked up to see who had caught the Irish accent. Frankie . . . I wasn't sure about the others. Any of them might have heard something they managed to keep out of their face.

'Who is this?' Glen asked on the tape, and you could hear the suspicion enter his voice. He was forty-eight, plumpish and wore, probably defiantly, unfashionable glasses with heavy rims that gave him a perpetually quizzical look. The diametrical opposite of his brother. I wondered where was his wife – the diametrical opposite of Sylvia?

'Listen to me now. I won't be repeatin' and I won't be on long, neither.' You could hear him breathing; he was frightened. I thought he sounded like a dangerous man, over and above the evidence of his having shot Freddo three times at point-blank range.

'We're holdin' your brother and we want a hundred

million for him . . .' You could hear a collective inhalation in the room and Glen swearing under his breath on the tape. '. . . New bills, none over a hundred. You understand, do you?'

Sylvia flashed Duchow a look of despair, a little theatrical but that didn't necessarily mean it was false. She lit a cigarette and began to pace. I glanced at Frankie to see if she had reacted to the absurdity of the demand, but she remained impassive, focused.

Glen showed, for him, some presence of mind. 'How do we know you're the ones who have Jim?'

The voice on the tape bent away as it ordered, 'Say hello to the little brother, Jimbo.'

After a moment we heard James, voice tired and raspy but clearly him. 'Glen, they're telling the truth. They shot Freddo— '

Sylvia murmured, 'Oh, Jesus.'

He had obviously been yanked off the phone by the mick, who spoke sharply to him, 'That's enough now.' Into the speaker, 'We'll watch the news for your answer before we contact you again. If you don't give us the money we'll kill him.'

A click and the dial tone. No one spoke as Frankie turned off the machine and extracted the tape, slipping it into an evidence bag.

I noticed Owen ease out of the room; too many questioners can muck things up and Frankie already had one more than she wanted. Anyway, his job was to keep working the body while she jabbed at the head.

'Anybody recognize that voice?' Frankie asked finally. 'Or know any Irish people?'

No reply; everyone studied the floor, a wall or a window. Sylvia murmured something about knowing hundreds of people. I decided to editorialize and see if that did anything. 'These clowns don't have a clue. A hundred million in hundreds, for Christ's sake – they'd need a derrick. There's no way to make a pickup like that. What are we dealing with here?'

'Someone smart enough to outwit your security firm and kidnap my husband.'

She had disliked my questioning more than I realized. That, or the distance I had maintained. Michael and Glen would take for granted this kind of jab from Sylvia when she was in pain – if she hurt, you hurt – but I think Frankie enjoyed it.

She turned to Glen. 'What made you think they might call you over there in the office?'

The corporation kept a modest office in West Palm Beach primarily for James's convenience, because this was where he preferred to live. Headquarters was in New York and top executives like Duchow did a lot of commuting.

'I didn't. I never gave it a thought. I just happen to have a tape recorder on my phone and when I heard a strange voice . . . for some reason I turned it on.'

'Oh? You have a recording device on your phone? Why is that?'

Obviously he had never thought about it, and now that he was forced to it embarrassed him. 'It's just a good idea sometimes. I mean, we're in business . . . people say things . . .'

Frankie moved on – Duchow. 'Your company have any business interests in Ireland?'

'Not much. We have bought some airplane parts over there.'

'Northern Ireland?' I interrupted, presuming on my ancestry.

He nodded. 'Belfast.'

Frankie took it back quickly. 'Any trouble with the IRA?'

'Not that I know of. And things are pretty quiet over there right now, anyway.'

'Even if they weren't, they get too much money from

41

the States, they don't want to jeopardize that.' I was presuming again.

Frankie gave me a baleful look. 'I know. From Boston and New York. They might not consider Palm Beach the United States.'

'On the other hand,' I went on, 'they'll be spinning off unemployed and unemployable thugs from that thing over there for decades.' No one was listening, they were on to other things.

'Michael, what are we going to do?' Sylvia pleaded. A suppliant tone with him surprised me.

He felt obliged to translate for Frankie. 'Nobody has that much in *real* money. Bonds, credits, mortgages, company stock . . . But in this economy it would take weeks to raise it, even if that was feasible.'

'What about the company paying?' I asked, and Frankie gave me still another look that said, 'Butt out!'

Duchow said that would require some study.

Frankie stepped to the center of the room. 'I want to make something clear, okay? We don't endorse anybody paying ransom. In our experience it doesn't work and only increases the future risk to the public, because it encourages others to try the same thing. What— '

'Sergeant, I don't give a rat's ass about the public. I want my husband back.'

Frankie chose her words carefully. 'That's what we all want, Mrs Chapelle. What we advocate is, you pretend to go along with the demands. When they do call again, and they will, you insist on speaking to them yourself. You tell them you're willing to do anything possible but you'll need some time. Maybe you can't raise quite that much but name a lower sum. Eventually they'll get desperate and greedy and arrange a handover. We take care of it from then on. You only need one of them in custody to break the case, and they're almost always caught.'

Sylvia observed, 'After they've killed their victims.' She

stood abruptly. 'Michael, you and I should talk. I need some air.'

He knew that if Sylvia said the interview was over, it was over, and was prepared to follow her out of the library. Glen, more timid, looked to Frankie for permission. She nodded, but added, 'One more thing. We'd appreciate it if at this stage nobody talked to the media.'

The three of them looked at her but nobody said anything, and they went out.

FRANKIE

Sean and I were alone. He examined the sound system and tape collection. I paced. For a minute or two we were both caught up in our own thoughts. Finally, he asked me, 'Think they'll listen to you about the media?'

'Haven't so far. Maybe you should ask her. Or maybe flash her would work.'

'Come on, Sergeant.' This time his smile was a little weary.

'You're trying to tell me it isn't you, she comes on to every guy on the planet that way.'

'In a way, yeah. But it isn't all that contrived, either. Everybody here is trying to either get or hold on to something. And they just naturally use whatever weapons they have. Being smart – and she is – isn't a very smart way for a woman to go in Palm Beach. It could make people self-conscious about all the really dumb chatter they normally lay on you.'

What was he talking about? I've never known a man to make such a big deal about denying that a gorgeous babe had slept with him. Most guys, just the opposite. Dunn was such a bizarro.

'Excuse me, your notes?'

'What?'

43

He handed me a frayed little notebook. 'Two-way street? Quid pro quo?'

I had to think a minute; I hadn't considered that he was really serious about this kind of collaboration; I thought it was just some kind of stall. But I couldn't see the harm, either, so I gave him mine.

'You think she's doing it with Duchow?' I asked when I'd finished my scan.

'She could be doing it with the dog next door.'

That surprised me coming from him; what didn't I understand? 'That's pretty crude. I thought you at least liked each other.'

'I'm a liberal, I'm supposed to like everybody. But that doesn't mean I'll lie to you. Here . . .' He poked at my notes. 'Duchow says Chapelle doesn't gamble much. Absolute bullshit.'

'Enough to put him or the company in trouble?'

'Enough to put whole countries in trouble. He's a stone gambler. The pros start dreaming about tax shelters when he comes into the room.'

'How do you know?'

'You hear things.'

'That's where you're gonna leave it?'

'Privileged.'

'Oh, terrific. Loyalty. Well, you're not withholding evidence on me.'

'If I thought it was relative, I'd tell you.'

'That's not for you to say.'

'Fran – Sergeant – trust me on this. Because you're not going to win.'

I wanted to kill him but he was right. I couldn't afford a big confrontation. Not yet. 'Any other contradictions you see in here?'

'Contradictions? Everything they've said since we got here's a lie, including "hello." Even the hundred million could be had somehow. Assuming the kidnappers are serious, which I doubt. Incidentally, did Duchow mention that the company he was with before this was mixed up with the BCCI?'

'You don't see it in my notes, do you? We hadn't finished when the tape came.' Listening to myself it sounded defensive. My old man, my stepfather who was a cop, used to say never explain yourself, it's a sign of weakness.

'"Bank of Crooks and Criminals,"' Sean said. 'Nice dating service if you wanted to meet ex-spooks and "hardboys" – as the Irish call them.'

'It'll be looked into.'

'See, they lie on principle. Because there's always something to be covered up even if they can't remember what it is at the time.'

'I got the message.'

'And yet . . .' He stepped over to the sound system and put in a cassette. Classical music boomed out and filled the whole room. I didn't know what it was but it was impressive. He said *The Brandenburg Concertos* by Bach. Him I'd heard of.

'This was the last thing Chapelle was listening to.'

He obviously liked it, and the fact that Chapelle did too impressed him a lot. I didn't know why exactly, but probably something about the guy not being a typical rich jerk. Nothing I'd heard suggested that anyway. But Dunn liked things, and people, complicated. I listened to it and kind of liked the music myself. The rest of the house must have thought we were off our nob.

Sean, head down, completely into the music, muttered, 'Go figure!'

'Good advice.'

The kitchen had been 'modernized' into Country French. I am a woman, I do read those magazines sometimes. Not often. It was as big as my apartment and might have enticed even me into cooking. Owen had bummed a couple of cups of coffee, espresso no less, out of one of the maids. Occasionally there are advantages to being black; help always treated me lousy.

There was some cooking and cleaning-up going on, although most of the sympathizers seemed to have gone home. Driven by the stench of police, no doubt. I watched the servants coming and going. 'Any of them have any kind of record?'

Owen had a mountain of notes that made mine look puny. 'Not so far. There's five fulltime, not countin' the chauffeur who didn't exactly think of himself in that category. You know, only worked for the Massa.'

'How'd he get on with the others?'

'Poorly to not at all. Spent most of his off-time down in Miami, carryin' on in bad company accordin' to them. And you know how these people here love to gossip.'

'About their employers too?'

'Oh, yeah. They not only know who's doin' what to who, but in what position wearing what funny hat, if you know what I mean. It was always that way. My mama worked in one of these homes . . .' His eyes were remembering.

'So did mine.'

'Go on!'

'So it's not likely he ever told them where he took the "Massa"?'

'No, just that he took him a lot. And they stayed away a lot. Carmen, one of the maids, thinks he used to deliver Chapelle somewhere, go hang out in Miami or maybe Hialeah, then come back for him, say, the next day.'

'Chapelle had a secret life and not a soul in this big old house knew what it was. That's amazing, Owen. Wouldn't you say it was amazing?'

'I'd say it was impossible.'

'To quote you, "Amen."'

'We'll make a good Christian lady out of you yet.' He knew better.

'What do they say about the family?'

'Whatever they do, they don't bring it home.'

'They fight?'

'Nope. They're not so sure about the Missus, but everybody likes "Mister James," as they call him.'

'I'm already getting tired of hearing that.'

'The brother's kind of a big nothin'. He can get real bossy, they say. Michael Duchow's here on business a lot, stays at the house sometimes, but they don't see him as belongin' somehow, so they don't pay him no mind. You forget sometimes you're still in the South.'

'Easy to do here. What about Glen's wife? I haven't seen her yet.'

'Just that she's tougher than him and kind of "foreign." Born in Italy, they say. Doesn't mix much. The son's kind of a weirdo. Spoiled, you know. But stays to himself.'

'They got a kid?'

'In boardin' school up north. Be home tomorrow, for the day at least.'

'Jesus, we got a cast of thousands.'

'Charlie's out huntin' down the dinner guests from last night.'

'Kissin' up the rich. He'll be in hog heaven.'

Owen chuckled. We all ragged on Charlie, who read the local paper over here, called by everyone 'The Shiny Sheet,' and was fascinated by the gossip. The captain assigned him; personally, I had doubts he could ask hard questions of people and suck up at the same time . . .

'First thing I want to know, did anyone get up from that table and make a phone call after he left?'

'We been askin' that and so far 'pears not. And he hasn't found any ax murderers 'mong 'em, neither.'

He looked over my shoulder at some commotion behind me. As I turned, one of the maids was reporting something excitedly to the two who were working. Then all three rushed out. Owen and I looked at each other, but we were already moving.

We went out a side door and hurried around the massive side of the house, following the buzz that usually signals some kind of public event or disaster, in this case both. In the front out on the lawn we found Sylvia, Glen and Duchow giving a press conference. The usual noisy, jostling cluster of journalists wriggling around them like worms in the sun. They're always so proud of being obnoxious.

Sylvia, for someone who seemed so languid, had surprising force in her voice, another indication of the steel beneath the iron. I noted she had made some small but crucial adjustments to makeup and hair since our interview.

'. . . received about an hour ago by telephone. They asked for a certain sum of money, and said my husband would be killed if we didn't pay . . .'

Owen and I joined the group of servants looking on. It seemed appropriate. The journalists began shouting questions all at the same time, each trying to climb above the other. Sylvia waited them out and stared them down like a pro until finally, helpless against this silent resolve, they quieted.

'Didn't wait long, did they?' It was bad-penny Dunn at my elbow. He always seemed uplifted when people turned out to be as jerky as he had predicted.

How much did they ask for? was the consensus question from the swarm. Sylvia glanced aside at Duchow who whispered something in her ear. So, she wasn't always totally in charge. 'I don't think I should tell you the amount, but let me say . . . I love my husband very much, and I would do anything to get him back, but the amount demanded is just impossible to raise. I hope these people know they're going to have to be more reasonable . . .'

Aloud, I said, 'Jesus, they're trying to get him killed.'

I expected Dunn to agree with me, but he had his own

speculation. 'Maybe not. Maybe he's a part of it.' Naturally he smiled at me.

SEAN

Frankie stomped away, 'stomped' the operative verb, before the conference was over, her face set, steam coming out of her ears. Owen followed, but straight up, non-committal; he didn't walk like a Southerner or a black man or even a Baptist; he walked like a veteran, a man who's been to see the elephant and hear the owl. A useful complement to Frankie's intemperance. If he had been a little more aggressive, or perhaps just white, he would have been minimally a commander by now. That he didn't like me, I don't require that from people. He cared and thought I didn't. Maybe he was right.

I drifted away myself then; I've seen better shows. Up to the house where I found Glen's wife, Amelia, in the doorway. She was watching the spectacle with even less pleasure than had Frankie. I had always found her a little strange. Addressing some inner audience, she demanded, 'Why doesn't Glen say something? He goes out there and stands around and doesn't say a goddamn word.'

I pretended I was the audience. 'There isn't that much to say that it needs three people. Matter of fact, it'd be better if nobody said anything at this point.'

She finally discovered me. An un-chic, full-bodied woman with slightly protruding eyes that gave her the look of a lemur. Thyroid, I suppose; at least that was the excuse given for my seventh-grade algebra teacher's ruthless behavior, and she had eyes like that. Amelia, from what little I knew, was born in Italy and brought to this country as a young child. Her father was supposed to be some big mover in Sicily and there was an industrial connection to the Chapelles. At the time I thought she was the least Italian person I ever knew. Although she could hate, I'll give her that.

'I suppose you're in charge.'

'More like a consultant. Sheriff Department's in charge.'

'Why hasn't the FBI been brought in?'

'Family doesn't want them, won't cooperate with them. The Bureau's too political to get involved in anything where they're not wanted. Besides, there's no reason to think it's not limited to South Florida.'

'Why don't they want them?'

'Mrs Chapelle, I'm just an employee, a kind of old family retainer who stops the conversation when he comes around. Why don't you ask your husband?'

'He won't tell me anything, even when he knows. He didn't tell me about the ransom call before he came over here. I heard when somebody from the company called.'

'Who was that?'

'Somebody. Are you making any progress?'

'Just started.'

'Well, I'm not surprised.' She had a way of sighing that carried a lot of moral freight. She also looked away.

Her clothes were expensive but the off-blonde hair was always in chaos; she poked at it, trying to stuff individual wisps back into the mass. It was a sign that she was agitated which, granted, was most of the time.

'What are you not surprised about?'

'James. Everyone thinks he's charming and bright and all that, but they don't know half of what he's into. Both of them. Something like this was bound to happen.'

'Anything you ought to tell me about?'

'I should think you'd know. Of all people.'

'Sorry. I don't socialize with him and I don't know anything about the business.'

'Don't you?' She could be formidable when she chose to emerge from her peevishness. I had always thought there might be an element of danger somewhere in her psyche.

Perhaps she was Italian after all. Fortunately I didn't have to worry about it. Not then.

She turned her attention back to the press conference. 'Her!' was all she said.

'You dislike her?' It was a little bold but with luck it could get me thrown off the case. Again she just looked at me with those starey eyes. 'How does Glen feel about his brother?'

'Take your own advice, Mr Dunn. Ask him yourself. I'm not supposed to have opinions.'

'If you were, if I allowed you to, what would you say?'

But I had lost her. She retreated to that place inside, the other audience. 'I used to be a Catholic before my marriage.'

With that, she disappeared back into the cavernous house. I understood that the door, still open, was not open to me.

V

FRANKIE

I went straight back to the station and the rest of that first day was spent, hazily, in contacts with other agencies, reporting to my superiors, all ten thousand of them, coordinating with the public relations officer, reading every statement and interview, given or taken. The brass were naturally pissed about the Chapelles' media statement. It was all over the news locally and even nationally, although I didn't have time to look at it. I'd seen it live. But, while they thought I should have prevented it somehow, no one was willing to call them on it or even allow me to.

I got home at eleven, got some macaroni and cheese out of the package and fell into bed. By midnight the heat hadn't brought any storm but the trade winds were active in tormenting the trees outside the bedroom windows. My nerves were ringing like a thousand church bells and I lay stiff as a board, trying to unravel my life in the shifting shadows on the ceiling. The lover tossed out at first light scarcely made an appearance, but something about this case brought around all sorts of childhood demons.

Maybe it was the simple fact of a servant being killed, and my mother having been one. I was one myself, 'civil servant.' That morning the late Freddo Carfagno had only been an ugly corpse, a hoodlum destined to get what he got one way or the other. A quick death, there are worse things. But now I felt pain for him. Why? I should have been thinking about the victim being physically and psychologically abused, wondering whether he would live, afraid to die in the dark among strangers.

I should have been, but it was that poor dumb blown-up thug in the canal that reached me then.

SEAN

I rented a motel room on a weekly in West Palm. It was necessary to go out and buy some things – cheap razor, underwear, socks, shirt – because I'd come away from Miami without taking time to pack. Normally I'd have gone home to my Munchkin hearth and home – it's not that bad a commute and there have been too many motels in my life – but Duchow and The Brother wanted to see me next morning before start of business. Anything's a long commute at that hour. I phoned in my report to the Miami office. The boss didn't care what I had to say so long as the Chapelles were happy. I watched an old movie and read my dog-eared copy of Suetonius, having a liking for ancient history despite the fact that I've never studied it and can't pronounce any of the names, most especially 'Suetonius.'

By the time I got up at six-thirty, God help me, over in Palm Beach gardeners were already hard at work in avoidance of the noonday sun. Automatic sprinklers were coming on. Paperboys on thousand-dollar bikes were delivering their loads to homes they could barely see through the gates, but of course they all lived in one themselves. Some of the wilder inhabitants, particularly the snow bunnies, would still be coming home from the dance clubs, hoping to sleep for the first time in days.

The Chapelles' maid, Carmen, had the coffee drill that morning. Since Sylvia arose late, James was absent and the boy at school, she went out for the newspapers in her bathrobe, shuffling past the armed guard who sat on a little stool back in the shrubbery beside the main entrance. A fellow Hispanic, she insists he was wide awake and greeted her, wishing her a good morning. He helped her open the big iron gates so she could pluck the papers out of the mailbox.

Back in the kitchen, she poured herself a cup of thick Cuban coffee which she brewed only for herself and the staff and sat at the table in the breakfast nook. The Chapelles took the *Miami Herald* and the overnight *New York Times*. Carmen read English well and, while she would have preferred 'The Shiny Sheet' for its gossip about her friends' employers, she would go through the *Herald* for news of Cuba.

She settled in, a nice quiet moment before the long demanding day, and sipped at the coffee. She removed the rubber band, unfurled the paper . . . and screamed louder than she ever had in her life. To look at Carmen, with her operatic thorax, you knew she could scream. It woke the entire house.

It had taken her a few seconds to realize what she was looking at. What appeared to be a small pink banded worm leaking blood across the financial pages. It was a man's little finger severed not too cleanly above the middle joint, grotesquely wearing a too-large ring. She tried to leap up out of the breakfast nook but, the table being fastened to the floor, she found the exit space small, crooked and unyielding.

Apparently she tried to do this several times, bounced back, leaped up again and again, but remained a prisoner until the houseman rushed in and yanked her horizontally. Afterwards, she was given one of Sylvia's Valiums and sent to bed for a couple of hours to quiet her nerves, but walked bent over for the next several days. I thought her eyes never quite looked normal again.

I wasn't aware of this at the time, being at the Chapel Corporation's high-rise in West Palm. Duchow's office was expensive but characterless, reflecting a nomadic business life and closed personality. The man himself was sprawled on a leather couch wearing exercise clothes. It was so uncharacteristically informal I assumed it was studied. Glen was wearing a sport coat and tie, which struck me as obscene at that hour, sitting up like the best-behaved boy in the class. I still had on my jeans, sneakers, and a 'golf jacket,' although I want to go on record that it's the silliest game on the planet.

Duchow commented sarcastically on my sartorial failings. It was just something he did in business; if you're going to contend, start by diminishing the other guy's confidence. Possibly it was territorial, too – almost everything was with him – the territory in this case being the Chapelles' approval. He could have had my share for the asking but the truth was he thrived on struggle. I didn't give a shit, I wasn't listening; a police siren going out of town in the distance rang some inner bell.

'I suppose we should be grateful you're here at all at this hour. And on time.' He made a kind of lolling, insouciant gesture with his hand; lying on couches brings that out in people.

'I'm usually not even up yet.'

'And proud of it,' Glen observed, accurately.

I indicated a bottle of Maalox on Duchow's arid desk. 'I never had to take that stuff.'

He sat up and looked as if he had never noticed it. 'You seem to have questions. We have instructions.'

'Why don't you want the feds in? It's causing a lot of comment in the media, and sooner or later . . .'

They exchanged a glance. Duchow said, 'Federal investigations have no stopping point.'

'Where should this one stop?'

'Let me put it to you as a question. How many corporations in America can afford the kind of heavy-handed scrutiny we're talking about? I'll answer it for you. Almost none. We're not into anything illegal, any coverups, there's no BCCI here. But still, we can't afford it.'

'You're broke.'

That upset Glen, which pleased me no end. He could almost make his nostrils flare. 'Absolutely not! That's a helluva thing to say.' He rounded on Duchow. 'Why do we have to put up with this crap from this . . . employee?'

I wondered if we would have had this outburst if I'd said they were crooked? 'In other words you are.'

Glen was prepared to storm again but Duchow put up a staying hand and he obeyed. Amazing. 'No, Sean, we're not. We do have a minor cash-flow problem and it would be an embarrassing time for that to surface. You see, there's a stock offering soon, and we need that capital. Simple?'

We all knew it wasn't. But I'm not a ledger-mind. A lot of people find corporate shenanigans fascinating; personally I'd rather watch bull-fighting. The fraud's more interesting. I figured I could learn more from the other one in the room. 'Your brother's gambling a factor, Mr Chapelle?'

Glen wiped his glasses with more deliberation than they required. 'I noticed you call my sister-in-law by her first name.'

'I call your brother by his first name, too. Of course you're not your brother, but I'll call you "Glen" if you want me to.'

He tried to work up something like a growl while he ran a search for an answer. Duchow said quietly, 'Give it a rest, Sean.'

I turned, feeling like a lion-tamer with these guys. 'You lied to Bodo about the gambling.'

His pupils disappeared in his tiny eyes; the effect was

androidal. 'And so will you if we tell you to.' Then, abruptly, tone and expression changed. I went on guard. 'By the way, she's pretty good-looking for a policewoman. Have you noticed?'

'Yeah. They usually look like me.' I can play the 'by-the-way' game. 'Your company have kidnapping insurance on its executives? A lot of companies do since the terrorism in the seventies.'

'I don't know,' Duchow said. He looked dyspeptic; I looked skeptical. 'The company's been around a hundred years. I've been here three. The by-laws have probably been amended dozens of times. And I don't pay any attention to them, anyway.' He motioned towards a sulky Glen for an answer.

The Brother shook his head. 'I'll go ask the attorneys, if anyone's in. Or I'll call New York.' He left the office and seemed glad of it.

Duchow watched him. 'You have to admire his brother's patience and loyalty.' Then he was quiet. Something was worrying him. 'I assume you didn't contradict my statement about James's gambling?'

'Why would I do that?'

He wasn't sure he believed it but the phone got me off the hook. His secretary hadn't come in yet so he actually answered it himself. Suddenly there was that rare thing, emotion in his face. As it turned out, it might simply have been revulsion. 'Oh, my God,' he said. I deduced it was Sylvia on the other end simply from the effort behind his attitude. 'Of course . . . yes . . . Sean's here, I'll send him. I'll be over myself as soon as I can.'

He put down the phone and tried to look shaken. 'We've heard from the kidnappers again. In a pretty dramatic manner . . .' It was, of course, his peculiar way of saying they had whacked off one of his boss's fingers, but I was gone before he could explain.

FRANKIE

I studied the ransom note under the desk lamp in the library, the one quiet refuge in the house. It swam a little in my big red eyes as I'd had very little sleep for forty-eight hours. Then the jarring awakening after I finally did manage to grab a few and the race over here. Owen waited behind me, holding the ring. We had our gloves on.

The words on the note were, as always, cut from something printed. All it said was, 'NOW YOU KNOW WE ARE SERIOUS.' I sniffed at it. 'From the *Miami Herald*.'

'You smelled that?'

'It's a girl thing.' I didn't know what I meant, but it was true.

'Mrs Chapelle says it's from her husband, all right.'

'She identified a finger?'

'The ring. She passed out when she saw the finger.'

He handed it to me and we both examined it under the light. A Harvard ring. 'I guess theoretically it could be his ring on somebody else's finger. I know that's a pretty weird idea. Got blood on it, anyway, for DNA.'

'Won't be necessary. Feebies got his fingerprints from some classified government project one of his companies did.' He took it back and placed it in an evidence bag.

'How's Mrs Chapelle now? Can I talk to her?'

'I wouldn't wait too long. It appears like she's decided Valium is one of the four basic food groups.'

I laughed – he's funny sometimes – and headed out to look for her.

Something I'd said had disturbed him, though, and he caught me at the door. '"Somebody else's finger?" You listen to that Dunn and you'll end up with the same kind of crazy-quilt mind.'

'Okay, Dad, I hear you.' He was a good straightforward

detective, and he'd gotten through all the years and all the
grief of the bad old days by insisting that everything was
simple.

I went out through the french doors at the back end of
the living room on to a stone terrace that overlooked the
expanse of carpet-perfect lawn which led to the sea beyond.
The water was Gulf-colored, blue-green, and very calm for
autumn, our stormy season. An on-shore breeze had raised
some whitecaps, rattled the palms and shoved aside the
humidity of the day before. The clouds on the horizon were
kind of bosomy and high-reaching but appeared friendly.
Sometimes you know why you live here.

Sylvia was still in a near-turquoise silk négligé that
matched the sea and sky as though the day had been
painted for her, and it might have been. She was reclining,
a little stoned on the Valium, on a chaise longue out on
the grass with a lawn umbrella overhead. Extra-large dark
glasses did not entirely hide wasted eyes when she tipped
forward to sip tea.

There was a young man with her; cops' instinct told
me immediately there was something schizy about him,
two people, two worlds. I can't explain it, but I'll take
credit for it. He was sitting at her feet like some poet
in a book, a thin young man in his early twenties with
a moustache and tiny ponytail. I wondered if he'd have
grass stains on those expensive white pants. Their faces
were inclined towards each other and he was touching her
hand, but I didn't know if they were parting or coming
closer. I cursed my timing, because I would have liked
to have known, and they self-consciously separated when
they spotted me.

We watched each other as I walked towards them. I
wanted them to know I had seen.

'Mrs Chapelle, if you're up to it I'd like to ask you some
more questions.' I directed my attention towards her visitor
in case there was any doubt.

'It's all right. Uh, this is William Beane, an old friend of the family. Sergeant Bodo.'

We shook hands and he looked away, admiringly or evasively at Sylvia. I kept my gaze locked on him. He was a good-looking kid with the kind of bones they call aristocratic. I tried to see the eyes but he also had on shades that precluded that, which I'm sure was the idea. I don't know if I ever saw him with them off.

'You from around here, Mr Beane?'

He returned to me grudgingly. 'I grew up right down the street.' I should have known; he had this light yellow sweater tied around his shoulders – tennis, anyone? The temperature was eighty. 'But I live in Miami now.'

Sylvia intervened. 'He came over to offer moral support. Very sweet of you, dear. Give my love to your mother and father. Tell them not to worry. I'm sure we'll get Jim back. I have a lot of confidence in the sergeant here.' She *was* stoned.

'What do you do in Miami, Mr Beane?'

'I'm a charter pilot.'

'What kind of charters?'

By now he seemed to be studying his Adidas for signs of alien visitors. 'Fishing parties down to the keys, businessmen to the Bahamas, real-estate developers, usual thing. Goodbye, Syl. Nice meeting you, Sergeant.'

Sure. As he went toward the house he picked up his pace.

'Sit down, Sergeant.' She waved toward the lawn chair opposite. 'I think I was pretty much the queen bitch yesterday. Whether you believe it or not I really do care about my husband. We've been together fifteen years. I'd make any sacrifice to get him back. I really would.'

'A good start would be to do what I asked. Make a public announcement to the effect that you agree to the kidnappers' terms. When they call you can try to negotiate them down some. That'll sound real since their numbers are so far out of the ballpark.'

'Of course, anything. I'll have our personal attorney with me and maybe I'll get better advice this time.' I took that to be a slam at Duchow, moving him to the head of the list of people who might be indifferent to Chapelle's return. 'I can't even think what Jim's going through, it's too horrible.'

'Yeah.' What else could you say? 'Tell me something. When was the last time either of you had dealings with Mr Dunn?'

She pretended to search her memory. 'Oh . . . eight or nine months ago. He lives and works down in Miami, you know. Most of the time for other clients. He only comes up here for special things.'

'What was special eight or nine months ago?'

'I don't know. Something Jim wanted looked into. We've known Sean since he was on— ' Her voice trailed.

She was either 'nodding' or had thought better of finishing that sentence.

'On what?'

'Well, on the Miami Police Department. He was a detective.'

'What were the circumstances of your meeting him?'

'I don't remember. You'd have to ask Jim.'

'That's a little hard to do right now.'

'Why all these questions about Sean? I think you're way off base, frankly. Surely there must be better clues or suspects for you to chase.'

'Yes, ma'am. Can I talk to your son?'

'I can't imagine what there is to be gained by that either, but if you think it's necessary.'

'Thank you.' I stood to go.

'I don't think he likes us very much, though.'

I looked down at her but she was gazing at the ocean.

You didn't get the idea that she thought she'd said anything extraordinary.

Sean was in the doorway, leaning against the frame with his arms folded as if he owned the joint. Looking a little self-satisfied, I thought. 'You still believe the man's involved in his own kidnapping?' I asked him as I approached.

You could never get to this guy. He just smiled and said, 'I don't think he wanted to hand over his finger. Hey, it was a hypothesis – one of many.'

I stood next to him by the doorway for a moment and looked back across the lawn. 'You see that young dude was talking to Mrs Chapelle?'

'William Beane the Third.'

'You would know him. So?'

He nodded. 'Billy's a runner.'

'Who for?'

'Medellin mostly. But anyone.'

'He needs the money?'

'Does it for the life, I guess. They get bored.'

'He's a dealer?' My hand took in minimally all of Palm Beach.

'No, no. He just brings a little blow to hostesses. The way you would flowers or a bottle of wine to dinner. Good manners.'

'So everybody knows what he does.'

'They're not very judgmental. If Saddam or Fidel came here in exile, it would depend a lot on the quality of their parties. You got to remember, most of their family fortunes came through some kind of piracy.'

It was all right for him to accept it. I started past him on my way to see the kid, but he asked, 'You find out where Chapelle was headed the other night?'

'First thing on the list.'

'What's second?'

'Why you've been lying to me.'

I went on into the house but behind me I could hear him
with that shrug in his voice. 'When in Rome . . .'

The mansion was literally big enough to get lost in. The
Hispanic houseman showed me the monster staircase and
gave me directions to the boy's room. I wondered whatever
happened to all the black servants they used to have over
here? Were they all sent to an island some place? I had to
count doors going along the upstairs hallway, so I was a
little tentative when I knocked the first time. I heard some
rustling but no response. I gave it the warrant-whack and
tried the handle. It was locked, but he was in there.

'Gerald? It's Sergeant Bodo. Sheriff's Department. I
want to talk to you.'

I finally heard his voice, which came down to more of a
snicker. 'Dodo?' We were off to a great start.

'Look, I know you're upset about your dad, but— '

He was moving around in there. Loading his gold-plated
Luger for all I knew. 'I'm not upset.' I believed him.

'Didn't you hear what happened?'

'Yes.'

'Gerald, your mother said I could talk to you.'

'So what?'

He was starting to get to me, this rich kid. If this had
been a street bust I'd have been in there in three seconds
bouncing him off all four walls. I tend to get very precise
before I lose my temper; it's the way I shift my gears.
'I'm not your mother, I'm a police officer and this is
serious business. You understand? Your dad's life may
be at stake here.'

He snorted or some sound like it; whatever it was, it was
negative and there was a strong suspicion that it was 'Dodo'
again. I could feel myself starting to burn. I looked around –
no one in sight – leaned close to the door and lowered while
intensifying my voice. 'Listen, you little jerk-off, if I have
to shoot the lock off, I'm getting in there. And when I do
I'm gonna whip your ass, mister.'

I heard another snicker, then locks, three of them, being turned. For a sinking moment I had this vision of a teenage prep-school pervert eager for what I had rashly promised.

The boy, grinning uncertainly, backed away as I entered. He had on glasses, was wearing one of those school blazers and loafers. I thought, what kind of a kid wears a jacket and creased pants at home at eleven in the morning? It was as if he was already on his way to his father's funeral.

I laughed, awkwardly I'm sure, and tried to sound convincing when I told him, 'Just kidding.'

He maintained that goofy grin and a certain amount of space between us, but didn't say anything. I looked around at a room packed with electronic gear of every kind. It looked like a thieves' warehouse. There were a few toys and games, a Metallica poster on one wall which gave me the creeps and, of course with a kid like this, Dungeons and Dragons. I moved around examining a VCR, tape recorders and a transfer machine, film and tape editing consoles, a fax, short-wave radio with transmitter, three computers . . . and that was only the beginning.

'Is all this stuff legal?'

'I don't know.'

I didn't either, and it was just as well. Time to try a softer approach. 'You gotta be pretty scared for your dad, right? I can see where that could shake you up a little.' I took a step toward him merely to signal contact, but he backed into a casement window like it was a cave. More secure, he could say, 'Not really.'

'Wait a minute. You know your father's been kidnapped, okay . . .?'

'Sure, but we're too rich for anybody to hurt him. There'd be a humungous stink.'

'They already did.'

He giggled. 'Yeah, they cut off his finger. Really gross.'

'Yeah, "gross." Also scary as hell.' Normally I wouldn't say that to a kid, but I seemed to be having trouble getting through here. 'Don't you love your dad?'

He had to think. 'Better than my mom.'

I could have said that, too, and I had never even met his father. So much for the appeal to sentiment. 'Why don't you relax, Gerald. I want to ask you some questions, is all. There's nothing to be afraid of.'

'I'm not.' He seemed to remember something. 'My dad took me bone-fishing last summer with a whole bunch of men.'

'Well, that's nice, isn't it. Tell me, do your parents get along?'

'I guess so. I'm away at school all the time. But I know what you want.'

'What are you talking about?' I had no idea. But he did.

'Does my dad have a girlfriend? That kind of stuff.'

'Gerald, you're a smart kid. I see that. A little twisted, but real smart. So, I'm saying don't mock me. You may feel safe because you're rich and in your own home and you're a little boy. And I'm a woman and we're supposed to have a maternal instinct. And I do. But the situation is, right now you are locked in a room with a crazed cop who has a "humungous" stake in solving this case and bringing your daddy home to the bosom of his loving family. Is there anything you don't understand about that? No? Good.' I thought I'd made an impression.

'He has one.'

'What?'

'A girlfriend.'

I needed a moment to regroup. 'Okay. How do you feel about that? Do you mind?'

'Why should I? When I'm grown-up and have money I'll have lots.' He looked like a petulant child talking about coconut creams, which I guess he was.

'I hope it brings you better luck than it did him.'

He stared at the floor and for a moment I worried that I'd hurt him. I mean, he *was* a kid. I also began to wonder if I hadn't assumed too much too soon.

He read my mind. 'You thought I was just making it up.'

'What made you think I wanted to know about any possible girlfriends?'

'TV.'

A reasonable answer, I had to admit, but I didn't entirely believe it. 'And he does have one. How do you know?'

He gave me the goofy grin again, the one little boys call 'shit-eaten.' It was obvious he would have liked to have strung this out, but his eyes betrayed him when they darted to some electronic equipment on a wall shelf. Gotcha! I moved to look, picked it over and suddenly turned to him in amusement. 'My God, you've bugged the house.'

He was so delighted with himself he came right out of his cave, brave in his precocity.

'You listened to us question your mother and Mr Duchow and the servants and . . .' It was really a queasy thought.

But he nodded enthusiastically. 'I haven't had time to listen to all the tapes yet.'

'Wait a minute. You weren't here yesterday.'

'I can turn it on and off with an electronic signal through the phone lines. When my mother called me at school to tell me what happened to my dad I knew it would be juicy stuff on it.'

'Okay, how do you know about the girlfriend when no one else does? Or'll admit it, anyway?'

'I accessed his computer. That's how they talk to each other.'

I was starting to get excited and trying not to show it.

'Annie Robertson. But they use real pukey love names sometimes.'

'How do I find her?'

'I don't know. Her apartment's near a lake, I guess.
'Cause he asked her if she wanted a canoe for a present
and she said, "Ha ha!" And she talks about the cute little
ducks. It's real dumb.'

I caught myself beaming at him. 'Have I told you you're
one weird kid?'

'I know it.' He was so proud.

VI

Finding the girlfriend was easy after that. It wasn't far from the scene of the kidnapping actually, and the fact that it was inland, nearer the Everglades than the ocean, limited population density a lot. The thing that surprised me as I approached was the modest nature of the apartment complex. What kind of rich man's girlfriend was this? A high-priced hooker would have demanded more.

It was boxy, caramel-colored; the planting was too early in its growth to provide any grace or shade for years to come. But there it was . . . the small lake in front. There weren't any canoes, but there sure as hell were ducks.

Her name was on the mailbox. I buzzed, no one answered. Going around to the back I looked for someone to ask. The pool was in the rear surrounded on three sides by the apartment and some scrubby palms that would provide privacy in the year 2000. It was very quiet even for early afternoon and you got the feeling the place was only half rented. Welcome to Florida.

There were two little boys playing Marco Polo in the near end of a pool that would not have been disgraced by some energetic use of a rake and net. At the far end a woman was doing bend-and-stretch exercises with her back to me. She was wearing a maillot cut all the way to the hips on the side, and cropped, low-maintenance hair. A fitness freak, or athlete if you prefer.

'Excuse me! You know Annie Robertson?'

She was serious about that workout, but called back over her shoulder, 'Not as well as I'd like to. Why?'

'I need to talk to her.' I went towards her, figuring that kind of cute answer deserved further exploration.

She turned around – an athlete, all right. 'You are. Mea culpa.'

I showed her the shield and introduced myself. She shook hands, vigorously as you might expect, and indicated I should sit in a deck chair. She had oil all over her body – I wondered who for – and started wiping it off with a big towel. 'I've been expecting you. Sit down. Be drinks along in a minute.' Maybe that was who for.

'We understand you're a friend of James Chapelle.'

'That's right.'

'Was he on his way here when he was kidnapped?'

'Supposed to be. 'Course, he was late, but then it was his wedding anniversary.' She looked up and flashed me her wicked grin which she probably had patented for its great effect on the guys.

First one tanned leg went up on a chair to be rubbed off and then the other. They were shapely but muscular. I found my mind wandering to the question of whether guys really want this and why? They used to like to slide between soft thighs; now it was hard bodies. Why couldn't they ever get it right? Maybe it was some kind of fantasy thing men had about being gripped and imprisoned by strong female legs. Whatever, we were getting stronger and they were getting wimpier and that wasn't the way it was supposed to play out.

'Sergeant?'

The job, Frankie! Off guard, I scrambled. 'You don't seem very upset about his disappearance, Ms Robertson.'

She flopped down in a chair off to my side, so I had to scoot around to confront her. For a moment she stared at the pool and her tone darkened. 'I am. I was up all night, crying. No one to tell it to, that's the hard part, how it feels. I'm devastated.'

'Could've fooled me.'

She wasn't offended and I had hoped she would be. 'This

is just how I act when I'm upset. I turned off the television and radio the minute I heard. It's the only way I can deal with it when the pain gets too much.' I wondered if she knew about the little digital message of the morning. 'How did Mrs Chapelle take it?'

'About the same. How close is your relationship with Mr Chapelle?'

The widow's weeds were not discarded, they were flung up and out. 'Well, he was on his way here to fuck me stupid – or the other way around. Does that answer your question?'

I took off my dark glasses and put them in my jacket pocket, the better to let her see what I had in my face. I don't know if it had an effect but the mood swung wildly again.

'Sorry, I didn't mean to sound like that, deliberately raunchy. If you want the honest truth, James and I didn't have a particularly hot sexual relationship. Mostly we were friends. *Are* friends.'

I looked at those strong, practiced legs again and didn't believe a word of it. We were interrupted by a man's voice calling, 'I couldn't find any soda. Mineral water all right?'

We both turned towards the apartment although she knew whose voice it was. Dunn!

'Hi, Sergeant.'

SEAN

My legendary charm wasn't going to do it this time. Frankie was trying to burn holes in my face with her lethal eyes. I put the tray down on a little table between them, a bottle of Amstel for me, a Scotch for Annie, the mineral water and a couple of glasses. 'What can I get you?' I asked in my best maître d's voice. I knew she wouldn't drink on duty; she wanted to be sheriff some day. I wouldn't have enjoyed partnering with her in the old days.

She didn't even want to acknowledge much less answer me, but looked to Annie. 'What's he doing here?'

Muscles was too smart to get between. 'Ask him.'

Frankie had to turn back, her tone that used on third-time felons. 'If you knew about Ms Robertson and didn't tell me, I'll have your ass, Dunn.'

'You can have it as a present.'

She wasn't listening. 'I swear to God, I don't care who you know.'

I didn't want to embarrass her but . . . 'The truth is, it was just old-fashioned detective work. We heard Chapelle was this cautious, discreet guy who wouldn't even use the office phone to call here. Sorry, Annie.' I used 'Annie' deliberately, just to cause trouble, which I was kind of enjoying. Find your fun where you can.

'No, James is considerate of everyone. Even the world-class bitch he's married to. And I admire him for it, it's rare.' She looked to Frankie as if to say, you should be so lucky to find one like that in today's market.

'Anyway, we also hear he's this big romantic. So I just called all the florists within a few blocks of his office in West Palm. I scored on the third one.'

'Oh.' She was embarrassed. 'Freddo brought him here all the time and he was your buddy, you got him his job, you're in charge of the Chapelle's security— '

'I told you before, I'm not. The company is. I'm not the company. I barely know these people.'

'But he just never happened to mention Ms Robertson here to you. I find that impossible to believe.'

'Sorry.'

Annie, watching us, was grinning. 'Say, you two are *not* friends.'

That was bound to draw Frankie's lightning. 'How did you meet Mr Chapelle?' You could have filed your nails on the edge in her voice.

'I backed into him. Literally. My Honda, his Merc. I was

in the parking lot of a bank up in West Palm and I guess I was in a hurry to get back to the office. He was so nice about it he almost convinced me it was his fault.'

'So you naturally gave him your name and phone number.'

'That's what you do when you hit someone, isn't it?'

I just kicked back and nursed my beer, which is the only safe way for me to drink it. I thought I'd let them work out on each other for a while.

The boys got out of the pool, toweled off and went in. They looked at us a little dubiously. I didn't blame them.

'So you started going out with him.'

'Well, a week later he called and . . . yes, I had lunch with him.'

'Did you know he was married?'

'Yes. Everyone in Palm Beach is either married, getting married or getting divorced, and the three are pretty much interchangeable. Does that help?'

'I'm not interested in your morals, Ms Robertson, except where they might affect the return of Mr Chapelle and the prosecution of his chauffeur's killers.'

'That's a relief.'

'Why, if he was so discreet, would he risk leaving his anniversary dinner to come here?'

You could see Annie savoring her reply and a taste for irony. She smiled sweetly. 'It was our anniversary, too. The mating of the Merc and Honda.'

Frankie looked at her notes. 'You called Mrs Chapelle a "world-class bitch." Do you know her?'

'He told me a lot of things.'

'They always do, don't they.' Oh, this was getting mean. 'Had you ever met either of the Chapelles before the "mating of the Merc and Honda"?'

'I'd seen them around, I guess. We used to live in Palm Beach, you know. We were part of that whole crazy scene up there.'

'"We"?'

'My late husband and I.'

'How long ago did your husband die?'

'"Die"? I should be so lucky. Mr Robertson's doing fifteen to twenty in Atlanta at the pleasure of the Securities and Exchange Commission. Federal sentencing laws being what they are, it's just too bad he wasn't smart enough to rob a string of video stores with a machine-gun. He would have been out in five.'

'The lady knows her law,' I pointed out to Frankie. She was not grateful and, indeed, both women turned to look as if they had forgotten I was there and wished I wasn't.

'I learned it the hard way, and I take no pride in it,' Annie said.

'How did people treat you?' It was a question Frankie wouldn't have thought to ask.

'Like a leper. Stone-cold broke and not a friend in the whole bloody town. After all the entertaining we'd done, the clubs we'd fought our way into, the boring, self-congratulatory charity affairs we'd waded through . . . it meant zip. Can you believe it?'

I could.

'So, anyway, I moved down here and rehabilitated myself emotionally and physically. Getting in shape's one of the greatest things I ever did for myself. I got a good job in real estate and I'm doing great, thank you. I'm entirely independent, and I really like that.'

'Not entirely,' Frankie told her.

'If you mean James, forget it. A watch on my birthday.'

'You're saying you've never profited from your relationship with Mr Chapelle?'

'You bet your booty I am, lady. You want copies of my bank statement, income tax or any other damn thing, you're welcome to it.'

Again I had to put in my oar. I never learn. 'A look around makes a believer out of me.'

Frankie gave me a stare this time that was intended to stop my heart for ever. 'Mr Dunn, are you working for Ms Robertson or are you just a very close friend? Because I was under the impression you were being paid by Mrs Chapelle to help recover her husband.'

'How about the latter?'

Annie had had enough; she yawned, stood and went to the edge of the pool. 'I think I'll do a couple of laps before I go in.'

'Ms Robertson, what did you do when he didn't show up the other night?'

She looked back at Frankie over her shoulder, and suddenly they were in the sisterhood. 'What do we always do? Blow out the candles, sing a sad song and go to bed.'

She jumped in. Big! We had to duck, which was the idea, and got a little wet anyway. But Frankie didn't get mad. I think she understood. Instead, she decided it was my fault. 'Mr Dunn, I want to talk to you.' She marched off, convinced, of course, that I would follow.

Annie, bobbing at the other end of the pool, sleeked back her already sleek hair and called to me, 'Come on in, Dunn. You don't need a suit.'

I pointed a minatory finger. 'You're a troublemaker.'

'Trouble's fun.'

I told her I was a man staunch in my devotion to duty and 'fun' did not even enter my lexicon, or words to that effect.

She said, 'Go with that one and it'll cost you one of what you now got two of.' She was already climbing back out of the pool as I trailed after Frankie.

We stood around arguing in front of the apartment for a few minutes. Or Frankie ripped me up and down for unprofessional behavior and I listened. For one thing, she was convinced I had known Annie previously, and I did nothing to disabuse her.

I have no doubt now that the woman herself was looking

down at us from her apartment window even as she picked up a cellular phone and punched in a number. We do know that she placed a call at about that time, and the content.

'Hi, this is Blair. Guess who just came to see me. Call me when it's, you know, convenient. Bye-bye, love.'

FRANKIE

Dunn insisted we stop at a little waterside restaurant in Del Ray Beach on the way back. He was one of those types who thought he could win anybody over, even a hard-case like me, and you couldn't discourage him with a club. I only agreed because it was almost three o'clock in the afternoon and all I'd had to eat that day was a candy bar Owen had slipped me back at the Chapelles' when he thought I looked peaked.

The restaurant wasn't much; a little wooden deck wide enough for a row of tables-for-two ran along the back. It was surrounded by a wooden rail encrusted with gull guano. To us, gull guano is decor. Despite my hunger I was having trouble eating and picked away at a club sandwich. Dunn ate everything in sight, even the pickles, and drank a beer. I give him credit for watching me sip iced tea without comment.

He asked me, 'How come you didn't tell her about her lover's new handshake?'

'Nothing in it for me. She's too tough to rattle, Ms Pecs.'

'You're not exactly silly putty yourself.'

'Why didn't you tell her, then? Hate to see the girls cry?'

'As a matter of fact, yeah. I was raised a lot by my grand-mother and a whole other gaggle of women. Who I loved, but I think sometimes it can oversensitize you to them.'

'Where was your old man?'

'Dying. He was always dying. He spent more time dying than most people spend living. Anyway, when I was in

Homicide I was always chicken about taking the news home to the victims' wives.'

I must have made some noise under my breath that sounded contemptuous to him.

'You, on the other hand, probably enjoy that part of it.'

'Come on,' I muttered. I was a little embarrassed that I might have come off that way. Nobody likes that duty. He was feeding the gulls, encouraging them to make pests of themselves. He was always feeding or taking care of something – his face, some animal, probably orphans, whatever. Saint Francis with a mouth on him.

'I think she looks pretty good, Annie.'

'What I think is you been pokin' her on nights the boss was home with wifey. Somebody's wifey.'

'Wrong. I told you how I found her.'

'Yeah, yeah.' The trade wind ruffled napkins and hair, stroked our faces, washed away the humidity. I turned mine to it. The smell of distant islands and things washed up . . . There were a few squalls out in the direction of Miami but there always are at this time of year and it gives an energy to all those delicate colors we live with. 'You told me you hadn't seen the Chapelles for two years.' I had to turn back to see his reaction. 'Missus said eight or nine months.'

'They have a different sense of time.'

'She also said they met you when you were with the Miami PD. Did that have anything to do with your getting dumped?'

He threw a piece of turkey high into the air and a gull swooped in to capture it just before it hit the deck. Its shadow or fluttering of wings alarmed a nervous tourist at the next table. He glared at Sean who smiled back. 'I backed over my captain's legs.'

'Wonderful.'

'He thought it was pretty funny at the time. Between screams. Have I got time for another beer?'

'No. You were wasted, right?'

'Hell, we all were. Why else would we be in the parking lot of a cop bar at two in the morning? He didn't want anyone to go home, though, so he plops down on the pavement and starts shooting out tires.'

'A captain did this?'

'That wasn't so bad, but his aim left something to be desired. So naturally, we were all in kind of a hurry to get out of there. I suppose I should've looked in the mirror.'

It was all so dead-pan, matter-of-fact, I wondered if he wasn't shining me on. But then you always wondered that.

'You got fired for this? It wasn't your fault.'

'Frankie, get real. I crippled the man. My superior. But, hey, you thought it was going to be bigtime sleaze, didn't you? Like I was on the pad or shot a kid or— '

'I'm supposed to be reassured you're just an alcoholic?'

'I wasn't an alcoholic, I was a drunk. If I was still a drunk you think the Chapelles would want me?'

'I don't know what they want you for.'

'I'm a reference point in an uncertain world.'

'Whatever the hell that means.'

'Listen, you could work for these people. Make big bucks, see the world, like me. No more decomposing corpses of five-year-old children, no more fifteen-hour days, drunken cops playing grab-ass at the lieutenant's retirement party . . .'

'Why would they want me?'

'For one thing, Duchow thinks you're pretty cute. Intelligent too, of course.'

'You're making me sick.'

'No, he's right, but— '

I ran up a warning hand – train coming, you horny bastard! 'Don't start with me.'

All innocence. 'What? You mean me? You don't have to worry about me.'

'And the Pope's not Italian.'

'He's not. And I'm celibate.'

'You're gay?'

'That's not what the word means.'

'I know what it means.'

'I like football and I'm a messy dresser.'

'You're not gay. You had an accident?'

'Had it shot off like Jake Whatsisname in *The Sun Also Rises*? Very romantic, but no, I'm all here. It just saves a lot of trouble.'

This wasn't making sense. 'But you're a guy. That's all you think of, all day every day. You spend your whole goddamned lives trying to scratch this big itch in the sky that never stops itching.'

'You exaggerate.' He fed another swooping gull; I was learning to hate those fucking gulls.

'You just hate women, don't you?'

'I like women. I even go out with them sometimes.'

'Nuns?'

At times men become these serious, sincere little boys when they want so much for you to believe them. This one was a real man, I admit that, but he could do it with the best of them. 'I just wanted you to know that, with all your other problems, you don't have to worry about me hitting on you.'

'That's nice, but it's a little extreme.' I suspected that 'all of your other problems' was patronizing, but I didn't want to appear paranoid.

Looking past him, I could see inside through the sliding glass doors to the bar and the television set above it. On the screen, Sylvia Chapelle, Duchow and a lawyer-type giving a press interview in an office, the kind those expensive firms have where a soccer game would not be out of the question.

I stood and pressed closer to the door in order to see better, and Sean joined me, standing a little close behind for a celibate. By the time I had noticed the interview, it was almost finished, and it was impossible to hear much over the bar talk, anyway. I told Dunn I hoped to hell she was saying she'd cooperate and deal and would the actors for God's sake get back in touch.

He sat down again and seemed to be remembering something. 'Sylvia's not quite what you think she is.'

'What is she quite?' I came back and sat, mildly interested.

'Actually she was raised dirt poor. Chapelle met her when she was a saloon singer in New York. She didn't pursue him, he pursued her. The guy was really bonkers over her and still is in his funny Palm Beachy way.'

'That's it?'

'For years now she's been commuting to the University of Miami, all the way down there, to get a degree in English Lit. She's involved in a lot of charities— '

'I know, I know, and she's got great tits. Let's get going, huh.'

I move very quickly when I move. It's a habit. I was already on my way inside. I saw him, unhurried, slug down the remainder of his beer – waste not, want not – and stroll after me.

SEAN

She insisted we take one car from there – hers. I couldn't see the practicality of it and suspected it was because I was a suspect, the only one she had a hope in hell of keeping under the microscope long enough to discover anything. She didn't have that hope in hell, but I didn't mind.

We went along Ocean and then South Ocean and found ourselves on one of the grander streets, Vedada Lane. I couldn't tell if by design or what, because the route seemed uncharacteristically random, and yet Frankie drove like someone definiitely on the prod. I assumed at the time it reflected her disquiet about the case and maybe even my part in it.

The mansions were lovely in their colors but there was also something monstrous about their very size and cost, like gliding between two rows of brooding, watching tyrants. It diminished you, which was their intent, of course.

It was the right place for Frankie to ask, 'How come you hate rich people?'

'My old man was a coal miner.'

'Oh.' She seemed to understand that. 'What happened to him?'

'Black lungs and amber bottles.'

'You some kind of Communist then?'

'I'll tell you, I was down in Nicaragua on a case, and all those red-hot revolutionaries? They're now living on the same big estates they took away from the dirty rotten exploiters in the name of the poor and exploited. Right?'

She wanted an answer. 'Yeah, but you want to get rid of all the rich?'

'Can't. "For ye have the rich with ye always." I just think we got it backwards. Instead of oppressing the poor we should oppress the rich.'

She turned her head to watch the estates sliding by, seemingly giving respectful thought to my great wisdom. 'You could be talking about me, you know. I could be an heiress.'

I expressed a natural skepticism.

'No, I could. My old man lives in one of these.'

'I thought he was a cop?'

'My stepfather. Before that, my mother was a maid. Real good-lookin' lady when she was young.'

I interjected, 'I can believe it,' but didn't get anything back, not a smile, not even a shrug. Okay, it was clumsy.

'Anyway, she got knocked up.'

I made a hum of sympathy. 'And she never told you who he was? You could sue, get rich, retire to . . . Palm Beach.'

She stared ahead, giving nothing in tone. 'She might have when I was little, but later on I just didn't give a shit.'

'Where's your mother and stepfather now?'

'He's dead. She's in Fort Lauderdale with two cats and five thousand bottles of gin.'

I started to ask something else but she cut me off with, 'Subject closed.'

We went back over to West Palm after that. A call from the Medical Examiner asking us to come to the morgue had ended our brief wanderings. My favorite place.

Cops see every kind of horror, of course: floaters falling apart when you pull them out, burn victims, child victims. They find themselves standing in brains at an accident scene. But the thing about the morgue is the smell. It's driven me back to smoking more than once. Most officers are nonchalant about the place, and I believe some of them, but the people who work there all have, figuratively, an extra eye or finger or breast. Their greatest joy is flaunting its awfulness as close to your face as they can and still avoid being knocked on their ass.

I was beginning to know Frankie; she'd never allow herself to have any feelings about it. The drawer was pulled open and we were looking down at poor old Freddo after the band-saw. There wasn't any reason for it except to provide some sort of sick visual aid for the ME's informational. 'Canoe-maker's getting sloppy,' I told him.

Neddy gave me a baleful look; he was proud of his work. 'Our customers never complain.'

Where else would you find wit like that except at a morgue. 'Humor,' I pointed out to Frankie, in case she missed it.

'Here's the cleanest entrance wound of the three, the one

that entered the left thorax and penetrated the ventricle, shutting everything down. It entered at a little less than a forty-five-degree angle. The one in the face did so much structural damage it's hard to say for certain, but the guesstimate's about the same angle.' 'Guesstimate?' I hate that word.

Frankie and I looked at each other, just like partners. She started to pace, acting it out, her hand the trajectory. 'Shooter *was* laying down. Playing an accident victim. Forty-five degrees means Carfagno was right on top of him. Either Freddo was rushing him, which doesn't make a lot of sense because he had a gun . . . Would he hesitate to use it?'

'He once shot a dog that kept him awake.'

'Or he bought the act till the very last second.'

'The distance between where the Merc skidded to a stop and where the shooter was wouldn't leave time for anything except dumb instinct.'

She frowned. 'Took some kind of guts to flop down there in front of an oncoming car at the last minute. Tells us something about the actor.'

'Yeah, he's playing with fifty-one cards.'

The ME suggested that forensics had a couple of bullets and some other items that would be of interest to us. We were keeping some cadaver waiting, no doubt. On the way out I told Frankie she'd been right all along about it being a set-up and she seemed pleased. Actually, I'd never doubted it.

The forensics lab was at the Sheriff's Station, one floor up from Frankie's office. If there's a single universal artifact for future archeologists it's the police station. From Belgrade to Biloxi, electronics aside, they have the same basics – lockers, holding cells, squad rooms, interrogation rooms, going back to old Bobby Peel. If they put one on Alpha Centauri it will be indistinguishable.

Mel, lord of this manor, wore a white gown, latex

gloves and a plastic shower cap that made him look like some bleached-out jive-ass street person. He went all the way, Mel. Owen was there on a stool at a counter looking through the microscope. We followed him.

'It's a thirty-two-caliber from, we think now, a Fabrique National.'

'A what?' Frankie asked, not surprisingly.

'Yes, this particular model's rare in this country. Belgian manufacture.'

She extracted the bullet and tossed it in her hand, feeling it, weighing it, communing with it. 'IRA?'

'Not necessarily.' He paused. 'But they are used by the security forces in Northern Ireland.'

Even in the face of that distinctly mick voice on the phone I had trouble accepting some major Irish involvement. We're chocolate, they're vanilla. It's true, we get a lot of tourists from the British Isles in the winter; it's cheaper than Majorca or Ibiza since the dollar committed suicide. But their relentless good manners and the tentative way they put their ivory feet down on the hot sands is distinctively unmenacing. And of course the Irish are the palest of them all with their red hair and pink necks, looking as if the sun coming up out of Africa is going to serve them barbecued for breakfast. It seemed to me that even the hardboys from the Falls Road would melt into surfers or mamboistos soon after their arrival on our decadent shores.

There was no reason for Frankie to think that way; she'd never been there, never been anywhere. Since the province of the detective is human nature and nothing else, it was a shame.

'Owen, you'd better get with the Immigration, the feebies, Secret Service . . .'

'Don't have much to give 'em.'

Mel said no fingerprints, no fingerprints anywhere except for Chapelle and the bodyguard. He brandished the ransom note. 'Yes, from the *Miami Herald* financial pages.'

Owen suggested they were already planning on how to invest their money.

'Of course,' Mel pointed out, 'it's sold all over the state and the Bahamas on the same day.' He moved toward a cabinet but paused to touch a drawer. 'The finger and ring were Chapelle's. Want to see?'

Lab nerds are only a little less ghoulish than morgue trolls. Frankie ignored him. He went on to unlock the cabinet – locked against thieves who could only be policemen – to expose a lot of admirably hi-tech sound equipment. 'Something potentially of use on the phone tape . . .'

Slipping in a cassette of the phone call from the kidnappers, he ratcheted up the volume to the point where I, at least, winced and everyone had to shout over it. 'I had to send it out for the clean-up and to have the background amplified. Hear something over the traffic?'

We all strained to listen, not without pain.

Frankie jumped first. 'An airplane.'

I said I thought it was landing, another leap but a good one.

Owen was skeptical; it was his role. 'So you are all sayin' the actor went to a phone, likely a booth, near an airport. What's that help? He could be squirreled in ten miles from there.'

I'd started my police work in New York and I'd noticed something then. 'They're lazy. They're all lazy, these bastards. Even Mafia dons won't go away from the neighborhood to place a call. My guess is we're in the area.'

'We still don't know what town that airport's in,' Owen argued.

I looked over at Frankie, who had her ear plastered to that damn speaker at risk to her hearing. 'That's four engines.'

I listened hard and, by God, she was right.

'They got four-engine airplanes comin' into Miami, Fort

Lauderdale, here and right on up the coast,' Owen pointed out. 'So where's that take us?'

Nobody said anything for a minute. Frankie was especially remote. The tape went on to the end of the conversation and ran out.

'Not much help, I'm afraid,' Mel said. He started to extract it.

'No, wait a minute.' Frankie came alive. I could see the break-out in her eyes. 'Play the last minute or so.'

Owen asked her what she'd heard, but she didn't answer. Mel rewound it to James's last couple of words and let it play. When it had run out again none of the rest of us had heard anything. We looked at each other, then at Frankie.

'Another plane.'

Mel said, 'So what?'

I thought I had heard it too, but the significance had escaped me.

Frankie knew what she believed; only the kick from a good insight lights a hunter's face that way. I saw her fingers form a fist. 'Time it.'

'Time what?' Mel asked.

I understood then. 'Two flights. Landing close together. Very close together.'

She popped up and began moving quickly around the room. 'You got it! There's only one airport around here has that volume of traffic. Miami.' Now she was pumping that fist. 'Owen, call Miami PD and tell them he's down there. No ifs, ands or buts, we want them focused, want them to go flat out.'

'That's kinda stickin' your neck on the block, Frankie.'

'Time I did.'

She marched out and as usual I followed. 'Want my opinion?'

'No.'

VII

Frankie drove me back to my car and I started for the motel in West Palm. I wanted time alone to think, but there was no chance; my boss called saying Amelia Chapelle wanted me immediately, claiming to have some information. More likely, I thought, she wanted attention.

I called her from the car. She wanted to meet me – she said it was the cocktail hour – at the Au Bar, of Kennedy infamy. I said no, the bar of the Royal Ponciana Hotel. Getting along with these people is a lot like dog-training – something I tried to communicate to Frankie – they're used to you jumping when they bark, so you have to keep them off balance to gain any measure of respect. Not that their respect is worth much, but it can be useful. She wasn't happy but I wasn't surprised that she gave in, either.

The Ponciana was old man Flagler's original creation, at one time the largest hotel in the world. The old pirate invented Palm Beach, if not the whole damn state. He once invited in a lot of workers to help realize his dream then, when their modest little houses began to look to him like urban blight, had them all over to a circus picnic while his thugs torched the neighborhood. An apt beginning.

I had to go home and gussy up for the hotel, so she was waiting for me, sitting back with a martini already in hand and her legs crossed under, barely under, the mini-skirt of a yellow linen suit. The mere fact that she had legs was a whole new perspective, but good ones set off by yellow pumps was a revelation. Through amber glasses the hyperthyroid eyes were suddenly very active and sexy.

Formerly untidy hair became feral. She indicated the low leather chair next to her.

When she smiled I realized for the first time that she was younger than her husband by a decade or more. But then weren't they all? I wondered why she had been hiding all this.

I wanted to get it on a business level as soon as possible. 'Mrs Chapelle, I understand— '

'Amelia. We don't think of you as an employee, Sean.'

'That's reassuring . . . Amelia.'

'I noticed you call Sylvia and James by their Christian names, so why not me?'

'Why not? I understand you have something to tell me.'

She leaned closer and I realized that about a thousand dollars' worth of perfume had gone into the preparation for this sharing a little drink together. That was scary.

'You know what the French call this time of day?' I could honestly say I didn't. 'L'heure bleue. It's the time when the bourgeoisie visit their mistresses before going home to the boring little woman who scrubs their floors, cooks their meals and raises their brats.'

'Ah. For the Irish, it's time for half-and-half.'

'Oooh, sounds kinky.'

'Actually, that's half-Guinness, half-ale.' Her attempt at a sexy smile thinned and then dribbled away. 'About this information?'

She sat back. 'All right. I thought you should know, James took his son, my nephew, to karate lessons over in West Palm. You know, to toughen him up, make him self-reliant. Fathers always think that's important. Of course, karate studios aren't usually in the greatest of neighborhoods, but somebody had told James about this one at a party and the "master," or whatever the hell they call them, was supposed to be super. Anyway, you can meet all kinds of people there. People not from here.'

Did she hear my groan.

'James met a young housewife who was bringing her son of about the same age for lessons. I doubt they got along because Gerald doesn't get along with other children, and the karate thing was of course a complete washout. He's the same nerdy little monster he always was— '

'James and the housewife?'

'I'm getting to it. Are you that anxious to be out of here? I'm in no hurry at all. Would you like another beer?' The word 'beer' made her nose twitch with disdain. 'Or perhaps something else?'

I turned down that offer but she made me another one, or started to. The tables were low; maybe this was why, because I felt her stockinged foot glide on to my shoe. She smiled, I left my foot where it was and we went on. I've suffered greater indignities.

'This, believe it or not, was just an ordinary little housewife from up in Jupiter. But I imagine she was a sexy little piece who knew something about fucking, and of course James is James. Forget his usual charms and delights, everybody around here's heard of the Chapelles so I'm sure she was impressed. *Le droit de seigneur?*'

I agreed. I would have agreed to anything. Her foot massaged my ankle and still I was brave. 'Did you ever screw him?'

'What?'

'James. Everyone else has.'

'I'll be damned. I'd heard about you, but you really are a cheeky bastard, aren't you?'

'Where did you hear the other from, about little Miss Nobody?'

'Never mind. Here's her name and address.' She pushed across a piece of paper.

'You don't have to answer about you and Jim. Just curious.'

'You're damn right I won't answer, and I ought to slap

you hard. Am I a suspect now? Or Glen, who has to call a servant to throw a spider out of the house.'

'Your husband, whatever his failings— ' There were quite a few, she let me know immediately, with an attitude that suggested most manifested themselves when horizontal.

'Whatever his failings, he's always struck me as an angry man behind it all, and angry men can be violent and even brave under certain circumstances. Courage is often just showing off or playing a part or— '

'I'll bet that isn't true of you.' She was shameless. Her foot ran up my leg to the thigh and kneaded. I wondered if she expected a response. More likely it was enough to be in charge.

'Come on, who told you about this business?'

'Never mind. I am Italian, and we have our ways. Machiavelli, you know.'

'Yeah. Jupiter was married, right?'

'Yes, and hubby found out. That's when James asked you to get him a bodyguard.'

'That was why?'

'You're going to pretend you didn't know, as usual. That gets very boring.'

'Someday you may want me to do something for you without asking questions.'

She liked that, but it was dumb to play around with an unstable woman. She moved her chair around closer to mine. The foot wouldn't bend that way, so it was a relief in one way, but on the other hand I was near enough to find out that her breath was warmer than the room.

'Why was James afraid of this guy? He's always skydiving or running rapids or ballooning up the Amazon.'

'Well, he was a big young man, I guess, and kind of tough and working-class, and . . .' She brightened. '. . . he said he'd kill him.'

'"Working-class"? What did this guy do?'

'I think he owned a fishing boat.'

I groaned audibly. 'And what did he fish for?'

'Fish, I suppose. Isn't that customary?'

'Not any more. Smuggling, running dope from a mother ship . . . was this guy connected, that you know of?'

'No, I never heard anything. Why did you groan? I thought I was helping you.'

I was wishing I had that second beer. 'For one thing, it ought to be a simple kidnapping and it's not. Also, if this guy has anything to do with it then the chances of getting James back frankly aren't very good. I was hoping the answer would be simpler, like your husband set it up. Or you.'

She at least pretended to be surprised and offended. 'What are you saying? My God, what's wrong with you? We were kidding before, I thought. Why would we do such a thing?'

'Who'd run the corporation if James didn't come back?'

'Glen, of course. Well, Michael would run it, just as he does now, but Glen would get to look like he was in charge. Come on, surely you don't think he— '

'He doesn't like hand-me-downs. You can see it in everything he does. And you're a frustrated woman who's a lot brighter than her husband, so you like it even less. Not to mention the joy of forcing Sylvia into suttee.'

She didn't ask me what 'suttee' was, just shook her head. 'You're really too much. I can't believe this.' Suddenly she hissed, 'You bastard!' and reached under the table to grab my crotch. It was the move of an accomplished predator, managing to gather in all the utensils in a single swoop and hold them fast in red-nailed captivity.

For a second I didn't know if it was love or war. We both sat there, smiling at each other like a pair of idiots. I dared to look around because I had this fleeting fantasy that every couple in the bar was doing the same thing and it was perfectly normal behavior here. If they were, I couldn't make it out.

My voice edging up half an octave, I managed, 'Now I believe you're Italian.'

Her voice went down to husky. 'You better believe it, mister.' She began to work her hand with the effect she wanted. I don't know what I wanted, but first there was a shiver – I know she caught that. Then the tumescence became apparent, and you could see some sort of female equivalent creep into her face. Lust, but also a sense of real power.

I managed to get my voice under control. 'I have to go.'

'Why?'

'I'm beginning to like it.' I got up quickly, trusting that she would let go when my privates and her hand reached the light, and hobbled out of there, trying to pretend I was walking normally. I could have pointed out, 'Because there's a serious crime here, lady, and your brother-in-law's life's at risk,' but what I had said was the right thing; she was still smiling when I went out the door.

The address in Jupiter turned out to be a dumpy little house of vaguely Spanish design with a lawn two feet high and a lot of blocks between it and the ocean. By the time I got there it was seven-thirty, not a bad time to catch working people, and I wanted to see the husband. Some investigators like to call first, but I'm not one of them.

I knocked and waited, looking around. It's easy to see a life in dissolution – the lawn goes first. But everything was either dead, dying or overgrown. A lot of touch-up jobs needed doing: paint, plaster, drains. Sometimes that just means the man moved out. I'd had to step around a boy's bicycle coming up the walk; no one to tell him you don't leave it there.

Finally a female voice from inside asking me what I wanted. There was a peephole in the door so I held up some ID. It so happens it was fake, left over from my time with Miami PD, illegally obtained and several years out of date, but no one ever looks at the date. Still, the door didn't open. I could hear a small child crying.

I asked to speak to Lelani or Daryl Grosbeck. 'Daryl?' The tone screamed incredulity. I told her either one, but eventually we determined that they weren't there and she was Lelani's roommate. It's rare when people are too frightened to open the door for a cop, but this one hung tough, if that's the word. 'Not after what happened,' she said.

'What happened?'

'Go away or I'll call the police.'

'I'm the police.'

'Oh, yeah.'

Always nice to have an intellectual for a roommate. I had to lean on her with the only tools I had, my voice and her seeming obtuseness. I was going to come back with a warrant claiming among other things that we had a new process that could scrape marijuana smoke away from where it had embedded itself in the walls. Something worked. Lelani was at her aerobics lesson in downtown Jupiter. I asked again about the jealous husband but it seems the interview was at an end.

'Betty's Bodies' was on the second floor of a building old enough to suggest that period when every dink town in Florida thought it was going to be the pearl of the Atlantic seaboard. Opening the door, I was assailed by a musky effluence of sweaty air and rap. Everything in the studio bounced, flailed, flapped, stomped, pulsated. And sweated.

'One . . . and . . . two . . . and . . . up! Up! Higher! Buns-of-iron, buns-of-steel, buns-the-boys-will-long-to-feel!'

I was willing to bet that Betty herself made that up. It went a long way toward validating celibacy as a lifestyle.

The crazy thing was, most of the women there were

already attractive. What did they want? It's becoming a very strange country; people who can't afford to have the roof fixed join health clubs while others who have to borrow to pay their kids' tuition take a Caribbean cruise to get their minds off what they owe. I watched for a while . . . all this activity made me want to lay down and drink a beer. Maybe even smoke a cigar if it annoyed a yuppie.

It wasn't hard to spot Lelani. I knew James's taste, morganatic or otherwise, was limited to every attractive woman in the world. But to give the devil his due – and people always did with James – it didn't necessarily run to huge jugs or dancers' legs, but might mean a brilliant smile or lively mind. Lelani did happen to have good breasts and legs and the face was cheerleader-cute, framed, as it was, by layered blonde hair. But it looked tired from something other than exercise. All of which suggested a story to tell.

There was another reason I knew she was the one. I'm not pretty but nevertheless ladies sometimes pay me heed. Not here. You'd think two dozen women, yes, working their buns off, working harder than any slave in history to torture their bodies into superior sex objects, would at least be cognizant of the presence of a rogue male among the flock, but no. Total self-absorption. Except for one whose eyes slid sideways. Lelani. That's what James had seen.

She wasn't any trouble. Accepting me and my purpose without question, she went willingly to a nearby coffee shop. You can't invite these healthy women to bars any more. I mentioned the kidnapping and, now that the adrenalin was down to sludge, her face turned as gray and worn as the coffee they serve in those joints.

'You had an affair with James Chapelle.'

She was silent, studying her napkin. 'Yes.' It emerged like a berthing. Even the one word said 'Southerner.'

'Lelani, I'm not a real cop, you know that. And in my line of work we don't meet a lot of church wardens. So I don't judge. Have you ever had a shrink? Think of me as your shrink. Even if your husband's involved in Chapelle's kidnapping, you can tell me.'

She started to cry. I gave her a piece of Kleenex and asked the waitress to bring her a couple of aspirins for no reason I can think of now. 'What is it?' I asked, very soft, very gentle, Sean-the-shrink.

'My husband's dead.' I waited. 'At least I think he is.' I had to urge her on. 'Some Seminoles found him, or someone, way back in the 'Glades days after he disappeared. Near that reservation at Big Cypress. Police said it was him but the 'gators and all those awful things that live in there'd been eatin' on him. There was nothin' left for me to see except some jeans and a shirt and there wasn't enough of them.'

'What about dental charts?'

'Daryl didn't like dentists. When he got a cavity he just filled it up with wax or something or had a friend pull it.'

If she heard a sound, it was me summoning 'Jesus' under my breath. I was looking for the Terminator.

'Actually, he had great teeth. I should know, he used to bite me.'

'In ecstasy or anger?'

For the first time I saw her smile; it was wan but showed nice promise. 'Both. Mostly the first, though. He was a terrific lover.'

'Not terrific enough, I guess.'

She actually blushed. 'Oh, James was a great lover too. And really nice for somebody so . . . well known and rich. You know, I was flattered. Daryl was never home then, not since— '

She was nobly trying to protect the terrific lover/biter/cuckold beyond the grave. If that's where he was. 'Since he got into the life?'

'Huh?'

'Dope.'

'Oh, yeah. That was terrible. We had a lot of money all of a sudden, or he did, but he got mean and ran around and . . . you know, hit me. He even got into this religion with the Cubans he was working for, Santa Maria or something they call it, where they kill poor little chickens.'

I thought that if James were there and I had remonstrated with him about getting involved with the mate of a gorilla in the dope business who practiced voodoo, he would have laughed. '"Santeria." I don't blame you about the chickens, although I eat a lot of it.'

'Me too,' she said sadly.

'How did the authorities determine that the corpse was Daryl's?'

'I don't know. Clothes and hair and size, I guess. Also, he had broken knuckles from hitting people and so did the body.'

I looked down at my own knobs and gnarls.

'If you want my opinion, they didn't seem to care if it was Daryl or not. You know, just another dope runner. One officer said to me there were more smugglers than mosquitoes in South Florida and as far as he was concerned their lives had equal value. That's a fine thing to say to a grievin' widow, don't you think?'

'Whoever it was, the man they found, how'd he die?'

'Shot in the head. Several times, they said.'

Once is usually enough, unless you're mad at someone. Or want to screw up the identification of the body. 'Police ever report any leads or suspects?'

She teared up again and since she was drinking decaf, I asked the waitress for hard stuff to kick in some endorphins, get us off the self-pity.

'I told you, they didn't even care.'

'You think it was him? Daryl? If it wasn't, wouldn't you have heard from him?'

'Not unless he was horny.' Then she started to get mad, which was good. 'All he ever wanted was to have sex with me. James treated me different. He was a real gentleman, classy, like I was smart and a worthwhile person. Put me right on his level.'

'Yes, he does that.'

'What?'

'How did your husband find out?'

'My son told him. Told him enough anyways.'

'He did threaten to kill Chapelle?'

'Oh, my God, he was insane. I was scared to death. I told James, you know, warned him.'

'Then what happened?'

'I don't know.'

'What do you mean?'

'Daryl disappeared right after that.'

God, the pussy factor in history; without it there'd be no original sin and the human record would be practically spotless.

On the way back to the motel I struggled with the question of whether or not I should tell Frankie. I decided against it for the moment. There were reasons.

FRANKIE

A week later I found myself staring at a newspaper heading some shit-for-brains, probably my wonderful captain, had outlined in red and left on my desk: KIDNAPPED MILLIONAIRE STILL MISSING. It sure as hell was the captain's voice I was listening to. '. . . Not one damn lead. Not one. That don't cut it, Sergeant. Not one damn bit.' He was one of those no-neck bulls that can fill most of the space in a cubicle the size of mine, so you could feel or maybe it was smell his breath when he bellowed. A loud voice was a bellow in there. I knew that everyone out in the larger office was listening, and probably enjoying it like the sadistic bastards they were.

'I got leads, Captain. And we finally found a judge'll give us a tap on Annie Robertson's phone. I just don't have enough to bring forward right now. The thing we can't figure is why the goddamn actors don't get back to us on the ransom. Unless they totaled Chapelle already and— '

'You mean "Mr Chapelle."'

'Yeah, Chapelle. And they're running.'

'That what you think?'

'No. I mean, I don't know. So far they strike me as having more guts than smarts. The kind who always fuck up. Unless, of course, they're smart enough to look dumb, in which case— '

'What the hell are you sayin'? Look, Bodo, the Sheriff's back from El Paso on Thursday and you goddamn well better have somethin' solid by then. And in case you got any doubts, I was against givin' you this assignment in the first place.'

He rumbled out. It was like an elephant's behind going away from you into the jungle. 'Yes, sir, Captain Dickhead,' I muttered, but it was dangerous; he had fantastic hearing for dissent. I didn't care. Through the door I could see everyone go back to whatever useless thing they'd been doing. Was my neck red? I'll bet it was, but he was right in a way; I was beginning to sound like that whack-off Dunn.

Owen slipped in and asked me how many real leads, he meant 'hot' leads, did we have? Dispirited, I merely made a zero with my thumb and forefinger. 'That's what I figured. What you gonna do?'

'Question everybody again.' I indicated the files, over a hundred interviews with friends, employees, rivals, lovers, and police reports on practically every violent criminal in the state of Florida. Then there were all the transcripts of telephone intercepts sitting in boxes on the floor around my desk. 'Go over these again. Pray.' He reached for part of the stack but I told him to go home. 'You got a family, Owen. All I got waiting's Stouffer's meatloaf, and it's never in a hurry.'

He gave in, promising to hit it hard in the morning. The rest of the office was emptying out, everyone headed for the pool, driving range, tennis court, windsurfing or whatever the rest of the world down here seems to do with their spare time. Dunn looked pretty urban but I was willing to bet even he had something stupid like that to do. I never seemed to do anything except be a cop. How did they manage?

My phone rang, which is just as well because philosophical thoughts make me depressed. The sound brought me back to life immediately, brought me back to the job, and I started shuffling the files like long-awaited presents even as I cradled the speaker between my shoulder and my neck and barked out my name.

It was a male voice, ineffectively muffled. 'Bodo? There's a dude you oughta talk to. Right away.' I had a sense of someone trying to sing the song of the streets and failing. 'Reuben Rodriguez, down in Miami.'

'Who is this?' He wouldn't answer, but I knew that when I asked. 'Why should I talk to this Rodriguez?'

'He was runnin' his mouth in the Rebel. You know it?'

Who didn't? A hotel and private club down in Coconut Grove on the south side of Biscayne Bay, frequented by the boys in the life. Bimbo heaven, too. But believe me, don't touch the cantaloupes, everybody's packing. They all wear dark glasses to protect their eyes from jewelry glare. Colombia should have a consul in the lobby. I know the Rebel.

'It was all about how he was into some bigtime kidnapping and it got all fucked up, so he bailed on it.'

My mind was starting to boil. 'He walked?' The voice on the phone made a sound. I assumed it meant 'yes.' 'And he's still hangin' out? What about the other doers?

Doesn't he worry just a little bit about that, for Christ's sake?' I already had him on longer than any tipster in history, which went toward confirming what I'd thought about him.

'I gotta go.'

'Wait a minute – what kidnapping? Who?'

'Hey, that's no place to ask questions.'

He was certainly right about that, but I was still jumping on the ends of his sentences in an attempt to hold him. 'Where can I find Rodriguez?'

'That's your problem. I said enough.'

Finally the click and dial tone. I put the phone down slowly to prolong the pleasure, because I was convinced. Cops' instincts. I was so stoked I slammed the desk with both fists. 'Yesssssssss!!!!'

VIII

I picked up Sean at this motel where he stayed when he was in town. I should have thought with a big rich company like that it would have been fancier, but he said he didn't care. I had the impression he was a hair-shirt kind of guy, and I'm not crazy about that.

By the time we headed south on 95 it had started to rain. Not hard, but the sea on our left disappeared in the murk.

'You recognize the voice?'

I told him no, but I'm not sure he believed it. He looked sideways at me. 'Anyway, Miami ran Rodriguez, he's a Marielito with outstandings and priors up the kazoo. Heavyweight, a shooter.'

'And his "last known's" somewhere near the airport.'

'You got it.'

Actually, I was in a great mood, adrenalin running a motocross with the rest of my glands. It was beginning to look like I might have a career after all, with a chance of saving the vic's life. It wasn't all about me; I really did worry about what the poor bastard was going through in the hands of these cockroaches.

Dunn noted that I was 'uncharacteristically cheerful,' as he put it. I didn't know if that was a slam or not. Kidding on the square, I told him that I hadn't felt this good since my stepfather died. He laughed, but again I didn't know what he thought; hell, I never knew what he thought.

I wouldn't have admitted it to him, to any guy, but while I was waiting in my apartment for the Miami PD to run Rodriguez I heard from an old boyfriend, and even though he was the cheap date from hell, we girls can use those validations from the suckers now and then. Of course, Dunn had to put all of this good feeling in the crapper with his comment. Maybe he was right, it's not my natural state.

When he suddenly told me he'd been holding out about how Chapelle was catting around with the wife of some dumb-ass runner and gotten his life threatened, I wanted to castrate the sonofabitch. I could have charged him right there with withholding evidence and interference with a criminal investigation and all that garbage, but I didn't have enough experience with the politics involved to know the cost. I promised myself that by the time I was through with this one . . .

The fact that the runner had ended up 'gator lunch soon after his threat disturbed me. Money can buy violence, although nothing I'd heard yet about Chapelle suggested he'd be capable of having it done. Matter of fact, you don't need all that much money; there are plenty of hitters on the street and in the bars who'd kill the Pope for five thou. I think one tried once. On the other hand, you never really know what will happen when a powerful man feels threatened. Because they don't ever feel as if they should be.

Dunn claimed he'd done a thorough job of investigation on this angle, yet he didn't have anything to show for it and even he wasn't arrogant enough to think that was going to satisfy us. So by the time we got to the station in Miami I was really pissed and I didn't care if it showed. But then he didn't care, either.

The lieutenant in charge of the bust was a Cuban named Estrada. He was wearing a Marlins cap and a black windbreaker like he thought he was in SWAT or something, but you could tell he was a stand-up guy. Thorough, too; he had the whole operation outlined on a blackboard with a sketch of the target apartment by the time we got there.

A couple of plainclothes and two uniforms were sitting around the ready room on desks or chairs or wandering around the way you do when your heart thinks it would like out of your chest but you can't admit it even to yourself. Everybody had a cup of coffee, donuts, pizza, there were three smokers, and so a certain amount of trash laying around. We're a lot more GI up north. That with the dim light and rain on the windows made me start to feel a little gloomy, a little tight. Maybe it was just Dunn. It was always convenient to blame my unwanted appendage.

'. . . All we got's this anonymous tip, so like we're not going in there with SWAT or the Marines or nothing. Why should they have all the fun, anyway?' He picked up a pointer and moved to the blackboard. 'Just us lucky band of hermanos, right? Here . . . the den of Mr Reuben "Badboy" Rodriguez. Or I shoulda said, "Señor." One of my people. Which means I will have to kick his ass all the harder.'

The box that represented the apartment, really a two-storey house divided into flats, had a tiny walkway on each side and a small yard in back. With chalk he filled in the rest of the block.

'. . . Four doors down, from Mira Flora. Yellow stucco. Dirty yellow's a safe bet. Bottom floor.' He turned to one of the plainclothesmen who oddly enough was a burly Pole or Eastern European or one of those. 'Ernie, you take the front with me and the Sergeant here. I definitely want a shotgun.' To the other one, 'Carlos, you take the back . . .' He indicated the uniforms, rookies, 'You two take the sides. He's a long-termer with warrants out and just maybe he's involved in this bigtime kidnapping the Sergeant's been so kind to bring to our attention. So watch it, manos. Any questions?'

There weren't any so I moved up to the front. 'I just want

to say one thing. Chances are, Chapelle isn't there now, if he ever was. The informant claims Rodriguez skipped out on the others. But if he's not there, I sure as hell want this sucker in shape to talk to me.'

They gave me that cynical body language cops have, letting the world know where I could stuff that last little request. As they got up and moved around, collecting weapons and gear, the big one called Ernie said, 'Shoot the gun out of his hand, boys.' If it had been me, I'd have felt the same way. No offense taken.

I'd been so focused on what we were doing I forgot about Dunn, who had been unusually unobtrusive in the back of the room. I heard Estrada say, 'Hey, Dunn, what do you think you're doing?' While I had never met any of these Miami cops before, I suspected Dunn had, or there was some sort of acquaintanceship between them, maybe only on reputation or rumor. It was obvious they didn't like the idea of a private security firm being involved. Join the club.

'I've been deputized by the Sheriff of Palm Beach County.' He was checking the clip on a Beretta that he carried in a shoulder holster when he wore a jacket. Now he paused and flipped open his wallet to show the ID to Estrada.

If I'd been ticked before I was berserk now. I didn't care what any of them thought. I shouted, 'Nobody told me that! Goddammit! That sucks!'

Estrada stepped in, using his rank, and cut it off. 'Doesn't matter. This is Dade. You'll wait by the car, Dunn.'

Sean shrugged, slipped the gun back into its holster, saluted with two fingers to the brow, and strolled out easily behind the other cops. Estrada and I watched him.

I tried to sound calm when I asked, 'How come he got bounced off the force down here?'

'I don't think he did. I heard he resigned.' He obviously wasn't hearing any special interest in my voice and set about getting himself ready for the raid, checking equipment, collecting the warrant and collateral papers.

'Why? Was he dirty?'

'I don't know. I heard he was a good cop. But yeah, maybe something.' He finally looked at me. 'If you really want to know, if it's important to you, go through channels, they'll tell you.'

'I didn't want to get into all the bureaucratic thing.' I was feeling a little embarrassed. 'Forget it.'

'Then let's play ball, okay? I'd like to see my wife before breakfast. And I guess you'd like to see your husband or boyfriend or whatever you got waiting for you.'

'Right.' He didn't read my expression and wouldn't have been interested, anyway. I followed him out, both of us moving on the balls of our feet.

The neighborhood was marginal, mixed racially. Sure enough, you could hear the planes landing and taking off. We passed a phone booth that the locals had savaged for fun or profit and I wondered if that's where the ransom call had been placed. Most of the Irishmen I'd seen would stick out around here like a pickle in ice-cream. There were a few tacky little houses but mostly it was tackier duplexes and apartments. Streets and yards, if you could call them that, were littered with auto parts, beer cans, broken toys, and God knows what else.

We rendezvoused at the corner, two unmarked cars gliding in silently except for the hiss of tires on the slick streets. The rain had almost stopped; that was a good thing. I glanced at my watch. Two-twenty. Everybody got out, moving softly on rubber soles, hushed voices speaking in the familiar shorthand of professional jeopardy.

I saw Sean leaning against Estrada's car, arms folded, distancing himself. He was getting wet but didn't seem to mind. I gave my stubby little thirty-eight-caliber revolver a last check, the tenth and absolutely last check. My stomach was up above my tonsils. I'd fired my gun a couple of times when I was in uniform but hadn't hit anyone, and as far as I knew nobody had ever aimed rounds directly at me. We all get stoked on a raid, no denying that, but only a few mad bulls really get off on it while most of us are rightfully terrified.

Estrada led off for the objective and we all fell in behind. The rain had become a light mist. I was last to go and Sean reached out to touch my arm. I jumped and immediately tried to cover it. All he said was, 'Careful, huh.'

But his concern threw me for a minute; I didn't know how to react. Mainly I was anxious to get away. 'Hey, I'm a killer.' I left him there and hurried to catch up.

There was a wooden porch along the front of the apartment. It looked so rickety I was afraid it wouldn't hold all three of us, and maybe not Ernie alone. It also creaked; that caused a certain collective pucker. A dog began to bark somewhere, bringing a cold hand to clutch at my heart. Ernie moved to a big window next to the door and peered in through the dirty windows and the dirty curtains inside them. He whispered, 'Light's on in back.'

He stayed by the window and Estrada stepped to the side of the door, reached over and pounded. We hadn't brought a ram or anything so he gave it all he had. 'Police warrant! Open the door!' He gave it another hammering for punctuation.

Ernie, still whispering for some insane reason, said, 'I see movement.'

Estrada backed up for kicking room and I got ready to join him. Granted, I'd worn my running shoes and he had on boots, but I like kicking doors and they never want the girls to get in on that. Suddenly it was like the world blew up in our faces, even though it was only three rounds coming through the door and splintering the old wood.

Everyone ducked frantically and used up their life's accumulation of obscenity. We all asked each other if we were okay. For a few seconds there we strangers were soulmates in terror. Ernie never went down, just out of the window, and now he jumped back to fire two blasts into the living room from that big shotgun. God bless him.

There were so many sensations in the next few minutes I lost track of what was real. Glass flew around, gunsmoke up the nostrils, someone scrambling and knocking over things inside. More dogs and now people yelling questions out into the night without even knowing what they were saying. Just fear.

Ernie shouted, 'He ran in back. I think I maybe hit him.'

What we should have done was fall back and call for SWAT, but surprisingly nobody even thought it. I wanted the guy too badly myself and I guess they were just so used to violence down there in Miami everybody was a cowboy by instinct. Anyway, Estrada and I fired through the door and then hit it with hands, feet, gun butts, and for all I remember now I might have bitten or belly-bumped it open. We went in screaming like maniacs, into the darkness and trash and debris and overturned furniture. It was all training then, reflex, no thinking allowed, run into an area, and point, adjust, scream and scramble out again using any and every cover available.

I could hear the other two bulling around, kicking things over, swearing and shouting at Rodriguez to give himself up. On my side of the apartment – I was in a hallway leading to the back – there was another shot, the sound of glass shattering, a window being slammed open. I thought I saw the reflection of a muzzle flash although I never figured out how that could have happened. And the worst, a yell that sounded like death.

Putting it together later, the officer on that side of the building had heard the shots and, gun in hand, tried to look through a small back window that was in a toilet behind the kitchen. His bad luck that the actor was thinking of coming out that way at exactly that moment. Further, there was a light outside and he was looking into total darkness. Dumb or inexperienced; I didn't know him well enough to have an opinion, and who gives a shit anyway. Rodriguez fired through the window and hit him in the throat half an inch from the trachea. The blood was everywhere – the concrete walkway, the side of the building, his face, uniform.

I'd be a fine one to rag on the kid; that last gunshot drove me right around the bend somehow. I pointed my gun straight ahead like a battering ram and charged, screaming, at the sound. I don't know who I thought I was, but for a few seconds I would have blown away anyone in my path. Fortunately Rodriguez had already dived out that same window and the other cops had gone to ground. Plunging straight through took me right out a back door. No one there so I doubled back along the side where I thought the yell had come from.

The first thing I saw, and I wished to God it had been the second or third, was the kid sprawled on the concrete and all that blood pumping. I heard his hoarse gaspings for air. I can still hear that.

I never saw Rodriguez until Sean shot him. In the back, twice, as he rose from behind a collection of trash cans bunched against the fence that separated the apartment from its neighbor. He claims he shouted my name in warning and it's possible, although nobody else heard it. I do know Rodriguez's gun was still down when I first saw him; Dunn claims it was coming up in my direction but we'll never know. It was being raised by the time he'd been hit and was spinning toward his attacker. Dunn fired again, as cool as if he were on a range, catching Rodriguez on the side of his face as he spun and blowing him back into the metal cans, collapsing among them, sending them clattering all over.

It's such madness after a shooting and if a cop's down it's that times ten. The rest of the party came running. Dunn was already kneeling, alternately giving CPR to the wounded officer and trying to staunch the flow of blood from his neck. I should have helped. Instead I went to see about the slimeball, I guess because he was my slimeball, my case, my life. I'm not proud of that part. There were some sounds and twitches like you always get, but on the whole he was deader than usual. I went bananas, all hope gone.

To my credit I held it in until things settled into routine chaos. I think, too, I was a little dazed for a minute. I recorded but wasn't really aware of what the others were doing or saying . . .

Sean's voice cut right through. 'He's going. Call it in, for Christ's sakes!'

Then Estrada. 'Code Three! Need an ambulance immediately. Read me? Immediate!'

I didn't come all the way back to life myself until the ambulance cranked up its siren and burned some rubber getting out of there with the kid. Rodriguez would wait; he wasn't going anywhere except a very cold drawer. The ME's people had just arrived and were already unzipping a bag, although it could be hours before they took him.

Dunn was standing with his hands in the pockets of his windbreaker, watching the ambulance go. It had started to drizzle again but that didn't discourage the locals who were standing around outside the barricades with raincoats over their bathrobes. He looked more serious than I had ever seen him and I noticed he avoided the corpse. At the time I thought maybe he'd never killed anyone either. Later I knew better.

Turning away, still trying to control myself, I heard Estrada say to him, 'Good goddamned thing you were sworn, Dunn. Could be some real heavy shit in the fan with you being here and being the shooter, man.'

'Better judged by twelve than carried by six.'

'Yeah. You'd know.'

Out of the corner of my eye I saw him go on to join

the 'shooting team' that comes out to investigate these
things, and turned on Dunn. I began in a restrained
voice but it didn't last long. 'You didn't have to kill
him.'

'Judgment call.'

Typical Dunn, viciously calm. If I hadn't started screaming I would have hit him. 'You shot him in the fucking
back, for Christ's sake!' People turned to look but nobody
interfered.

'His back was facing me, but his front was facing
you.'

'You're goddamn right, and that's how I know his
goddamn gun was pointed down.'

'It only takes a second to bring it up, and then they're
shoveling dirt in your face, okay? I've heard too many
pipers play "Amazing Grace." If there's any doubt, I waste
them first.'

'Bullshit. You know what I think? I think you knew
they'd had Chapelle in there. And Rodriguez could have
told me where he is. But you shut him up— '

Miracle of miracles, he got really mad. Dunn lost it.
What happened in his face surprised me and, to tell the
truth, was a little scary; the blue eyes took on a peculiar
light, harsh and cold as a winter sky, while the muscles
behind turned the skin into something that looked like
cast iron. Compared to that, anyway, his voice was
almost mild. 'Jesus, Joseph and Mary. You honest to
God think I'm involved in this? That I'd be stupid enough
to work with that pile of bleeding dogshit back there?'
He glanced at the walkway but the corpse was obscured
by technicians plying their trade, like ants swarming on a
dead beetle.

'I don't know what you've done or what you're capable
of. I only know you're hinky as hell. Sometimes I'm with
you, things you say or do, or don't say when you should,
the hair stands up on the back of my neck.'

'Very scientific judgment. I'd hate to have you on a jury.' He was sneering, and it wasn't very attractive as he went on, 'Are you sure it isn't my broken nose or knobby knees, scar tissue around the eyes or maybe my breath?'

I was embarrassed for him and starting to lose my steam. 'All I know is I had a chance to save him – Chapelle. Now, thanks to you, I got nothing.'

'You got something.'

I had enough energy for one last yell. 'What?'

'Your goddamn life, lady.'

He stalked away after that. Estrada took him back to the station to fill out the five thousand forms that go with that kind of incident. I stayed on with forensics, since finding Chapelle was my responsibility. They went through the house carefully even though the kidnapping wasn't in their jurisdiction.

I've seen homeless jungles that were cleaner than that apartment. There was no doubt several men had been holed up there. Besides the usual mess there were the plugged-up toilets and they had even ground out cigarette butts on the floor and in the carpeting. The refuse must have been two feet deep in some places. I didn't envy them the amount of fingerprinting and chemical tracing called for. There were no apparent signs of Chapelle on the scene but we did find two bottles of Bass ale and I didn't think those were likely to be the common fare of Reuben 'Badboy' Rodriguez. I told them to look for his car in the neighborhood but of course they were already doing that.

At ten in the morning I gave up and went back to my apartment in West Palm, called in and slept until two that afternoon. Showered, down to the station, start over again. I didn't see Dunn for a while after that; he had his problems with the authorities in Miami.

111

SEAN

The boss raised hell about the shooting but I asked him why they gave me a gun if they didn't want me to fire it, and he saw the logic in that. Except, of course, I wouldn't get it back until after the coroner's inquest.

Not that I was totally indifferent to the fact of killing a man, anyone, even human waste like Rodriguez, but I learned a long time ago in these matters that the defensive loses. He was a cranky old bastard but he'd do right by you when he got through yelling.

'You had to shoot the cocksucker in the back, Sean. And twice, for Christ's sake. If you hadn't done that . . .'

'When you shoot them in the front they sometimes shoot you. And, hell, everybody shoots twice, you're supposed to shoot twice whether you're a commando or a traffic cop. It's just that nobody's told the ACLU that.'

'Nobody heard you shout a warning.'

'I'll tell you a secret, Emmett. I didn't. The sonofabitch was gonna burn an officer. I did call a warning to her.'

'Nobody heard that neither. I'll tell you a secret, too – we gotta get along with the Miami PD down here. Maybe you think you don't, 'cause you already didn't, but the company does and believe it or not, they expect you to. It's a pretty huge goddamn understatement to say the cops are a little hacked about having to take a private security operative along on a raid, having him waste some scummer and then they see the story on the six o'clock news and all the fruitcake politicians are bitchin' their heads off.'

'The story could have been about a female sergeant from the Palm Beach Sheriff's Department killed while in their company, on their turf, by said scummer. As far as my being there in the first place, not my idea, remember?'

'Yeah, yeah, I know. You still made 'em look like a baboon's back end, and they aren't goin' to forgive that fast.' He paced silently for a while after that.

I got up, went to the window and looked out over downtown. The Metro pulled up just below us and disgorged passengers. I distracted myself by wondering, as I always do, what their lives were like, who was sick, angry, in love, headed for marriage, war or just dinner with the kids. What else was there to say? I had no regrets. Unless it was about Frankie.

Emmett started to stuff a pipe and pretty soon the rugged odor of Balkan Sobranie told me the storm was over. Our firm was countrywide, founded by FBI and Secret Service veterans who could call at least the Vice-President by his first name. It had security contracts both with the state and federal governments. They were often involved in controversies far nastier than mine, which is not to say the next few days or weeks would be a Caribbean cruise. For one, I didn't like losing the gun.

Everyone has their own way of dealing with the shit blizzard. Me, I took a gig the next night with a salsa band at a little club off Flagler. Actually, Afro-Cuban with a jazz tilt, like the great Tito Puente. The group didn't normally carry a trombone so I could 'casual' myself in any time I wanted. I was the only Anglo; for some reason Latinos don't take up that instrument in any numbers.

Anyway, I loved the music, knew the charts, and the guys were great to me. I always considered it a vacation. They would insist on paying me and I'd try to refuse, but in the end you risked being insulting. Usually I cleared about fifty dollars which I spent on smuggled Havanas that I passed around.

That night I had that wonderful feeling of ease you always experience when you climb on to a bandstand. Nothing could have been more remote from the realities of my 'day job.' No politics, violence, suffering, moral ambiguities. You tune up, talk some trash with the guys – I speak a rudimentary Spanish – check out the pretty girls, fool with the lights and sound . . . joy.

JAMES DAVID BUCHANAN

It never would have occurred to me that the whole madness could follow me to that unlikely place and taunt me in the middle of a chorus of 'Noches de Habana.' But there in the noisy, eddying crowd around the door I thought I saw James.

The absurdity of it was apparent, over and above the fact that the poor sonofabitch had been kidnapped and we had his severed finger as proof, but also the surroundings. El Tropical was a pit. It suggested the way clubs must have looked in Miami thirty or forty years ago when, before the Cuban immigration, Miami Beach was everything and the city proper sleepy, run-down, irrelevant. Or it could have existed on a backstreet of Havana where tourists never went during the time of Batista or 'Machado the Butcher.' Small and dark with a lot of twisted Moorish pillars to screw up the sightlines and squeeze the tiny dance floor, artificial palms, inlaid tiles, and the inevitable whirring fans. No air-conditioning and when it was humid as it is during the mean season the band would look as if it had marched through a car-wash. Of course, so would the customers. No one cared.

A friend of mine said he had once played in a club out on the Coast with the irresistible name 'The Kiss Kiss Continental.' It would have been perfect for the Tropical. The dancers were wonderful, so jammed together that their frenetic gyrations constituted group sex, and the extravagant clothes often bordered on costumes. To move like that in a skin-tight skirt and stiletto heels is a gift from God. They were indifferent to everything but the rhythm section, which gave the horn players *carte blanche*. It was beautiful and a hell of a long way from Palm Beach.

I noticed the woman first, tossing her head and laughing, a profusion of shiny black hair whirling, neon lips, teeth so white they could be seen across the room through the dense smoke, and with a large pinkish hibiscus in her hair – a Cubana. I couldn't make out her escort at first except

114

for the gray hair and a head that was . . . different. If I'm honest about what I thought at the time, it was somehow 'aristocratic.'

It's possible all I meant was 'Anglo' in a place where there were very few. When I remembered it later the figure was tall, very straight, a certain carriage and attitude. James had told me once that his ancestors had gone to England with William the Conqueror, the name was originally LeChapelle, and there was something like that here.

I was improvising, sub-conscious right up to the front, totally absorbed, so it took a minute for the idea to penetrate. What it comes down to, I recognized him after he was gone out the door. As soon as my chorus was over I plunged off the stand, startling the trumpet players next to me who thought it was narcs or the Migra, knocking over a stand in a crazed dash after this phantom.

Rushing out on to the street I found only another couple getting into their car. No one else in sight. Vanished. Coming from that superheated interior gave me a cold shot up the spine. Either that or the thought that it really could have been Chapelle.

I looked up at the sky. There were stars spotted among the clouds but also the reflection of lightning from the direction of the sea. I knew where I would go after the job.

We got off about one, something about the fire laws which I would have thought were violated every night. I drove alone out across the Bay on the Rickenbacker Causeway to Key Biscayne and along Grandon Boulevard to near the end of the island where there is a state park that is really a miniature jungle. It had rained while I had been working and the residue hung in the air as luminous dust around the street lights. The Key projects well out into the nighttime Atlantic and is remarkably quiet, even the few hotels, with a wide white beach that's largely deserted at night.

When I have things to hack through I like to go over there and sit at the outdoor bars at the Sheraton or adjacent Sonesta Beach. Then I stroll the sand with a keen sense that I'm looking at Earth from another planet. You can't buy that kind of loneliness very many places. And when there's a squall line offshore with plenty of lightning in it you march with the gods.

At that late hour there were no other customers inside or out. I sat on the terrace. A couple of lovers were strolling way out by the surf with their pants rolled and arms around each other, watching the display across the water. The lightning flared and slashed this way and that through rips in the layered clouds, themselves often escaloped by moonlight and so fat with energy they seemed to be pulsating. Beneath it, down on the world, whitecaps caught the light and turned luminescent as they tumbled toward shore.

The waiter wanted to close up and go home so I paid the tab and wandered off on to the beach. The couple had disappeared and I was alone and remembering. It could have been Chapelle. He liked jazz and God knows he loved anything Latin. He'd always been amused by the idea of my playing the trombone and had once brought Sylvia to where I was working in a really bad joint, one that made the Tropical look like La Cirque.

To say they stood out – it was like a couple of Venusians had dropped by Earth. I never would have taken a woman, especially a woman who looked like Sylvia, in there and I'm armed most of the time. But James was always remarkably fearless. Or crazy. That possibility always existed as there was insanity in his family.

I plodded along through a sudden shower with my hands in my pockets, wet sand sticking to my shoes, looking a little crazy if there had been anyone there to see. Some distant thunder rolled shoreward behind a big crashing wave to remind me where I was.

Frankie disturbed me and I suppose if she could have seen where I was right then I would have disturbed her too, more than I already did. I could never quite summon her up, see her as she actually was, but always seemed to be looking for her in my mind.

Hair not as short as Annie's, not an athlete's hair. I'd hardly seen her legs but that wasn't her fault. Carried herself straight, GI. And those opulent eyes, that was the only thing I was certain of. The bones in the face were not high fashion like Sylvia's, but were pronounced as if they might have had a little Hun in them. She had a stubborn will and a tumultuous Balkan soul. I wondered how much my perception of her had changed since that first time we met out at the death scene, and decided not much since my disturbance had begun at that moment.

I cursed the Chapelles. They were like the Chinese curse, always bringing interesting times. This time they had added Frankie to the mix. My life had just reached some kind of equilibrium and now I had to watch it burn. I found myself walking toward the end of the island, toward the lightning to the southeast and the jungle at the tip, and the appropriateness of it made me laugh.

IX

FRANKIE

I was very down after Rodriguez's death. And I didn't feel any better after they found his car parked three blocks away. This was pretty standard in Miami if you're in the life but too broke or too lazy to secure your wheels at night. It's not just bombs under the hood. I remember one instance of a coral snake, Florida's equivalent of the cobra, on the driver's seat. Forgetting that, none of these hemorrhoids want people to know where they live.

It was an old Cadillac. The tires appeared to fit the imperfect prints formed·in the sand out at the kidnapping site. Not definitive enough for court, but useful just the same. No fingerprints, except for Rodriguez who had likely gotten careless after he dropped out of the loop. In the trunk they found a small bloodstain and two hairs. Preliminary DNA analysis indicated it was Chapelle's. It was enough to make you cry.

There was a surprising upside, although short-lived. Headlines screaming KIDNAPPING SUSPECT KILLED IN SHOOTOUT sounded like progress to a lot of people, including my brass who should have known better. But, hell, I'd take it.

I wasn't going to waste the time bought with Rodriguez's blood, and we had some leads now. The deceased had a buddy-in-crime who was rumored to have stayed with him on and off at that same residence. Better, he was known to have once kidnapped and tortured a dealer, for which he served a lousy nickel on a dime. Alfonso 'Pants' Utrillo was a long-time violator with enough aliases and convictions to blanket the Vietnam Memorial. Our interest heightened when a stolen credit card with his fingerprints on it was found among all the garbage in the house. Miami put out an APB on him for South Florida.

We were pretty sure there had been three kidnappers at the scene, but couldn't be certain because of the sandy terrain and breezy weather. If it had rained the night before the case might have been over. As it was, one was accounted for – Rodriguez. We assumed that either this Irishman or a hell of an actor was the second. Now we were digging for the third, Utrillo. But it figured that the smarts to set it up resided in the head of whoever knew these people. The losers in our cast so far couldn't have parked cars for them.

My guess was that the third man, Utrillo, was still in it with the mick, because it's just about impossible for one person to hold another prisoner for long, go out for food, make a ransom call, even to sleep peaceably. Sooner or later the captive makes noise, works free of bonds or does something to screw you over. Drugs can pacify a captive but it takes some skill to administer them safely. Of course, all bets were off if Chapelle was dead.

The Sheriff traced Duchow's supposed tie-in with BCCI. They weren't going to let a mere female sergeant get into that. It turned out he knew some bad guys but the only fact was that a company he was running got a short-term loan from them, which they repaid. Some of the Chapelles' friends and servants over the years had sheets but it was soft stuff, nothing life or death. It's always amazing to me how many of these millionaires have brushed against the law. Owen had followed that without finding anything useful.

So now there was this whole stupid line about the jealous husband to investigate. 'Stupid' because of the way Dunn had laid it on me, and how long he took to do it. Actually, it should have been a good lead. I went over to see the sister-in-law, Amelia Chapelle, the afternoon after Rodriguez, wondering what Dunn did to earn her confidence, besides wear pants. Further evidence of how he was tied to these people.

I decided I wouldn't call ahead. You had to admit, Dunn was turning out to be a prophet on that; politeness did not earn respect. I drove around the island by myself for a while first, trying to see it through new eyes, old eyes, anybody's eyes but my own. I had to talk with a veteran detective, Bruce Brown, who was about to retire and knew the town better than any of us. Owen, I suppose because he was black, hadn't been over there a lot, working mostly the County. What was weird, Brown was Jewish but nobody ever seemed to catch on and he got along with the natives real well. He figured it was because he didn't look Jewish and had a neutral name.

'They think they're sharp about spotting us, but the truth is they think a Jew has to be named Shapiro and look like Yasser Arafat in a yarmulke.' He was a funny old guy, kind of bitter and cynical; I liked him. He was smart, too.

I drove along South Ocean Boulevard. The big metal shutters were being rolled up on one mansion, and they were raking the gravel driveway of another. Sure sign that summer was over. Soon the two thousand turkey buzzards that migrated here every winter would be showing up. Dunn said they came for the companionship.

Most of those houses along there have a tunnel over to the beach. State law says everybody's equal beach-wise from the high-water mark to the surf, but somehow that never has applied on the island. I remembered how once as a kid a bunch of us worked up our courage, probably on beer, and went over there to try and go swimming. The police arrested us and practically frog-marched us right through town. I was so embarrassed, and got the hell beat out of me at home. I often wonder why I ended up doing what I do. Maybe to get it right.

These other Chapelles, Amelia and baby brother, lived

near the south end of town in a condo, where there were a lot of them. My 'source,' Brown, said the white bread called it the 'Gaza Strip' down there.

You had to wonder why, even if he was a mere vice-president and James always got the long end of the stick, Glen didn't have his own mansion. A family that rich, there's always enough to go around and keep everybody proud. Not that this condo was slumming; in size and cost it would probably take in every residence my family had occupied back to the fifth or sixth generation. Maybe it was his own version of the hair shirt, wanting people to feel sorry for him; 'I'll show you how deprived I am!' I could see that in him. I wasn't sure about her.

Amelia wasn't in but the maid said she was due back from shopping any minute. I went down and waited in my car. She showed up in about half an hour, parked on the street and got out, pulling her packages after her.

I watched her; you learn a lot about people that way. Good legs with fairly high heels and fairly short skirt that showed she knew it. Hippy, the way Italian women get at a certain age if they're not careful, although nothing else about her said 'Italian,' except the big hair which was near-blonde with roots. The dress cost a fortune; this for shopping.

Her movements were quick and nervous. When she had trouble getting one of the packages out of the back she almost destroyed it in her frustration. A woman like that with a passive whiner for a husband, it must lead to some interesting evenings. She wasn't much like Sylvia and I couldn't see them getting along.

I got out quickly and hurried toward her, intercepting before she got away from the car. 'Mrs Chapelle. Sergeant Bodo. Could I have a word with you?'

She was a strange woman with those perennially hysterical eyes that made you want to give her a laxative. I don't know if she was good-looking but I was willing to bet the local studs thought she was hot. The kind who would lock her legs around you and not let go until one of you was dead. She stopped and gave me the ray.

When she found out I wanted to question her about the babe with the husband up in Jupiter she went nuts. Speaking of nuts, I seem to remember she yelled that she was going to have Sean's pickled for telling me about it. According to her it was family business.

I got between her and the condo, leaning on the fender of the Beemer, which you don't get to do a lot in police work. 'Mrs Chapelle, we got two people dead now, and your brother-in-law's still missing. There isn't any private family business any more.'

She drew herself up and rested her packages on the car. 'We'll decide that, Sergeant . . .' She couldn't remember my name.

'No, ma'am. We definitely got a police matter here. Look at the papers or TV if you think you still got that kind of privacy. The only way you'll ever get it back is to help us solve this thing.'

She made an exasperated sound. 'I'm tired of all this. You got one of them, why don't you go out and get the rest? Do your job, and leave us alone.' She picked up her packages again.

'What about Mr Chapelle?'

'What do you mean?'

'You said how we should get the perpetrators. You didn't mention getting Mr Chapelle back. That's our first priority. Is it yours?'

'I don't know what you're talking about. I'm going in.'

She made a move around me, but I blocked it long enough to ask one more question. 'You seem to know a lot about family goings-on. Are there any affairs you haven't told us about? Annie Robertson, for instance?' She shook her head slowly, hating me. 'How about Mrs Chapelle, the other Mrs Chapelle. Anything there might help us?' I waited. 'You two are not friends, are you?'

She continued to glare at me before saying very deliberately, 'Fuck you.' Then marched straight ahead; if I hadn't stepped aside she would have taken me out like a linebacker. Nothing ventured, nothing gained. I knew one thing, she'd never complain to anybody.

On the way up to Jupiter I found myself wondering about James Chapelle. Everybody liked him; he was supposed to be friendly, democratic, well-mannered, charming, all that shit. So he liked the girls, I liked the boys, although I imagined he'd gotten a lot more out of it. But how could you put him together with this bunch, with his whole world? If we got him back, maybe I'd find out.

Sexy little babes who live in Florida beach towns always have names like 'Lelani,' which usually means their old man was stationed in Hawaii in the Navy and wanted to memorialize his johnson's finest day. I caught up with her in the local bank where she was a cashier and took her to lunch, which was a sacrifice, believe me. First I had to make it right with the manager, saying I was the law and it was about a distant relative.

She was dumb, soft with big soft boobs and a letterbox for a mouth. I was a little disappointed in Chapelle; evidently a sexy bod and spread legs was the only thing he asked for. That wasn't how I'd come to think of him even if he was a member of a despised race – men.

Some women see female cops as a safe father figure – if that's the way to put it. She didn't give me any trouble, but she didn't give me any help either. It was all about what a wonderful guy her husband was, even though he whacked her now and then, but Chapelle was even more wonderful. Mainly, putting aside all the charm, manners, intelligence and sophistication, because this exalted creature from another world had deigned to be interested in a little housewife from Jupiter. She seemed to think that if her creep of a husband hadn't discovered his horns so quickly it might have turned into the love of the century. It was enough to make me want to barf my lunch.

I had to hold myself back from suggesting you should have tried 'My pussy belongs to Jesus Christ,' and then you'd have seen how long he was interested. But I didn't. After I got over being irritated I felt sorry for her and listened patiently to the long whine about how hard it was to get along with a growing boy and without her dead dope-runner husband. It seemed to go on for hours but really it was only a bank lunch, which is shorter than a shrink's hour.

In the end, I don't think she had anything to tell. At least about what had happened in the past. The present, maybe. I had figured originally that Sean, confronted with a nice lit-tle piece of Southern poon pretty enough to have attracted the Great Lover, had let her off easy. I didn't get any more from her. So I headed out to the local cemetery to make sure that someone named Daryl Grosbeck was planted there. He was, and there were flowers. I was touched.

For some reason having to do with boundaries, or local politics anyway, the autopsy had been performed under state auspices at the little town of Dickerson on Lake Okeechobee.

I like the lake, it's real South, even if it's swampy and the mosquitoes are big enough to carry off small children. I had a departmental car with a sick air-conditioner and my blouse was soaked through by the time I got there. The main street ran along the lakeshore so I stopped and let the breeze off the water air me out. Small, mostly wooden houses with docks and little boats, fishing tackle and nets strung, mongrel dogs in the yard. None of the boats had been painted in this century.

I leaned against a willow whose branches trailed down into the water. We used to swing from those when I was a kid and pretend we were Tarzan in those corny old movies on TV. They always wanted to make me Jane, but I'd never have it. I got in a hell of a fight over it once, I remember, and broke the boy's arm. My folks had to pay for it. I wasn't easy.

There was an old cracker in a boat with his dog near shore, puffing on a corncob and trailing out an inert line like he was posing for a picture on a place-mat. Out on the water the distant putt-putt of a motor boat, a sound I've always loved, especially at night.

The morgue was a little less attractive; it was part of what had once been a meat-packing plant, this being cattle country, and nobody seemed in the least self-conscious about it. It was set close to the other county buildings surrounding the usual Civil War statue. We were a long way from Miami Beach.

The coroner, who was a moonlighting local doctor, had been alerted and met me in his little office in the morgue. He was sixty about, grizzled as grits and chewed tobacco even while he chain-smoked cigarettes. Both went into the spittoon at his feet. He had some of the Southern courtliness about him and wouldn't sit down until I did. I happened to be wearing a skirt and remembered that this was pull-your-hem-down-and-legs-together territory. He offered me one of his awful cigarettes and I almost took one to fight off the odor of formaldehyde drifting in from next door, but somehow the association with his chaw was a turnoff.

'What was the basis of the identification, Doctor?'

'The "basis"?' Cracker country, all right.

'Yes.'

The desk probably went back to the Confederacy and had all kinds of cute ugly knick-knacks on it, including a 'gator whose nose lit up. There was a big painted photograph of an owl on one wall with some kind of motto under it that I couldn't read, and on the other a painting of a likely ancestor. It seemed terribly out of place in an institutional setting with peeling paint, like it needed drapes and damask.

'Well, now, let me think. Mind you, it was a while ago. I . . . oh, yeah, I reckon it was his wallet. We sent to the Jupiter police for dental charts but there weren't none. No, it was the wallet.'

'The contents were legible?'

'We all didn't think so, but we sent it to Tallahassee and those boys did a real good job.'

'Was it still on the body?'

'Yup. 'Bout only thin' that was. 'Gators must've found it gristly.' He grinned, revealing brown-stained teeth. I tried to imagine having this dude leaning over a baby of mine during an examination.

'Were the state investigators down for the autopsy?'

'Nope, jist dropped him off. Nobody ever wants nothin' to do with the ones we find in the 'Glades. Jist drop 'em off and run.' He cackled.

I smiled to show I shared in the hilarity and wasn't just a sissy girl. 'So who certified him?'

'Me. Who else, girl? His little wife and son and a girlfriend of hers that's supposed t'lived with her come here to claim the body, but there was nothin' to look at. Nohow. I didn't like that girl come with her none, I tell you that. Kinda smart, asked a lotta fool questions. What for you care so much about this boy?'

'I'm investigating the Chapelle kidnapping over in Palm Beach. This man Grosbeck had threatened him.'

'What for?'

'Messing around with the "little wife."'

'That's all they do over there. Well, you can forgit it. He's dead.'

'Unless it was somebody else's corpse with Grosbeck's wallet in the pocket. So another person could disappear because they were in trouble.'

'Grosbeck hisself.'

'You're quick.'

'Well, little lady, now I wouldn't know 'bout that.

127

They're all scum, most ever'body ends up here, 'less it was fishin' or huntin' accident. But all them over there that's dealin' dope and fornicatin' each other's wife, whether they're rich or poor, scum. I say that to the corpses sometime when I'm workin' on 'em, 'cause these 'Glades are jist full of trash nowadays. I say, "You mighta thought you was awful tough or rich with all that jewelry you was wearin' when we found you, but look at you now. Now you belong to me, me an' the worms, an' how do you like them biscuits?" Makes me feel real good.'

That was about enough local color for one day; I stood.

'You figure he could be out kidnappin' your feller, huh?'

'Chapelle may be dead. They killed his chauffeur.'

'This feller here, Grosbeck, he was a smuggler?'

'He was a fisherman, but yeah.'

'Scum. Got what he deserved, two or three – I cain't remember – in the haid.'

'If it was him.'

He stood too, and lit another cigarette. 'If it wasn't, you ain't gonna prove it here.'

'I see that. Thanks for your help, Doctor.'

As I started out he asked, 'Sure you don't want to tour the facility? Come all the way over here. We're real proud of it, an' I got one in there now that's in jist about the same condition as Mister Grosbeck. Maybe you could compare.' Then he laughed and sprayed tobacco juice. 'Jist bein' humorous.'

I waved and went out. Dunn was right. They were weird everywhere.

SEAN

A few nights after Frankie and I shot up Miami – or at least I did – and cut each other up, an extraordinary thing happened, back where it had all begun. Nick of time for her, because the Department was starting to take a lot of heat, editorials about why feds hadn't been called in, questions at press conferences about her experience and, in all honesty, the real lack of progress. Frankie was within hours of being yanked.

We had no contact during that period; she considered me a suspect and I considered her a pain in the ass, if an interesting one. I spent my time looking into the life of Billy Beane Three. The man himself was supposed to be in the Dutch Antilles, having taken some wealthy scuba divers to Aruba where the reefs are spectacular. If he had he'd probably taken a day off and hopped over to some little jungle airport, and wouldn't the happy sportsmen be surprised if they knew what was returning home with them in some bottomless suitcase, tool box, spare tire, or even in the fish – that's been done.

I wanted to know where he had been on and about the time of the kidnapping, who he'd been associating with, his financial status, enemies, the usual. You've got to poke your head into a lot of snakeholes for that kind of info, but what am I except a paid badger.

All I could determine was that he had been in South Florida at least a week before, had expensive tastes, liked women of all ages so long as they were wealthy, and often needed money. Like James, he gambled, and in fact they had once flown to the Dominican Republic together for a few days in the casinos. I tried to find out if Sylvia had been one of those women; she had no aversion to youth that I knew of. At one time in my investigation I sniffed cop and it was only later that I found out Frankie had someone from Miami PD pursuing the same line.

On the night I spoke of, Syl had fallen asleep on the couch in the library about midnight. She admitted to me that she'd been depressed and had had several vodkas, rare because alcohol was one vice she didn't indulge in.

About 2 a.m. she heard the doorbell. It took a minute to penetrate, not only because she was tired and a little drunk but nobody ever uses the doorbell in these mansions. If you get past the main gate you're in. There was still a shotgun guard sitting down there every night, so it was either him or someone he had let in.

You don't normally need a lot of security in Palm Beach because it's a small place and at the first indication of trouble the police raise the three bridges that are its only access. Every crook worth the name knows this. There's often enough jewelry at one of their parties to buy a small planet, yet you never hear about anyone walking in with an UZI and grabbing it. Chapelle's kidnappers knew what they were doing when they waited for him behind Boca Raton.

Sylvia said she was a little alarmed and very woozy. She called for Carmen and the houseman but no one responded. She didn't have her pistol downstairs and was too out of it to go and get it. Instead she straightened her clothes, patted down her hair, and went to answer in her bare feet, swearing all the while because she couldn't raise anyone.

She punched off the alarm and opened the door carefully. James was leaning there, disheveled, battered, obviously exhausted yet grinning. 'Would someone pay the cab?'

Sylvia says she was frozen in place, unbelieving, and he just waited. The grin never left his face but it glazed and he began to tilt. She came out of her paralysis screaming and threw herself on him, almost knocking him over. 'Oh, my God! Oh, my God, James! It's you! Oh, darling, sweetheart, my God . . .'

The bandage on his mangled finger had unraveled and was hanging. He raised it to look at it with curiosity, as if wondering 'How did that come home with me?' That's when Sylvia came all the way back to reality.

X

FRANKIE

I was sleeping but not too soundly. The bed was all rumpled from my tossing and I hate that feeling of messiness. I've been known to get up in the middle of the night and make it up new. When the phone rang I didn't know where I was, but I shot up like those targets on the pistol range. The TV was on with the sound off, always a bad sign. I told myself, you're starting to lose it, Bodo, when you do that. One step away from sitting at bus stops with a shopping bag and telling your life story to pigeons.

I dropped the phone fumbling it to my ear, making a hell of a clang, but the dispatchers at that hour are used to loud noises. When they told me, all I said was 'Hoooooolllly shit!!!' and hung up. They're used to that sort of response too.

SEAN

Glen called, saying Sylvia had asked him to let me know about his brother's return. Fortunately I'd returned to the motel in West Palm that night. I was surprised, sure, to the extent that anything surprises me any more, but I took my time in the shower while I pulled my thoughts together. The story I got in fragments on the phone was that they had simply let him go, which was about the screwiest goddamn thing I'd ever heard of. I had no idea where it took the case.

By the time I got over to the hospital it was three-thirty in the morning. No media out front as yet but somebody inside would tip them; they always do. Frankie was sitting in the deserted lobby watching an old movie on TV with very old eyes. I suspect I care less than most people what others think of me, and as a result I don't suffer a lot of self-consciousness. I'm not sure if that's good or bad, just true. Yet I felt edgy about how Frankie would greet me. And I didn't like it.

She stood when I entered and behaved in a straight-ahead, businesslike way. It was absolutely emotionless, and in a way I think I was disappointed, but it was pro. She said Chapelle was in a private room with his personal physician and they had promised we could talk to him in a few minutes. While she was telling me a nurse summoned us.

James was sitting up on the examination table, stripped to the waist, smoking a small cigar, and when was the last time you saw that in a hospital? There was an IV on a long tether in the back of one hand. But his long gray hair was combed, there was a clean bandage on the amputated finger, his eyes were clear and bright; he looked like he had just come back from a sail to the Bahamas where he'd had so much fun what was the loss of a little thing like a finger?

The doctor's concession to informality at that absurd hour was to put on a red blazer over a polo shirt, white pants and deck shoes. As he moved the stethoscope around I watched his hands; he'd had a manicure, was wearing a gold wedding ring and Rolex. He'd never work on me. Nurses hurried in and out; I noticed one cast a dour look at the cloud of smoke overhead. Chapelle winked at her and she would have smoked the cigar for him after that.

Frankie was in her full-on professional mode and dress.

I wore shorts and a sweatshirt as it was a little damp and chilly at that hour. She had her notebook out and was very crisp while I slouched in a corner and tried to stay out of it. Our usual roles.

'. . . I was held in two different places. I know that. One was probably in Miami and the other out in the country.'

'But you were blindfolded and gagged the whole time, right?'

'Yes. The blindfold was never taken off until I was brought up here on the floor of a car. I'm glad they didn't take it off in daylight. It was painful as it was.'

'How could you tell first you were in Miami, then outside the city?'

'As far as Miami . . . well, I know about how long it takes to drive there from Boca Raton and I counted off the minutes.'

'Pretty cool thinking.'

She was looking down at her notebook, so it was more of a comment than a compliment, but it brought on the famous Chapelle grin when he said, 'What else is there to do on the floor of a car?' Frankie looked up, right into it and didn't blanch. I was encouraged.

'Still,' she said matter-of-factly, 'most people would be too scared to think of it under those conditions.'

They used to say the Vietnam War, or whatever it was, was fought by the poor and dark. James had volunteered. Of course, with his background and education he was assigned to Intelligence and planning in Saigon, but I'd had some experience in that world in another context and you could tell by talking to him that he'd taken it seriously, done it well.

The grin went suddenly and just as suddenly was replaced with the sober, responsible Chapelle. 'At least I was alive. Sean, Freddo gave his life for me. Syl and I would like to do something for his family.'

'I don't think he has one. At least not the kind you can do something for. What happened out there?'

'He was out in front of me, going toward this figure on the road when the man showed the gun. Freddo shouted "Run!" and threw himself on the guy. On the gun, really . . .'

'Did he try to get his own out?'

'I don't know. I was behind him. The shots came instantly. I heard them but I couldn't see them, just Freddo going forward . . . then falling forward. It . . . was awful.' I thought I saw pain in his eyes before he turned away from us, and I looked at Frankie to measure its effect. You wondered if she knew how unusual this was, this emotion. I knew him well and even I couldn't say how deep it went.

'What did you do?' I asked. Frankie snapped a look at me and my doubts came back.

'Tell the truth, Sean, I really don't know. To me it all seemed to happen inside of a minute. I'd been sleeping when Freddo hit the brakes and the whole thing was like being thrown off a cliff without having any idea why it was happening to you. Like in a dream. I think I froze for a moment. Then I think I started to run although I don't know where. There were two other men came around fast on each side and pointed guns at me. I gave up.' He gestured his surrender. 'Nothing to be proud of, I know.'

'Nothing to be ashamed of either, Mr Chapelle,' Frankie told him with another glance at me. 'There was nothing you could do. The chauffeur should have known that.'

'If you're armed you don't give it up,' I reminded her a little acerbically, even though I knew she was right.

'That's for police officers, Mr Dunn. Mr Carfagno wasn't bound by that.' At least her tone was no longer professional. She turned back to Chapelle. 'The two men who came after you, did you see them clearly?'

'They wore masks like the other one, the big one.

134

Except when they talked these two had Hispanic accents. I saw their hands, too, and the skin was dark. Not black, but dark.'

The doctor, who had to interrupt his examination continually, wasn't used to anything less than godlike deference. 'James, would you put out that damned cigar so I can listen to your breathing.'

'Sure. Sorry.' There it was, the democrat. A nurse handed him a saucer for the extinction. 'Oh, about Miami, I remember hearing a Miami radio station. You'd think they'd listen to salsa or Irish folk music or something but it was that godawful heavy metal. On the whole, I'd rather have lost another finger.'

'What made you think the second place was out in the country?'

'Insects. Birds. Otherwise, it was very quiet. Like the Everglades.'

'The first place, in Miami, did you hear airplanes?'

'Yeah, now that you mention it.'

'Did you overhear any conversation?'

'Not for content, but they seemed to argue a lot. It would get very heated and once one of them got so angry or frustrated he came in and kicked me a few times.'

'Were all three there most of the time?'

He thought. 'In the first place, where I was only a couple days, yes. I did lose track of time, then. There was some kind of big blow-up, mostly in Spanish and mine's pretty primitive, but then when I was moved to the second place I heard only one Hispanic.'

Frankie and I shared a look, but it would have been nice to have heard something we didn't know.

'Did they say why they were going to do that to your finger?' she asked him.

'Just that— ' He broke off and held it out to look at, wincing. 'Funny, isn't it? Hurts when you mention it. Like those war movies where the amputees think they still have a leg. Anyway, something about having trouble getting people to take them seriously.'

'What people?' That was me, the nasty one.

'Didn't say. They were so crazy and hyped I don't think anyone could have given them what they wanted fast enough.'

'Did they tell you what they were asking for?'

'No.'

We weren't asking the right questions for the doctor. He held up James's mutilated hand. 'They gave him two aspirin and used whisky for an antiseptic. He's lucky he didn't get blood poisoning.'

'Must have been rough,' Frankie sympathized.

'I've had better nights.' He studied it himself. 'What do you think? Wear a black glove? Make me kind of exotic.'

Frankie addressed the doctor. 'We've got a couple of things we'd like to ask in private, if you don't mind. If you've got him put back together.'

He was a little peeved but he went at a nod from James that suggested we should be humored.

'How many people knew where you were going that night?'

Anyone else would have given some indication as to how awkward they found it to answer that question, some little flinch or glitch, but James was accomplished and engaged on terrain he knew only too well. 'I announced it at the dinner table. Everyone knew.'

Of course, as smooth as it was, it was instinctual; he was much too smart a man to think he could keep up that pretense if he had thought about it.

'Mr Chapelle, we know where you were going.'

'Ah!' He grinned, charming the room now even though there were only two other people in it. 'Of course you would. It's insulting for me to think otherwise. I'm afraid what you got was just the instinctive reaction of a guilty man.' That smile was luminous. The guy was a genius.

136

'Who else?' Frankie asked, her face neutral.

'I don't know. Maybe Annie told someone. Michael might know, or Glen or his wife, Amelia. She's like the Italians say about the tomato, "it's in everything." Don't misunderstand, I like her. I mean, everybody at the party knew I was going someplace. Everybody gossips, there are no secrets.' He turned it on for Frankie. 'I'm not proud of it, Sergeant, but I'm reasonably sure my wife knows. It's sad, but things happen in the best of families, and . . . that's the way we live.' He opened his hands, a monk pleading with God to lead him to something better.

'Did Mr Dunn know?'

Unexpected, although it shouldn't have been. Good for her; she was a cop. It seemed to me that James was, for the first time, a little uncertain, shifting his eyes. Frankie wouldn't fail to pick up on that.

'I don't know. Why don't you ask him, since he's standing next to you?'

We had become very serious, the three of us. Chapelle abandoned his *joie de vivre* and I couldn't think of any dumb jokes or wise-ass remarks. Remorseless Frankie.

'I'm asking you, Mr Chapelle. Mr Dunn and I would have been over this territory.'

He kept his eyes on her now. 'I'm afraid that's the only answer I can give you. We've never talked about it. He got Freddo from New York for me.' He glanced at me, a look that seemed to say 'I hope I'm not betraying you, but I have to give her something.' He had reasons for not betraying me. 'Freddo knew for sure, since he almost always took me there. He was very loyal – God knows – but servants always talk in my experience.'

'Freddo wasn't a servant,' I reminded him sharply. 'Servants don't do what he did.'

'No, of course not, you're right . . .'

Had anyone ever seen James Chapelle unsettled? Maybe over manners. He put a lot of store in manners, was very

JAMES DAVID BUCHANAN

gallant, and that's how he would see a slip like this, as a breach of manners, not callousness. For a minute I almost enjoyed it simply because it was rare, then I began to feel guilty. The guy had been so thrilled to be home, to be alive, he was bursting with it.

'Ah! Something I should have told you right away. I watch detective stories. When Freddo and I got out of the car and went towards this "victim," at least that's what we thought he was, the first words out of his mouth as he pointed the gun at me were "Happy Anniversary, Motherfucker."'

I muttered, 'Black Irish?' but nobody got the joke.

Frankie asked if his anniversary had been mentioned in the local press, and with a little thought he remembered that it had, the *Post* and 'The Shiny Sheet.' Still, it added a certain shading to the idea of an ambush.

It was obviously on Frankie's mind. 'Mr Chapelle, do you have any reason to believe that someone could have conspired at your kidnapping?'

We watched him intently for the slightest betrayal by a muscle. He seemed genuinely puzzled. 'You mean other than the men who took me? Who I'm sure I didn't know.' We didn't answer. 'Well, no, I don't. You can't have a company or money or . . . without someone disliking you.' I assumed he had dropped out 'or be catting around.' 'I usually try to deal with those things as positively as possible. Quarrels, rivalries, hating . . . all that's a big waste of time. Life's too short.'

'I assume,' Frankie said, 'your answer's "no"?'

'That's right.' Her bluntness seemed to amuse him.

'I'm sure you'd like to get out of here and rest. Just one other question.' He nodded. 'You say the Irishman drove you up here and let you out. What kind of a car was it? Did you see the license, anything at all we can use?'

Chapelle shook his head. 'I was blindfolded when he put me in and made me lay on the floor in the back. When he

138

got me out he kept it on and told me to walk away from the car. I stumbled but got up and kept going. As he drove away I did get just a glimpse of it but except for the fact that it was a dark color and kind of large . . . I'm afraid I don't know much about cars. American cars anyway. Please don't quote me to the workers at our Seattle plant.' He tried to work it for a laugh but it died. 'I honest to God don't even know exactly where I was let out. I was tired and scared and I guess run-down, they tell me. I just started wandering to where I found that cab. Maybe half an hour. It was like dream-time. I was stunned I was free.'

'That's the big question, Mr Chapelle. Why would he do that?'

He raised his hand in a fictional oath as far as the IV would let it go, conveying a shared frustration. 'You'll have to ask him. All I know is both Hispanics seemed to be gone by then. By the time the Irishman came into my room and woke me up. He said something to the effect that the whole thing was a wash, but when you asked this gentleman for any clarifications you got hit. And I'd been hit enough, thank you.' He had managed not to make that sound self-pitying. 'He did say one really weird thing. "I'll let you go, but you've got to promise to pay me a million dollars later on."'

Nothing in Frankie's experience, or mine for that matter, had prepared her to absorb such an idea. 'Just like that? He'd let you go if you'd *promise*, not give, promise him a million dollars? When, for Christ's sake?'

He brightened. He liked this Frankie, I could tell. 'Didn't say. Soon. He'd get in touch, that kind of thing. Pretty bizarre, huh?'

'What did you tell him?'

'What you tell any eight-hundred-pound gorilla.'

'Right. You think he actually believed you'd pay him or was this just running his mouth?'

'I don't know. It was all so strange. He did threaten to

kill me if I didn't. That impressed me, the way he said it, the way they'd behaved, and of course what they did to Freddo, but I'm not sure it convinced me. It's possible, frankly, they were just glad to get rid of me. My wife told me they never even got back to her about the ransom.'

Frankie and I exchanged another of those little involuntary looks, and regretted it instantly. Fortunately, the doctor returned with Sylvia and distracted him. She looked a little haggard, had no makeup on, was wearing shorts and sandals and was still smashing. I saw Frankie looking at her and had a good idea what was in her mind, woman to woman. They have it harder than we do.

'Don tells me he's all through with you, darling.' She put her arm around her husband in a proprietary way that was very uncharacteristic, and gave us both a reproving glance.

While a nurse removed the IV, the doctor, arms crossed, leaned against a wall and studied James as if he'd performed a medical miracle. 'Eyes clear, reflexes good, a little dehydrated and lost some weight. Contusion healing nicely. We'll have to keep an eye on that finger, but I have to say, you're a remarkable man, James.'

Everyone was beaming. What else would we do? And he was 'remarkable.'

'We'll give you some antibiotics and something to help you sleep. That's what you need now.'

James slipped off the table and started putting on his shirt. Sylvia helped, the solicitude continued – but I'm being unfair. They loved each other. I knew that more than most. 'I'm taking him right home to rest. You'll have to question him later.'

'Honey, I feel great.' He rolled up the Venetian blinds and you could see the first pale salients of light clutching the eastern horizon. 'Look! I haven't seen daylight in – how long?' It was his riff, no one was going to take it away from him. 'Hell, I'm not going home to bed.' He told the doctor, 'No pills. What I am going to do is get a bottle of Dom Perignon and a Churchill and a chair out on the lawn. When the sun comes up I'm going to be there to toast him like an old friend.' He threw his arm around Sylvia, who was smiling tolerantly at him. 'Right, sweetheart?'

'Mr Chapelle. When you were in captivity, did you ever hear the phone ring or anyone come to the door?' Frankie wasn't going to give up on that, and he knew it.

'No, I don't think so. Well, wait, the phone did ring a few times. I suppose that could have been, "Do you want to have your carpet cleaned?"'

After a significant beat, Frankie allowed as how 'It could. Thanks. We'll come around to the house later.' I appreciated her including me.

The hall was empty at that hour except for some pre-op work. One poor devil went by me on a gurney looking as if he would rather be vacationing in Bosnia. I gave him a thumbs-up. We were both fall-down tired but somehow Frankie kept up her usual pace, our footsteps echoing like horses clopping in those scrubbed silent corridors.

'"A few" phone calls,' I said out loud to myself. 'Don't telemarketing firms tend to target only affluent areas? Who was the phone listed under, anyway?'

'Previous owner.'

'You could check the telemarketing companies. We should have asked if there was any movement after the calls.'

'I wonder how she'll tell him there wasn't enough money for his ransom? And she went on TV to say so, which maybe cost him a finger.'

'She'll find a way.'

'Sean, listen . . .' She put her hand on my arm, stopping me. It felt peculiarly warm. 'What I said after the shooting was . . . a little extreme.'

I couldn't help myself. I laughed. 'Frankie, you are extreme. C'mon, I'll buy you breakfast.'

She surprised me by accepting. As we went off down the hallway she asked, 'Can you believe that Chapelle? How cool he is after what he went through?'

'I don't believe anyone.'

'I've heard your song, thanks.'

'Okay. It's just that I know him, so I'm not surprised. About that.'

As we went out the front door she said, 'I'll tell you, he is really somethin',' but I don't think she was talking to me.

In the empty, still-grayish parking lot with little trails of fog running through it, the reporters were starting to arrive. The morning air was like putting your face to the ocean's spray. I would have liked to have stood there and sucked it in but that wasn't possible. We ran for it.

It took a while to find a restaurant at that hour, but every good-sized city has to have a central produce market where people are well along with their workday by sun-up, servicing restaurants and stores. We settled for a little cantina with only a couple of customers where we could sit in a booth by the window and watch the buyers and suppliers come and go in the early light. I like this hour if I'm not getting up and *huevos rancheros* and beer has always been my favorite breakfast, although it can make the rest of the day anticlimactic.

'You've been looking for Billy Beane, Owen tells me.'

'That's right.'

'Why?'

'I don't know. Just hoping to get us off the dime. He's real tight with the Chapelles, especially Sylvia – I know that look.'

'You probably would, wouldn't you.'

You had to learn to ignore a lot of things to get along with Bodo. 'But also with James. They gamble together. Remember, a lot of people in Palm Beach are rich but don't have any money. All the big money's in dope these days. It's replaced US Steel as an American commercial artifact.'

'You're pretty well educated for a cop, aren't you?'

'What's that got to do with it? Everybody uses big words nowadays. It's television. That doesn't make them or me smart.'

'Could we get back to it?'

'I figure if the company was in trouble, or the Chapelles personally, Billy would be able to put them in touch with some very rich, very bad people. Anything can flow from that.'

'Companies as big as the Chapel Corp., they don't get in with dope. That's crazy.' She pushed her breakfast away, largely uneaten, and pulled the coffee close.

'I have four initials for you. BCCI.'

'Look, if it was bigtime crime they wouldn't use three losers who couldn't find their wee-wee with their finger. Who all they got to recommend them is their brutality.'

'The kidnapping itself wasn't a loser. Coordination was tricky on that. And they didn't leave a lot of clues, either. Who knows what happened after that.'

'Why'd they let him go if it was like Medellin or Cali or those guys?'

'I don't know. That's when the doers, I admit, begin to look like idiots. Unless there's a whole agenda here we can't see yet.'

'It's not about dope. Whoever's involved, it's not about that.' She leaned on one elbow and stared out the window at the market workers, gray ghosts in the half-light, trundling crates of produce in and out.

'You know, when I got that call about Chapelle, I was dreaming. I was walking down this long, dark, slanty corridor that didn't go anywhere, except I knew I shouldn't go down it so it must have eventually gone somewhere pretty bad. In this dream – I have it all the time – I know better but I can't help it. And I want to go in a way, but it's bad for . . . someone. Maybe me, but not necessarily.' I didn't say anything and she thought about it for a while. Finally she said, 'Pretty obvious shit, huh?'

'You going to a shrink?'

She snorted with derision worthy of a beer-truck driver. 'That'll be the day. But I read articles, you know, and watch TV, and I took psychology in community college. It's just I hate that goddamn dream. It's probably 'cause I knew I was going to get dumped within a few hours if I didn't make any progress. Then this call about Chapelle probably saved my ass, in fact my whole career from flat-lining. But, shit, I didn't have anything to do with it. That's what sucks.' She hung her head between both hands.

'You nailed Rodriguez, didn't you? That probably scared them into giving up Chapelle.'

'Yeah, I nailed him on an anonymous tip. Big deal.'

I picked up my napkin and threw it down on the table. I wanted to make an emphatic point but not enough to break the crockery. 'Jesus H. Christ, Bodo! What the hell do you think police work is? Agatha Christie? Crossword puzzles or Rubik's Cube?'

She looked up at me glumly. 'What do you think it is?'

'It's just knowing people, pushing them a little out of their orbit, befriending them or making them mad or scared, until the fact that they're human does them in, and they give it to you. A detective's a confessor. With luck. Luck doesn't always show up, though, so for Christ's sake when it does take advantage of it. And credit for it.'

'Sounds a little lazy to me.'

'Man, you're hard, lady. You can't win with you.' I threw the napkin back on my lap in another gesture of frustration.

'I suppose not.' For a moment she went back into her funk. Then she remembered something and cheered up. 'I hope they do let me hang in. I've got a couple of new leads. If they don't, you run with them. First, I checked with the State Department on a hunch and found out that last year Sylvia and Amelia went to the British Isles for three weeks. Two of the three in *Ireland*.'

'Northern or southern?'

'Both.'

'There's sure a helluva talent pool for mayhem in the North, but if either of them was looking for a hitter why go all the way to Ireland? There's as many stone killers per square foot in Miami as anywhere in the world outside of the Middle East.'

'Maybe it was accidental. Met somebody in a pub.'

'I'm more impressed with the idea that those two would go anywhere together. I've misjudged. What was the other thing?'

'I went out and talked to the coroner that did this guy Grosbeck. There's no real proof that the man's dead, considering the tricks of that trade.'

'Any proof he isn't?'

'No.'

After that we sat for a while, pretending to eat or drink, listening to fatigue shut down our systems one by one.

It was hard to stay awake even driving the short distance to the motel. I fell on the bed in my clothes, slept for six hours, got up, showered, and started all over again. I don't know what Frankie did, except that she had to go over to the Department and make her report, so she was bound to get less rest than I did. Yet when I saw her she was as chipper as a Vegas whore at an undertakers' convention. I was on my way over to the Chapelles and she called me on my car phone, suggesting we coordinate our arrivals. I found myself wondering why, and on what occasion she had gone to the trouble of ferreting out my number?

There isn't a lot of parking over on the island so we met at the Palm Beach Police Department and left her car. The hope was that the media wouldn't think anyone important was arriving in a dirty Jeep.

As we approached the gate there they were, vans and

remote trucks hunkered like nocturnal animals caught in an unexpected sunrise. The reporters themselves were very active, bunched around Glen who had come outside with what looked like the lawyer we'd seen on television beside Sylvia discussing the ransom. Glen looked at us as we turned into the entrance, not an especially friendly look, but it could have been my disreputable wheels.

His glance tipped some reporters who broke away from the pack and ran to badger us. The gate guard was a little slow in getting it open; one reporter managed to thrust his yammering face into the vehicle. I snarled 'Fuck off!' with as much menace as I could manage and he jumped back.

Frankie laughed; she always thought I was too laid-back. I reminded her that it would probably end up in the paper as 'Police officer in charge of case has temper tantrum when confronted by reporter.' Her laugh faded. She had to care; I didn't.

There was a swarm of luxury cars parked all around the grounds. It was like the morning after he disappeared, only more so. I left the Jeep smack in front of the portico just to be bad. We went through the house, led by a maid.

Frankie, looking crisp, glanced at my attire. 'I see, as usual, you dressed up for the occasion.'

Well, I had put a khaki canvas sport jacket on over my jeans, and wore my best Reeboks. Anything to please.

The maid led us out on to the terrace by way of the french doors at the rear of the living room, or 'great hall' as I liked to think of it. Spread out before us was a garden party out of *Town and Country*.

There were about forty guests in all their pastel glory. To me it looked like a cross between a banana split and a Dufy. Out on the lawn was a portable bar surrounded by umbrellas. It was manned by the houseman and on the end of it was a cassette playing reggae tapes. No time for a band, evidently.

Everyone was drinking, laughing, talking animatedly,

James included. He wasn't even sitting down. The colors in the sky, lawn, sea, the quality of the air, were so pristine it suggested that God was a Republican.

'Aren't these people ever alone?' I asked myself, knowing I sounded weary of it. A good thing I had other lives.

Frankie had a different expression on her face. 'It's just what he said he was going to do. You got to admit, the gentleman's got class.'

Billy Beane was out there, entertaining three starved and pampered matrons who found him hilarious. I wondered if he'd given them a hit? That was the only way he'd get me to laugh.

Something, some criminal instinct no doubt, let the back of his neck know it was being stared at. He turned and looked, but at Frankie, not at me, which I found perplexing. His expression took on a certain penumbra, then finally he looked away. Why?

James and Michael were talking and it looked a little more heated than animated. They were out of earshot, but the intensity was unmistakable.

Frankie, watching them, mused out loud, 'I bet even if I knew what they were talking about I wouldn't know what they were talking about.'

'You think every time these types get together it's about some complicated high finance, right? Who's on top. And that's something every cop knows about.'

She tilted her head and looked at me, her whole tone suddenly light and teasing. 'That's very smart of you, Dunn. I think I should go and find who is on top, don't you?'

She didn't wait for my opinion. I strolled across the lawn toward the other wing of the party. You had to wonder how 'they' got grass like that – thick, springy, and a slightly phosphorescent emerald color. Not a brown spot in sight. I could never get anything like that going.

The first group I would have to pass was that of Billie and the three old darlings he was seducing, but even that much proximity was too much for him. He caught me coming out of the corner of his eye and jumped. Always nice to have an effect. I knew that he'd heard I'd been looking for him, because I had seen to it that he would. He made an immediate decision to fade on us but I was between him and the house. He put his head down and tried to make a wide sweep around my oncoming figure.

I hailed him anyway. 'Hi, Billie. How was the flight from Colombia?'

'Fuck you, man.'

I laughed but those guys never have any sense of humor. My target was Sylvia. There was one more obstacle; Amelia broke away to intercept. As usual she was being a little obvious and I wasn't sure that was healthy in this company.

'Well, Sean, he's back. Should we toast you?'

'Toast God. We don't know that much, and two of the bad guys are still out there.'

'Only two?' She was wearing a cream-colored suit, jewelry, heels, a big hat, overdressed as you might expect. And a quart of perfume again. Unfortunately I have no standards as to quality or volume – it all turns me to jelly – so she had me there.

'Are there more?'

She wagged her head. 'You don't know the half of it.'

'Enlighten me.'

'Why don't you come see me, and maybe I will. I'm getting tired of their little games.' Amazing how quickly the attitude could turn.

'Whose "little games"?'

She threw yet another switch, from anger to gloom or self-pity. 'I don't know what I mean. It's just not fair, that's all.'

'What?'

'Things.'

It was like questioning a guilty nine-year-old. I looked

down to where she was watching one of her high heels sinking slowly into a turf that had obviously been watered that morning, the automatic sprinklers knowing nothing of human perversity. When she pulled it out it made a sucking noise. I put out a hand to steady her and she looked up at me with a look of such gratitude it was unnerving.

'Thank you.' She glanced around at the other guests, some at least with a history of tabloid exposure. 'You might not believe this, but I've been a good person all my life.'

'Why shouldn't I believe it?' I could see past her that Sylvia was waiting for me with her eyes, talking absently to some elderly gentleman wearing a rosette and, I swear to God, pince-nez.

The channel changed to harsh. 'I'm fucking sick of it.' Abruptly, she started for the house, then stopped and looked over her shoulder at me like 'naughty Amelia.' 'I meant it. Come and see me when it's safe.' She went on.

'"When it's safe,"' I repeated. What the hell did that mean? I went on to Sylvia who joined me halfway. A sleek young man tried to get to her first but she warned him off; she could do that better than anyone.

'Are you still working or are you here to celebrate with us?' she asked as we came together.

'I wouldn't get too cheerful until a few people are dead or off the streets.'

'Boy, you're depressing. Come on, we might as well have a drink, then.'

She led the way over to the bar, ordered up a beer for me, accepting my limitations without argument, and a gin and tonic for herself.

'I didn't think anybody drank gin any more. Frankie says it's mother's milk to her mother.'

'It's a little retro. I never like to be in step.'

'I heard you were in Ireland last year.'

She didn't blink. 'It was great. Something really atavistic

149

happened. You know, my ancestors are Irish on my mother's side . . .' She went on like that for a while.

I don't mind being stiffed or startled, but I wasn't in a mood to be jerked around. 'I know ethnicity's in right now, Syl, and you like to stay current, but you're about as Irish as Kielbasa.'

She put her shades down on her nose. 'You're a lot of fun. Don't be so goddamn serious, Sean, and such a goddamn wise-ass, either.'

'I have fun. I just laugh at you all in private. To make a public display you got to have job security.'

'Oh, God, the unregenerate socialist.'

'Only in Palm Beach. Otherwise I recognize its demise.'

'Well, I should think you'd have job security with us.'

'Not asked for.'

'Do you have to be difficult today, of all days? You're such a fake. The truth is, you're an absolute nihilist.'

'Not true. Pure projection.'

'At least I'm honest. I'll make you a bargain. We'll wait till we're both very old and compare notes on how we've lived our lives.'

'If we live that long.'

'I intend to. It's idealists like you claim to be who die young. I'd say in your case it depends a lot on what you do from here on.' When I didn't respond to that she down-shifted. 'Ever been to Ireland?'

'Once. Briefly.'

'That's hard to believe. Wonderful people, language, music.'

'That why you went?'

'I went because it's what I was getting my degree in, English Lit.'

'I thought we were talking about Ireland here.'

'That's where most English literature comes from.'

'Good point. How come with your sister-in-law?'

She shrugged it off with a grin. I always thought she

got a lot of enjoyment from lying. 'We're family. Why not? Families travel together. Our husbands happened to be working on a buy-out.'

'You're trying to tell me you're friends?'

'Sure. You have different information?'

It was my turn to be enigmatic. I sipped the beer, watched the other guests, and decided that hers had been a serious question.

Especially when she began to gild the lily. 'We're not very similar, I know, but we're not enemies. Not that I've heard. But then I tend to love everyone, don't I. Not wisely but too well.' I refused to play. 'Why is this trip interesting?'

'C'mon, Sylvia, you're too smart and too honest for this kind of bullshit.'

This was not something she wanted the houseman-bartender to hear, so she moved away and I, of course, was expected to follow. I assumed it was the same way when she danced. 'I suppose that's a compliment. We do treasure your bluntness, Sean.'

I wasn't sure what to do with that. We made a collective study of the grass while I spoke confidentially. 'Syl, a lot of people are taking a long, hard look at young Billy. Whatever you two . . . well, I wouldn't stand too close.'

'Thank you for the advice, but if you mean his alleged profession, I am not currently a user and I have certainly never been a provider.'

'Anything else?'

'I'm not sure what you're getting at. He just happens to be a socially correct neighbor of the oh-so-venerable Chapelles of Palm Beach and New York and name-it.'

'Okay.'

She put her public face back on and used it to smile at the world. Raising her voice to the bountiful, she asked, 'Beautiful day, isn't it, Sean? With Jim back . . .'

'Looks good.'

'Do I owe you for bringing him home?'

'Sergeant Bodo.'

She followed my gaze to where Frankie was in earnest conversation with her husband. Suddenly Frankie laughed, big and bright, and something dropped away inside me.

I vaguely heard Sylvia's voice. 'Looks like she'll get her reward from James. I swear to God, he's worse than a Kennedy. Although at least he doesn't kill them.'

I turned back when she said that but, whatever I was expecting, she seemed serene. 'Why her?'

'She has two legs and a cunt. And a policewoman, that's a novelty, isn't it?' She turned to me theatrically and lowered her voice. 'Sean, is this jealousy I'm hearing?' Naturally the idea amused her.

'She's just out of her element, that's all.'

Sylvia studied her again. 'She looks like a pretty fast learner. Actually, although she doesn't like me, I think she's quite intelligent. And why should she like me, really?'

To hell with it. Frankie was a grown woman. 'Sylvia, what's coming off here is a feeling that it's all over. It isn't true.'

'Is as far as I'm concerned. I have him back.'

'But the Irishman and one other, at least one other, are still out there. I think there's more, tell you the truth. Then I get a call from the office before I come here telling me you already intend to cut back on security.'

'Just being prudent and thrifty. We're having an austerity program, if you didn't know. And your bunch are bloody expensive.'

'Our company's on retainer. You practically own us.' My gaze led her in an encompassing sweep of the little home-coming drop-in around us. 'Anyway, some austerity.'

'You're becoming oppressively serious again. They're just petty thugs involved in this kidnapping. We'll keep the armed gate guard for a while, okay, but frankly I'm tired of the whole damn thing, and I don't care what you think.'

'I think you people have a short attention span.'

'Maybe so, but from now on I go where I want when I want.'

'And no bodyguard?'

'Oh, sure. Here . . .' Cheerfully, she pulled a Ruger automatic out of the pocket of her jacket. 'I'm a helluva shot, as you know.'

I knew, but the sight of the pistol didn't make me happy. 'I was going to tell you where James was headed that night. Now I'm afraid you'd shoot her.'

'Pu-lease. When have I cared? Do you want another drink? I want another drink.'

'You know who she is?'

'I don't care.'

I didn't entirely believe that. Why should I? Her husband didn't. 'You know, Bodo's right. It is some kind of weird conspiracy. When we know why, or at least how, we'll know who. Probably somebody you've known and trusted for years.'

At last I was rewarded with some slight trace of confusion. In testimony to her extraordinary self-control, it was there for the snap of a camera shutter. It seemed like a good time to exit. I left her and went off in search of someone else whose life I might make miserable.

XI

FRANKIE

On the way to connect with Chapelle I was confronted
by Duchow, who had quickly stepped away from him
and come to intercept me. These parties struck me as a
lot like those dances in old movies about Europe where
people broke off from one group, came rushing to you,
spun you around a couple times, and then were gone on
to somebody else without you even learning their name.
Maybe that was the idea and I was missing it.

'Good job, Sergeant,' he told me with his thin professional smile. I thought it sounded condescending but maybe
I was being too hard on the guy; when I thought of it he
was the only one in the whole frigging case who had given
a few honest answers to my questions. Except about the
gambling.

I consider myself an honest person, so what I should
have done was tell him I didn't deserve any praise. Yet.
But I caved and accepted it simply because I wanted so
goddamn badly to stay with the investigation. As it turned
out, I could have decked him and it would have come to
the same thing.

The odd thing was, he went on to make the same case
for me as Sean did, about how I spooked them into giving
up Chapelle and it didn't matter that it took an informant
to bust Rodriguez because that's what good police work
was. Blah . . . blah . . . blah. But to be perfectly honest,
by the time he got through I almost liked this guy.

'Remember, Mr Duchow, we only got one of the actors.'

'One down, two to go.'

'I don't think so.'

He looked a little edgy. 'What do you mean?'

'The profile on these perpetrators – it doesn't convince me they were capable of dreaming this up. I've got to question even the ransom motive.' Bringing a few of these people into reality might have its uses.

'And who else do you think is involved?' The nice friendly tone had gone south and by now was somewhere off Brazil.

I looked very serious and shook my head, as if I knew but refused to answer.

'Too bad Sean killed your suspect. Kind of left things dangling, didn't it?'

'He was a violent felon, a fugitive with a gun in his hand, Mr Duchow. He'd already shot one officer and he was getting ready to fire at me. Mr Dunn probably saved my life.' Did I believe that? It didn't matter. In a situation like this where a soft, safe, pompous little citizen in a two-thousand-dollar suit tells us how we ought to behave when some evil sonofabitch is seriously trying to end our lives by firing bullets into our hard, unsafe, non-pompous cheap suits over precious bodies, then cops go balls to the wall. Or maybe in this case ovaries to the wall.

He didn't look like he believed it either. 'My understanding is the shooting's not that simple. They're taking a long, hard look at it down in Miami.'

'"Long" is right. These things can grind on you for ever. But "hard," I don't think so. There's a young officer down there who'll be turning his head funny the rest of his life and talking like a frog, which the girls won't find the least bit sexy. This kid was done by human slime who never worked a day in his life and preyed on people from eight to eighty. Do you have any family, Mr Duchow?'

Now he merely seemed uncomfortable. These types can only go one way, and that's to always know what's going to be said or done next. You can in business if you're sharp, I guess, but in my world, huh-uh. He had to answer something. 'I have a daughter in New York.'

'If this Rodriguez had ever gotten hold of her, you'd be kissing Dunn on the mouth right now.' After I said it, it sounded kind of extreme.

He gave it a grim little laugh, though, and said, 'I understand your loyalty.'

Sure you do.

'What's she been saying to you?'

I wasn't looking at his eyes so this was a real *non sequitur* there for a minute. He was staring through me at Sean and Amelia in a big convo across the lawn. You might say 'the women's side,' because it kind of broke down that way. Dunn appeared mainly to be listening. I couldn't read anything myself into the way they looked, but it seemed to upset Duchow.

'Not much,' I told him. 'I'd need a rubber hose. Ask Dunn. He's her favorite.'

'The woman's a little crazy, you know.'

'Is she? In what way?'

'Ask her husband. Ask anyone.'

'I don't have any right or reason to. Unless you can tie it into this case for me.'

His head snapped around at that and he gave me a very sharp look. 'Of course not.'

'I didn't think so.'

I felt he didn't know whether he wanted to keep this going or run like hell, so I made up his mind for him. Chapelle was waiting, sitting by himself, speaking to people briefly but then pointing to me, apparently fending them off. He even lifted a glass of champagne to me as an invitation, grinning. Duchow wasn't aware, it was behind his back, and I was starting to find it distracting, so I excused myself.

In the hospital room I'd been too busy, too close, maybe too tired to really see him. I had a lot of notes and few impressions. Now, walking directly at him as he rose from his chair, smiling, I thought he was about the most gorgeous man, certainly for his age, I had ever seen.

I wondered if he had been prematurely gray. I knew a boy in high school that happened to, because the face under it looked twenty years younger. The skin was a little pink from this first exposure to the sun after his long captivity, but not so much so that you couldn't see it was perfect with hardly any lines. Sean's looked like unfinished concrete; he said it reflected character. Chapelle had dark, deep-set eyes with lashes as long as a woman's, yet it didn't make him look feminine. In fact, his body and every movement were precise, controlled, straight-ahead. No fullback but an athlete. His mouth was sensuous like an Asian's, with those beautiful teeth they have. He was wearing white topsiders, white pants and a white dress shirt the sleeves of which had been rolled back. To his credit he wasn't wearing a Rolex – to me they mean dope dealers – but some kind of antique gold wristwatch that could have been his dad's.

Standing, he pulled a chair over. From that point everybody knew not to bother us; some code these people have. He offered me champagne. I refused. I asked about how he felt; he expressed his gratitude. But I didn't have a lot of time for pleasantries and that thought fortunately banished all the silly indulgent stuff about his looks and charm and all that.

When in doubt, cut right through. 'Annie Robertson?'

He took it well, smiled, a little embarrassed, which on him looked good, sat back and lit one of those little Dutch cigars. Of course he asked me if I minded, and we were outdoors. I gave him his space; the man had been through a lot. That reminder made me look at his finger but he had already adopted the black glove he had talked about. If it had been his right hand that might have been a little sinister, but this worked okay for cosmetics.

'Nice person. We've been having an affair. But then you already know that. What else can I say?'

'How much do you contribute to her financial support?'

'Nothing. She's not a whore, mistress or concubine, Sergeant, but a very independent lady. She's had a hard go, recovered, making it on her own and damned proud of it.'

'Did you ever offer to support her?'

'No. Never came up. I assume she would have resented it.'

'Then this is a real love affair?'

'Just an affair, Sergeant. I wouldn't read anything more into it. Lovers, yes.'

'You ever given her any lavish presents?'

'No. A moderately priced watch she had admired. Lots of flowers. Some intimate apparel. That what you want to know?'

'Did you know her when she lived up here?'

'Not really, although I think we must've met at parties. Sometimes there are three of those a night during the season.'

'Three parties a night? Night after night?'

'For months.'

'Pardon me, but doesn't that get monotonous?'

'You know it.'

'Why do you do it, if I'm not getting too personal?'

'Inheritance.'

'Come again?'

'Some people inherit the obligation to maintain a kingdom, a class, tradition, or even the rights of the poor and oppressed. Ours seems to be to sustain a party schedule.'

These people did it all the time, but I didn't much care for constant put-on even when they were laying it on themselves, and I didn't see the use of it. It was an excuse. I suppose my look told him that, because all I said was, 'Sure.' It could be the way I said it, too.

To his credit, he looked guilty. 'You're right. Sometimes we're a little ridiculous, maybe a lot ridiculous, around here. Sylvia, especially, doesn't like it, so we try not to get caught up in it very often. A lot of them are charity events, of course, but that . . .'

'You must have known her husband, after all the trouble he got into. Or do people around here go to prison all the time?'

'No, although some of them should. I do remember him, or I did after the trial when we all talked about it. "Gossiped" is more accurate, since we're having a soul cleansing here. But no, Annie and I have wondered and joked about how we could have missed each other so completely in a small town and such a crowded, inbred society. Our loss.'

'Know any of her friends?'

He shook his head. 'We seldom went out.'

'Why?'

He had to think about that. 'Sure you won't have a glass of champagne?' I shook my head. 'I admire your discipline. I've heard how hard you worked on this, Sergeant, and I'm not sure I've adequately expressed my gratitude.'

'It's my job, Mr Chapelle. Why did you seldom go out?'

'I said you were disciplined. Well . . . there was the question of propriety or delicacy or whatever. I don't know everything you've heard about our quaint lifestyle, but I can imagine. Despite that reputation, I don't enjoy creating gossip or hurting people. Why do you want to know about Annie's friends?'

'The people who kidnapped you knew you were coming. I just wondered if she knew anyone with a criminal history or connections.'

'Ah. But we all meet criminals now and then. It's the

times, it's Florida. Not out-and-out hoodlums, though, I don't think.'

'It's all over America, Mr Chapelle, but personally, I don't hang out with them.'

'You're pretty unforgiving, Sergeant.'

'I am. A real hardass.'

He laughed good-naturedly at that so I guess it didn't hurt anything. We talked for a while about various things. He was so open it was amazing. And funny; once I caught myself laughing out loud, and then I look over and what else but Sean and the guy's wife are watching us. I don't know if he noticed or not – Chapelle seemed to pick up on things very quickly, almost like he could read your mind, but he suggested we go down on the beach and take a stroll while we talked. He said this was police business and all these people were a distraction. Worked for me.

On the way across the lawn I felt, never saw but really felt, Dunn watching us. I don't know why but it gave me the willies. You never knew what he was thinking. Like, why would the guy care if we talked on the beach? When we reached the sand I had to stop and take off my shoes because of the heels. Fortunately I can get away without wearing pantyhose because my legs tan well. I snuck a look back up at the house and Dunn was gone. That was another thing that always drove me nuts. He was a goddamn phantom.

'I noticed,' I told Chapelle, while hopping on one leg like a flamingo trying to get a shoe off, 'that you kept referring to Ms Robertson in the past tense.'

'You're right on top of it, Sergeant.'

'Can I ask why is it suddenly over?' I left my shoes on the seawall and we started to walk.

'I'm tempted to say no, it's personal and doesn't come under the purview of your investigation, but I suspect I owe you a lot. I also suspect you'd give me no peace. Look, it's just been too messy. It's out, everybody knows about it or will, and I don't think any of us need more complications in our lives.'

'Does she know?'

'I haven't talked to her since I've been back. There just hasn't been a time for it.'

'So she had to hear about it on television?'

'I'm afraid so. That's what I'm talking about, fairness to her.'

'How will she take it?'

'I think she'll be relieved.'

There had been a heavy surf the night before and the sand was still a little squishy under my toes. It was a nice healthy feeling in these circumstances. It was getting on in the afternoon and the clouds looked as fluffy and pinkish as that awful cotton candy they sell in arcades. You could feel the evening breeze coming up from the south and see how it ruffled the tops of an otherwise placid ocean that seemed to stretch out for ever. It was impossible to tell where it met the sky.

There were a few sailboats coming in, a yacht that you would expect to see around here and a big cruise ship headed for the Caribbean. At night they look like Christmas trees in space. I always wanted to take one . . . right off the edge of the Earth, dancing the samba with a marguerita in my hand and a flower in my hair. Whooooaa, Frankie!

That's the kind of mush my brain was mired in when suddenly I realized Chapelle was telling me something very strange . . .

'. . . What they did was lay me down on the floor and put something sticky on my face and head. Of course, I was still blindfolded, but it had a very distinctive smell. It could even have been catsup – is that possible?'

'Possible, not smart.'

'Anyway, I'm sure it was to simulate blood. This was on the first morning so I was still a little disoriented. I was able to handle the stress of captivity a lot better as the time dragged on. But that morning I was still hurting and pretty scared, so my perceptions were fuzzy. They told me not to move a muscle and arranged my body to look . . . I don't know, unnatural, sprawled. Then they took my picture. Several, actually.'

'How do you know?'

'I could see the flash through the blindfold.'

'Did they say anything?'

'Just directions and threats if I moved. Why would they do that? They didn't send copies to the family or company or Annie or anyone.'

'I don't know. Usually it's to convince someone, some-one who's paying them or they're afraid of, that they carried out orders and executed the victim. When they haven't for some reason.'

'What do you mean?'

'Like if somebody comes to the cops and says a woman just tried to hire them to knock off her old man. We put in an undercover officer acting as the hitter. Meanwhile, you tell the intended victim and get his cooperation in staging a fake homicide. It's a sting. The "killer" goes back to the wife wearing a wire, shows the pictures and gets paid. She's thrilled. Then they move in and bust her. He gets to marry his daughter's best friend in high school.'

'I can't imagine how any of that could apply here.'

'Except in movies, things never go exactly the way these people plan. Thank God.'

We went past a dock with some kind of speedboat tied up to it, but I didn't think anything of it at the time. It was our autumn and we were moving through that slanting orange light you get when the sun starts its dip toward the Everglades. I love that time of day but I'd rather have been on a balcony with a drink in my hand and the promise of a date with a decent guy – not even handsome, just someone who would make me laugh and wouldn't take a swing at me.

'Can I ask you a question? About your investigation?'

I realized he had stopped. When I turned to face him I had the sun directly in my eyes. Typically, he shifted so I could avoid it and still look at him. A girl notices those things.

He had that special quality of taking people very seriously, intently. When you talked, he looked into your eyes no matter what the quality of the bullshit. Real or fake, everybody seemed to be fascinating to him. And his tone could get so earnest. Not many can resist that but I did my damnedest.

'Depends.'

'Is my wife having an affair with Michael Duchow?'

I was surprised and thrown for a minute. 'I can't answer something like that, Mr Chapelle. You should know that.'

'I know, but something strange is happening.'

'Professionally, I have no evidence of it. In this kind of an investigation you do look for things like that, connections that might lead to motives. All I can tell you, personally, my instinct says no. Whatever that's worth.' I surprised myself by adding, 'Would you care?'

'Probably, but not for the usual reasons. Tell me, is that a personal or professional question on your part? About whether I love my wife, I mean. You also wanted to know if I was still involved with Annie – Ms Robertson.'

That had me a little flustered. I meant it when I said, 'I don't know what you mean.'

He never got to answer. Suddenly there were all these loud, obnoxious voices coming off the water. We'd been so involved with what we were saying, paparazzi – that's what they were, not journalists – had snuck up on us. Dunn says they like to see themselves as 'raffish,' whatever that means. To me they're just scuzzballs. They don't shave, they don't wash their hair, and the way they dress, just a little up from street people, could give grunge a bad name. Some have got gray hair and it makes you wonder what they've been doing all their lives, because it defies logic that anyone could do this and not die young.

There were about a dozen of these jerks crowded in this little speedboat that had cut its engine just outside the surf line. That isn't always smart, but that particular afternoon the sea was a bathtub practically, and I suppose they had to reduce vibration for the camera.

'Hey, Jimmy! Hey . . .!'

'Jimmy, look this way!'

'Chapelle, give us a break. C'mon!'

'Over here! Over here!'

They were all jostling each other like a herd of cattle trying to get through a small gate, shooting and shouting in a perfect stew of accents from New York to Arab.

Chapelle instantly turned his back on them. You could tell this was not his first experience. He looked pained. 'I'm sorry . . .' he told me. Later I understood his concern; this wouldn't be the way the public would want to see one of their detectives investigating a crime. Strolling on a beach with the great-looking rich victim in my bare feet – oh, God.

He asked quickly, 'You ever been in a Cigarette Boat?'

'No, not— ' Grabbing my hand, he yanked me off in the direction from which we had just come. Reluctantly I found myself running like I was in a meet, listening to my hard breathing, my feet pounding on the sand.

He was in good shape for a guy who'd been tied up all that time, because I'm very fast and he stayed ahead.

The paparazzi had to start their engine and the fact, when I looked back over my shoulder, that there were so many of them bunched together seemed to complicate that ordinarily simple task. They were screaming and waving and shaking their fists as if we'd done something dirty to them; the boat rocked and rolled. It looked like a gerbil stampede and I laughed. That distraction is what led me up the primrose path. Before I knew it we were racing out on to the white wooden dock. He jumped down into the boat, spun and pulled me down after him, protesting all the way.

'Mr Chapelle, I can't . . . go . . . running off . . .' But to be perfectly honest, how hard did I object? I mean, how many times in my life has someone made me do a thing I really didn't want to do?

The paparazzi had to swing out to sea in order to turn and jam back in our direction. By that time Chapelle had the engine cranked and roaring. He shouted for me to cast off and I, a loyal crewman, did. We left the dock with such an insane burst of speed I fell down. As we went out through the surf, the boat leaping off the top of one wave and slamming down on the next one, lying on the bottom was like being trapped in a washing machine. I scrambled to my feet and sought out a bench.

Chapelle yelled – you had to yell, the noise was incredible, it hurt the ears – for me to stand and hold on to the cross-bar.

'Don't sit down, you can break your spine.' Lovely idea. 'And bend your legs, move with it. It's like— '

'I know – sex. I'm supposed to be working.'

He ignored that and studied my form. 'Now you got it.'

I know these stupid boats, the fastest in their class in the world. First the smugglers bought them, and then the customs service had to in order to keep up. Even the Israeli Navy is supposed to have some, but mainly they're the beloved of rich *Playboy* subscribers who believe that all that roaring, vibrating and battering will somehow send bimbo blood racing to the desired bodily entrances. Or exits, as the case may be. I don't understand that, since the ones I've been on didn't even have a bathroom. Yuk.

'Look back!' Chapelle yelled, grinning like a kid.

The paparazzi boat was falling rapidly behind, all the bearded bandits waving frantically and some screaming obscenities now that there was nothing to lose. I had found it funny, sure, but what surprised me was this delighted, triumphant look on Chapelle, Mr Sophistication. God, I thought, they're all just little boys, even him, this . . . god.

I shouted, 'Why didn't we just go up to the house? Would have been a lot easier.'

'But this is a lot more fun.'

'You must've dodged these jerks before. Is it always this crazy?' I had to keep reaching up to grab my dark glasses with one hand when I really needed both on the rail to stay upright; it was a juggling act. My over-the-shoulder bag was flying practically straight out from my body and the spray was soaking my hair, blouse and suit. It was terrific.

'Sometimes they win, sometimes I win. Today I win, and in good company. What a great way to celebrate freedom!'

I started to remind him that while it might be great for him the Sheriff would have my pelt on the barn door if he found out, but it was just too much effort. I clung to the hope that none of the bandits had gotten a clear shot at me.

We went around the north end of the island and doubled back through the Lake Worth Inlet to the Intercoastal Waterway, cruising south in calm water with West Palm on our right, or is that the starboard? Opposite Currie Park he took it in close to shore, cut the engine and threw out a sea anchor. Before I could protest he ducked into the interior and returned with a couple of German beers. I figured, to hell with it, and took one.

He pulled off his shirt and sat down with his back to the gunwale. 'Sergeant, I don't think anyone would hold it against you if you took off that damp jacket and maybe rolled up your sleeves.'

'You don't know my captain.' But I did it – I was already in my bare feet – and joined him on the deck, sitting opposite. I even opened the top two buttons on my blouse and let the last rays of the sun flow in. Suddenly I didn't feel like such a square geek. I moved my bag next to me and it made a clank when it touched down.

'Is that your gun?'

'Yeah.'

He shook his head. 'I keep forgetting.' I knew what he kept forgetting, or at least I was afraid I knew. 'You look so young and vulnerable and . . . even happy? . . . sitting there. It's just not what you think of when you say "Sheriff's Department." If you know what I mean.'

'I can't stay here, Mr Chapelle.'

'How's the beer? Is it cold?'

'It's great. But I can't stay here.'

'I know. I just needed to rest. We'll go in a second.'

He did look a little drained and I felt a tug of that feminine sympathy that gets us into so much trouble. Why God stamped 'nurse' on us I don't know, but we all have it inside us.

He gave me that brave lopsided grin of an ill person, which can make them so attractive. 'You liked the ride, didn't you?'

I had to admit that I did. 'But I only went along with it because you'd been locked up and under all that stress.'

'It is thrilling, though, isn't it? The speed? Lets you know you're alive.'

'There's enough thrills in a cop's life, Mr Chapelle.'

'I imagine. But there wasn't any real privacy to talk back there.'

I think I went on point a little. 'Do we have something private to talk about?'

He was obviously torn about how far he wanted to go with this. 'I came back to find Michael Duchow and my brother trying to take over the company. My company. The one that was left to me, anyhow.'

'I guess we do. How did you find out?'

'Michael just told me. Glen wouldn't be up to it. He'll skulk around till he sees how I take it.'

'I don't know a lot about corporations, Mr Chapelle. What is it they want?'

'Control. Glen would become the acting chairman of the board, Michael would be president as well as CEO. I'd become a figurehead, emeritus chairman. We're having some cash-flow problems. Like a lot of companies these days we got a little overextended, so the minute I was out of the picture they went to the board, secret meeting, and asked for the changes.'

'And— ?'

'Got them. Michael, it turns out, knew a lot about different problems I'd had. I don't mean anything dishonest. Personal problems.'

'What about your brother?'

'I never tell Glen anything. The charge, I guess, is "dilettantism," but it's not true. I've always worked hard for the corporation and kept my personal problems, and I have made some mistakes there, but I've kept them out of it. They've never impinged in any way.'

'That why you asked if he'd had an affair with your wife? You figure she told him about the gambling, the different women or whatever?'

He looked at me with a new shrewdness I took to include respect. 'Maybe my life isn't as private as I thought. You have been working hard, haven't you, Sergeant.'

'It wouldn't have to be your wife. Somebody else told us about the lady up in Jupiter, and her fisherman husband wanting a piece of you.'

He just shook his head and looked a little more wan than before. With effort he managed a pitiful smile. But it worked; I found myself again feeling sad for the man who had everything.

'I'm trying to imagine,' he said, 'what I must look and sound like to you.'

'Like a man who's been the victim of a vicious crime, Mr Chapelle. It's not my job to judge you. It was my job to get you back and, now that you are, take the people off the streets who did it.'

'Right. And I have no business to expect anything more.' He stood and leaned against the top of the gunwale. Finishing his beer, he tossed it overboard. You know, like in *Robin Hood*, where the noble of the castle throws the bone he's been gnawing on to those big dogs. 'I'm sorry. I need a friend and I thought maybe . . .'

'What are you talking about?' I stayed down on the deck, keeping a certain distance; seemed like a good idea.

'Look, I know it's ridiculous, and it's not fair to you to even say it, but . . . I just hoped we could be friends.'

'Mr Chapelle, you're a zillionaire with a lot of powerful and famous friends who runs a huge corporation and went to Harvard. I'm a forty-thousand-dollar-a-year detective with two years of community college and friends who think a big night out is bowling. What could we possibly have in common?'

'I like bowling.'

'I don't.'

He considered or pretended to. 'We like each other?'

'I have to get back.'

'I'm sorry. Of course.'

The time for cuteness was over, and I was grateful that he understood that. He moved to the cockpit and revved up the engine. We went back slower than we had come, both of us a little subdued.

XII

SEAN

When Frankie left with Chapelle I figured that it was her
show and there was nothing more for me to do there.
I hoped I had at least spooked Sylvia and moved the
sister-in-law a few more inches toward some kind of
catharsis or explosion or whatever served the cause. But
on the way up to the house I met brother Glen coming
from his press conference. You could tell how it had gone
from the way he put his feet down, stomping on that fine
grass hard enough to leave prints. They feast on his type.

I had nothing to say to him and sometimes he didn't
bother to speak to me, so I was prepared to smile
(thinly) and wave (half-heartedly) but he reached out
and grabbed my arm. I stopped, making a point of
pulling free.

'That detective's been harassing Amelia.'

'Her version is she tried to talk to her but didn't get
very far.'

'My wife doesn't have anything to do with this mess. I
want her left alone.'

'Tell the Sheriff.'

'What are we paying you for?'

'Beats me.'

I figured he'd get mad at that but instead the bluster
evaporated so swiftly I listened for a hissing sound. 'She's
not strong,' he said, 'and there's no reason for it. I'm afraid
. . . Please do what you can.'

'How'd she know about the Grosbeck couple up in Jupiter?'

'Who?'

'Your wife.'

'I don't know what you're talking about. Amelia lives in her own world, she doesn't get involved.'

'I must be confused. Sorry.'

I went past him and on to the house. It seemed to be my appointed role that day to leave everyone sitting on a pointed stick.

I went home to Miami for the night, tired, a little sick of it all and wanting some distance. I even put off dinner until I got there knowing fully that, at the lugubrious pace at which I cook, it would be a late one. A lot of my recipes require endless chopping which creates an atmosphere similar to the shower for thinking. I put on a tape, sharpen the knives – that can take five minutes – and hack. Most of it ends up in a wok, pitta bread or a tortilla. Given a good bottle of burgundy I like my own cooking, and how many chefs can say that. It's even by accident healthy. It wasn't a bad life I'd contrived down there.

I was married once back in New York when I was working as an investigator for the DA's office. My wife was from a wealthy Bucks County family and I always suspected that having a coal miner's son from the other end of the state for a husband satisfied some warped impulse for the exotic, some overdue youthful rebellion. Given her personality, that was one possibility.

Then, too, she might have been fooled by the job description, when in reality I was just another low-paid cop and had needed a service-connected recommendation to get that. How she deluded herself about my job I don't know, since she was an attorney herself and should have known better. Granted it was with a tony litigation firm and those can be a world of their own.

The inevitable came quickly. It was a Wellesley and Yale

education versus two years on a scholarship at Penn State and night school at CCNY. The funny thing is I never saw her read anything other than a law journal in all the time I knew her, whereas I'd stolen Melville from the library in order to pore over it in the privacy of an outdoor privy behind a miner's shack in the Appalachians. If lawyers are any kind of literate in this country it's probably movie-literate.

Anyway, she figured out all these contradictions and walked. I can't remember now which lasted longer, the marriage or the job. To be honest, I'd probably been guilty of a reverse snobbery, but whatever was the lure she had for me, I was crazy about her and the breakup put me right in the dumper. That's when the drinking started, but New York's a lousy town to be a drunk in. Florida, with its grace of nature and easy ways, sounded like a better idea.

A lot of people, like cops or my musician friends, thought it was strange for a single man to live in a little suburban house, but I was very attached to the place. I had so much vegetation around it I didn't need air-conditioning, which was a good thing because I didn't have it. Also, I could practice my horn without driving the neighbors up the wall; try and do that in an apartment.

The interior was strictly import-store classic. A tropical motif, you might say, with a lot of straw, bamboo and rattan. I threw in some big pillows, bright flowered prints and a couple of Gauguins, and the only thing missing was recognition from *Better Homes and Gardens*. Hey, look, whatever else it was, it was cheerful. What more could a celibate bachelor with irregular tastes and habits want? Sometimes I used to garden at midnight.

When I got home that particular night there was the usual accumulation of junk mail and phone messages on the machine. An old friend from New York, I'd missed him, an offer of a gig with a big band at a big blowout Cuban wedding, I'd missed that, the boss three times and notes from an old girlfriend. Also Mrs Cardoza, who implied that Fidel's declining health was due to my prolonged absence and obvious indifference. She said he didn't like walking with anyone else.

I made my favorite quick dinner, vegetable burritos full of onions, eggs, peppers and potatoes fried in olive oil and garlic, accompanied by Dos Equis. Haute cuisine. At eleven I watched the local news and then started to practice to one of those tapes of an unadorned rhythm section laying down accompaniment for horn players. I had mine made up for me by friends; this one was Ellington tunes. At midnight the local public broadcasting channel was showing *The Maltese Falcon* uninterrupted. Who could ask for a better night?

Then at about eleven-thirty I received a strange phone call from Frankie. I don't even know how she got my number; it's more unlisted than most. I didn't particularly like that idea and it cost me a few music jobs, but certain old cases dictated caution. Even the special kind of work I did in the service had at one time carried the potential for trouble.

'Too late?'

'No, no, I told you, I'm a night person.'

'Oh, yeah, one of them.' Good old Frankie; this was her as the blue-collar puritan. I suppose I could have said, 'What do you mean by that?' and got into it with her, but I was more interested in her whole tone than the joys of sustaining our combat. 'What are you doing?'

'Practicing.'

'Yeah, you probably do a lot of that if you're celibate.' I didn't get a chance to respond, because she followed up with, 'Sorry, I didn't call up at this hour to be a pain in the ass. What are you practicing?'

I told her to hold on, picked up my instrument, sat on the piano bench and played a few bars of 'In a Sentimental

174

Mood,' a celestial standard designed by God for trombone players alone or lonely. The rhythm tape was still running and I improvised a couple of ideas that so entranced me I was in danger of running on. I had to force myself to break off the chorus and put down the horn.

'Hear it?'

'That's totally weird.' I could see her shaking her head, trying to decide if I was bonkers beyond hope. In that I misjudged her. I made a lot of mistakes about Frankie, mostly confusing attitude with conviction, which was easy to do because the attitudes barked and the convictions waited for better times.

'It's a Duke Ellington tune. And no, he doesn't play with Guns 'n' Roses.'

'Hey, I went with a musician once, I know who Duke Ellington is.'

I expressed a certain skepticism and she confirmed it.

'An old dead black guy in a white suit.' She couldn't sustain it. Not that night. No sooner was it out of her mouth than she rushed for another judgment. 'Just kidding. Listen, you really play that thing?'

'What do you think? You just heard me.'

'I don't know much about it but it sounds like, yeah, you really do.'

'Where are you?'

'At the station. Cleaning up some stuff.' When I didn't say anything she thought she had to defend being there. 'It's a good time to play catch-up – quiet, nobody bothers you, you know? No brass.'

'You'd be better off home playing the trombone.'

'Yeah, maybe.'

She'd run out of excuses for the call. I could imagine the scene; very few places are as desolate as a detective squad room when only an occasional desk lamp is lit, most of the 'guys' are home with friends or families, and the cleaning woman, who's glumly banging metal wastebaskets around, looks as if she could use a raise to help with the six fatherless kids. You always pretend to work, but you know why you're really there and end up aiming crumpled papers across the room at those just-emptied baskets.

She forced energy into her voice. 'You got anything new?'

'Nope.'

'Me neither.'

'That it?' I had decided that the greater kindness would be to let her go.

'I had something else but I forgot.'

'Okay. Take care.'

'Right. You too.'

Even her hang-up echoed. I gave up practicing. Enough blues for one night. There was a time when I would have emptied a bottle of Irish after a late-night conversation that desperate. Now I got another bottle of Dos Equis and went to sit out in the yard where I could ask the crickets for answers. I missed *The Maltese Falcon*, but then I'd seen it thirty or forty times. I've always wondered what Spade would have thought about Intersec Systems?

I think that what she had wanted to tell me was about her time spent with Chapelle. She sure as hell should have. She didn't even mention the contradiction wherein James had maintained that he had had no contact with Annie Robertson since his release yet knew that the photographs of him taken by the kidnappers had never been delivered to her. Passing that on might have saved a lot of grief later. Was it deliberate? I realize now I had kidded myself about our working as a team. Frankie had too much to lose. And because she insisted on keeping that always in mind she lost it.

I went to bed about one-thirty, knowing full well I'd be up again soon to pay for those beers. I usually put myself to sleep dredging up batting averages or imagining myself bone-fishing in the lucent green waters of the Keys. I'm not complicated; women are. Before I went under, the phone rang again. Calls at that hour make anyone antsy – the Highway Patrol telling you your favorite aunt drove off a cliff on the way to take her vows.

It was Annie Robertson, drunk as a skunk. I was interested but tired and not a little confused at that point. One of the things that interested me most was where *she* had gotten the phone number? Frankie was a cop, that was one thing. The office never gave it out; no one did.

Chapelle had it, both of them did, but he wouldn't have given it to her because he was a naturally discreet man and I wasn't clued in about the affair. Whatever Frankie thought. I asked Annie how but she just laughed in that way drunks have of making everything hopeless. That was the only thing she laughed at; the rest of the time she cried.

'I haven't even heard one goddamned word from him, the bastard! Do you know what it feels like? I love him . . . and he treats me this way? After the agony I've been through . . . without even anyone to talk to, no one to tell how shitty I felt not knowing . . .'

I sat up on the edge of the bed and tried to massage or shake my head into some semblance of lucidity. 'Annie, can I ask one question? Why me?'

'Why not?' she wailed. I would have thought she was tougher than that. It occurred to me that I hadn't begun to understand this woman. For one thing, I had never believed for a minute that she loved him. Now I wasn't so sure.

'Well, for starters,' I suggested, 'we hardly know each other.' Trying to be logical with an hysterical drunk in the middle of the night.

'But you know Jim,' she pleaded. 'I had to talk to someone who knew him, don't you see? If I couldn't talk to him . . .'

I did feel sorry for her, caught in that timeless conundrum. Life is a soap opera. A soap opera with wild beasts abroad in it. She asked me how he looked, what shape he was in, if he had mentioned her. Knowing nothing of his conversation with Frankie, I was lying when I said he had, privately, spoken of how badly he felt about his inability to contact her.

I couldn't tell whether that made her feel more loved or increased her frustration; the sound at the other end was profound but undistinguishable.

Another thing held back from me at the time was the fact that he intended to dump this woman. For her own good and her ultimate relief, as he so ingenuously told Frankie. If I had known I don't think I would have gone out of my way to lead Annie on; it would have been kinder not to. I even said things like 'I'm sure you'll hear from him tomorrow.' I promised to remind him forcefully of the awful position he had put her in.

At the end, she asked a peculiar thing. Would I be her friend? Presumptuous, but then everybody wanted to be our friend in those days. Aren't there any fathers any more? What else are you going to say except 'of course.' I promised to come see her and keep her apprised, and yes she could call at any *reasonable* time. She thanked me profusely, apologized profusely as only a drunk can, and hung up.

I lay back on the bed, fully awake again, and stared at the show of wind-formed shadows on the white ceiling. The call had seemed mundane and pathetic. Only later would I understand how remarkable it had been.

The night wasn't over; at the time it felt as though it never would be. I went back to bed a little after two, and this time all the way down to sleep. About three I was awakened by some providential instinct, or maybe it was training, I don't know. It started as a buzz deep in the sub-conscious, as I remember in some kind of flaky, frightening dream about being stalked by faceless people. That turned out to be a prophecy.

The buzz was the idling of pistons, perhaps, because

there was a car out there on the street with the engine running. At first I was annoyed at my own paranoia, lying there, wondering whatever happened to sleep as a palliative. Someone who worked a late shift or was coming home drunk and loath to face a fed-up mate, lovers unable to break it off and return to a world without intense feelings . . . it was just a car nearby. Then I noticed something – where was Fidel? My, the neighbor's, demon watchdog? He hated cars at night the way a mongoose hates a cobra, and was a lot noisier about it.

They had suspended my right to carry a gun and taken away the Beretta as evidence but I kept a Colt at home, and now I retrieved it from the locked drawer of my desk. There was still no logical reason to be alarmed, but out-of-control DNA-driven senses were ascending to some new level of acuteness. Just in case there was a sabertooth outside the cave.

The birds seemed to have stopped singing. What did they know that I didn't? The car moved a little. I couldn't be sure but it seemed to have come closer. Then I became aware of a gliding beam of light on the ceiling, where it had leaked in across the top of the louvered blinds. Looking down, the glow of it could be seen against the closed slats. The car had moved to fix its lights on the front of the house. I looked to the panel beside the bed to make certain I had turned on the alarm system.

Gripping the pistol, I got off the bed without sitting up. I was wearing pajamas but I know better than to meet these things in bare feet so I slipped on a pair of deck shoes. The light on the ceiling broadened and brightened as the driver edged further into my driveway. I tried to peek through the bottom of the blinds but I was looking straight into the glare.

Keeping low, I dodged back through the house – the bedroom is in front – and, after checking outside and then turning off the alarm, slipped out a side door into some shrubbery. Most likely the lights directed at the house were supposed to draw me to the front door where, if I opened it, I would be silhouetted and blind. If that was their intent, clearly it was someone who didn't know me.

I could have simply set off the alarm or called 911 and a unit might well have gotten there in fifteen or twenty minutes, or on the other hand someone could have torched, blown or shot the house to hell in the next few seconds. People are armed these days with things like the Kalashnikov, which will drive right through a concrete block. One reason not to stay inside.

I crept forward through the bushes and vines until I could see around the corner of the house and at a better angle, one that allowed me some relief from the beam of the headlights. My pajamas were filthy and sweat ran from my scalp to my fingertips, gluing my palm to the pistol butt. I wasn't sure but the car itself looked like a Buick, possibly a LeSabre. There was a man, or at least a form, outside of it, and I thought someone, some blob, behind the wheel. There was the faintest hush of voices on the heavy air. It's strange, but even under those conditions I was fairly certain that I sensed indecision.

That indecision echoed in my head. If they weren't going to frag or burn the house I considered going back in and calling the police. As it was, I had nothing to shoot at; that is, no justification. I started to edge back when the man beside the car suddenly raised his arm. I heard two cracks and saw the muzzle flashes as tiny bright tongues in the dark. My first, and good, instinct was to flatten. I heard the engine roar into life and took that as my cue to leap up. The car door slammed as the shooter jumped back in, then slammed again as panic induced chaos. I made it to a crouching position and fired twice at the general shape of the car. Whatever the effect, it kept moving.

Backing out, the headlights swept over me, and that put me into another dive towards the earth. I don't care what the movies tell you – caught flush in a strong light anyone with any acquaintance with violence ducks. And by the time I got up again they were gone. To follow would have meant going back into the house to get my car keys. By then there would have been dozens of alternative routes they could have taken.

I went inside and called the police, although it wasn't necessary. Neighbors had been alerted by the sounds of combat. I think a couple had been at the Bay of Pigs. They were already out there wandering around in their nightclothes with flashlights, asking each other what had happened, probably armed to the teeth. Other dogs were barking but still no Fidel.

I didn't know any of the cops who came but later, the next morning with the detectives, we had some acquaintances in common. They treated the whole thing as routine. By 'routine' I mean they assumed I was probably into something hinky now that I was 'retired' from the force and this had been payback time. I didn't try to disabuse them. The whole idea of Intersec and the case I was working on had for them all the appeal of a head cold. Cops, striving in a complicated world, prefer things simple, and who can blame them.

One bullet had hit the front of the house next to the front door but the other was never found. The spent round was a hollow point or, more likely, notched by the owner and flattened into a lead patty by the impact. A ballistic washout. They did find casings by the car. I didn't mention the shooting of Rodriguez; that would only have made it more complicated. There was no problem in my, along with millions of other Floridians, having a gun in my house and shooting it at shooters. The American way. I would come in and fill out a report. That was it.

I never did get much sleep and woke up sweaty and drained. Anyone who tells you they were not frightened before, during and after a shootout is lying or some kind of freak. But finally I had the Cuban coffee going and the smell brought me back. When I went out for the *Herald* I found a note under the door from Mrs Cardoza. I guessed that she had missed the whole thing the night before because she turned off her hearing aid at nine. It said I wouldn't have to walk Fidel any more, he was dead. She speculated that he had bitten a Communist and been poisoned.

That last part I suspected might be the case. A strychnine meatball for a pesky dog was not unheard of on a hot prowl. I thought about pursuing it further and even arranging a secret autopsy – I could have swung that through some old contacts if she hadn't had him cremated – but what would have been the point? I already knew somebody meant me no good at home, and it might end up causing the old lady pain.

Before I went over to the Coral Gables station for the paperwork I stopped at the office and laid it out for my boss. Like me, he assumed the night visitors might have come to kill me but more likely were sending a message of some kind. He was more concerned by the fact that they had been able to find me. The company takes security very seriously and as a matter of course protects the privacy of its operatives. In my case they had made a special effort.

'Anyone we should be looking at?' I asked him, meaning the departmental employees.

'Currently there's only three or four have access.'

'"Three *or* four"? You don't know?'

'I don't include our president as an employee, okay? Anyway, no, not a chance. What about the hall of records? You own your own home? Or somebody coulda got into the unlisted numbers at the phone company.'

'I bought my house and listed my phone under another name. I use my own with the neighbors just to keep from going goofy. I've seen what happens to those guys who live clandestine for years. When they get their pension they don't recognize their names on the check.'

He lit one of his collection of pipes and took a couple of puffs. He thought it made him look sage. 'I'll tell you what I'm worried about – a hacker. Illegal accessing.' The man would always have trouble liking computers; that was a given, even if we were called Intersec. 'Raul thinks somebody got in recently. He's had to change the codes. Anybody in this Chapelle deal a digit-head?'

'I imagine all the males and probably a couple of the females are literate. I don't know if any of them are capable of hacking.' I didn't know what Frankie knew.

He sat way back until I was afraid he'd tumble, swung his feet up on to the desk and rubbed his never-quite-shaven chin. There was a hole in the sole of one shoe. Even when you didn't like this boss there was always some reason to like him. He grinned. 'On the one hand, somebody's tryin' to kill you. On the other, you must be doin' a great job. Isn't that where you been all your life? Now what's wrong with that?'

Evil old bastard.

FRANKIE

When I got through talking to Dunn that night I just sat there like a lump for about half an hour. Couldn't get my butt off the chair with a crane, dreary as it was in that hole at that hour. Even the cleaning woman had gone home.

Why the hell had I called him in the first place? And then I didn't say anything, except to mumble and make a goddamn fool of myself. As far as the shooting at his house, he withheld that information until much later. You can imagine my temper when I finally heard.

In the meantime, things Chapelle had said disturbed me. Christ, being within ten feet of the man disturbed me, but I thought some of these anomalies (another word from that frigging Dunn) were serious. Lying in a crime victim is always serious.

At the same time I actually believed that there was something sad, almost tragic about him. I just couldn't put my finger on it. My head warned me that he could probably manufacture and call up any kind of emotion he wanted and then insinuate it into others. The guy was an actor; it would be good to remember that.

With some effort I stopped myself thinking about it. There was no magic, even of the heart. I was a practical, determined person. But, Jesus, men were confusing. From now on I would only take cases where everybody was poor, ugly and had bad breath. If there were any more cases.

I had no idea how they were seeing me over at the Department. I knew I had one bit of unfinished business that I'd goddamn well take care of in the morning no matter what happened. I crumpled papers and tried for a few more baskets, missed them all – what else was new? – and went home to my cell.

A sleepless night and up early. Everybody in the Department was in one meeting or another all morning, which suited me fine. I finished my report, made some calls, found out what I wanted and bailed.

I bet nobody in history ever arrived at the Everglades Club in a Toyota, unless they were working in the kitchen. I drove right up in front – so I'd have to put in for the dollar tip.

It looked like pictures of castles or at least fancy hotels in Italy, kind of square-cut with big arched windows and red-tile roofs. The color was sandy, or maybe that's 'sienna.' The hedges looked like they'd been trimmed with nail clippers by midget slaves. I could smell snobbery coming off the stones in this place.

I was learning as I went that this area called 'between the clubs,' meaning the Everglades on the north and the Bath and Tennis to the south, contained a large amount of the richest people in the world. And here was little Frankie come to bust their chops. Weird.

The doorman didn't like the look of my car or me, but I wouldn't expect him to. I jumped out, told the kid who took my keys I wouldn't be gone long, headed for the entrance under the green-striped awning. And all the time the doorman's up on his toes like a shortstop, ready to go to his left or right. He made his move, but before he could say a word I had the buzzer in his face. He wasn't the first person to be surprised I'm a cop, and it threw him for a minute.

'I'll get the club manager.'

'I don't have time for that.' I swept right by him, the same way those sharky ladies do. It worked.

I asked one of the employees where my guy was. He didn't try to stop me but he sized me up pretty good, so that I had that cheap-suit feeling. Of course it was a cheap suit. The squash court. I knew that was some kind of game like handball or badminton or something and my people never played it.

Beane was really into his game when I entered, and I got a chance to observe him. He had his hair tied back with a headband but otherwise he could fit right in. All in whites, clean-shaven, earrings left in the drawer, in fact no jewelry at all. You could get away with any one of those attributes of the life around here, but not all together, and obviously Billy-boy had been swimming in these waters long enough to adapt to different currents.

His opponent was a lot older, very distinguished-looking, but in great shape and giving Billy a hard run. He seemed a little cranky about it. I suspected they played for money. Big money, for sure. How many times and how much had Chapelle lost at deals like this? You read how a big basketball player lost a million and a half in a golf game, and you wonder if the goddamn country is worth defending. Which is what I thought I did, anyway.

I found myself getting impatient so I barked his name. He broke play and got hit by the ball while turning. It's soft – I looked it up in the dictionary afterwards and found that's how it got its name – so he wasn't hurt. Just pissed to find me there giving him my worst stare.

He came over. 'How come they let you in?' Even his voice had taken on the superior, laid-back tone they used for complaint around there.

'Why not? I'm not Jewish.'

Mr Distinguished didn't like that at all. 'We're having a game here, young lady. Who the devil do you think you are?'

I was learning – it wasn't enough to stonewall or carp, you had to take it right to them. I give Sean credit. I went straight at this old bastard, waggling the shield out in front of me like he was a vampire and I had the garlic.

'I know who I am, sir. I also know what happens to people who lie down with dogs. Now why don't you give us a few minutes, okay?'

He stopped in his tracks, scowled, but apparently he understood. Turning snappishly on his heel, he showed me how to walk out of a room when you've been insulted by a nothing. I watched him, pleased.

'Man, you don't care who you fuck with, do you?'

I rounded on Billy. 'It's good you know that.'

'Yeah, well he happens to be— '

I jammed my face right in front of his like a DI. 'Shut up!'

'Whoooa, hey . . .!' He tried to grin like he wasn't impressed, much less intimidated, but like everything else about the guy it was bogus.

'It was you, wasn't it?'

He couldn't look at me for a minute, so I backed off and let him breathe. 'Yeah, it was me. I did you a favor.'

'Oh, sure. You did somebody a favor, asshole, but you didn't do it for me, so let's not fill this beautiful room with bullshit, okay. You *overheard* it in the Rebel?' I put enough sarcasm in it to draw flies.

He was panting a little, and to show that it was from the exertions of the game, which it wasn't, he strolled over to a bench, put down his racket and hid his eyes behind a toweling-off. I followed and stayed close.

'Okay, not exactly "overheard." I know the guy. Or did before you went down there and smoked him, you and that goddamn Dunn. Anyway, I admit I knew him, we'd done some business. He was real hammered that night, mixing all kinds of things like black rum and beer, and he was probably high too. He usually was. He said how he'd gotten into this thing, the kidnapping, after he met some insane mick through some bitch or something. I don't know. I was a little zoned myself. They hid at his place for a night or two with . . . you know, Jim. Then he, Rodriguez, got spooked and, when they moved, he bailed on them. He was scared they were going to come after him, because they were all wired on everything but mostly panicked, and couldn't risk him ratting them out.'

'Did he tell you they were supposed to kill Chapelle, but tried to double-cross the buyer instead?'

'What are you talking about? That's insane.'

'Why'd they panic?'

'I don't know. Look, that's it. What he told me, and I told you, so just leave me alone now, okay? Or you're gonna find yourself in a world of trouble, I promise you.'

'There's only one of us here sweating. You willing to take a poly on all this?'

'I got no problem with it.'

'Sure you don't. This big act of charity on your part, how come?'

Billie started to pace along the bench. I noticed he was all right as long as we were both in the world of the streets. He liked the chameleon thing; he was proud of it or it amused him or something twisted. But when I touched him in this

world, 'between the clubs,' it made him very edgy, like he
didn't know the rules any more.

'Well . . . I mean, the Chapelles are old family friends.
You know.'

'Birds of a feather, huh?'

'Something like that.'

'Tell me something. Is there anything they could do that
you'd disapprove of?'

'Why would I do that?' It was the first straight thing he'd
said to me.

'Fair enough. Nobody ever disapproves of you. Why
should you disapprove of them? You guys got your
rules.'

He looked sullen. 'I don't know what the fuck you're
talking about. So I was born rich. That doesn't mean I
got to be a fuckin' artichoke all my life. In another time
or place I would've run off to join a circus or be a pirate
or something. I *need* the excitement.'

'Me too. So, I guess polo doesn't cut it. You ever see a
crack baby?'

'Shit, I love it when cops preach. Like the fuckin' DEA,
there's a church choir for you. C'mon, Sergeant, okay? I'm
a big boy and you're a big girl and— '

'Have you ever seen a crack baby?' I reached into my
bag – I'd love to use a shoulder holster but it just doesn't
cut it with breasts – and pulled the pistol out far enough
for him to see it. He would know I wasn't going to use it in
there, but he was soft and the mere sight of it would make
a point about how I felt about him. It served also to remind
that there was that more basic world outside which we really
belonged to and how sooner or later its rules would have to
be obeyed.

I don't even know if he saw it but his mood changed. 'I
don't make anyone use,' he said glumly.

'I want to find the two who are still out there, or who
brought them together, or the second hideout, or who

started the whole goddamn fucking mess in the first place. Especially that. *Comprende*, Billy?'

'Dream on, man.'

'If you don't know, and I think you do, you find out.'

'C'mon, lady, you can't rag on me, with my family. You'll be out on your ass.'

I smiled sweetly. I could afford to. 'No harassment. Promise. What I can do, though, and happily, is put the word around about who ratted on Rodriguez. They'll understand the motive, because everybody's got to wonder how come you're in the life, and that breeds suspicion and those Colombians, they sure as hell understand group loyalty. *Padrón! Padrón!* and all that *la familia* shit. They'll be looking at you saying, "Sure, he'd do that for those rich gringos who gave him his milk when he was a little *infante*." You'll look funny with your tongue wagging through your neck.'

There it was, the kind of thing we do sometimes. You can't clean streets with white gloves. At least I had the satisfaction of having made a definite impression; fear climbed his face like a monkey on a vine.

'You fucking bitch. You wouldn't dare. I'll have you crucified.'

'Billy-boy, there are some things you can't prove. And some kinds of justice you can't buy. Go back to your stupid game.' I started out but he had to try to get something back. A grown-up criminal would have swallowed it. Choked on it, but swallowed it.

'I've seen Dunn in the Rebel.'

I turned very deliberately. It was infuriating that, searching for the worst, most painful shot he could give me, he came up with this crap. What the hell did he think? I looked; his face was redder than it had been when he was playing. 'Am I supposed to care?'

'You care.' He was breathless, as if from climbing. Rage, I guess. 'Ask him what's his deal with Jim and Syl.

I never figured it out, but I can smell dirty or I wouldn't be alive.'

I waited, because I'm good at it. The look said, 'You tell me, asshole.' Eventually it worked; it usually does.

Nervously, he said, 'I figured you'd know, since I heard you two were gettin' it on.'

I managed a very controlled 'Why do you think that?'

He tried to look as if it was the most obvious thing in the world. ''Cause I know Jim's jealous.' He hesitated; should he go on? 'I've never seen that before.'

It was ridiculous. I could have told him so, but I was blinded by this flaring red screen that came down over my judgment. I heard someone, logically it had to be me, say with absolute indifference, 'Boy, are you misinformed.' Then I kicked him hard in his kneecap, causing him to scream and collapse on to the bench in agony.

Kneecaps are underrated. I know nowadays it's popular to go for their stones – sure, if they're frog-marching at the time – but the truth is they're a very hard target. Nature recessed them there between the thighs in order that they can go on, with a little help from us, propagating the race. If you miss and catch the stomach you can kill the bastard, and then you're in a whole world of trouble. Also, for short women, it can be a long reach up there, especially in heels. I'm not short but I did happen to be wearing those and believe me they are not ideal kicking-wear.

In this case, Billie was wearing shorts and that vulnerable cleft in the knee loomed like a bullseye, crying for it, heels or no. The shoe flew off, causing me to scramble for it and ruining the movie-smooth exit I had in mind. All I remember mumbling to him was, 'I been too fuckin' polite lately,' but I don't think he heard me.

I didn't know anyone else had seen me, didn't know the trouble it would cause, and didn't give a shit.

By the time I got back to the station doomsday had arrived. I sat up straight in the Captain's office in a chair

I had always felt made me smaller, surrounded by bowling trophies and pictures of his triumphs as a Pop Warner coach, and listened to him bellow, which like I say is his normal speech.

'The club manager called the Sheriff. You actually kicked a man in the Everglades? A man from a prominent family? I can't believe it. Are you out of your goddamn mind, Sergeant? Explain it to me. I dare you to. I mean, what the hell were you even doing in there? We don't go in there. For sure, unless we're invited. You could lose your shield over this, for Christ's sake, and you just sit there.'

'You haven't let me talk.'

'Talk, goddammit!'

'I don't care if he's from a "prominent family," he's a scuz. He flies for the Medellin. And he's also a suspect in this case, and when I tried to question him he threatened me with his squash racket.' It sounded so funny even to me I almost laughed out loud. The look on the Captain's face . . .

'With the what? He did what?'

I explained, with of course the little embellishment that enabled me to claim self-defense. My view was that if he had not exactly threatened me with a squash racket he had certainly threatened my good nature with his repulsive one. Fortunately, the Captain understood less about all this than even I did. He seemed to calm down.

'We still don't kick people in the Everglades. Or the Bath and Tennis, either. You understand?'

I nodded.

'As far as him being a suspect, that's not your business any more. You go on that jewel robbery in Boynton Beach where they shot the owner.'

'What are you talking about?'

'The FBI's been watching this case and they've ID'd the Irishman.' He consulted a readout on his desk. 'Name's Harry Feeney. Six-one, two hundred and twenty pounds, thinning blond hair and facial scars on chin and above left eye. Born in Boston, worked for different mobs – loan-sharking, extortion, union strong-arm – wanted on a felony warrant. He's left the country, they think to Puerto Rico.' He made a particularly obnoxious snort. 'Ought to look like a roach in a bathtub down there.'

I knew what he was saying but I sure was having trouble accepting it. 'What the hell do the feds have to do with this? This is our case, for Christ's sake.'

'You don't understand English? They're over at the Chapelle house right now doing their number.'

'Chapelles didn't want them.'

'I don't know from the politics, and neither do you. The Sheriff told me how they been watching and come up with the doer, this mick.'

'Jesus, they're like vultures.'

'Cold War's over, they don't have as much to do.'

'But it's my fuckin' case, and I don't believe that shit about this Feeney jumping to Puerto Rico.'

'How would you know different?'

I didn't, but I wasn't going to let him know that. If I'd told him 'instinct,' I would have had to listen to a whole symphony of those snorts. So I lied. I told him I had very reliable word from informers about a whole other dude. I even made up his sheet, his MO, and how he was hiding in Miami. I think he actually bought it, but it still didn't mean a goddamn thing.

'Forget it, Bodo. The vic came home on your watch, that won't hurt you at all. So let it go now. Metcalf will liaise with them.'

'Owen? Why Owen?' My voice, despite hard effort, was going up and coming on.

'Because he's older, smarter and easier to get along with. Besides, the feds got to get along with a colored – the Democrats are in power. Now get out of here and don't give me a lot of mouth. I got work.'

It was good advice. I should have taken it but I was really upset. I wanted to stay on this case more than I had wanted anything in my adult life, even if I didn't know why. I rationalized it was simply that this was the big time professionally and I had come an awful long way to step up to it. Okay, that was part of it.

They heard me yelling out in the squad room and that's never a good idea, embarrassing a captain. I even threatened to resign but he called my bluff. I thought in the end he was going to throw me out physically, but I came to some sanity not a minute too soon.

It was necessary to go outside for a few minutes to untwist the pretzel. I was young to be a detective-sergeant. Young and female. I was never going to be a young female detective-lieutenant. Swallowing a few deep ones, I paced around on the sidewalk and gave myself my patented too-oft-used pep talk. Then I went to look for Owen to tell him, if he'd heard, that there was nothing personal in it, but he was over at the Chapelles. Sitting down at my desk I tried to pretend that I was finishing my report and everyone left me alone. I didn't blame them. Poison Bodo.

XIII

SEAN

The boss waited until eleven o'clock to call me; in itself a bad sign indicating the opposite of imperative. Even routinely he was contemptuous of my slovenly habits and liked to wake me up as early as possible.

'Forget about the Chapelle case, okay.'

I expressed confusion and, what surprised me, disappointment. He reminded me none too gently that I hadn't wanted to be connected with it in the first place.

'What about the investigating officer – Bodo?'

'She's history.' He explained the FBI involvement, but we both knew they were still obligated to work with the local authorities. Or at least pretend to.

'Who called you?'

'What?' He'd heard. 'What do you care? You wanted off, now you're off. Aren't you ever happy? Take the day, go to the beach. The client's back, New York's happy, God's in his heaven and all's right with the corporation.'

'I don't like the beach.'

'You like to fish, go fishing. I don't give a shit. Check about noon tomorrow, if that's not disturbing your rest too much. I got something for you down in Key West.'

'Who called you?'

He waited, deciding. 'I don't know what the fuck difference it makes, but Duchow. And the brother was there with him, Glen, got on the horn too. They said you did a great job, they're happy . . . I'm happy.'

'I don't suppose you asked them why they're so anxious to get rid of us?'

'Oh, sure. I asked them how many times a day they whack off, too. When you're older and smarter you'll see the less you have to do with these pricks the better. Do your job and out.'

One thing only Frankie and I had in common – we never took advice.

I might not find turning myself into *carpaccio* at the beach exactly thrilling, but I've also never had any trouble filling days in South Florida. Granted, it's a little short on museums and libraries, but if worst comes to worst I'll drive down the Keys or just go sit out in the Everglades with a book. There are coves, islands, swamps, relics – it's an explorer's dream.

Miami is a Spanish city, but I love that, too. I go sit in the Plaza on Calle Ocho, sip that blacker-than-black coffee through a sugar cube and listen to the domino players tell tales of old Cuba. Sometimes we speculate about how to kill the current occupant of the throne. God knows what they'll do when he goes. No, I would have been fine if I hadn't agreed to take that one last call.

I was sitting on the front porch with my morning espresso watching a chameleon seeking its breakfast – I'd already had mine, such as it was – on a camellia bush. A little sticky that morning, a reminder that you were in the tropics. They always say 'semi-tropics' in the literature but that's so as not to scare off the tourists. I've been in the tropics and Miami is tropical, although fortunate enough to have the trade winds.

I was worrying about Frankie. To be released from the case might be a mixed blessing for me but was a real blow to her future. I thought about calling her. She would, of course, act as if it was the last thing she wanted, but that didn't mean it wasn't a good idea.

The phone rang and it was the boss again. Amelia was

desperate to talk to me. He said if I didn't want to take it he'd cover for me. I was either mellow or insane that morning, and agreed. She insisted I come all the way up to her place that night.

'Does your husband know you're calling me, and where is he going to be?' Might as well be blunt.

'No. And New York.'

'Do you want to tell me what this is about?'

'No. I don't know what it's about. I have to talk to someone and . . . you're sympathetic.'

'Thanks, but, uh, what happened last time . . .'

'I'm not asking you to come fuck me, Sean. I'm just desperate . . .'

Hard to turn down an invitation like that. 'There's something you ought to know. Your brother-in-law's kidnapping, I'm not on it any more. Neither's Sergeant Bodo.'

'Why?'

'You tell me. Something about the FBI, but also the family wanted it like that.'

'"The family."' It was like a kid saying 'castor oil.' 'Glen and James's sister are here now. Did you know that? They'll all gather . . .' She broke off self-consciously.

'Like vultures, I think you want to say.'

'I don't care what your status is or who doesn't like you. I want you to come. Please.'

I told her I would and set a time after dinner. Dinner was too intimate. I couldn't imagine why I was doing it anyway, why I felt a tug of excitement.

FRANKIE

I don't know what I accomplished the rest of that day. I just tried to look busy and didn't talk to anyone. Fortunately for me, anyway, there was a lot going down during that period and all the investigators were out in the field. About five o'clock I lost my mind and called Chapelle. I don't know what I was going to say to him, and don't know what I would have done if he had come to the phone. The maid said he had flown up to his son's school in Pennsylvania and would be back late that night or early in the morning. Did I have a message? No, I didn't.

Before I went home, my ass really dragging though not from work, from lack of it I did something I've regretted ever since. I called Estrada in Miami and asked him for a favor.

The only contact we'd ever had was when we went after Rodriguez together. That had actually turned out all right for him in that he was in charge of the team which, well, 'brought one of the Chapelle kidnappers to justice,' not to put too much of a fine point on it (still another screwy Dunn phrase). And the fact was, I didn't know anyone else down there.

I asked him to put the word out on the mean streets how Billy Beane ratted out Rodriguez. No questions, no problem. He agreed right off because it's not a big deal. They kill, we kill. Like the song says, some people do it with a gun, some do it with a pen. I was willing to do it with my mouth.

I told myself it was a last grasp at the solution that had eluded me all along, that it had a legitimate objective in that I was trying to roll a witness, someone we would certainly protect if he cooperated. I might take two brutal killers off the streets and protect Chapelle from a still-secret and dangerous enemy. You tell yourself a lot of things when you're fooling with people's lives.

But I was off the case and Estrada didn't know that. I don't think he ever knew it. And the thing that will always nag me, I thought about but for some reason failed to call Beane and give him a second chance, to warn him again. Sitting there in my cubicle with everyone gone or going to their nighttime lives, I told myself I'd already warned him and if the sonofabitch thought because I was a woman, because I was wussy or simply because he was so fucking arrogant he couldn't believe the rich die, it was his fall.

When I got home I defrosted some dinner and wandered around the apartment looking for something I hadn't seen before. It looked so bleak I couldn't imagine why I had never put any thought or effort into decorating it. God, it was like the interior of a monastery, except not that attractive. Not even comfortable. Dunn had talked a little about this dinky house he had down in Coral Gables and I found myself wondering what that was like. Probably worse than mine.

I had a beer, even smoked a very rare cigarette, which tells you something. My television set had broken down and I'd forgotten, so there I was channel-surfing a blank screen. I never seemed to have time to wait for a repairman. It was such an up-tight night I called my mother, and naturally she was drunk. The woman was amazing, a liver for all seasons. I put on another U2 tape, my favorite group that year.

Sitting in a chair assembled from a box, staring at the blank TV screen while Bono's voice charged around the room, I tried to remember my feelings before and after calling Dunn the night before. I couldn't, so I called him again. After all, I hadn't told him about my questioning of Chapelle. Would I have told him about – okay, 'confessed' – to my heavy move on Beane? I think I would have felt better if he'd understood. He was, I found out, as practically the whole world found out, with Amelia Chapelle that night.

I was thinking of going to bed; I didn't have anything to read and the alternative was to become a bottle jockey like my old lady. The phone rang, scaring me out of the chair. I should have been used to strange calls at strange hours, so it must have been the mood. When I answered it was a man's voice, one I'd never heard, which put me on edge right off. It wasn't threatening; just my healthy paranoia.

'Is this Francis Bodo?'

'Francis?' Who was this guy?

'Please look outside your apartment door, Ms Bodo.'

'What? Why . . .?'

'Have a nice night.'

Jesus, I'm thinking, what kind of stupid game is this? I hate games. One of those treasure hunts, or did some old bust want to decapitate me? I got my gun from the bedstand, turned out the lights, checked the street below. It was as square as ever, a quiet neighborhood where most of the residents lived in small houses and owned RV's with bumper stickers like 'I'm spending my children's inheritance.' But tonight even less than nothing . . .

Next, I get the idea the door might be booby-trapped. A pretty insane idea when I thought about it later and could afford to get embarrassed. But it was the only entrance to the apartment except for second-floor windows, and I would rather have died than call the bomb squad only to discover it was nothing. I got behind the wall and opened the door with my left hand, keeping the pistol, safety off, down by my side. No big bang, no smoke, fire and flying Bodo. Carefully, I peered out.

Roses. Yellow ones, hundreds of them billowing in clusters and waves on the steps, the landing, in baskets and vases. The incredibly sweet odor almost knocked me down and I can't imagine why I wasn't aware of it before i saw them. I just stood there in shock; nothing like this had ever happened to me. How had they been delivered without my hearing? No card, no word. I asked myself the obvious question – who could afford a gesture like this? No one I'd ever known. Until now.

Still paralyzed, it seemed I could hear my own heart rattling along and my insides felt peculiarly warm. When I realized that I was also smiling I knew I was in big trouble.

'Oh, Frankie . . .'

SEAN

It's a nice little hike up and back from Miami. I had left some things in the motel so I could rationalize that I would have had to make the trip anyway. In some instances a call to the boss will get you a plane and a rental but he would only have reminded me that I was off the case, and I didn't want to be reminded of that.

I went up 95 to Southern Boulevard, turned right over the bridge and took Ocean Boulevard to the neighborhood where the Glen Chapelles lived. I was due at nine and arrived at eight-thirty, which is a good habit to cultivate in my line of work. We're in the watching and listening business; that's all, watching and listening. I parked a half-block away and sat – watching. Not long. A Jaguar came up out of the private garage under the building, the big iron gate opened and it turned to go past me, accelerating rapidly, anxious to get away. I was in shadow but slid down a bit anyway. The driver was Michael Duchow. I said it was good practice; sent me in with a whole new topic of conversation.

Amelia buzzed me inside. If we'd been anywhere else there would have been a guard in the lobby. I took the elevator to the third floor. Very lush building; the carpeting between there and the apartment was worth more than the total of my three pensions. She came to the door herself in a yellow négligé with a lot of décolletage which she could handle very nicely, although it was a bad sign. I always had the feeling about her that she could have been a really good-looking woman, but the hair never worked and now there were some clunky glasses not unlike her husband's. Funny how sometimes we imitate the people we despise.

Other bad signs – a nerve jumping beneath the flesh of her cheek, the quick, brittle moves and febrile eyes. Febrile body, because she was a little flushed. The eyes

. . . amphetamines? Did I want a beer? Oh, yes. If only it could be Irish.

She sashayed into the kitchen and kept up the conversation from there. 'Maid's out. Out permanently – I just fired her. She was always spying.'

It didn't seem to call for an answer. I looked around. I was sitting in a lucite chair with a granite-topped table in front of me that made me long to put my feet on it. It was all glass, pale woods, large empty spaces, starkly modern, or post-modern, or whatever they were calling it then. Not offensively ugly, but cold and soulless. You'd think she would have had at least some Italian furniture or paintings or something beautiful from that beautiful country. A twenty-five-watt bulb like Glen wouldn't know about decorating a home, so it had to have been her.

'Glen's in New York,' came the voice from the kitchen, reading my mind.

'Business?'

'He's got a girl there.'

'Your husband?' Why was I surprised?

When she reappeared the unflattering glasses were gone. She was carrying a very large vodka, my beer and some cheese. 'Yes, my husband. I don't envy her, or them. He's no good to me.' She raised her middle finger and let it droop, before putting the beer and snack down beside me. 'I like serving men. Sicily,' she added for explanation. Her eyes followed mine in another involuntary sweep of the apartment. 'Ugly, isn't it?'

'Doesn't look like . . . Italy. Or you.'

'The company sent a decorator. They decorated, they paid, they decided. And it all came from taxes, or so my husband told me when I made a nice mousy little comment at a party about it resembling an expensive pile of plastic shit.'

'Speaking of the corporation, I saw Michael Duchow coming out of here when I arrived.'

'Did you?'

'You two lovers?'

'What would that have to do with anything?'

'You never know.'

'Haven't you heard? There's a little power struggle over the family firm. James is up and out, Michael and Glen take control. It's been a mess, you know, trying to convince James that the eighties are over.'

'So Duchow came to talk about that. But Glen's in New York?'

'Glen can be difficult. Michael often runs things past me first.'

'Why is that?'

'The American language is a wonderful language. Have you ever heard the saying "If you have them by the balls, their hearts and minds will follow"? Who is going to have a firmer grasp on a man's balls than his loving wife?'

'Right.' She crossed her legs as a form of punctuation, the négligé fell open and I understood that she was wearing high-heeled sandals (around the house?), one of which now dangled as if it might begin tinkling any minute. The toenail polish was Chinese red. They were wonderful legs.

She looked at me appraisingly, long and hard, squinting, as if seeing me for the first time. It was a little unsettling. 'I can't seem to remember why I asked you to come. Although it's nice to have an attractive man admire your legs.'

'You noticed.' She gave me a smile so pleased it was a visual purr. I fixed that. 'When you were in Ireland together, did Sylvia meet anyone? A man? An Irish man?'

'We met lots of people. The Irish are very gregarious.'

'Please, don't waste my time, huh? I'm tired of it. Tired of you all. If you don't want to talk about these things, don't get me all the way up here.'

'She's a married woman.'

I stood. 'Thanks for the beer, or as much of it as I got a chance to drink.'

'No!' she said a little desperately. 'She didn't meet any Irish men. And neither did I. You were going to get around to me, I assume?'

'You have more motive than anybody.' I sat down again. It had been a bluff, anyway.

'We weren't even at the party, Glen and I.'

'You wouldn't have to be. There were other ways to know. You knew about Annie Robertson.'

'Yes. But why do I have a motive?'

'You're the only person I've ever met who doesn't like James.'

'What about his wife?'

'Sylvia? She's crazy about him.'

She laughed and it sounded as if somebody's brakes had locked; you looked for the accident. 'Neither of them are capable of loving anyone. Those two . . . they fuck anybody they want and flaunt it. Does that sound like love to you?'

'No, but it does to them.'

She popped a pill right in front of me. With vodka, yet. I started reviewing my resuscitative knowledge about these things, just in case. 'I think you're very naive for a detective.'

'And I think you know a lot of things that could have ended this a long time ago. But you like secrets. You like the manipulation that goes with them. But you're smart enough to know that if actions have consequences, so does inaction.'

She suddenly turned off the light beside her, casting herself into heavy shadow while leaving me exposed. The effect was dramatic in its directness. Even with that much cover she wasn't looking at me. I heard her murmur, 'This family . . .'

To even things, I turned off my lamp, leaving only peripheral light from other rooms and through the huge expanse of rectangular curtainless windows. You could see the stars now. She seemed to be studying them too. 'Why did you marry Glen?'

'I was sold to him, to them. I hated it, the whole idea, and I hated him. Chinless wonder, the English would say – I went to an English school when I was little. I hated it but I adapted. Because I had to. This family could teach Sicily.'

We sat there in the semi-dark for a while. I think both of us recognized the impossibility of reaching the other, but we seemed driven to keep trying. She lit a cigarette and I found myself following the glow as her hand moved around.

'You're very light-complected for a Sicilian.'

'You're very dark for an Irishman.'

'Black Irish. Supposed to be that the sailors from the Spanish Armada came ashore when their ships were smashed along the rugged coast. The people took them in and hid them, because they both hated the English.'

'Is that true?'

'No. How do you explain you?'

'Rape.'

Something unusual and unexpected can make us laugh, of course, but this time I strangled that sound aborning. I don't know what kind of noise I made, but it was ambivalent.

'By some Frank or Lombard or Visigoth. Everybody's left their genes in Sicily. The whole island's been raped many times over.'

'The Irish feel that way, but the English found ways other than sexual to do it.'

'Less honest, you mean.'

She got up and moved around the darkened room. I could hear the rustling of the négligé and occasionally catch a glimpse by moonlight of white thigh or calf passing. My gaze followed her. I wasn't letting her out of my sight.

'That's what it's all about with men, isn't it? Combat.

Warriors through history. You haven't really conquered anyone until you've ravaged his wife.'

'I'm afraid I haven't had much experience of that.'

'Still works the same way. Only now warfare is mostly corporate.' There was a silence, except for the rustling and the click of the heels and then the ice rattling as she drained her vodka. 'Still, it must have been very exciting for some women, if they didn't kill you afterwards, to be taken by force by a strong man.'

She seemed lost in some fantasy, some fantasy it was not my business to discourage. 'Not exactly politically correct,' I suggested, 'but it could get you on a talk show.' I'm not good with women's neuroses; I'd rather deal with a biker on crank. I sounded so lame I actually found myself wishing Frankie was there.

'My mother was taken – you know, kidnapped. In the Sicilian tradition, by my father and his brothers. A broken hymen makes marriage a *fait accompli*. I don't think she minded at the time. He was very handsome and powerful. Very strong. A lot of people were afraid of him. Still are.'

'Amelia, look around you, we're in Palm Beach, Florida. It's got nothing to do with Sicily.'

'Think so?'

Her sudden proximity jarred me. This figure looming over me, next to me, so close I could smell not perfume this time but simply that wonderful, soft female odor no one has ever been able to give a name to. The silk rustled in my ears like a waterfall. And the heat from her body; I had the sense that it came from where the peignoir offered freedom and access at the top of the thighs. I thought in the dark I could see the even-darker triangle. It had been over a year since I'd been in this kind of intimacy with a woman and it sent everything rushing and spinning inside me. See the strong man grow weak! If only they knew what power they have.

My breathing stopped for a moment and, as that's one of the most powerful silences in the world, I'm sure she knew. I looked up, feeling my passive, childlike state, and saw her face coming down over me. The silk spread, exposing her breasts and opening a new cave of scents inches from my face. Her open mouth covered mine in a way that made it seem magically huge. It was a pillow of flesh yet I could feel all the small muscles moving beneath the skin like a working vagina. Moist, encompassing and then finally, with equal gentleness, penetrating. I returned the probing gratefully.

It was, I suppose, exactly the way women are always telling us to kiss. I believed them before, and I believed them even more afterwards. It gave me an instant erection, the kind that threatens to club you to death if it's denied another second, yet she hadn't touched it physically. She knew I had it though. Somehow.

Withdrawing slowly, sighing as though we had just loved to exhaustion, she raised herself to full standing height, the silk pulling curtains across her body. I had a lot of trouble getting my mind going again. She moved away and the darkness took most of her.

She seemed to be going on about her childhood and Sicily or Italy for no apparent reason. That wasn't what we were here for, not that I understood. The odd idea occurred to me that it was someone evoking their life at the end of it. Strange, but then it was a strange evening.

Trying to organize my thoughts, I simply blundered in with some of the questions I felt compelled to ask. What did she know about Billy Beane's relationship to the Chapelles? Her response was a bored 'nothing.' Drugs? The Chapel Corporation's financial troubles, his gambling, her affairs with . . .? Did she know more than she had told me about the couple up in Jupiter? Then I realized she was talking about Sicily again. It was getting eerie.

'. . . There was no divorce, of course, not in those days,

JAMES DAVID BUCHANAN

and even now it would be unheard of and would probably
lead to killings. But my mother simply wouldn't take it
any more, so she brought me over here. Father made one
unsuccessful attempt to kidnap us – he would have to for
his honor – but afterwards he agreed to support us in grand
style. In the old country I wouldn't even have been allowed
to go to a university and here he paid for Miss Porter's
and Smith. He visits us every year. He's a count. Did you
know that?'

I didn't, and didn't get how it could inform me. But like
I said, I see my job as listening to people far more than
collecting hairs in plastic bags. This crazed, remarkable
woman had the key and I knew it.

'. . . I used to like his visits, a little girl and a handsome
powerful father who brought presents, but later, as I grew
up, I realized that what my mother had always said was true.
He still controlled us. Controlled everything we did and
even what we thought from thousands of miles away.'

'How?'

'They have magic in Sicily the rest of the world doesn't
recognize.'

'Magic?'

'Yes. For lack of a better word, maybe. I wouldn't expect
you to believe me.' She sounded sad. 'Do you pray to the
Holy Ghost?'

'I don't, but that doesn't mean I think you're nuts, either.
There are more things in heaven and earth . . . right?'

She laughed to herself. 'Why am I saying all this? You
couldn't understand.'

'Try me.'

'What do you know about, what does the modern world
know about evil . . . sin . . . redemption through the Holy
Ghost . . .'

'A lot about the former, actually, not much about
the latter.'

'I know about them.'

208

I got up, but stayed with my hands on the chair as some kind of anchor in a dark, unpredictable landscape. 'Look, all this, I don't want to be a pop shrink here, but . . . does it have to do with, like, being molested as a kid, or abused or . . . Did your brother-in-law ever make a pass at you?' I was flailing now.

'Oh, yes. James raped me.' She laughed again, the fragile, tinkling sound they used to depict scarily calm madwomen in movies. I thought maybe they'd had it down after all.

'I find that a little hard to believe.'

'Why?' The one word was almost musical.

'I know him. I know who he is, where he came from and how he thinks. He's an explorer, he's looking for something, not a control freak.'

'Are you saying he could never be violent?'

She knew, I don't know how, that I couldn't. 'Sorry, I just don't buy it.' I didn't believe he had ever made a move on her.

She floated to the window, where I could see her silhouette, and went on in that fanciful tone that made it difficult to know if she was serious. I couldn't tell if all that business about sexual violation meant to her some kind of crazy symbol or metaphor or what, but her voice got increasingly detached and remote as it went down to a near-whisper . . .

'The family is a thing, you know. It dominates, like it was male, like a single living entity with a cock that's endlessly erect, looking for victims. I've been assaulted by them everywhere, in dreams in bed when Glen is sleeping, on those few occasions he sleeps with me, but it can happen in the shower, even during the day . . . There's no getting away from the power . . . and the company's just another part of the family, another predator . . .'

I didn't think she was talking to me but that didn't stop the hair from raising up off my neck, and I've dealt with every kind of loon. I realized what it was, why this woman so disturbed me, and it wasn't simply because she looked well turned out, satisfied, under control. I felt great sorrow for her. I don't know, won't ever know if she was insane or it was all that bizarre dislocation she described as her life.

I didn't exist for her any more. Her voice became a distant hum that could have been a chant. I believe, against my pragmatic nature, that any Seminole out in the 'Glades would have understood it was a death chant.

The Jeep was open to the wind and sky all the way back to big, raw, violent, but very real Miami. I played my horn for a while when I got home; it had a calming effect most of the time, but not that night.

FRANKIE

The Captain said we were overburdened and tossed the jackets of three new cases on my desk, in addition to the jewelry store robbery. I had a feeling that they were trying to keep me so occupied I wouldn't have anything more to do with the Chapelles. I didn't know what they'd heard, and I couldn't believe that Owen would have ratted on me. Besides, they were worrying for nothing.

About noon Sean called me. Neither of us knew why the other had been yanked from the case, although he said he had an idea. It would have been the first time if he didn't. The following day he was scheduled to go down to Key West on something new and that was that. Still, he waltzed me around for a while; obviously something was nagging at him. I don't know if that was it, but finally he asked me to ask Chapelle if he had his address book on him when he was taken.

'You got a hearing problem? I'm off the case.'

'Yeah, but not off Chapelle.'

'Whooooaa. What kind of shitty remark is that? I mean,

we're not even working together any more and you still rag me.'

'All I meant was you'll be seeing him again.'

'Give me a break, huh. I've got work to do, even if you don't.'

He would have gone on but the Captain invited me to come into his office. My favorite thing to do. I started to sit down, but he said I didn't have to. The Chapelles had asked that I be put back on the case. He said whoever spoke for them laid on a lot of crap about they'd never feel safe until the perpetrators were off the streets. Of course this was just him shoveling it deep. Owen told me who had insisted on my return. Although he didn't have to.

I handed off the cases I'd been given, reorganized the Chapelle file, and prepared to head out to the house. I intended to have a go at the heretofore sacred Sylvia. At this point there wasn't anything to lose, and if her husband was going to mess with my head maybe this was the way to turn him off. When I got her on the phone to tell her I was coming she seemed amused by the whole idea, and we left it at that.

'Oh, by the way,' she put in just before I hung up, 'did you know Sean's going to be back, too?'

I didn't, of course, but I was no longer surprisable. Or I thought so until the call came in on the other Mrs Chapelle.

XIV

It's a terrible thing to say, but at the time I felt a tremendous rush of excitement and could hardly wait to get out there. Owen jumped in the car with me. The on-again-off-again nature of our status didn't seem to bother him at all.

The Palm Beach cops had roped off the scene. I told Owen on the way over I was worried we'd have to waste a lot of time on jurisdiction, but their chief and our sheriff had settled that even before we got there. There's only ten thousand people on the island so they had a real small department; that was the reality. Put a face on it and say it was connected with the kidnapping. And who was to say it wasn't?

Upstairs in the hallway a Palm Beach officer named Papasian, the only Armenian I ever saw with blond hair, briefed me. He said the husband had been in New York overnight, arrived home at 1.35 p.m. and found his wife as we would see her, dead in the living room of strangulation. Also, she had been raped. There had been a major struggle obviously, but no sign of forced entry.

'Where's the victim's husband now?'

'In the bedroom grieving. Actually he's zonked on the bed. Some kind of downer.'

'Shit! That's these people's answer to everything.'

Always the philosopher, Owen said, 'They just can't stand pain. Not even for a minute. You wonder how they all know they're alive.'

I gave him a look I usually reserved for Dunn before

turning back to Papasian. 'Why did you let him, for Christ's sake?'

'Are you serious?'

I wasn't. We went into the apartment. As usual the ME was already there. We have the fastest-reacting forensics people in the whole goddamn country. It drives you nuts.

Photographs of the scene were already being taken and we couldn't really do anything until they were completed, so we went on into the bedroom where Chapelle was 'grieving.' It was necessary to step over and around the victim and a lot of overturned furniture. She was sprawled in that awful, flopped attitude you would never strike in life. I glanced down – you can't not. She'd been wearing a yellow silk négligé with apparently nothing underneath. It was mostly torn off so she was mostly naked. I hate to see that, with my fellow ghouls wandering around like it was part of the furniture.

'Jesus, Neddy, do your work and cover her up. Bunch of perverts.'

He just grinned and pulled out the thermometer. He had to take off his glasses to read it. She'd been strangled with some kind of cord – tongue out, eyes bulging, face purple. You get familiar with it but you never get used to it. There was a lot of blood on the floor, between her legs and on her thighs, indicating the rape had occurred where he killed her, maybe after he killed her, although that called for expertise I didn't have.

Glen was on his back on this frilly bed with his eyes closed, and even when he opened them they were pretty much closed. He was in his stockinged feet but otherwise dressed as he'd been when he arrived. Owen and I walked right in. Of course we apologized for breaking into his grief, but we didn't mean it. Another murder on my case, on my watch; I would have walked through Attila the Hun to ace it.

'What kind of drugs have you taken, Mr Chapelle?'

He fumbled on the bedstand for his glasses but remained prone. I guess the better to see us with. His eyes were red and his face puffy, making him look more than ever like a large stuffed doll. There was a damp washcloth crumpled in one hand. 'Valium.'

'How much?'

'Fifteen milligrams.'

I'm wondering, yeah, and three drinks on the plane coming down? 'Can you talk to us? Because as much as we hate to disturb you right now, time is crucial in these matters.'

He said he didn't object and was capable, although you could see him start to nod off periodically and jerk himself back. Left New York early in the morning, commuter flight from Miami International to Palm Beach International, limousine home. Walked in and there she was. He described, with as much emotion as I suppose he was capable of, what he confronted, how it affected him and the horror he was feeling. You can't take that away from them. I was convinced he wanted to cooperate, at least at first.

The condo office had a key that was available to their security personnel. There had been only one full-time servant, a maid, but she had quit a couple of days before to follow her boyfriend to Tampa where he had a new job. At some point he realized we were not dealing with it as a break-in, a crime of opportunity by a stranger, and became a little agitated, but those were the facts.

'Have you ever had any male friends who were overly interested in Mrs Chapelle? Any incidents? Did either of you have personal enemies?'

He didn't know of or couldn't remember anyone like that, any unpleasant occasions involving his wife . . . and began to cry. More of a snuffle, really. Owen, always kind, handed him some Kleenex. He said his wife was very cautious about letting people in, and it was unlikely

215

she would allow anyone to enter that she didn't know well.
When he realized the implications of what he was saying he
grew silent and closed his eyes, fading away from us.

'What were you doing in New York, Mr Chapelle?'

'I had business there.'

'Could you be more specific, sir?'

He either thought about it for a long time or had dozed
off. 'No.'

Owen and I looked at each other. He tried. 'Sir, you all
could save us a lot of trouble. Because we're going to have
to find that out one time or another.'

'That's right. We'll have to hand it off to the NYPD,
or possibly, since it's interstate, to the feds, to track your
visit for us. If there's any question of discretion, sir, I'd
think you'd be better off to let us help you. New York,
well, up there, that's an open wound.' It sounded a little
melodramatic but I'd guessed right about his trip, so it
worked.

'I was visiting a long-time woman friend.' He struggled
to sit up, trying to swing his legs down on the floor while
supporting his wavering frame with one hand on the bed.
Owen had to help him. 'Goddamn it, I don't see what business this is of yours. You think I raped and murdered my
own wife, for Christ's sakes? Leave me alone! I'm sick!'

I was reassured; this was the jerk-off I knew. Nevertheless, after a lot of whining and bitching, he gave us the
girlfriend's name and address, the maid's and then the
airline and limousine schedule he had followed. Owen
hurried off to start checking.

'What's the matter with you people? My wife's just been
murdered. I should think common decency would make
you leave me alone at a time like this.' His voice rose
alarmingly; in a minute it was going to start calling dogs.
A hell of a moment for the other Chapelles to walk in. Or
'stalk' in would be more accurate.

They were both wearing all-white tennis clothes and the

effect was just about blinding. Even he had good legs. He was as cool as always, but she was more energized than I would have believed possible. Her attitude was basically 'Whatever they're doing to you, Glen, we're not going to put up with it.'

'We're taking you home, dear. Get dressed. Staying around here would drive anyone crazy.'

Not a word of sorrow or sympathy. Like the family dog died. It was incredible. She looked at me as if I was some kind of intruder.

'I'm sorry about your sister-in-law,' I said to both of them. 'I know that's not easy to look at out there.'

'No,' was all she said, but James, perhaps embarrassed, stepped over to his brother and held out his arms. Sylvia helped Glen up off the bed so the two men could embrace. Glen began to cry again.

'How could someone . . . be so vicious? She never hurt anyone . . .' I noted the word 'love' hadn't been used yet, either.

James was quite gentle with him, though, patting him on the shoulder while they embraced. 'I know, I know, Glen, it's hard to understand. Life just seems so goddamned unfair sometimes.'

'Mr Chapelle . . .'

Sylvia looked at me again; it was her 'don't fuck with me' look. I'd seen a lot of it by then. 'We're taking him to our place. You can talk to him later.'

'I need him now, Mrs Chapelle. The first forty-eight— '

She cut me dead. 'I'm sorry. We're out of here. Glen . . .! James, help him.'

They got his shoes and started packing some things. As much from disgust as anything, I started for the living room. I wouldn't give them the satisfaction of seeing me angry, so I refused to look at them, but still I caught a glimpse of something from James that was a plea for patience or understanding.

I stopped. Although I try hard, I'm not very good at sarcasm, which I think is a male thing, yet I had to give them a shot. I reminded James, 'He's not heavy, he's my new boss.'

That brought his sad smile, which could be pretty devastating, I had to admit. 'He's my brother. The other's nothing.' Pretty noble shit.

As I left I heard Sylvia say, 'Suzanne's come down to be with us,' and then someone, I think it was Glen, shut the door behind me.

'What time, Neddy?' I asked, bodyside again.

'Until I check what she had for din— '

'I know, I know, what time?'

'Ten to eleven last night.'

I looked around at the signs of struggle. It wasn't right. I waited until they finished photographing and went over to this big old heavy chair Neddy said was a Marcel Breuer, whatever the hell that was, and picked it up. Then I knocked it over again. Everybody jumped and looked at me reproachfully. It sounded like an earthquake, only we don't have those in Florida.

You try to imagine the struggle, how this piece had been knocked in that direction, on its back, and that lamp the other way and this other chair on its front. It wasn't real. I was willing to bet there was very little struggle here and the rest was a stage-set. I went over to Owen, who was on the phone doing his checking, and told him, 'Check out all the neighbors, especially downstairs, as to where they were between ten and eleven last night and what they heard. Ask them if they heard me drop that chair just now.' Of course we would have seen them routinely but I wanted to know sooner.

'Where's the murder weapon?' They had removed it already, leaving an indentation so deep I could have put my hands all the way around her neck with fingers to spare. Neddy took a cord out of an evidence bag and handed it to me, indicating the drapes where it had done its duty up until eleven o'clock the night before.

It was thick, had been severed with a knife. 'This would take some strength.'

'Sure would,' Neddy agreed. 'If you were planning it this way you'd have brought a wire or fish line or any one of a couple dozen things that work better.'

'So you figure it was an intruder who talked his way in somehow or was surprised? That'd have to be somebody pretty good with locks and systems. But violent. A hot prowl, in other words.'

'I figure. What else?'

'I don't know. If you got a knife to cut a cord with why not just use it on the vic? Could be somebody smart who wanted it to look your way.'

'When was the last time you met a smart killer? Most of the time they don't even know why they did it.'

'Among these people you could find someone.'

I went over to the sink where there were some dirty drink glasses. In the trash was a beer bottle. I examined the glasses, smelling them, and failed to find evidence that any of them had contained beer. The techies were still vacuuming for hairs, lifting fingerprints. While I watched, they moved to the contents of the trash. When I thought about a beer bottle without a glass my stomach became a bottomless pit.

I found Owen, who was interviewing the neighbors, and told him I was prepared to leave, but then an officer came along and said a Michael Duchow was outside raising hell about seeing me. I said I'd talk to him in the lobby, and followed him down.

The man was wearing a gabardine suit and flowered tie when the temperature was about a hundred outside. But he wasn't sweating; his eyes glittered and every move was quick and definitive. You could see where it might be a good thing for the cooler-than-thou Chapelles to have a furry little flesh-eater like this running the family cash cow.

He looked so stoked I thought I'd preempt him. 'Okay, the Chapelles are inside with him while the body's still there, and you probably want to know why you can't go in too. The answer's they're family and I couldn't keep them out. So if you push your way in too, what am I going to do? Arrest you. But I'd rather you didn't.'

I don't think he'd heard a word of it. He took my arm – he was one of those – and steered us into a corner. There were people going back and forth behind us. I couldn't be sure they wouldn't bring the corpse out. Without knowing anything about his relationship with the victim you had to figure this dude wouldn't fall down in a fit if it was his mother on the gurney.

'I have to speak to you, Sergeant.'

'You are.'

'I was here last night.'

Sure had my attention. 'What time?'

'About seven-thirty to . . . roughly eight-thirty.' It wasn't his usual voice. Of course, he was keeping it low, but there was something else pinched and tentative. If a voice could walk a high wire . . . 'It was business, strictly business. In fact I thought Glen would be here. He was supposed to be.'

'Where was he?'

'I understand he went to New York on . . . a whim. The kind of thing I had hoped was over now that the two of us . . .' He trailed off. 'Utterly irresponsible,' he muttered to himself.

'You said a "whim." What whim?'

'Well . . . Amelia said it was a woman. A girlfriend.'

'The victim told you this?' He nodded, uncertain. 'You couldn't have been too surprised. I mean, his name is "Chapelle."'

'I don't care how many mistresses the man has, I was

just upset he had me come over here – we have a crucial presentation at a bank coming up – and then he forgets to tell me he won't be available.' He gestured, dismissing a whole world of moronic millionaires or executives who can't keep their dicks in their pockets.

'Tell me something. You came expecting to find Mr Chapelle. You must've been a little ticked to find he wasn't here. Yet you stayed an hour or more?'

'His wife . . . Amelia – I'm having trouble believing this – but Amelia is, was, very clever about the business. Talking to her sometimes gave you a leg-up on trying to convince or even explain things to her husband. If you don't believe I was supposed to meet Glen here, ask him.'

'We will. What was her mood when you talked to her? Was she upset? Expecting anyone? Did she— '

'Dunn. Sean Dunn.'

'What?'

'She was expecting him.'

I tried to hide the feeling it gave me – whatever that was – but I failed. Confirmation in regard to the beer bottle, for one thing. I swore under my breath. Doctors and cops shouldn't do that. 'Why?' was all I managed for the moment.

'I don't know. It's none of my business. She was anxious to get rid of me before he came, though. He was due at nine, she said.'

'Sounds to me like a woman juggling lovers, Mr Duchow. Is there anything in that?'

'Absolutely not. Not on my part, certainly. I resent you even asking the question. As far as Dunn goes . . . I told you she was a little crazy, about men especially, and I'd seen indications that she found him attractive. On the other hand, I can't think why he'd have to rape her, or why anyone would, for that matter.'

If he'd smiled I would have hit him in the mouth, and there would go the whole career up in flames and flying

221

teeth. As it was I gave him the dirtiest look in my arsenal and asked him, 'Want to see the body, Mr Duchow? Want to see what rape really looks like – the blood, the ripping and tearing, the agony on her face . . .? I can arrange it.'

He looked a little caught-out, and that cheered me. Very tightly, he said, 'That won't be necessary. I've told you what I came to tell you. I've tried to be cooperative. If you want to ask any more questions, call my lawyer.' He spun on his little Gucci heel and hurried out of there.

I dashed upstairs and told Owen to bring Dunn in right away, even if he had to put out a warrant.

SEAN

'I don't know why she had me come up there last night.'

'You have no idea why she invited you?'

'No. She invoked the Holy Ghost. Something that hasn't been done in Palm Beach since the Spanish owned it.'

'It's going to be a long afternoon if you keep that up. What time did you leave?'

'A little before ten.' I had agreed to having this 'interview' in an interrogation room because there was precious little privacy in Frankie's cubicle. They promised to turn off the mike so it would just be the three of us. Now, as I was sitting at the scarred wooden table with its bulging ashtray and obligatory cup of gray coffee in a styrofoam cup, where a thousand felons had sat before me, Frankie seemed to have forgotten the deal; she was circling me like the bad cop, firing off questions fat with scorn and skepticism.

I could have reminded her, but I was enjoying it. Good cop Owen leaned casually against a sound-proofed wall in the time-honored posture the role demands. I had the feeling I was trapped in a movie.

'Did you have sex?'

'No. I mean, well, in a way.' She was standing behind me but I could hear her reaction in some nameless form.

'You'd better explain that.' She was sounding very tough now.

'She kissed me.'

'*She* kissed *you*?'

'Right. I was sitting there listening to her ramble, hoping to make some sense out of it or maybe she'd come back to reality— '

'What was she talking about?'

'Italy, her childhood, school, men, sin, her husband, how he had a girlfriend, or many, and they didn't have sex and so on. She seemed to think all men were predatory and that all sex was basically rape but she didn't mind too much.'

'Jesus,' Frankie said, this time in front of me. 'The woman must have been psychic.'

'I know. All the talk about rape was in terms of ancient chiefs taking the wives of enemies they'd conquered and how in Sicily men kidnap the women they want to marry and stuff like that. It was, a lot of it, pretty bizarre.'

'About her kissing you,' Frankie reminded.

'I came in— '

'Was she especially careful about letting you in?'

'No. There was no looking past the chain or any of that. I gave my name downstairs, she buzzed me in. The door was open when I got up there. Why?'

'Her husband said she was real careful.'

I just shook my head. 'She got me a beer – you'll find my fingerprints on it – and made herself a drink of some kind. Vodka. Said she'd fired the maid— '

'"*Fired*" her?' Frankie repeated.

'That's what she told me. Anyhow, she sat and talked for a while. I tried to get her to come to the point. Suddenly she turned out the light.'

'Why?' Frankie asked.

'Damned if I know. Just another example of the craziness.'

'This part of the move you say she made on you?'

I laughed at her choice of words but nobody joined in. It simply got quieter. 'No, not then, anyway. She wandered around the room talking about all these things. Then, when she came by once, she leaned over and kissed me. On the mouth. The real thing. Neither of us said anything and then she just started wandering and babbling again.'

I realized that had sounded a little harsh, and Frankie let me know it. 'You didn't like the victim.'

'No, I did.'

'How? Sexually?'

I looked at her and noticed she was averting her face. She looked as unhappy as I'd seen her in our brief acquaintanceship. 'Nope. I felt sorry for her.' Out of respect for the dead, I decided not to tell them about that time in the bar when she had effectively groped me. It could serve no purpose. 'Sexually, it was that one kiss. I'm not that easy.'

'Did you know Duchow was there just before you?'

'Yep.'

'How? She told you?'

'Yes, but I'd seen him driving away.'

'He didn't see you.'

'It's my job, it's not his.'

'Speaking of "job," you were off this one at the time. Yet you still drove all the way up from Miami without even a promise of information?'

'Wouldn't you?'

Owen cackled, for once on my side. 'Gotcha there,' he told Frankie softly.

'Did she say why Duchow was there?'

'That he wanted to talk business with her. I suppose about them taking control of the company away from

James. She was proud of it. She knew her husband was a zip.'

'Nothing about Glen was supposed to meet him there regarding a bank, but instead ran off to New York after this babe without notifying him?'

I shook my head. 'I try not to get into all that corporation crap. If I do I'm obligated to respect their privacy.'

'How about respecting a murder investigation?'

'Sergeant, you got your employer, I got mine.'

Her face was flushed; I didn't really get what was happening. 'Mine can put you in a cell,' she snapped, leaning in on me.

Frankie's scratchy charm was wearing skinny with me. 'Then you tell him to take his best shot, Bodo, 'cause I'm going home. All the way home.'

'I thought you were back working for the Chapelles.'

'Maybe, maybe not. I'm an employee, not a field hand.'

'They don't own you, you're saying.'

'Take it to the bank, lady.'

'Bullshit. I've seen you two together.'

We just looked at each other.

'You know what I mean,' she persisted. 'People aren't stupid. Anyone in the room would know that there was a bitch in heat. I don't know what it is, she's bored married to this super-desirable guy and you provide the opposite. But don't try to tell me . . .' She simply ran down, emotionally spent.

It was getting a little close to the bone. I looked over at Owen and even he seemed uneasy. I stood, vindictiveness rising in my gullet like a rejected oyster. 'You know, the Yakuza cut off their own little fingers as part of the initiation, and it's no big deal. Think about it.'

I left. That was as mean as I got.

FRANKIE

Owen and I went over to the morgue. I figured the sight of a few corpses might cheer me up. Sometimes I hated Dunn's guts. Sometimes he made me feel ashamed, a privilege that I give to no one except myself. Occasionally, very occasionally, he could be infuriatingly likable, even nice. I knew one thing – he was different. I didn't know how different – good different, bad different or just weird – but not like any guy I'd ever been with. Starting with my biological father who I only knew while a seed in the womb, through that world-class prick, my stepfather, and including every three-legged bastard I ever hoped could fuck me into oblivion – 'cause that's what it was. Enough to make you puke, right? Maybe it was just because he was a eunuch.

The ME showed us the victim, already on a table under a sheet, although he said he had a few others scheduled before her. Something about a big accident on the 95 and a murder-suicide in Ocean Ridge. Wealth and status lose a lot when you're wearing a toe-tag.

It was all right; I had only a couple of questions that I hoped would be factored in when the autopsy came around. Most of all, cops hate sex crimes, and the worst of those are against kids. You can joke and make remarks about almost anything, no matter how horrible, except kids. No one does that. With a grown woman I can handle it like the guys, putting up barriers of grossness, being even more obscene than usual, and fake indifference. You got to get through it somehow.

I wanted to see the vulva. Maybe 'wanted' isn't the word. It was about as torn-up as you'd expect from the bleeding. I asked Neddy to humor me and examine it while we were there. He grumbled, but he did it.

Finally he looked up at me. 'Well?'

'I don't believe it.'

'You don't believe he raped her?'

'I don't see this damage is a guy. If it is, he's got a dick like King Kong.'

'What the hell else is it?'

'Rape with instrumentality. After the fact.'

'Ah.' You could see he was considering it.

'Frankie's got an idea the victim knew the murderer— '

'And it was only made to look like a sex crime, something spontaneous,' Neddy said, finishing it for him.

'Owen asked, and nobody downstairs heard the struggle, yet the apartment looked like a bomb hit it. All that heavy furniture was set down very gently.'

'And this?' Neddy asked.

'You tell us. Looks like a baseball bat, for Christ's sake. Something the actor took with them to destroy.'

'Does at that. But the amount of blood suggests the victim was still alive, or at least expiring. Nothing as big as a bat, of course, but if it was wood we'll probably find something.' He was studying it with a light and glass now, caught up in the puzzle. 'You're right, didn't penetrate very far. Anxious to get out of there, I suppose. Interesting . . .' He gave us his best horror-movie grin. 'I'll give it priority. Lots more fun than a five-car crash or a murder-suicide. Something for the mind. Keeps us young.'

Owen kind of rolled his eyes at me and I rolled mine back. 'Yeah, right,' I told Neddy, playing his own game, 'get out your saw and create a masterpiece. Let us know.' Although we knew.

I used the Lord's name – whichever Lord I forget – a lot on the way out and didn't worry about how many of the Baptist equivalent of novenas Owen would have to say for me on Sunday. I was thinking about dropping in at church myself one day, which shows you how things were getting to me.

SEAN

I knew Sylvia could be generous but never had any reason to think of her as solicitous, yet she was treating her brother-in-law like a pathetic schoolboy and he was loving it. They had him in an upstairs bedroom that had its own air-conditioner. Many of these big old mansions, being on the sea, are not fully air-conditioned. To their credit, owners worry about the process being damaging to the architectural and esthetic integrity of the ancient Mizners. Anyway, it was so cool he had a light blanket over him . . .

He told me he was sickly as a child, asthma among other things. 'When we were at home in New York in the winter – we had a place in Mount Kisko – our mother would always make me get in bed after a warm bath. She believed that you were vulnerable when your pores were open. It sounds silly now, but she was very solicitous. And I was the one who'd had pneumonia three times.'

Considering how this man thought of me, as some kind of rude, uppity tough guy, I can only explain a confidence like that by suggesting he was stoned to the bone. I understood he had taken a large Valium, then someone had probably given him an upper to prevent him becoming complaisant with the authorities. Meaning Frankie and maybe me, I suppose. Then there was a half-empty glass that smelled like Scotch on one bedside table and, as counterbalance, a porcelain tea-set on the other. He sipped from the tea daintily, being now glint-eyed and stoned. And he seemed downright friendly, which made me wonder.

He gave me his story, same one he did Frankie. Recalling his first view of his wife, he began to cry. Most of us would, I imagine. It seems he had gone to the bathroom and vomited, but then was meticulous in cleaning up so there was no way he could prove that.

'No reason you should, Mr Chapelle. Throwing up on

these occasions is not an obligation under the law.' Most of the time he would not have understood my manner of speech, would have taken it for sarcasm or, minimally, callousness. Not that day; another reason for suspicion. 'I don't have any trouble with your cleaning up like that. Under extreme stress people do all kinds of crazy, compulsive things. Every investigator knows that.'

If he had tears in his eyes, they were of gratitude. 'Thank God, you're on our side now.'

'I always have been, Mr Chapelle. Within the boundaries of the law.' He looked a little disconcerted. 'Which I'm sure is the only way you'd want it.'

'Of course. Of course . . .' His mind fled the room, as is often the case when the questions become painful. Finally, he spoke in a subdued, distant voice. 'She was a wonderful woman. Nothing like the women around here. Very European . . . with ideals, morals. I feel terribly guilty that I had this affair . . . that I told you about, but she understood. Amelia was very loyal, very pure.'

I'm fortunate; I've got one of those faces that gives nothing. Of course, it's all just rocks and gullies anyway. Frankie was still trying to learn how to do the same thing with her own pretty face.

Chapelle went on like that. 'I loved her, Sean. As God is my witness. I really did. I hope you believe me. We were married ten years, you know, and despite the fact that she was Italian we almost never quarreled. Now this . . . it's unbelievable.' He shook his head so long I was thinking of getting a grip on it.

I was more interested in his reactions – I always am – than any details. So I asked for his first impression when he saw his wife lying there, vaginally bleeding, near-naked and garroted.

'I told you, I threw up.' He took great satisfaction in that.

'No, before that. Even before it reached your stomach,

before you understood it. When it was strictly between the
eye and the brain.'

'Well, what anyone would think, that my wife had been
murdered. Isn't that perfectly normal?'

No, it isn't, but I didn't say so. 'Normal' is to reject what
you're seeing, to refuse to take it in and process it. This can
take from microseconds to years, but it's 'normal.' 'Did you
realize that she'd been assaulted?'

He was watching me now like a sparrow watches
a circling hawk. 'Of course. She was almost naked,
after all. And there was blood . . . there. Between her
legs. I didn't know she'd been strangled, but I got the
rest of it.'

'Got the rest of it.' Interesting choice. Technocratic? I
said, 'But she was wearing a négligé which had come open,
could have been in the struggle. Did your wife do that, walk
around the house naked under a robe?' Apparently, no one
had told him.

'I don't know. I wouldn't notice something like that.'

No wonder the woman tried to light my torch in a public
place in the middle of the afternoon. I wasn't going to argue
the point with him; everyone's entitled to their illusions and
life would be unbearable without them.

'Did you ever find out about the kidnapping insurance?'

'Ten million with Lloyd's. But why are you asking me
these kinds of questions?'

'I'd ask them of anyone, Mr Chapelle. They go with the
circumstances.'

He cocked his head for a moment, then decided it was
all right. 'Please call me "Glen." I feel like we're all on the
same side now.'

'Sure.' The man *had* just lost his wife. Did he have any
part in it? The facts of his own alibi would be easy to check,
but he could have had it done. In cases where a husband
hires someone it's not unusual for the doer to commit or
fake a rape to cover the obvious.

I was ready to go but he started asking me questions about my experience with sex crimes. He asked too many and wanted too much detail, to the point where I suspected his palms were sweaty. I know that I had an uncomfortable feeling about it somewhere in the southern latitudes. More reasons.

When I did head for the door, he asked, 'Do you think, could it have . . . anything to do with what happened to my brother?'

I wanted to say, 'Bright boy,' but I didn't. Instead I said, 'No reason to think that at the moment, Mis . . . Glen. I'll let you know everything I know as soon as I know it.' Liar.

I got as far as the door this time. 'Don't you have any idea who's responsible for all this nightmare?'

'Yes.' His mouth started to open and I got out as quickly as I could. Let him chew on it.

On the stairs going down I met James coming up. He looked like he intended to go right past me with a nod but I stopped him. 'Jim, when you were kidnapped, did you have your PDA on you?'

He had to think. 'Yeah, sure. They took it. They took everything. But they've never used the credit cards, so I suppose they're a little smarter than the average crook.'

'A little. Did it have my address and number in it?'

'Of course.'

'You ever give my number to Annie Robertson?'

He chuckled. 'That would be the day.'

I nodded and went on down, very fast. Sylvia was approaching from the dining room. She didn't say anything, simply gave me her strange, knowing smile and I returned my even stranger one on the way out.

In front Frankie was just pulling up as I got to the Jeep. She didn't exactly bubble over in friendly greeting, just gave me a frown and went in. Back on the case but certainly not popular. The only one who wanted to talk to me was the geek. Ten million? Add a zero and you got the ransom.

XV

FRANKIE

The houseman answered the door and I asked to speak
to James. Sylvia was around somewhere, I could smell
Arpège, but it was her husband who came into the foyer.
I told him I wanted to talk further to his brother, but he
said Glen was a little tired from Dunn's questioning and
needed to nap. And since he had taken some pills, there
wasn't a hope, anyway.

I had to fight to control myself. I hadn't really blown
the whole gourd in a long time, but the quiver in my voice
indicated something like that was dangerously close. All I
needed was the departmental shrink on my case.

I got real boisterous about how Dunn was not entitled
to interfere with a police investigation, the first few hours
were crucial, and all like that. Pretty soon I caught on
that Chapelle was enjoying seeing me struggle to keep
from doing what would have come oh-so-naturally. Like
it's cute or something.

'Go on, Frankie, blow!' And he laughed.

'My name is "Sergeant," and I don't know what the
hell you're talking about, *Mister* Chapelle.' That felt a
little better.

'It's okay, I've been yelled at before. It might make
you feel better. Then we can have a pleasant drink on
the terrace where you can ask all the questions you want.
We'll probably solve the whole miserable affair, you and
I. What do you think?'

'C'mon, nobody ever yelled at you.'

'Of course they have. I had to get used to it very young. Our mother was mentally unbalanced. Or mad as a hatter, crazy as a loon – pick your cliché. Birds and dogs heard her. If we hadn't been so rich we'd have been run out of the neighborhood. Come on, we'll go outside.'

Damned if he didn't get me out on that terrace. And it was so beautiful – the evening breeze cool, churning my hair, which happens to look better churned, the smell of brine, wet grass and gardenias, the calm and the colors. I sat on an old-fashioned glider and rocked back and forth. James sat in a chair next to me while we both studied the ocean. A pelican waddled across the lawn with a fish in its beak and I had a sense, without looking, that we were both smiling at it.

The houseman came and this time, under sway of the powerful idea that here you could just have anything you wanted, I gave in. A beer would have tasted great but I thought white wine would be more sophisticated. Whiskey definitely wouldn't be a good idea because I had to go back into the station. As it was, the old Binaca in the glove compartment would be getting a workout – the cops' best friend.

'I had Dunn brought in for questioning this afternoon,' I told him after a while.

It got his attention okay; he turned to me with this puzzled, almost pained expression. 'Sean?' You sure got the idea they were buds. 'Why do you keep suspecting him?'

'He was in your sister-in-law's apartment just before she was murdered.'

He went from puzzled to ashen. 'Why?'

'We haven't determined that yet. He says she invited him, said she wanted to tell him something but then changed her mind. So he left.'

'You believe him?' He clearly expected *me* to.

'Not entirely. Did your sister-in-law have lovers, Mr Chapelle?'

His face took on shadows. 'I wouldn't know about that. But it was a rape, wasn't it? Someone who broke in. I mean, a sex crime. You can't think Sean . . .'

'I'm not sure it was a sex crime. Just made to look that way.'

He was quiet for a moment and then let out this little moan that startled me. It was so damned vulnerable. Softly, he said, 'My God, it has something to do with my kidnapping.'

We left it there, sitting each with our own thoughts, watching the boats hurrying in off the water as a slight chop developed and darkness threatened. I don't know what he was thinking but I wondered if I should have told him so much. He always had that effect on me, of wanting to confide.

Later that night I'm sitting there staring at my sick TV set, trying to figure out how to get it fixed. It was either that or buy a dog I wouldn't have time to take care of, I was so goddamned lonely. I had an Agatha Christie in my lap. I used to read them to help me get to sleep when I was wired from the job. I liked them but I could never remember one from the other. The phone rang. I looked at my watch – eleven-thirty. It was Chapelle.

'How'd you get my home phone number . . .? Yeah, it probably wouldn't be for you, would it. You probably own the phone company . . . Look, this is definitely not a good idea. I'm trying to have a career here, Mr Chapelle, and you're definitely a threat to it right now. I got to keep my objectivity. You're a job to me, don't you understand?'

I went on, a little breathless, and then he told me his sister was in town because of all the family grief and wanted to meet me for lunch. I didn't understand.

'Your sister wants to meet me? Why? Does she have information about this case?'

He laughed at the idea. 'I don't think so. But you'll like her, she doesn't approve of the rest of us. Never has. Saint Molly of Detroit.'

'You're telling me it's like some social thing? What about your wife, will she be there? I'm not a relative or friend of the family.'

'C'mon, Sergeant, cut us some slack. Cut yourself some and get rid of that hair shirt.' I'm wondering how does he know to use that on me? 'I don't know why she wants to meet you either. One of us must have told her how extraordinary you are.'

I looked around at my cell and said yes. I have no excuse.

In the morning I told my captain that I believed Amelia Chapelle's murder was not a sex crime and was probably connected to the kidnapping of James. He believed me, he even complimented me. The sky was falling. He wanted me to come to a meeting about the case at noon but I told him I was seeing the Chapelles and he said fine, let us know. I didn't tell him it was lunch on a white tablecloth.

We met at some place called 'Doherty's' that was supposed to be owned by this guy named Pulitzer. Like the prize. So why wasn't it called 'Pulitzer's'? Normally I'd like a place called 'Doherty's,' but everybody in here was long, thin and had a lot of teeth like any one of the fish that eats people – take your pick. They'd wear designer jeans to take out the trash, if they took out the trash. Well, it was interesting and not a place I would ever have entered without the Chapelles, in this case brother and sister. Where the hell *was* the guy's wife all the time?

'Molly' already didn't sound like a Chapelle. But that's later; he came first. I'm standing around with my thumb in my mouth, wondering whether I should beg the maître d' on my knees, flash my buzzer at him or simply tell him that Mr James Chapelle's starting to look at me with that look. I didn't have to; the man himself swept in and carried me right along to this little table. It was like the Red Sea opening.

He told me I looked beautiful, which wasn't true, but who doesn't want to hear it. I had gone off the departmental standard a little, going so far as to put on perfume and higher heels in the car, but only, I told myself, because I was going to this fancy restaurant. It was nice that he noticed, but then he would.

'Mr Chapelle, I'm really busy, so I don't know why I'm here meeting a member of your family, or why you're calling me up at night or sending me roses or being so goddamned nice to me, which I appreciate but don't get, except I guess you're coming on to me. Is that right or am I nuts? There, I said it.'

'"Coming on to you"?' He thought about the phrase and then smiled. 'I don't think I'm doing anything that crude, am I? Or maybe I am.'

'You're never crude, it's just that something's happening here which I've experienced before so I think I recognize it. Like the sap running in the spring, they always say.'

I guess that was funny because, grinning, he said, 'Well, what's wrong with that?'

'I told you what's wrong with it. For one thing, I have to keep reminding you, you're married. And by the way, while we're on the subject of people's feelings, how come nobody around here seems broken up about the murder of a member of their own family? I mean, Jesus . . .'

'Kennedys don't cry.'

'Who?'

'It's what Jacqueline Kennedy said to her son when his father was killed. That's the code we were all raised on. We grieve privately. A very antique idea, I know.'

'No, if I cried I got a hit on the head.'

'Also, we weren't close to Amelia. No one was.'

'Okay. Should I know more about that?'

'There's a memorial service in the morning. Only for the

family, a few close friends, and of course any members of
our staff who want to. Episcopalians don't have funerals
any more, they're too depressing.' He reached out, leaning
across the table. I could have moved my hand, but I didn't.
'I'm not a cold man, Frankie. Whatever else you think
about me, I'm not that.'

'None of my business.'

The sister showed up then and sat down with us. She
called her brothers the 'boys,' and appeared very youthful
herself with her mop of short, light brown hair, perfect skin
and upturned nose. A little plump, didn't dress any better
than I did, and seemed terminally pleased. She took out
some glasses and squinted through them. The better to
see us with, she said, and laughed. One thing, she was
smart, you could tell by the way she observed and took
in things.

'You no doubt heard I was the disreputable member of
the family. I work for a living,' she said cheerfully. 'Or at
least, I work.' She was a professor, English Literature at
Wayne State University in Detroit, but I noticed she lived
in Grosse Pointe, which I believe is not residential chopped
liver. 'The boys claim I'm their older sister, but I deny it
and I'm by far the most truthful member of the family, as
you're about to find out.'

'If you mean about the death of your sister-in-law or
any— '

'I don't. I really don't know anything about the crimes,
and I'd only met Amelia about a half-dozen times. We're
not a warm, cuddly bunch, I'm afraid. James, why don't
you go and chat with the dozen people you must know in
here at any given time? You can show them your glove.'

He just grinned at me and shook his head, as if to say,
'Isn't she the wild one?' But, you know, affectionately.
And then he did what big sister said.

I was still watching him walk away – a mistake, because
she was watching me – when she said, 'We all opposed his

marriage to Sylvia. Including our mother and father, who were still alive then. Not what you might think, not out of snobbery. People down here, at least, are always making déclassé marriages.' I wasn't going to ask her what that was, but I didn't have to. 'Chauffeurs, bodyguards. Even beachboys, until we understood what caused skin cancer. Then some of their luster went. At least Sylvia was smart and had a certain talent in her singing. She was very good, actually, and I also admire the way she went about getting her college degree, but— '

'Ms Chapelle, I don't want to be rude, but is there a point in all this for me?'

'Probably not the one you'd like; but I suspect you'll listen anyway.'

I didn't much care for the sound of that, and started gearing up for a fast exit. 'Don't count on it.'

'The problem was, she was too beautiful . . .

'"May she be granted beauty and yet not/Beauty to make a stranger's eye distraught."'

Oh, man, now they were using poetry on me. Time to leave. But cops always have to have the last word. 'So, she's beautiful. So's he.'

She laughed, but it wasn't with much enthusiasm. 'That's true, but there's something in French called a *folie à deux*. Madness of two, basically. It's usually applied to crime.'

'Like the Hillside Stranglers out in L.A. They said if they'd never met it might never have happened.'

'Yes. Of course, that's certainly not what I'm talking about here.'

'What are you talking about, Ms Chapelle?'

'Molly, please. About feelings, personal relationships, love. See, when two people that rich and beautiful, that bright and charming, get together, it's always dangerous.' She gave me one of those dramatic pauses the whole family was good at. 'Because they can do anything they want.'

'No, they can't.'

Did she hear me? 'My brother talks about you all the time, and you can deny it, but I saw how you looked at him when he left the table.'

'How was that?'

'Hungry for his return, for his presence at the table.'

'That's silly. It's not true.' I was too embarrassed to get mad and tell her where to stuff it. 'The man . . .' I started to list all the usual reasons I had given him, and a few more that were less kind, about how he was a gambler and a womanizer and totally irresponsible and even a little old for me, but I sensed I wouldn't score with any of them. She knew him.

'I hope you know, I love my brother.'

'Most people do. Love their brothers, I mean. So, who are we protecting here? Him from me? How could I ever get to be a menace to a guy like that? A working cop, for God's sakes? It's ridiculous. And if you want the truth, I haven't given him zip. Ask him.'

'A woman committed suicide over James a few years ago.'

'How'd he take it?'

'He was devastated. I had to come down on that occasion, too.'

'He looks okay now.' I pointed to where he was standing at the bar showing a woman his big, beautiful, sun-tanned, white-toothed grin. 'By the way, how'd his wife take it?' She didn't have an answer. ''Cause if he was my husband and women started killing themselves like that, I'd take a sharp point to him. Myself, I'm only interested if she had friends or relatives who might just now be thinking of a little revenge.'

'I don't think she had anyone.'

'Well, it doesn't have spit to do with me, then. I've been stupid about men, okay, but my inclination is to kill them, not myself.'

'Am I supposed to feel relieved?'

'I haven't body-bagged one yet.'

'You really don't understand, do you?'

'I think I do. You're afraid if I get close to him he'll tell me something the family wants kept secret. Men do lose it in the sack.'

She looked more puzzled than offended. 'I don't know what you're talking about.'

'I bet you don't.' That was more bitchy than I wanted to sound. Anyway, I didn't think she got it.

'He's a fantastic lover, you know. Not from personal knowledge, of course – incest's about the only sin our family wasn't guilty of. But it's his reputation, and you do seem to me like a woman who might be . . . vulnerable to that.' Maybe she'd 'got it' after all. 'I don't tell you that as an advertisement, Lord knows, but just as a warning.'

'I don't take warnings.' There was no taking any more of that, period. I bounced up and got out of there, not even looking to see if *he* noticed my going. I never saw her again, except at the memorial service. On that occasion she smiled. I looked through her – sayonara. I never knew whether she was a mother hen, a pimp or, like I said, she suspected something really dark and wanted to push me away, although I had an idea.

SEAN

I didn't go to the memorial service. Frankie had to. I couldn't see any point to it; if any murderers showed up they'd look like the family or friends, and I already knew what they looked like. It's something else they do in the movies.

Anyway, a couple of days later a strange call came into the office and was passed along. It seemed Count Giovanni Benedetto de Carini was in town to take his daughter's body back to Sicily for burial. He hadn't attended the memorial service – wrong religion and, as I found out later, wrong family. He wanted to see me, of all things. I didn't have to go, wasn't sure how smart it was, but I was curious.

He was staying at the Breakers, which was only natural because it's a wonderful old antique going back to Flagler and about as Mediterranean as you can get on this side of three thousand miles. You go up a long driveway past rows of white-trunked royal palms, maybe the definitive old-Florida experience. Nobody wants to wait for them to grow any more; they would rather paint them on a building. The lobby is updated but still looks as if it should have counts and duchesses from 1905 sitting around waiting for their daily fix of noxious mineral water when the spa opens. I love it.

There was no trouble getting up to the rooms; the way had been smoothed. A young man waiting amidst the polished antiques in the dark lobby got up and followed, stepped in the elevator without looking at me, then escorted me down the hall and opened the door. That was strange enough, but his dress made it stranger. He was all in black down to his cheap foreign shoes, wore large sunglasses, one of those peaked Sicilian caps tilted forward, and even black gloves. We were in Florida in September, for Christ's sake.

When we entered the suite he wasn't crude enough to stand in front of the door, but went off to a far end of the suite and gazed out the window with his hands clasped in front of him. I never did see his face clearly and am not sure I would have wanted to.

The Count was more contemporary, but not by much. Nobody had ever told me what the family did for a living. Somebody had said he was an industrialist, which would have made sense if he was from Milan or Turin. He was very thin and weathered with black pits for eyes. Even though it was hard to see them, you sensed they could come out on demand and burn holes in concrete. His expensive English suit hung on him, giving the appearance of illness.

There was grief on his face, and hatred and suspicion and bewilderment and a whole lot of things eons old. He shook my hand softly and his was hot. Smiling without meaning it, he went to a mahogany bar in this vast suite and indicated an array of Italian liquors, liqueurs, wines and waters. I chose Pellegrino and felt to see if I'd worn the Colt, since this was beginning to feel like the 'fine Italian hand.' They hadn't searched me; that was a plus.

He sat on a brocade settee and indicated a chair opposite that looked like it might have supported a conquistador but was a little delicate for my peasanty frame. His legs were crossed and when he bobbed the top one you could see skinny old ankles over the thousand-dollar wing-tips. I told myself not to be lulled; he also had a large nose and those guys are to be taken seriously. Especially when they're rich, from Sicily, and have a bodyguard like that hanging out.

'My understanding is, you investigate this case of my daughter.'

I nodded. 'Starting with the kidnapping. I represent a firm that's employed by the Chapel Corporation. In other words, the Chapelle family.' He didn't look pleased by that decision to preempt, so I took it a little further. 'I thought you should know where I stand. Where I *have* to stand.'

'Thank you.'

'*Niente*.'

'I am also to understand you are with my daughter when she dies.'

'I saw her earlier that evening.' I emphasized, 'She asked me to come see her.'

'You are fucking her?'

I hadn't expected anything like that and was very anxious to disabuse, at the same time knowing better than to appear anxious. 'No. I was not her lover, or the lover of anyone else in this case.' I sure as hell was too smart to try to claim celibacy as a defense. 'The truth is, I hardly knew her.'

'How it is you are alone with her the night when she dies, eh? And her husband is away?'

'I told you, she asked me. Supposedly to tell me something important, but evidently she changed her mind. She seemed upset.' No way I'm going to tell this sucker the seed of his loins was bonkers, drunk, horny or anything else less than noble and pure. Wisely, I added, 'She didn't seem to trust the Chapelles.'

His disdain was epic. 'Not even her husband?'

'I don't know if she trusted him. He didn't have her respect.'

'How could he? How could he have anyone's?' He got up as suddenly as a grasshopper leaping off a leaf, and went to the window, so he could keep his back to me. 'You work for Chapelles . . . so why does my daughter trust you?' He didn't want to say 'Amelia,' and I could understand that.

Best to be honest. 'I don't know. People do sometimes.'

He turned to look at me, study me. The sun streaming in behind made him a gaunt, other-worldly silhouette, a theatrical phantom. It was pretty impressive. 'Who killed her?'

'I don't know.'

'What sort of detective are you? Americans should be able to do these things. If you wish to.'

'I want to. But I'm not the police. I work for a security firm, like I told you.'

'And have conflicted loyalty, eh?' He turned his back on me again.

'If I knew who it was, no matter who it was, I guarantee you I'd nail their ass.'

'Maybe. Maybe it is you.' His voice trailed away. Wherever it went, I didn't want to follow.

'If it was,' I told him, 'I wouldn't be here. I'm not stupid.'

'I take her back to Sicily now. To home. And put her in our family crypt. And then I wait. If you have killed her . . . there is no place to hide from me.'

I stood up, resisting the impulse to clear my throat. 'I don't have any problem with that. In your place I'd do the same thing.'

He turned and looked again; still I couldn't see his face. Finally his attenuated fingers fluttered from the shadows in a gesture of dismissal. The young man stepped over to the door and opened it. Fortunately, they have a bar in the Breakers.

I looked into some things and two days later decided to call Frankie from my motel, see if we couldn't start sharing information again and finish off this sonofabitch before it killed us both. She wasn't there, but Owen was, getting on the horn and actually chatting with me for a minute. Obviously he was headed somewhere with it but by way, as my family used to say, 'of Robin Hood's barn.'

'If you really want to know where she is,' he said, lowering his voice until his drawl made it practically unintelligible, 'it's havin' lunch with Mr James Chapelle. Somewhere real nice, I suppose.' That last was definitely unnecessary unless you were a malicious type, and Owen wasn't, or wanted to make a point.

I thanked him and hung up. It shouldn't have bothered me but it did. So much so I went over to Palm Beach and drove around, past all the major restaurants, without the slightest idea why I was doing it or what I intended to do if I spotted them, beyond maybe following them. And they could have been in Fort Lauderdale or Boca Raton, anyway.

It wasn't likely he would take her to any of the more prominent places. Certainly not the Everglades or Bath and Tennis. The social rules on that were shaky, but they could get away with the investigation 'beard' only so long. I wondered was Frankie still rationalizing it as that?

I didn't find them of course. And as this was about the loopiest thing I'd done in many years, I soon gave it up in embarrassment and went back to the motel to sulk. There were other lines to follow, not all specifically aimed at who killed or kidnapped whom. When I arrived there were calls from Sylvia, Annie and Glen. I ignored them all. That night I went out on a relatively deserted beach and played my trombone, prepared to punch out anyone who objected.

Of course it had been none of my business. My business was this case and then on to another and another and the sun rises and the sun sets and . . . I did care. It got crazier. I had never touched the woman. Oil and water, or better, dog and hydrant. She despised me; I found her impossible.

I asked a contact in the phone company and found out Chapelle was calling her both at the station and her apartment. An apartment I'd never seen, by the way, although I cruised by it the next night late. The lights were off but I refused to ask myself to what purpose. By an effort of will I managed to draw the line at checking credit-card expenditures and florist shops.

The next day I stopped by the station and caught Frankie in her office. Owen was with her, smoking a Marsh Wheeling. The place smelled like an alligator farm. She seemed more accepting about my working the case again and gave me a catch-up on things like a flight to Colombia by the second perpetrator. No surprise.

'Of course, we put through a few pounds of paper. DEA's trying to track him for us, but . . .' She spread her hands. We all knew the dismal odds on getting him back.

'The mick's out there alone,' I said.

'Maybe,' Frankie agreed the way she always agreed, by half. 'If it's the actor the FBI says it is, this Feeney, "out there" could be Belfast or Libya. They think Puerto Rico. Okay, let them play their games. Personally, I think he's still here.'

'Amen.' Only one of us would have said that.

'Why?' I knew she would have had to answer 'instinct' and wouldn't want to. Okay. 'I've dug up a few things.' I just threw it out there so she had to ask me.

'You going to tell us or you going to put down roots? I've got things to do here, Dunn.'

'Beane was involved with Annie Robertson's "late" husband in some kind of half-ass business deal.' I should have known right then, because I pay attention to faces and hers took on a certain look, defensive or apprehensive, at the mere sound of Beane's name. That's in retrospect; at the time all I knew was I'd seen something. I remember I even looked to Owen, but he was off to her side in his wall-leaning stance. 'My guess is it's Billy told his employers how he knew this highly respectable crook up in Palm Springs who was in the dumper with the feds and needed money to fight it. They'd gamble on something like that.'

'Then they lost. You got anything concrete?'

'He's been up to Atlanta to see Robertson a couple of times.'

She looked at Owen. 'Worth asking about.'

He nodded, then gave her this Old South patriarchal 'do the right thing, chil'' look. Call it 'dour.' 'You gonna tell the man?' he asked.

It did not make Frankie happy. Of course, she turned the glare on me. 'I suppose he means about how it was Beane who tipped me to Rodriguez.'

Now I wasn't happy. 'Oh?'

'He claimed they were just casual friends and he ran into him in the Rebel. Probably both were on big rock candy mountain, running their mouths. I interrogated him pretty thoroughly and— '

'She kicked him in the Everglades Club. That is, in the knee, in the Everglades Club,' Owen said, chuckling.

My mouth must have fallen open, and then I know I gave a surprised laugh. 'You did that? I knew you

were a little gonzo,' I told her admiringly, 'but that's
. . . terrific.'

She wasn't mad at Owen this time; instead, proud of it.
'You believe Beane?'

'I believe a snake's got a belly, but I've never seen it.'

'I made another connection. Beane and this clown up
in Jupiter who's deceased or missing or whatever, the one
who threatened Chapelle for doing his frau— '

She snapped, 'We know who you mean!'

'They've both, at various times, worked for a smuggler
named Anselmo Porto Carrero who currently resides in
Key Biscayne. Although home is far over the seas to
the south in a quaint little city ringed by mountains.
Supposedly in the furniture-importing business, bringing
to a lucky world the best craftsmanship Colombia, Bolivia
and Peru have to offer. Actually he was sent up here a
few years ago by the late Pablo as a kind of underboss
for southeast Florida. Good family man, never done time,
some say because our friends in D.C. have rolled him over.
Whatever, he's employed the two gentlemen in question as
runners.'

'Man-oh-man-oh-Birmingham,' Owen exclaimed, softly
world-weary. 'This never stops gettin' more complicated.'
The rest of us were left to wonder which 'Birmingham' and
how it got in there.

Frankie seemed to have her own agenda. She turned
dark, on me with the singular eyes stripped for action.
'Beane says he's run into you in the Rebel.'

I tried to smile, but admit it was a little thin. 'So
what?'

'You tell me.'

'What is it, now you think I'm dirty? Because I went in
a bar?'

'Private club.'

'You see any chains or white loafers on me? Have you
looked at my car lately? Jesus, Frankie, give it a rest.'

'Nobody rests until this sucker is broken or it breaks me.'

'I think it's starting to do just that.'

'I don't give a shit what you think.'

Owen started to pull her off, but the desk phone rang.

She growled her name but the instant she heard the voice on the other end her whole demeanor changed, closing down emotional signifiers to guard against our curiosity. She couldn't hide her voice; it filled with smoke. 'Oh, hi . . . No, no, but . . . you shouldn't have . . . No, it's okay . . . Well, if you want to, sure . . . Right, I'll be there.'

She hung up and started to shuffle papers without looking at either of us, so transparent I was embarrassed for her. 'Not a good idea,' I told her, deliberately low-key.

Never mind; she came up like a bear defending her cubs. 'Just what the hell does that mean, Dunn?'

I looked to Owen but he wasn't going to get into this. 'She's a grownup lady and an officer. I got two daughters of my own at home that's 'bout all I can handle.'

Frankie refused to take him at his word. She looked from one to the other of us. 'What is this sudden sick bonding between you two?'

'He thinks Chapelle's your bad news as much as I do. I can tell.'

She threw down a pencil and started with a snarl that crescendoed to a shout. 'Christ, you piss me off! What are you, my fucking shrink? *Who* are you, anyway? I don't even know you! Get out of my face, Dunn!' In an unintentionally funny gesture, she flipped on her dark glasses, as if they could hold back the torrent of her rage.

She was right. I told her so and stood to leave.

'Wait a minute. Hold it!' I paused in the doorway. She stayed seated but whipped off the glasses and looked up into my eyes. 'Let's say some things straight-on here, okay? Is it . . . somebody told me you had a thing for me. I mean,

JAMES DAVID BUCHANAN

it's bananas, but is that what's going on all the time? You got some kind of feeling for me?'

'I do.'

Startled, she brushed back her hair, as if to clear the idea away. 'What?'

'Pity.'

'Oh, wonderful. He pities me 'cause a guy's coming on to me who's gorgeous, generous, rich, kind, funny, sweet and a regular fella in spite of it. That's a terrible fate for a woman, isn't it?'

'You left out "married."'

'Not what I call marriage,' she said quickly. Her voice fell away then. 'Anyway, there's no big thing happening here. We enjoy each other's company.'

'I believe you,' I told her, going out the door. 'But then I'm Joe Montana.'

Two nights later William Beane the Third inadvertently brought things to a head. 'Head,' in the chemical sense, being the relevant term. Whether out of stupidity – he went to Dartmouth; I looked it up – or arrogance or despair, he spent the evening cruising the clubs in Miami Beach's Art Deco district, South Beach, with two flagrant blondes propped up in his Merc convertible. The only thing missing was a flashing sign or a target on his pink Armani jacket.

South Beach is very special, a Fred Astaire/Ginger Rogers movie, everything in peach, lemon or lime outlined in neon. On that particular night the streets were wet and would have been splashed with multi-hued reflections; rain is particularly kind to the area, giving it a gentler Oz-like unreality. Sometimes I found it attractive, others I could choke on it. The inhabitants pretty much always gave me a hairball.

The two women were with him when he ate dinner in Coconut Grove across the bay where he ordered a hundred-and-fifty-dollar bottle of Margaux. What followed was a tangle of dance clubs – I understand he favored the merengue – and blow, walks and sex on the beach to clear the head, smoke to come down, more dance clubs with champagne and then brandy to clear the head. He spent a couple of K's and hadn't even had to pay corkage on the blow.

About two o'clock they came out of a club called Surf Bleu halfway to Mars, laughing and staggering around on the sidewalk in front while they waited for their car. One of the dope groupies had had her dress ripped so badly that it kept falling off her breasts. That was one source of their hilarity.

Apparently they were totally unaware that they were being stalked by two Hispanics in a Trans-Am across the street. Normally these chili peppers wouldn't be seen anywhere in a redneck short like a Trans-Am. Mercs, Caddies, Dinos . . . but they see Trans-Ams used for getaways and chases in the movies and they believe everything they see in movies. The man in the front passenger seat got out, leaving the door open, stood up on the floor frame, steadied a Czech machine-pistol called a Skorpian on the roof, and blasted off.

One of the girls was lucky. She had dropped an earring and stooped to retrieve it. Her upright friend received two bullets, in military terms 'collateral damage,' in the throat, severing her jugular and killing her outright. A lot of blood found on Billy, sprayed from two or three feet away, was determined to be hers. The real target caught five bullets in the head, chest and shoulder, blowing him back into the doorway, where he collapsed and sprawled. People inside panicked when they found their egress blocked by a blown-up corpse. There was so much blood around, the crime scene team hadn't understood at first that his jacket was supposed to be pink. One of the first uniformed cops to arrive slipped in it and fell.

The hitters lost a couple of inches of rubber making their Smokey-and-the-Bandit getaway. The technicians actually found significant amounts on the pavement along with a dozen or so shell casings. Never happen in New York; up there you get careless and you're very quickly, permanently, out of business, but down here they have it pretty much their own way. The sheer volume of drug killings usually mitigates against a serious investigation.

Miami is run a lot like the old British Empire; understanding that they were so few and the small brown people were so many, they let them fight each other to a standstill for several centuries. The only difference in Miami is, the brown people are in charge. Human nature, go figure.

Some drunk sitting on the curb down the street from Surf Bleu, and alerted by the horrendous screeching, actually got a partial on the license. A hobbyist, no doubt. Didn't matter. The car, which had been stolen anyway, was found two days later on a backroad in Homestead, wiped, burned and abandoned.

The rounds were soft-nosed, so the easiest way of identifying Billy on the table was by his ponytail. He was a mess. The girl I never looked at; she was an accident, one of hundreds who get too close to the flame every year. I noticed he was wearing a uniform established for the boys in the life by the actor Don Johnson in that TV series – designer jacket over what we plebeians call a t-shirt and the usual crap that goes with it. Of all the people involved in that long ugly scenario I liked him the least for what he was, what he did and why he did it. To be truthful, I didn't give a pig's whistle that he was dead. In his world it was inevitable and this was one of the easier buys.

XVI

I didn't know at the time what Frankie had done, but it wouldn't have mattered to me. If you're a detective, especially a narc, you have to threaten to hang people out all the time. If you don't actually do it now and then who'll believe you? If death isn't an option you have no credibility on the street. Of course, I'd worked in Miami and New York and some worse places in the service, whereas Frankie's whole career had been in Palm Beach County. Look, I told her, the bastards always have an option. They don't play, fuck 'em! It didn't help.

With her, I think it was all the other things. You always investigate a crime involving a family from outside; the Chapelles and that whole goddamn matrix sucked you in, made you a part of them, a part of the problem so you could never quite get a clear line to the solution. When I said Beane brought things to a head I was thinking of Frankie. I knew we had to end it after that, no matter what.

I'll probably never hear all of what she did to calm that turbulent spirit, to ease the guilt, but I sensed that James had a lot to do with it. He could be an impressively sympathetic man, a talent that in myself regrettably remains underdeveloped to this day.

The next morning, when the news reached Palm Beach, I got a call from Owen. He said Frankie had come a little unglued about the death of this Beane guy and he was afraid people in the Department were going to start looking at her.

I didn't know why he thought I could do anything

about it. But as I was already up there, staying in the motel . . .

'What is she doing? Is she crying, is she hysterical?'

'No, nothin' like that. It's hard to describe. Maybe I'm seein' things other folks aren't. But they already got an odd idea about her, some of 'em here.'

'It sure as hell isn't because she kicked the little shit in the kneecap.'

'No, I don't 'spect it's 'bout that.'

'Okay, I never know if she's even speaking to me, but I'll try to find out.'

I don't think he knew either when he called that Frankie had left the guy to twist slowly unto death in the wind. He really was at heart a smalltown Southern cop, not to mention too nice a man, to think those thoughts. A less nice man, I guessed.

Surprisingly she agreed to meet me for lunch in West Palm. I named the kind of restaurant with a counter, naugahyde and Formica booths, big dirty windows, comfy waitresses and the bad food that all cops are used to. Something perverse in me, I suppose, because it was obviously the polar opposite of the kind of place Chapelle would take her. She came in wearing her nerves all over her. When we sat down she asked me if I had a cigarette?

She didn't want lunch, just coffee. She never seemed to eat when I was around. I got a Denver sandwich and a salad. Now that I had her there I couldn't think why, but on the other hand she didn't seem to care. We made small-talk as if there was nothing unusual about our having lunch, as if she didn't have deep suspicions about me and I didn't have serious reservations about her.

Finally she said, 'If this is about Chapelle, you can just forget all that. I won't go out with him, okay? And that's it. I don't want to hear any more.'

'That wasn't what this is about.'

'Oh.'

'Did you hang him out?'

'Who?'

'Who died last night?'

'Oh, him.'

'Yeah, "him." You hung him out and somebody blew him up and now you feel shitty about it, although God knows why. Is it because he's one of them?'

'Why don't we just eat?'

'You're not eating. Did you notice?'

'Well, maybe I will. I don't have any appetite.'

'Don't get the Denver, it's runny inside, and according to the FDA that means there's a good chance I will be too before long. Is it because he's one of them?'

'What do you mean by "them"?'

'You know what I mean.'

'Jesus.' She went over and bummed a cigarette off the waitress. When she came back she asked, 'What do I care what he was? I killed the sonofabitch, didn't I? If I cared, why would I waste him? And some poor clueless bimbo stupid enough to go out with a slimeball like that, I killed her too. She probably had a family, maybe even a kid at home with grandma. Hell, they always have kids. But that's not my problem.'

She was as dark as I wanted to see her, although you had to assume Frankie was down the hole a whole lot worse when she was alone.

'I don't know why we do this, why any of us do. I don't know why I fucking do anything? Do you?'

'Not for me to say.'

'My life doesn't work. If work doesn't work, what's the point? I thought I could find some goddamn reason to get up every morning in serving. I was supposed to stop people from killing, not do it.' She put her head in her hands. 'Shit.'

'Look . . . um . . .'

'Yeah, give us your wisdom. Your good advice.'

I shook my head at her and ordered a cup of coffee for myself.

'Sorry.' She didn't look sorry, just unhappy.

I leaned over the table into the smoke to get closer. 'So Beane's dead. Judgment call. And the woman, that's true. But it's just a mistake, an act of God, like getting hit by a meteor. If you want to think you're responsible, I can't stop you.'

'I thought I could roll him, and he didn't roll. What was the point? I wasn't even sure he could break the case.'

I tried to talk about how I didn't think life was sacred, except in the abstract. That we gave it its value ourselves, and if we didn't we didn't deserve to have it. She listened in disbelief for a while and then told me to stuff it and left. I decided she was right and considered going home to burn my library; I wasn't born pompous.

When I went out to the parking lot I could see Frankie's Celica tearing off down the street. The phone rang in the Jeep, a call from the boss. Sylvia wanted to see me, making it clear that it should be sooner rather than later. Granted, I'd been ignoring her, had not even answered the last two calls. I didn't bother to phone but went straight out to the estate.

Prescient, she was watching and hurried out to meet me. At the time I wondered why, since there was so little kept secret from James. If anything. Maybe she just needed the exercise. We walked around the house and out towards a gazebo on the waterfront, talking as we went.

She made an attempt to appear despondent about the fate of Beane, but I wasn't sure I believed her. Oh, I know she liked him the way they like anybody and felt badly about his death, but it was a question of was it tragedy or momentary regret. I asked her if they had been lovers and she told me it was none of my business without resentment.

'He was a pretty bad boy,' I told her.

She shrugged. 'Part of the attraction, I suppose.'

'I don't mean in terms of what constitutes "bad" around here.' I gestured around. 'I don't mean bad and beautiful.'

'I know what you mean. At least he wasn't boring.'

'Is that all it takes? How come I'm not prince of the city?'

'You're boring.'

'Why?' I tried to sound indignant.

'Because you have all these ethics. Or pretend to.'

'If Beane'd had a few he might still be doing the merengue.'

She made a little gesture as if shooing away a mosquito. 'Is his murder tied in? I need to know. I insist on it.' She said it like she meant it, all right; it was no stomping of tiny feet.

'Indirectly, yes. Actually, I doubt it. Remains to be seen.'

'How "indirectly"?'

'I'd rather not say at this point.'

'I don't give a shit what you'd rather or rather not say, Sean. I told you, I want to know.'

'We don't always get what we want. Not even you.' We stopped at the base of the gazebo and she started to open her mouth to let me have it, but I preempted. 'And don't threaten me with a lot of childish crap about getting me fired or run out of town or any of that shit. You know better and it's beneath you.'

Her leopard's eyes had 'kill!' in them. The mouth closed slowly but she continued to stand there, staring into my face from a couple of feet away. Some of the white rage showed through the tan, set off by the tight lines around her mouth and jaw.

I assumed that even James seldom said 'no' to her. However, we were old antagonists with that certain regard you get for each other when you've both stayed in the ring for time beyond reason. And in truth it was more complicated than our simply being 'antagonists.' I waited her out; she glared long enough for me to have time to think how much I liked the sound of gulls and never got tired of it.

Finally she broke it and stepped up into the gazebo to sit, plumping herself down petulantly. I expected her to ring for the houseman or a maid to bring us something, but not today.

She appealed to me. This whole thing was starting to tear her, tear them apart. By 'them' she meant to include James.

I pointed out that it wasn't my job to solve the crimes. 'I was brought up here to represent and protect your interests, remember.'

'People keep getting killed, Sean. Is that your idea of protection?'

'I'm sorry about your sister-in-law. You're right, I am responsible. I screwed up.'

'And what about Billy?'

She had said it a little too quickly. 'I didn't know he was one of your "interests."'

She stood, groaning, and looked up at the house with her hands gripping the railing and her back to me. 'Oh, God. Okay, I did him once. On somebody's boat one afternoon. Is that what you wanted to hear?' There was moisture on the railing and she wiped her hands on her pants.

'No. I don't care.'

'He was lousy. Light-years from James, who's absolutely the best. I think God or Mother must have raised him just to be that. I feel selfish just being married to him. Although, of course, it's not all that much of a hindrance.'

There are times when honesty can be ludicrous. 'I'll have to find out some day what he does.'

'What did Fats Waller say to the woman when she asked him what jazz was?'

I often forgot that she'd been a singer; this made me smile; I couldn't help it. '"If you gotta ask, lady, you don't have it." Thanks, by the way.'

'Oh, you're not so bad.'

'That's one area where no man wants to be damned by faint praise.' I seemed to be taking a hell of a battering from the ladies lately; they were lining up.

'I'm scared, Sean.'

'Well, it's a new sensation. Enjoy it.'

'That's pretty damned flip. And a little callous, don't you think?'

'It is if you're serious. I'm just having trouble processing that.'

'I'm scared. About Jim and your Sergeant Bodo.'

I had to shake my head in disbelief, even at the risk of appearing callous. 'First of all, I keep telling you, she's not "my sergeant." She doesn't even like me. She may, I don't know, hate my guts.'

'But what do *you* think of her?'

'That's got nothing to do with anything.'

'The hell it doesn't.'

'This is crazy. You're beautiful, she's . . . mortal.'

'She's quite attractive.'

'Okay, pretty, but . . .'

'Good body.'

'I wouldn't know. The Sheriff's Department has that under control. Syl, this really is ridiculous. The two of you can't even spell "jealousy." And for good reason. You couldn't count— '

She cut in to insist, 'It's different this time.'

'It's different every time. For five minutes.'

She whipped around to snap at me. 'Stop your patronizing. I'm trying to tell you something.'

I stood and went over to join her at the railing, so that our shoulders would touch now and then when we turned from the house to the sea or back again. It was what we could allow ourselves. 'You can't make this some big deal. Jim jumps every female who shows up, from Airedales to grandmothers. Granted, sometimes he stops at dispensing charm.'

'You're so crude sometimes. And disrespectful. God!' Still, she smiled. 'But you don't understand. James is in a crisis lately. His whole life. Nothing's worked out – our child, the business, marriage. He's feeling useless, wasted. What you get off Bodo is an incredible energy and purpose that none of us seem to have.'

'Neurotic energy. She's mad and confused. But then aren't we all.'

'I don't care. It's enormously attractive to a man who's emotionally and spiritually blah.'

'What right's he got to feel like that?'

'There's nothing in the world so wasting as having everything you want. I think you've said that yourself a few times.'

I looked over at her. 'You remember when I used to play piano and you'd sing?'

'Yeah.' Her tone softened noticeably; the past, whatever it was in reality, is always gentle in evocation. 'Everybody was bored except us. We used to have a lot of fun.'

'I'm making a point.'

'I know you are. I haven't sung in a long time. It doesn't seem to go with this life.'

'I met an Episcopal priest out on the Coast who manages to play in jazz clubs and concerts, says mass and runs a religious school.'

'Thank you, but if you want to save me, save Jim for me.'

It was so entreating and simply put I found myself taking her hand, and by the time I realized it it was too late. 'You weren't worried about Annie Robertson, and that seems to have gone on a while with all its little rituals and sharings and . . .'

'No. I talked to her, did I tell you? That was no more serious than a new body-type.' She smiled again, but forcing it this time, which made it wistful and in turn gave the lie to her words. 'New muscles for new feelings. I can see where that would be exciting.'

'I hope you mean all this.'

'Jim's told her they're all through.'

I nodded. 'I heard that. But you claim it didn't cut you at all.'

'It didn't. Don't you see, she's one of us. Bodo's not.'

'She's also not going out with your husband. I just saw her. She told me she had no intention of getting involved. It's strictly the job.'

Sylvia didn't reply for a long time, then she told me quietly, 'They're having dinner tonight.'

I went back to the motel and rested, having some idea of what lay ahead of me. At six I drove over and sat outside the offices of Chapel Corp. in West Palm. Sat there in a car for two hours. As usual when I have to stake someone out I rented a nice neutral Honda. You can't get anything more neutral than America's bestselling car. The Jeep's just too quick a read.

I didn't start at the Sheriff's station – I'd stick out around there, and had much the same concern about Frankie's apartment, which I knew to be on the second floor with a clear view of the street in both directions. She was a pro, however much she might be excited by the prospect of seeing Chapelle.

Maybe there was another reason – seeing her come out of there with all that wonderful high-color anticipation you get in women, dressed in a way I'd never seen her, maybe that was too personal. Anyway, you never knew where she was and I did know where he was.

It got dark and started to rain. Finally he came out and stood under the overhang. He was wearing a white linen

suit with a red tie. You've got to be good to get away with
that. He practically glowed in the dark.

I sat with my head against the rest and watched him.
The windows were open so I could feel and hear the
rain. A young woman came out, spoke to Chapelle and
hurried off to a man waiting in a Chevrolet, holding a
sheet of plastic over her head. She made little cries of
delighted alarm at getting wet. I wondered had he fixed
dinner for her, were there children waiting? Would they
go out somewhere nice? Would they make love or discuss
a divorce? Were they cheating on someone? All the things
you do to pass time on a stakeout if you don't want to turn
into a turnip.

I had situated myself in such a way that I could see both
the main entrance on my right and straight ahead along
the street where their private garage exited. Frankie came
past me and turned right to where Chapelle was waiting,
making a U to stop in front of him. Obviously she hadn't
made me sitting there. Rain helps. They talked through an
open window for a minute and then he climbed in. Frankie
drove off more demurely than usual; she didn't understand
what he wanted from her.

I followed at a distance that entailed uncomfortable risk,
but which I thought unavoidable. I couldn't count on her
distraction for ever. What I did count on was that he would
take her to Lauderdale, Boca Raton or at least West Palm.
And I was wrong. The Celica turned east and went across
the Royal Park Bridge, on to Royal Park Boulevard like
they were driving an arrow into the heart of Palm Beach.
The sonofabitch was smart, and he didn't care; she must
have been as surprised as I was.

The doorman may have been surprised to see a Celica
drive up under the striped awning, a mouse in a parade
of cheetahs. A Rolls preceded and a limo followed. I
could see because by the time the attendant opened her
door I was already sliding into a parking space across the

street. What I saw didn't make me happy, but it was a revelation.

When she stepped into the light she was wearing a red sheath mini and red shoes with heels high enough to arch over an anaconda if one happened to be coiled on the sidewalk. Her hair was different, that was indistinct, but I thought I could make out her earrings from clear across the street. It would have looked great with salsa. Still, I didn't think it would hurt her when she got inside, except to draw the usual male approval and female disapproval while each sex lied to the other about their motives.

Not everyone in there was an American aristocrat like the Chapelles, and probably a third of them had started life as some variety of criminal or hooker. James wouldn't be embarrassed or even self-conscious; he had never been either of those in his entire life. He was above them.

The waiting was painful. My anxiety rose by small increments, but it didn't let up. I was afraid for her. After a while I had to get out of the car, although it's seldom a good idea, to stand in the shadows, first on one foot and then the other. I would gladly have given one atrophying testicle for a cigar or a drink, any drink.

They came out after another two-hour wait. That was all right, I was used to that, but it went downhill from there. Chapelle said something to the doorman, slipped him some money and they went off down the deserted street. Where? I never found out, although I followed for a while.

It was still raining but they didn't seem to mind. They had their arms around each other and he made her laugh as they struggled against the elements. I had seen it so seldom I'd almost forgotten what a terrific laugh she had, and what it did for her. It lit up the block and made her extremely desirable.

They stopped against a brick, vine-covered wall and he encircled her, pressed up against her, the rain wetting their hair, running down their faces, dampening their clothes. His face moved slowly toward her, melding with hers until finally they kissed and her arms went around him. One long stockinged leg rose and bent, sliding upward, rubbing along his. Their hips began to move subtly, unconsciously. They were preparing themselves. I left.

FRANKIE

I had an awful time getting ready that night. For one thing I hadn't been out like that in a long time. I mean, dress-up bigtime. Then I couldn't really remember what these people wore in those places. Sure, I'd seen them and certainly I'd seen pictures of them in magazines and 'The Shiny Sheet,' but it had never registered because I didn't care. Now I had to care. And I didn't have anything, anyway. I decided that if I was going to be looked down on, at least it would be after I'd knocked their socks off.

Of course, I never realized it would be on the island. I assumed, like with all married guys, it would be somewhere along the lines of, say, the dining room of the hotel in Boca Raton, which was pretty fancy and far away. Or in Lauderdale or wherever. When he asked me to pick him up at the office and then said we'd take my car I began to worry he'd booked a reservation in Orlando. How he could do what he did with him knowing everybody in town for a hundred years and them knowing his wife I would never understand. I just told myself that it was his play and if he wasn't ashamed I had no reason to be, and that's how I conducted myself. Even if I didn't believe it.

He said hello to some people going in, easy as pie, and I tried to look a little haughty the way they all do. I got a lot of glances and a few stares that usually I would have stared down, would have had to, but not tonight, tonight I was above that. And the whispering, and a couple of guys smiling at me in secret. I couldn't help thinking that in the normal run of things in my normal clothes they wouldn't even recognize I was in the room. Heady stuff.

James ordered the wine. I asked for a screwdriver first even though I don't like them, and he got that French mineral water. When they came with the menus he asked if I wanted him to order for me. Even though it was written in French and the waiter had a broom up his ass I said no way. I didn't know if it was the custom or that's the way he saw me, but you can only accommodate so much. I made out tornedos on there and I like them so I asserted my independence. If James noticed, you couldn't tell. He just changed the wine order to red.

'Where are you supposed to be tonight?' It probably wasn't the smoothest transition into conversation I ever made.

'That's a terrible cliché. And so far nothing about you's been predictable.'

'Okay, but where *are* you supposed to be?'

'Anywhere I want. And what I want is to be here with you. Do you mind being here with me?'

'No. Not as long as the Sheriff doesn't come in.'

'Not, I think, on what we pay him.' It was remarkable how he could always get away with saying things like that without sounding snobby. It was his special talent.

'What about Annie Robertson? Did you ever bring her here?'

He shook his head but he didn't strike me as irritated. I supposed he'd had this conversation about a thousand times. 'God, you're relentless. If only I thought you really cared.'

'I do. For a lot of reasons.'

'But some of them professional, right? Is that why you agreed to go out with me? I don't know what I can do to get you to see me in another light.' He made that pathetic wounded sound men do. 'Annie was different. She hated

Palm Beach because of what had happened to her here. I could never get her to go out. And it's over between us, anyway. She knows that.'

'You always tell *them*?'

He looked at me full on, reeking sincerity, and those eyes would have convinced the Devil. 'No,' he said, 'sometimes they tell me. I've had my share of rejection, some of it pretty painful.'

'So long as you don't expect me to believe that.'

'Why not? I'm suffering it now. Can't you see it in my face?' Like always, he smiled after he said it, so you could never know if he was serious.

Frankie, I told myself, you are so out of your element. What are you doing sitting and trading banter with this cool, smooth aristocratic guy like you lived here? So I was glad I had laid on the deodorant and thrilled by the arrival of the screwdriver.

'You believe me about it being over with Annie?'

'Yeah, I suspected it.'

'Oh?'

'Dunn told me he thought you'd dumped her from what she'd said.'

'She told him?' That appeared to trouble him.

'They seem to be getting on okay.'

He worried that. 'How are you getting on with him lately?'

'I don't. I still think he's involved.'

His expression took on a firmness you didn't see there every day, but made you realize he could run a big corporation when he put his mind to it. What I never did see there was the killer instinct, like a good boxer's got to have, for instance. But then I've seen killers who didn't have it, either.

'No,' he told me, 'you're way off. I know him very well. There's things he'll do and things he won't, but money's just not important to him.'

'He seems to think he knows you pretty well, too. He's always warning me about you.'

He laughed good-naturedly. 'Does he? What does he say?'

I had the feeling I'd gotten in a little deep, but on the other hand what did I owe Dunn? 'Oh, mostly it's about me personally.'

He nodded, confirming the obvious. 'He doesn't approve of how I've lived my life. But then I don't myself.'

'Having second thoughts?'

'About everything.' He raised his gloved hand. 'I am the victim, remember. It changes you, an experience like I had.'

'So Dunn's wrong about that?'

'He wouldn't have been once. Now . . .' He opened his hands, begging acceptance.

I was a little embarrassed about what I was about to say, but it was better to clear the air. And I owed it to him anyway. 'That's funny. You think I'm here just to get something out of you, and I wondered if you asked me out because you thought I knew something. Like about your CEO and your wife or your brother's wife or something.'

'I asked you to have dinner because I'm fascinated by you. If I ever mention the company again you can just hit me on the jaw and walk away. You have my permission.'

'Dunn knows something about your company, but he wouldn't tell me.'

'Sean's very loyal.'

'Maybe. On the other hand, he did tell me you were a stone gambler.'

He seemed to find it funny, so I had to figure I wasn't going anywhere on this track. Laughing, he admitted, 'It could be pertinent, couldn't it? He was just doing his job, like you are. No, I trust him and I'm going to need him, too, in this fight for the company.'

'Does it worry you that your wife trusts him, too?'

'I'm not sure what you're getting at. But in answer to your question, we trust him for the same reasons.'

'Which are?'

He put one finger on my lips. The touch in that intimate place surprised and jolted me. It was strange, pleasurable like one of those encompassing orgasms women have, but like them, also frightening. I don't think he had any idea what he'd done.

He said, 'Please, I thought we weren't going to do this.' It really sounded imploring and maybe that felt wrong to him, because he lightened it. 'I'm trying very hard to be romantic here. To live up to my awful reputation.'

Then he took my hand. A lot of guys do that when they're coming on but usually they grab it, squeeze it or creep up it. He examined it and, sad to say, the effect was just like his putting his finger on my lips. I had a total sense of losing control and I didn't like it one bit, but I also liked it too much.

All I could manage was a dumb response in a weak voice. 'You're not going to read my palm?'

'I was just struck by what beautiful hands they are for someone who's made their living wrestling with drunks and burglars.'

'They're pretty strong.' I studied them myself. 'I never can wear polish. I just put it on tonight.'

'I'm flattered.'

'Short nails. Not what you're used to, I bet.'

He suddenly became very intense; it came off of him like those waves rising from a road in the hot summer. 'I'm sick to death of what I'm used to! You let the air in, Frankie.'

'Thanks.' That was all I could think of.

He put down the hand, sat back and looked at me. It was friendly but appraising. 'Are you lonely?' That shook me a little. He went on, 'I see it in your eyes. They're beautiful, huge, but I do get that feeling from them. Some very old sadness.'

That was getting a little sticky, I thought, although I never doubted for one minute he was sincere. Of course, I'd never had anyone talk to me like that before, either, so I didn't have much to go by. Dunn knew a lot of words but he was different.

'I got a lot of friends,' I told him a little defensively. I didn't like him having this idea about me. 'And I work with a hundred apes every day. So how could I be?'

'Nothing wrong with being lonely, Frankie. I am myself.'

'Oh, sure. You know half the world and live in a house bigger than Cleveland.'

'Doesn't matter. I am.' Then he gave me that killer smile. He had the most beautiful mouth I'd ever seen on a man. 'Or I was,' he said. I felt the old earth opening up right underneath me.

We ended the fencing after a while and it was a relief. He even stopped coming on to me; finally, a man who understood the most effective way to seduce is not to seduce at all.

Instead we talked about our childhoods. He asked you questions about yourself all the time, until you got the feeling like you were the President of the United States and they were preparing a biography. Not only that, he actually appeared to listen to the answers. Of course, there's things about myself I don't tell anyone, and if I did it would probably be a fellow loser like Dunn, but Chapelle still got a lot out of me.

I was amazed at how much grief there was in his family. Even rich, you can evidently spend time in hell. Believe it or not, his father took opium, and he never came home. When he did he was very, very cold. His mother he described as a coquette but a real loon, and a drunk. Another thing we had in common. He became an athlete in this private school they all went to in order to protect his brother who was the dweeb of the century. The only member of the family he seemed to have any real affection for was his sister, Molly.

I told him that I'd guessed that and it must be mutual because she was really hustling me on his behalf. I actually started to say 'pimped for' and he caught it before I could cut it off, so I apologized. But he waved it away, saying she had always known what was best for him; he just hadn't always listened. This time he thought he would. Since I'm not usually thought of as what's best for people, I liked that.

When he asked me what I thought were the differences between our two childhoods, money aside, I told him how once when I got hit at home I went straight out into the neighborhood and broke another kid's nose with a board. Chapelle thought it was wonderful and laughed harder than he ever had around me.

'And did it feel good?'

'Wonderful. For me. His nose was too big anyway.'

'You're right,' he said, still chuckling, 'I never had that alternative. That was what was missing. Why didn't all those shrinks at two hundred dollars an hour understand that?'

I said, 'Because they never had that much fun in their whole dink lives,' and he laughed hard again.

We had a lot of laughs during that dinner, more than I'd had in a long, long time. He could laugh at himself, which I had never seen among those people. And believe it or not, he almost had me shedding tears once about my life; he could do that, dig deep without being nosy or creepy, but just sounding like he really had to know.

We drank a lot of wine. I forgot a lot of things, but mostly I forgot to have any more doubts about what I was doing there. When we went out and walked in the rain in that crazy mood, and he kissed me up against the wall, I was nailed. Figuratively and literally, as Dunn would say. At the time it seemed like one of the best nights I'd ever had.

XVII

SEAN

As love-making goes, if that's the term, and it isn't, whatever took place on that bed and floor and God knows where that night was probably the strangest I'd ever experienced. The phrase 'making the beast with two backs' is a lot more appropriate. I was black and blue for some time afterwards, and they were not the kind of wounds you treasured.

It was vertical, it was horizontal, but mostly it was just violent; I was hit, kicked, pinched, and stabbed. The energy level was truly awesome – and usually that's what we want, right? – but this was more akin to aerobics or Desert Storm.

She hated me and I knew it almost immediately but there was no question of stopping, not only because of the many months my libido had spent in jail, but for the very reason I was there in the first place. She was telling me something, she was telling me a lot, it just took me a while to equate it.

In my heart I knew there was also for me an element of despair from that moment of seeing Frankie against that wall, but as I don't much like theatrics based on self-pity in others, I wasn't going to admit it in myself. Not then, anyway. The sex ended when we were mutually exhausted and I, perhaps to maintain the fiction a while longer, rolled over and addressed the ceiling just as if it had been love-making.

'Jesus, I thought you were trying to kill me.' I was still breathing heavily and hoped it would pass as a compliment.

'Maybe I was,' Annie said indifferently.

'I haven't done this in a while.'

'Yeah, I thought you were celibate.'

'All good things must come to an end.' I'm not claiming that I'm totally above the usual male vanities, because I brightened and tried to sound macho. 'Came back to me, though.' Of course I had just handed her an axe.

'If you're begging a compliment, forget it. A kangaroo can fuck. I can do it anywhere, any time, with my eyes closed or open, and still be the best lay in Florida without feeling a goddamned thing.'

'Thanks.' I must have sounded unhappy.

'You guys always say you want the truth.' She rolled over then, putting her formidable back to me. I didn't think it was inviting sodomy. 'You're not going to stay, I hope.'

I did.

FRANKIE

About one o'clock I found myself driving James back over to Palm Beach, right to the estate. Not my idea, it made me very antsy; he insisted it was perfectly okay. He said he had been given a lift over to the office by the houseman as they had not replaced Freddo as yet. I had seen at least three or four cars – a Merc, a Beemer, a Range Rover – yet people were always driving them places. I never figured that out.

Glancing in the mirror and then down at my dress, I was a mess. Makeup beyond repair, I would have had to have started from point one with a good scrub. Sexy before, now I looked cheap, a hooker on a bad night . . . although actually it had been a good night up to that point. The closer we got to the house, the less I liked the prospect.

'You expect me to drive you right up to the door in this outfit? What do I say? "I was taking his statement and I always wear catch-me, fuck-me shoes when I do that"?'

'Frankie, nobody's going to come running out to look at you at this hour, I promise.' Boy, was he wrong. 'Anyway, I don't sneak around.'

'I'll say.' I admit I was distracted; sex like that and I go all fuzzy mush, no good to anybody including myself for hours. This time I didn't have the luxury. I came around a corner and turned into the driveway on automatic. The gate guard swung them open quickly, too quickly, and waved us through; all that energy, not to mention the expression on his face, should have warned me.

'Oh, shit,' I said. 'Oh, man.'

Ahead, grouped around the main entrance, were police cars with their stupid flashing lights, people milling, a couple of uniforms. No journalists as yet, thank you, Mary, Mother of God! Alarmed, Jim's voice became steely. 'Keep going.' As if I had a choice by that time.

The uniforms were Palm Beach PD. They looked a little wary at first but I thrust the shield forward out the window at them even before I came to a stop. It must have been a picture, me in that outfit, Chapelle in his ice-cream suit, stepping out of a little Toyota into a big nightmare. Owen spotted us first and came hurrying.

He held up his hands in a blocking gesture, addressing Jim. 'It's all right, sir. Nobody's hurt.'

'What happened? Is it my wife?'

It was dumb and certainly reflects on me, but considering where I'd just been I found those words painful. To cover myself I broke in, 'What's going on here, Owen?'

He made a point of recognizing me now and the tone was a lot like a daughter had come home very late from the dance with the wrong boy. And what happened? My ears burned red like any caught-out idiot teenager. The only difference was if it had been my old man I would have been ducking already. I could have hit myself in the mouth.

'Well, while you were gone . . .' He kindly addressed this to both of us, which took a little of the sting off me and didn't affect Jim one bit. '. . . Mrs Chapelle took a little drive down south. Seems like a man with criminal intent tried to force her over on US 1 just past Delray. She pulled off, stopped and got out of the car— '

Jim broke in excitedly, 'Oh, Christ, why?'

'No reason to upset yourself, Mr Chapelle. She took out that little pistol of hers and shot the stuffin's out of him. He's just 'bout as dead as a person can be.'

Jim sagged as if the surgeon had just come out and said, 'She'll live.' He murmured, 'Thank God.' And come to think of it, it was a great break for me, too. If I had been out with the man when his wife was . . . Well, you're not supposed to think like that, but the truth was I couldn't stand the woman, so it was easy.

I looked past Owen to see where Jim was looking. Sylvia was in the doorway, wild-eyed and bushy-haired. My God, she was a human. Jim went straight to her and threw his arms around her until she almost disappeared. Touching.

Then I saw one eye come out, a bloodshot moon rising over his shoulder; followed by the other. It sounds funny, like some furry little animal poking its head out of a burrow. If it was an animal, it was a wolverine. The eyes burned like the last two coals in a fire. I'd seen it on the streets; you know when somebody's trying to wish you dead. Looking down at my rumpled red dress I didn't blame her at all. I was ashamed.

Owen drove me to the crime scene, mercifully stopping in West Palm for the world's quickest change of clothes on my part. The car was a dark blue Buick LeSabre, though hardly recognizable as that after a lot of hard use by a lot of hard owners. Soap and water had never touched its lips and now, its driver slumped dead across the front seat, it had probably had its last swig of cheap, unknown-brand, pump-it-yourself, pay-the-toothless-person gas. After the inquest or trial or whatever it would likely be impounded, compacted, melted and come back in a Japanese VCR. What kind of a name for a car is 'LeSabre' anyway?

The driver-corpse was a large red-headed man in an especially gaudy Hawaiian shirt, dirty shorts and sneakers without socks. Examining him closely, I was struck by his outsized freckled hands with banana fingers. There were calluses on the knuckles; obviously he had done some professional fighting. His jaw was heavy and covered by red stubble. I felt it – Brillo. The eyes were open as in unaccustomed surprise. I read somewhere that people used to think you could see the last thing the corpse saw in there. Sure as hell make our job a lot easier.

There was a bullet-hole in the windshield and another in the window of the driver's door, which was flung open, and enough blood on his shirt for a transfusion. I asked Owen, 'Who is this broad – Wyatt Earp?' and he laughed, so I knew things were okay between us again. That meant a lot.

Sylvia's Beemer was pulled over at an awkward angle a few yards in front of his car with one tire up on the curb, which certainly told you something. Or was intended to. That's where we started our reconstruction, surrounded as always by cops from the local force, slowing motorists, although there weren't many of those on this dark little side street. The curious from the neighborhood, many in pajamas, robes, and hair curlers, stood and watched us silently from beyond the yellow incident ribbon.

'She says he was right behind her on the highway, right?'

'Couple feet from her rear bumper, she says, which scared her real bad.'

'There's a picture,' I said.

'Kind of hard to imagine, isn't it?'

We moved to look at the rear of her car. 'No sign he made contact.'

'No, she said he was 'bout to, comin' up on her real fast, and that's when she spotted the exit and whipped down here to try and get away from him.'

'That what you would have done?'

'No, sir.'

'Me, neither. Does she look dumb to you?'

'Real smart. But even smart folks can do awful dumb things when their teeth's rattlin'. Frankie, just 'cause you don't like the lady— '

'Let's not get into that.'

'I wasn't goin' to. But don't let it cloud your judgment, neither.' Then he added, 'Sergeant,' by way of reminding me.

I nodded. 'So anyway, he stayed right with her. You say down here he honked and tried to force her over . . .'

'That's right. And she really floored it for a minute, but then decided the best course would be to stop and have it out.'

'Man, did she ever.'

'She figured on he wouldn't expect a woman to come out shootin', so she'd have the advantage.'

We moved back to his vehicle. 'Must've come out of her car like a commando,' I said, shaking my head. 'Maybe . . . maybe I'm having trouble imagining it because I can't credit myself with the ability to act that quickly and . . . ruthlessly.'

'Efficiently?'

'Okay. But it sure is a stretch.' He started to say something. 'I know, I know, she's a skeet champion. Still . . .'

Owen took up her account. 'Got out with her gun down by her side. Soon as she had two feet planted solid on the ground she raised it and shot him once through the windshield.'

'Had she even seen a weapon? 'Cause she's in deep shit if she didn't.'

'Says when he tried to force her over he pointed it at her. Says the man looked Irish to her – she spent time in Ireland – and since her husband was known to be kidnapped by an Irishman she thought the same was goin' to happen to her.'

'Oh, man. "Looked like an Irishman"?'

'Jury'd believe it. 'Specially when it turns out he is.'

I leaned in and examined the corpse once more. 'No witnesses? No one saw them tearing up the countryside like this?'

'Not so far. Pretty quiet 'round here at this hour. Some folks heard the shootin' and come out. Ever'body knows what that sounds like these days. There's a couple of other bullet-holes on the other side we can't account for. We think they're old.' They were the ones put there by Sean; we just didn't know it at the time.

'Where was the gun found?'

'On the seat. Kind of in his hand, comin' loose like when he fell back and his arm stretched out.' He held it up in a plastic evidence bag. 'Fabrique National.'

'I'm not sure I've seen one before,' I told him.

'I'd say that makes the odds pretty darn good it's the same gun smoked that chauffeur, wouldn't you?'

Looking at the corpse's stupid, butt-ugly face I had to admit it was all going her way. 'Looks like a dead mick to me.'

'License says "Daniel Patrick Loftus." But I already started to run him and so far he's used half the phone book. Born in New York, we know that much. Could be down here for some R and R and decided to pick up a little change on the side.'

'Yeah, a hundred million worth. It stinks.'

'I don't know, kind of nice in a way.'

I twisted my face until it hurt trying to convey new heights of skepticism.

JAMES DAVID BUCHANAN

'It's not the same fella the federal gentleman claimed it was.' He looked as wicked as he ever looked.

'Okay, so she got him the first time when he was just rising up from behind the wheel. But he's an ox and one doesn't do it, he just keeps coming . . . flings the door open and starts to lunge out of there, but she nails him again through the side window and, by the looks of it, puts it right in the locker. This time he falls back, being squeezed between the seat and wheel but . . . his weight pushes him down through to stretch out on the seat. Thing is, he should've crumpled right there on the ground. The angle's about seventy degrees short of what would blow him straight back in.'

'Maybe he was just tryin' to duck out of sight. Threw himself in there knowin' the dashboard's more cover than a door. Maybe he was thinkin' on how he was shot and just tryin' to get away from there. 'Way from "Wyatt Earp."'

'You got an answer for everything.'

A coroner's assistant showed up and naturally addressed Owen, older and male. 'Can we take him now, Sergeant? He's getting wet and a little bit ripe. Pretty soon he'll start to sprout.'

'He's yours.' He turned to me. 'I figured it'd be better for you to see him here.'

'More like my ass would be grass if I didn't. Thanks, Owen.'

'We tried to beep you.'

I seemed to remember it going off in the course of the evening, but at that particular point God could have put in a personal appearance and I wouldn't have noticed. The remembrance brought the old glow to the ears again. More like leaping flames. 'I know,' was as much admission as I could manage.

We watched them haul the body on to a gurney. Heavy going. I think we both wondered what the other was thinking, which would never have been true on any

278

normal case. Normally you talked them to death. 'There goes another witness,' Owen observed, and it just surprised the hell out of me, because that's what I *was* thinking.

'Where'd she say she was going at this hour?'

'Miami. See Dunn.' He knew he had my attention. 'Wouldn't say why. 'Course she'll have to.'

'Could be because she knew he was the only person down this way who wouldn't contradict her.'

Owen got out his notebook and jotted down some things, making me wait, making me think. 'And may be she *was* goin' to see him.'

SEAN

I didn't sleep much but evidently Ms Robertson had less on her conscience; you would have had to have taken her pulse to know for sure she was still among us. Spoke well for exercise. That reminded me and I padded naked into the bathroom to examine my bruises. She hadn't looked *that* strong. I rationalized that my generation was the last to have a built-in reticence about harming women.

I dressed quickly and quietly and stole into the living room. It's one of my skills. Whereas the bedroom had been kept in darkness, out here the early-morning sun stormed in through blinds with a painful brilliance that brought home how little sleep I'd had.

I didn't know what I was looking for but a desk is always a good place to start. Fortunately, Annie was a neat freak of the first rank. Bank statements for the last year were bound with a rubber band in the lower right-hand drawer. I examined these for the previous three months but nothing stood out except the fact that she had written checks for a considerable sum of money. The real-estate business in South Florida must have improved when I wasn't looking.

The checks themselves, along with receipts and bills, were piled beside the statements and reflected her interest in matters of health – payments to a gym, incredible amounts spent at health-food emporiums, on exercise equipment, workout clothes and videos. No wonder she'd taken me three falls out of five. I got the idea that she might be starting a small business of her own, maybe producing one of those exercise videos herself. She would likely want to keep that a secret from her present employers, and it would go towards explaining the large expenditures.

There were also checks to individuals that I deduced to be family members – round sums like five hundred dollars are usually gifts or support. A streak of charity in our Annie. I scanned the phone bills without finding a single call to James, at least not at home or office. You had to assume the Department had been all over these anyway. There were a couple of amorous notes from Chapelle – he hadn't signed them but I recognized the handwriting – which didn't tell us anything we didn't already know.

There was only one anomaly, a receipt from a saloon in Homestead called the Six Counties Bar & Grille for a hundred-and-twenty-dollar tab. First the name struck me. What 'six counties'? Monroe, Dade, Broward . . .? It wasn't until I was long gone that it came to me. But it was also itemized and included fifteen dollars for cigarettes; not exactly Annie's taste, I thought. And the place itself, Homestead, is a long way south, basically blue-collar, military and elderly retired, folks who watch American Gladiators in their trailers by the light of a six-pack and forty-watt bulb. I thought it was probably just another loser relative but when I couldn't find a check to match it, meaning she had paid cash, I decided to take it with me.

Finally, in another drawer, I found her birth and baptismal certificates and marriage license. People usually keep those in safety deposit boxes. I jotted down the details and closed the drawers gently, disappointed, wishing for more.

I had no luck until I made the decision to give it up; that somehow made it possible to see more clearly. Standing in the center of the room in my bare feet, holding my shoes in my hand, I saw what I had gone past a dozen times in the last few minutes. There was a dark stain on the pale, flowered armrest of an easy chair. It was blood, and from its position I could pretty well guess who had left it there.

My hostess caught me in a particularly undignified and compromising position, on my hands and knees sniffing at the stain on the armrest. 'Going to piss on it?' she asked me in a voice that could have freezed mercury. I turned slowly, trying to think how I might scam the situation. Herself had a Mauser .380 automatic in hand and pointed, I had to hope symbolically, at my crotch. She was naked under a large terrycloth robe. I couldn't help thinking that the last time I'd seen that it hadn't turned out very well.

I settled back on my haunches; giving her the high ground seemed like a good idea. 'Good morning.'

'What the hell are you doing?'

I indicated the chair arm. 'That's blood.'

'Is it?'

'Right about where a man would rest his hand if he was dead tired. And had lost a finger.'

When she put the gun in the pocket of her robe I noticed that the safety had been on all the time. Just a show. She slumped down on to a couch, looking several years older and at least as tired as I felt. Her voice dropped with her. 'The kidnappers, or at least one of them, let him loose somewhere in Miami and he took a cab up here, which I paid for.'

'Why would he do that?'

'I don't know.' She looked as if she didn't, or didn't accept his explanation anyway. 'He said he'd had a lot of time when he was a prisoner to think about how he'd screwed up his life. I guess that meant with his wife or me or vice versa. I don't know.'

'Going to clean up his act?'

She shrugged.

I thought a dose of vitriol might help things along. 'Didn't last long. He's already doing his number on that sheriff's officer, Bodo.'

I thought I saw two little flares go off somewhere behind the pupils, but it was hard to know what it meant. 'No skin off my wherever.'

Penance done, I got up and sat in the chair with the bloodstain. Maybe some mystical waves would come off it and inform me of a solution. 'A guy who's been kidnapped, bound, blindfolded, beaten, had his finger cut off, comes to his girlfriend's house in the middle of the night after he's released from captivity to tell her the romance is over.'

I was wrong about the smoking; she took a nondescript little package out of her pocket, took one out and lit up. It took me a second to realize it was a joint. I'd never known anyone do this at that hour, unless they hadn't gone to bed, but it was none of my business. 'You know Jim,' she said, sounding lazy after only one hit, which had to be the placebo effect. 'Love comes first in everything. What can I tell you?'

'So you fixed him up and drove him to West Palm where he got another cab.' I started putting on my shoes.

'He was in real bad shape when he came in.' Her voice thickened and I thought she was going to cry. 'It broke my heart.' After a long pause she said in a whisper, 'I still love him.'

Why argue? I stood up. 'Forget him. Like they say in Hawaii, "You bettah off."' I headed for the door and patted her shoulder on the way past. Pretty much the way you'd pat a collie, I admit, but it was all I had.

Behind me, she said, 'I get the feeling this was strictly a professional fuck. Am I right?'

I had to stop. 'As long as my cover's blown, let me ask

you another question. How well did you know Amelia Chapelle?'

'I told you, I didn't know any of those jerks very well, except they were around.'

'Was she around?'

'With the Chapelle bunch, sure.'

'Did she get on with Sylvia?'

'I heard somewhere they traveled to Europe together.'

'Ireland.'

'Was that it? Well, they are related.'

'Would that be the reason?'

'How the hell do I know? Maybe they dug each other. You're asking the wrong person.'

I didn't think so. Trying to look regretful, I said, 'Sorry about, you know . . .'

'Hey, where's the surprise? You're all bastards.'

'We are.'

I got out of there, finally. I had a busy day ahead. So did Annie; she just didn't know it.

I went over to the Boca Raton Hotel, a huge old, coral-pink, Mizner Palaci overlooking the coast, for an elaborate breakfast. There was time to waste and I felt deserving (sorry for myself), plus it was not a meal I had normally so I thought, why not indulge myself? I could hear the boss: 'Now you're sticking us for breakfasts – since when did you get up that early?'

The way I looked they almost didn't let me in; a swollen lip for one thing. That woman was out of control. The hotel was a good choice, though, quiet at that hour and time of the year when I had thinking to do. One thing came out of it, no small thing; I remembered a song that explained the name of the bar in Homestead.

Afterwards, meaning I had gone through the entire morning paper, every box score, even looked for a movie to see if this was ever over, I had to head back up to West

Palm to reclaim the Jeep. I shouldn't have. I should have kept the rental another day.

Time was no problem, because what I needed then could only be supplied by people finally settled behind their desks and resigned to a day's work. Also, I wanted to check some birth records at the Hall.

Headed south again, I got on the phone and called the office in Miami. What we presumptuously called 'The Research Bureau' was really one young man. Fortunately, he had the illusions of youth, mainly that enthusiasm will make right an imperfect world.

'Listen, François, very big voodoo. You are the most important cat in *tout le monde* to me this morning.' He was this hip Haitian and seemed to love that kind of trash. 'The address of a woman in Fort Lauderdale named "Bodo."'

A true bureaucrat, he wanted her first name. 'François, how many "Bodos" could there be in Fort Lauderdale? In the world? I also need a photo of a woman named Annie Robertson. Lives in Coral Gables. Works in real estate. Her husband went up on a Boesky a couple of years ago in Palm Beach. That should help.'

When I paused for breath he dropped the bomb about Sylvia and the mick, and I cursed a lot for a lot of reasons, and heard him snicker. How did I get out of the loop so soon? It seemed that somebody in the New York office had heard it from Duchow, who was up there and had received a call in his hotel room in the wee hours from a distraught James. Of course, it was on local radio already, but I was listening to a Charlie Parker tape.

'Okay, a picture of this Loftus guy, too. The corpse, if that's all that's available. But I need it yesterday.' He said that's when I would have it, and the man was as good as his word. Of course, I had to go on down to the office in Miami to pick up these things, so it was afternoon by the time I got back to Fort Lauderdale.

It was a splendid day, coolish, possibly because of a major

storm building off the Antilles, so I had the top off to the sun, onshore wind and salt air as I went along the coast. I licked my lips and tasted the sea. The cumulus clouds that appeared to race along with me were miles out and white as swans, but when they bank that high, move that fast and follow that particular course it promises something ominous. It was only right.

Maria 'Mimi' Bodo lived in an ancient bungalow that would have been peeling had not the 'tin men' been along, peddling their tacky aluminum siding to a weak-willed owner. Imagine selling that stuff in the tropics. As it was, the house looked more like an equipment shed surrounded by a useless brown skirt of lawn. A number of asphalt shingles lay where they had fallen to the ground. I went up on the porch and knocked. There was a broken straw chair tipped against the wall. I suspected that was to prevent its befogged owner from unwittingly sitting on it.

The woman who opened the door I knew to be only fiftyish; she looked sixty-plus and hard-used at that. Slatternly in a stained robe and mules, she had thinning hennaed hair and a TV remote in her hand. Already she didn't like me.

'My name's Sean Dunn, Mrs Bodo. I need to talk to you.' I sought Frankie in that hard face without success. I was grateful.

She reared back with this false hauteur, as if she could look at me down her long, pale nose. But I was taller and it was quite a bend. 'I don't know who you are, but I sure as shit know what.'

She waited for me to fill in the blanks. The porous screen door wouldn't have kept out a mosquito much less the boozy effluence of her breath.

'I seen enough of 'em,' she said when I didn't respond. 'I was married to one of 'em.'

'I'm an *ex*-cop, Mrs Bodo, if that helps. And a friend of Frankie's.' I knew it was a gamble, but I threw it out there.

'More than I can say. I ain't seen her in over a year. Calls me sometimes, but it kills her.' She took her time, since I was the one who wanted something, and looked me over again. 'Okay, come on in. Maybe you'll break my monotony.'

I followed her in, repressing the inclination to hold my nose.

'Any money in this?' she asked without hope. I didn't dignify it with an answer.

In terms of cleanliness and order, the living room could have passed for a Hell's Angels' clubhouse. I like cats, or I don't mind them, but here was that awful odor that emanates from the homes of cat-ladies when they get old or indifferent. Abattoirs smell better. But I wasn't so much interested in the physical disarray as the psychic dissolution and when it had begun. I suspected a long time before. A long time.

'How well do you know Frankie?'

'A lot better than I did a few minutes ago.'

I'm not sure if I 'broke her monotony,' but we talked and after a while she came right out and told me what I wanted to know, or better, had to know. I'm not a social worker. I left while she was still talking and headed south again. That highway would get one hell of a workout before the day was over.

I continued on US 1 right through Miami and all the way down to Homestead. There was still damage from the hurricane of '92 apparent but the Six Counties Bar & Grille had probably always looked like that. From the West Side of New York to a cantina in Heroica Nogales there was a certain kind of saloon that was an artifact of the marginal world. This one was painted kelly green – or had been.

There was nothing particularly Gaelic about the interior; the decor was more like Youngstown 1955. The aroma of Jameson's and Harp is no different than Old Crow and Pabst when it's stale on a Formica bar. It did have an old-fashioned jukebox with an eccentric selection, everything from Bon Jovi to the Clancy Brothers and, of course, a lot of country. For some reason otherwise perfectly civilized people in those isles love that country crap.

I made my choice to make a point . . .

> . . . Death to every foe and traitor
> Forward strike the marching tune . . .

. . . and strolled over to the bar to be confronted by its tender, a large, sullen Celt with three days' growth of beard and a potato for a nose.

'People actually play those rebel songs?'

'You just did.'

'I'm peculiar.'

'The old fellas mostly. There's some get a real hard-on from it. Young ones don't give a shit. What do you want?'

'Harp.'

I settled on to a stool that turned out to be a little sticky, so I moved over. He didn't offer them but by reaching down the bar I corraled the beer nuts. I gathered I was being treated like a potential secret service agent, which might have made sense in Boston or New York or even San Francisco, where the IRA gunrunners and philanthropic Irish-Americans used to meet – and maybe they still do, I don't know – usually under some kind of dissemblance like 'aid to prisoners' families.' Or maybe he just thought I was a cop; Mimi Bodo had.

While I was waiting for the beer I made a 'sunny face' in the damp on the bar. Then under it I wrote 'Fuck you!' When finally he returned with a dirty glass I drank from the bottle. He gave no sign of having noticed my message and started to move away . . .

'I've lived in Miami for years and I never knew there were enough paddies down here to support a pub.'

'You ain't in Miami.'

'I'll be goddamned! That's why.'

He gave me a surly look. 'How'd you hear about us?'

'I found this.' I showed him the receipt. 'It reminded me of a song when I was a kid.'

'Congratulations.'

'"Six counties under John Bull's tyranny . . ."' I sang. Badly. 'The six counties of the North, right?'

He leaned over the bar at me, forcing me to pull back or fight. 'What do you want?'

I glanced around. There were only two other customers, old guys, afternoon boozers who wouldn't look up if Christ came back through the roof. 'Take it easy, pal, I'm not the feds. Not even local law. And to tell you the truth, I don't give a flying fuck about the "cause" either, okay? Not one way or the other. I do have a couple of pictures.' I took the two the company had obtained for me out of my pocket and placed them on the bar like an offering.

He didn't show any interest, but then I didn't expect him to. 'Naturally,' I told him in my super-reasonable voice, 'I wouldn't expect you to go to all the trouble of bending over the bar and straining your eyes without some compensation.' I laid a few twenties atop the photos; I didn't know how much and didn't care.

He glanced at the pictures indifferently, said nothing. I wasn't sure what to think; in my world no one ever turns down a bribe. What I did know was that if he reached for the twenties without talking we'd both be rolling on the floor. Another good reason to order beer in joints like this; you always have the bottle. The special worry with bartenders is they're apt to have a piece under there and then you have to shoot the bastard, hitting the fan in all directions.

I pushed forward the mugshot of Loftus obtained only

a couple of hours ago by fax from New York. 'Never seen him before.'

Okay. I unfolded a reproduction of a newspaper article, exposing a photograph of Annie as she appeared outside the courtroom on the occasion of her husband's conviction. She was not crying. 'How about her?'

He shoved it all back at me. 'Never seen 'em. Finish your beer and get lost.'

He turned away and went to the end of the bar where he sat and opened the day's *Herald*. Fortunately, I'm a peaceable man. You start duking it with every jerk you meet in this life and you could seriously hurt your embouchure. Still, I was sitting there thinking about how much I'd like to pop the sonofabitch and all the reasons I shouldn't when my eyes fell on a particular poster on the wall.

It was peeling, faded like everything in here, and as there were several travel posters in similar shape, all plugging some harp-hustler who claimed he could get you to the Ring of Kerry and back for a dollar and a half, I hadn't noticed it or its possibilities. The date was March and that seemed about right for the scenario I was suddenly putting together in my mind.

'Hey!' I called down the bar to my friend, pointing at the wall. 'Your bar have anything to do with that "Irish Faire"?' He just looked and then went back to his paper. So I added, 'Asshole.' That got him up snorting.

Time to play my ace. I whipped out the old ID, counting on gloom, distance and intimidation to obfuscate the reality. More like last resort than 'ace.' I shoved it up there where his rhino face would have run right smack into it if he had kept coming. After all, what else is being a cop but having attitude, heft? All he saw was the shield, anyway, and he stopped. 'Yeah, we had a booth. So what?'

I had quite a lot of beer left; I emptied it on the bar

and went out. Sometimes I'm vindictive. I find it saves doctors' bills.

The poster had had a number to call for ticket information. I used that for my starting point. Also the address of the equestrian center where it had been held, but it wasn't necessary to go all the way out there. By late afternoon I had the address of the woman who had chaired the committee, near the university in Coral Gables, of all places.

It was one of those sticky little 'shoppes' with the English china, mugs, figurines of this or that idiot prince on this or that centennial. Mementoes of all kinds of obscure royal occasions around the former empire, canned bangers, assorted teas. I like Brits; I hate kitsch. There was even a tinkly bell when I went in.

'Mrs Brown?' And she was, too – brown dress, brown hair, brown eyes . . . brown soul? She was about fifty, to be kind, a little frumpy with tight hair and no makeup. I was tempted to address her as 'Mum.' But she was a fake.

'Can I help you?' she asked in imitation of Elizabeth Regina.

'You were the chairwoman of the last Irish Faire Committee? In March, down near Homestead?'

'Richmond Heights, yes.' She looked around, I thought, nervously. 'Uh . . . who are you?'

I showed her my real ID.

'Oh. You're like a private detective?'

'Nothing that glamorous, ma'am. I work for a security agency. Mostly industrial espionage – is the boss's nephew hitting the petty-change drawer, that sort of thing.' No need to mention that we provided protection for embassies and missile silos around the world; better to keep it humble.

'I see you're also Irish.' That seemed to cheer her.

'If it helps. I'm here on a missing persons case.'

Mrs Brown's English accent was suddenly exchanged for a less deliberate, more assimilated Irish one. 'Tell the truth, the name's Shaughnessy. But there's more Brits than Irish in these parts by a long ways. 'Sides which, the Irish don't buy anythin' anyways. So I converted, you might say, for professional expediency.' She added, laying it on, 'Still a Galway lass at heart, though.'

I'd had enough distraction for one day, and enough stage Irish in my life. I trotted out the photos. 'I imagine it takes a lot of volunteers to run a fair like that?'

Mrs Brown was proud of what she'd accomplished. 'Oh, yes. Two hundred or so altogether, aside from the paid employees, caterers and so on. But we had thirty-nine thousand paying visitors. That doesn't include the comps.'

'Did you see this man?'

She began shaking her head before she looked. 'Oh, I don't know. There's so many and it's over so quickly.'

'He was born in New York but he's probably spent time in the Old Country because he's got a slight accent.'

She put her finger on the photograph of Loftus, which was obviously a mugshot although I'd taken care to crop it. In my experience, they only touch it when they recognize it. 'No . . . no, I can't say I do.'

I waited, letting her absorb the implications of her own actions. 'Mrs Shaughnessy. I lied. I'm sure you recognize in me a man who lies a lot. After all, we're both micks. The man I showed you is dead, and a good thing. He was a killer. So it's not a "missing persons" case, is it?'

'No,' she said weakly, struggling to maintain eye contact. I indicated some white iron chairs and tables in the corner where tea and scones were served. 'Would you like to sit down?'

'No. No, I'm fine.' She didn't sound it.

Okay. 'Now are you here on a Green Card or what? 'Cause push comes to shove, you'll deliver him.'

'I believe he may have worked the "hospital fund" booth. But I'm not sure.'

'You mean the IRA booth.'

'Absolutely not!' She put one foot down, not quite a stomp.

'All right, that's not what I'm here about. This man' – I tapped the photo – 'we both know him, don't we? And I think you probably know her too.' I showed her Annie.

Mrs Brown surrendered with an exhalation. 'They met during the fair. Lots of young people do. We don't see anything wrong with it. There's few enough places for the young people these days. But I haven't seen either of them since. Am I goin' to have trouble over this?'

'Not if you do one more thing. Call Mrs Robertson and warn her that I was here asking a lot of questions about her and the dead man. His last known's "Loftus," by the way.'

However peculiar that may have sounded to her, it didn't take her long to make the decision. 'Now?'

'I'll be listening.'

'And then I won't be involved any more?'

'You've got a better chance of that this way.'

She knew it. I always wondered what else she was involved in. Over the years I've come to think that almost everyone has something.

XVIII

FRANKIE

By midday we had an address for Loftus, or 'location' might be more accurate. It was out in the boonies, the fringe of the Everglades actually, not far from the Tamiami Trail that bisects them coming out of Miami where it starts as 'Calle Ocho,' the locus of the Cuban exile community. A cabin with a caved-in roof, buried in sawgrass, a rusted-out minimal percentage of a pickup in front, it looked truly abandoned. By the time Owen and I got there the Dade County Sheriff's Department was all over the place. We said hello and went in.

The interior was about as charming as the exterior. The decor was the 'siege look.' You had to wade in through milk cartons, beer cans, McDonald's wrappers, dirty plates, well-thumbed magazines full of nudie-cuties, some with obscene drawings imposed on the bodies, and even a broken TV set. A family of baboons could have hung out here; all it lacked was shit on the floor. Sometimes you're inclined to think that crime really doesn't pay. We put on our gloves and poked warily through this for about half an hour.

'If Loftus had ever been IRA, don't you think we'd find at least something political?'

'The man talked the talk but he didn't walk the walk. Just another run-a-the-mill high-steppin' low-life jive-ass muscle-head.'

'With an accent.'

'I got all that on my way over. Just come in. He was born in New York, all right, but he grew up over there. Might have done some political stuff but mostly he used it to impress the ladies. Whose companionship he seems to have spent most of his life in pursuit of.'

I wasn't sure why but that interested me. 'Do we have any names on the girlfriends?'

He shook his head while extracting a pair of men's shorts from the mess and throwing them into the corner. 'He did run with the Westies in New York when he was young. They were real violent.'

'I read where their big thing was kidnapping Mafia guys. They even snatched Carlo Gambino's son.'

'Well, this whole thing wasn't carried out by no genius, honey. Just dumb-butt brutal.'

I was starting to lose interest in the refuse. Like Dunn, I knew we were close and in the end it wouldn't be about hairpins or shell casings. 'Letting Chapelle go after somebody wanted him killed, that's the part I can't finesse.'

'Don't you think folks who were dumb enough to kidnap Gambino's son would be capable of trustin' in a millionaire's word?'

I laughed, and regretted that Jim wasn't there to join in. I would have to tell him.

An officer stuck his head in the door. 'Sergeant Bodo. A Sean Dunn's trying to get hold of you.'

'Thanks,' I said, and then aloud to myself, 'Fuck him!'

We headed out. Dade people are very efficient and we'd get a report on every mite and mote before the week was over. Eventually they did find evidence that Chapelle had been held there. By then it didn't matter.

'My one daughter talks like you and she had a good Christian upbringing.'

All the way to the car I bitched about how ridiculous it was that a hoodlum this primitive could set half of South Florida on its ear.

'Just a monkey on a string,' he reminded me. 'Even Dunn agrees with that now.'

'He always knew. That's just his bullshit way of being contrary. I never said he was stupid. Especially about people.'

Our respective cars were side by side. We stopped and stood there in the ooze for a minute, each with our own thoughts about the case.

'He might have somethin', you know.'

'Who?'

'Dunn. He's tryin' to reach you, remember.'

'Oh, yeah. Hey, Owen . . . did it ever occur to you he's Irish too?'

He didn't say anything, just got into his car and drove away. I stayed there in kind of a trance, staring out at the Everglades. I've read books and seen movies about them. I love them; the real Florida.

There's some good old boys out on the trail always want to give me free rides on their airboat. That's where I saw a rare panther, one of the most beautiful sights ever. Standing out on the flat water among the sawgrass, watching us without fear, very proud and terribly alone.

A lot of people just see the 'Glades as empty, endless and gray, but I've got this side to me I never show that's very romantic about such things. If I did, people would only shit on it, the kind I hang out with. Or Dunn, he'd want to make me a soul sister or something, sensitize me till I puke.

I'm rambling, but that was my mood then. All I know is, standing there leaning on my car, I wanted so much just to walk out into it and keep going to heaven or hell or wherever it took me. I don't know if I ever had a stronger urge in my life. I should have listened to it.

Two hours later I was in the Au Bar in Palm Beach with Jim. I was still dressed for work with mud on my shoes, although I'd made a pathetic attempt to shape up. I was finding out, if I didn't know already, that this having an affair, especially with a married man involved in the case, made for a hell of a busy life. Of course, he was dressed beautifully and so breathtakingly handsome he made my heart stagger. It was intimidating. I suddenly realized I had the walkie-talkie up on the table, like I would in any burger palace. I grabbed it and put it on the floor.

'A first for this bar.'

'That's all it is, just a bar.'

'Sorry, I'm having trouble changing worlds.'

'Would you quit apologizing. We wouldn't be here, in this world, if I knew any other. Maybe you can show me. In the meantime, don't make so much out of it.' He implored me to believe. 'You're a lot tougher and smarter than most of the people in this bar.'

'I just don't want to draw attention to you, is all. Embarrass you.'

'I thought by now you'd know me better. Nothing you do offends me, embarrasses me, makes me want to do anything except draw you closer.' And he did . . . reach over and put his arm around my shoulders, draw me closer. 'Besides,' he said, grinning, 'it's very sexy being with a woman who's carrying a gun.'

Sometimes even the foxiest guy says something that's death. 'It's not like you haven't had the experience before,' I pointed out.

'What do you mean?'

'I saw your wife's handiwork last night. She's a lot better with these things than I am. If that's what you want in a woman, you got it.' He looked at me blankly for a minute. I said, 'Sorry. Bitchy. I'm apologizing again, aren't I?'

He seemed to come out of his confusion. 'Oh. Well, it's a damned good thing she can use one, or she'd have gone the way I did. Only a lot worse for a good-looking woman. They were really brutal.' He glanced at his glove.

'I was joking. I meant it worried me how good a shot

she was. You know, after the look she gave me when I brought you home. I've seen that look.'

He dismissed it with a wave. 'You have nothing to worry about, believe me. We haven't had a real marriage for years. She was just scared, and we are friends. Naturally I had to go to her. You wouldn't like me if I was the kind of man who didn't. Didn't care about people's feelings when they were hurting. Even wives who aren't actually wives any more.'

'Spare me.'

'What?'

'Don't start. "My wife and I don't get along. We sleep in separate rooms. I don't think it'll last much longer," and . . . you know. I can get that from a car salesman. And I probably have. But I didn't respect them, and I do you. So let's both just be honest with each other, okay?' I found myself starting to choke up and fought it back. I hated women who did that.

His voice became very gentle in a way I was beginning to know, and like too well. I thought later it was like hypnotism. 'Boy, you have been badly used, haven't you?'

'No!' I said too loudly. 'Every stupid move I ever made, I made it. Nobody else ever made me do anything. I'm responsible. The way I'm responsible for this.' I was sounding awfully tough, and inside jelly was bubbling.

Taking my hand, he ran his lips across it. 'You don't have to demand my respect, Frankie. You have it.' He rubbed against my cheek, nuzzling me behind my ear. 'I give you my word, whatever that's worth, however hokey it sounds, everything I told you about Sylvia and me is dead-on true. But . . .' He kissed the back of my neck. '. . . you don't have to believe it. That's not a requirement.'

'Jesus,' I said, still sounding sulky in spite of what he was doing. 'You don't require anything.'

'Not from you. You'll never be hurt by me, darling.'

A waiter appeared, and it was just as well he did or

I might have started crying or yelling or falling in love or I don't know what. 'A phone call for the young lady, Mr Chapelle.' Jim indicated that he should put it on the table.

'More proof that I'm not sneaking around.'

'But I am. Nobody knows I'm here. Nobody. And if they did, I have a beeper.' My life was so charged at the time everything that happened seemed ominous, or wonderful.

'Bodo . . . How the hell did you find me? . . . You serious?' It was Dunn with the news of what he'd discovered. It gave me this jolt of energy and everything else flew out of my mind. I wouldn't be surprised if when I left they didn't have to mop up a puddle of adrenalin under my seat. I started grabbing up my things the second I hung up.

It was Jim's turn to be alarmed. 'What is it? What's happened?'

'You know it was your brother the one told Dunn you were here with me? How can you even talk to him when they're trying to screw you out of your company?' I didn't really care about that now; I was just excited and trying to get him off the subject of what Dunn knew.

He shrugged off his brother, as he must have on a thousand other occasions. 'It doesn't mean we stop being civilized with each other.'

'You have no idea how weird that sounds to people like me.'

'The phone call,' he reminded me.

'Sorry,' was all I felt I could tell him.

'Frankie, I planned an evening. What is it you can't tell me? I thought now— '

'Duty calls, sweetheart. This is what my life is like. Catch you later.' And I was out of there. I hadn't even touched my martini and as I went out the door I looked back and saw him reach for it. Maybe it was time to tell him I was a beer person?

Unfortunately Dunn was down in Miami again but he agreed to meet me halfway. I guess we could have phoned and faxed but this was too important. We met near Lighthouse Point between Boca Raton and Pompano Beach, a tacky little waterside open-air restaurant that would have been overrun with partying kids during the season or on a weekend. I got to have my beer; you'd look strange drinking anything else there.

'Did she really like this gorilla, I don't know, but no sooner did they meet at the fair than they're doin' the old in-and-out.'

'She knew what she was looking for. It's circumstantial at this point, but it's a helluva start, Sean.'

'I don't think you ever called me that before.'

'What?'

'"Sean."'

'What are you making something out of that for?'

He refused to fight; he was too pleased with himself. 'Here, I got a look at her birth certificate.' He passed me some notes. 'Born thirty-six years ago, Annie – that's her given name, not "Anne" – Annie Mae Blair in Catonsville, Maryland. You might want to check her out before she married Robertson. Maybe she was Ma Barker in another life.'

I just had to bust his bubble. 'Madame Chapelle says she was on her way down to your place when Loftus caught up with her. You want to explain that?'

'Why don't you ask her?'

'Owen did. She refused to say why. I can't come at her again without something else.'

'She wasn't. She didn't call, and if she had I wouldn't have been home.'

'Maybe she was just going to drop in.'

'It's a long way to go for that. Anyway, she wouldn't know how to find it.'

'Bullshit.' He just shook his head and looked disgusted, so we dropped it.

I asked to see the newspaper photograph of Ms Robertson again. Something about it was singing my song, and it was driving me crazy that I couldn't hear the lyrics. Something Sean had just said. I looked away, and tried to recall it. 'Annie Mae Blair,' I murmured to myself.

Sean sat and watched me like a Buddha. Any normal person would at least have asked me what I was at. Not that it would have done him any good. I told him I'd get back to him and left abruptly. He didn't ask me about that, either.

Soon as I got back on the highway I called Owen at the station. It was now seven o'clock and he was headed out to attend his daughter's birthday party.

'I don't care if there are crates full, I want them all. Just leave them on my desk.'

'Honey, I can't let you do all that by yourself. I'll hang around. Just tell me what you're looking for.'

I should explain. Palm Beach may not look like the South but under the skin it is, and we do not consider an endearment from a male over forty, and especially a gentleman such as Owen, to be an assault. Is that clear?

Anyway, I told him not a chance. 'I just wish I could be there. Kiss her for me, present to follow.'

He was right. There were reams of transcripts, telephone intercepts of calls coming into the Chapelle residence. Boxes, crates. Guys were still going home when I got back and stopped to ask what it was all about and was I writing a cop novel and all that. Eventually it got down to just me, the mountain of paper, an anchovy pizza and a fast-disappearing pot of coffee. On top of my excitement I was riding a caffeine high. Jim was no doubt in some elegant restaurant eating something with kiwis on it, but I didn't miss it.

Now that I was practically alone I put on my seldom-seen or used reading glasses. As the hours went by my eyes got so tired I went to the drinking fountain with a cup and

poured water into them, spilling it all over my clothes.
Since it was a particularly humid, hot night, it felt good.
I hadn't been paying attention to what was going on in the
outside world, but one of the guys said when he left that
there was a big storm coming in. I told him, 'You don't
know the half of it.'

At about ten-thirty I found what I was looking for, hoping
for, praying for. 'Hi, this is Blair. Guess who just came to
see me . . .' At the time I couldn't imagine why we hadn't
discovered it on her telephone billings. Later we found the
call had been placed on a cellular phone listed to a small
company she was forming under her maiden name.

I sat back, rubbing my eyes. Someone had turned off
the air-conditioner, no doubt a cost-saving measure, and I
hadn't noticed. I had some water left in the cup and poured
it over my head, assuming I wouldn't be seeing anyone else
that night. It was very quiet except for some wind outside.
I even turned off my computer so I wouldn't have to listen
to it hum. It would have been nice just to have enjoyed
a few minutes of idle self-congratulation, but the phone
rang. My phone.

Sean was sitting outside Annie's apartment, out of her
view, he said, but where he could see in with binoculars. He
kept calling her on his cellular and refusing to speak. When
she let the machine pick it up he kept calling anyway, until
she ran out of tape. It sounds childish but, given a certain
temperament and given that it's arrived at a certain point,
it can be effective. Creates a siege mentality. It was the
kind of thing he could do and we couldn't.

'Man, has that woman got a filthy mouth. It's wonderful
to listen to. She's on the edge, that's for sure.'

'She knows it's you?'

'She keeps asking if it is, but sometimes there's some
doubt. When Mrs Brown called her I just had her say that
a "man" had been in asking questions. But she does have
reason to think I'm on her case.'

'What's that?'

'Oh, I stopped by last night and got a little tough with her. That's when I picked up the bar bill.'

I heard a lie in there somewhere. The kind men tell women. 'How did she act?'

Something obviously distracted him. 'Uh . . . with warmth and charm. Wait a minute!' You could hear the excitement building in his voice and it suddenly reminded me of when I was a uniform and the calls would come in over your car radio on a Saturday night. Say, a rookie saw shots being fired. You could feel your own excitement soar and you'd take off. It might turn out to be something horrible, something you couldn't get out of your mind for weeks, yet at the moment it was thrilling. I got that same sense out of Sean's voice that night, and of course I was right.

'What is it?'

'She's spooked. She's running.'

I could hear the Jeep start up fast, the engine rumbling, then his tires as he took off. 'How do you know?' I yelled, sitting up on the edge of my own seat. You always yell when somebody's in pursuit.

'She called somebody— '

I shouted over him, 'How do you know that? You didn't bug it, for Christ's sake?' I closed my eyes and could see the whole thing blowing up on the inside of the lids. I was ready to start screaming about tainted evidence when he broke back in on me . . .

'I could see her through the living-room window when she started dialing. She was agitated, you could tell from body language, and whoever was on the other end didn't give in easy, either. But as soon as she hung up she was moving. I waited to see her car and it came out of the garage like it was leaving Canaveral.'

'Where are you now?'

'Headed north on 1. She drives like she swears. I'm doing seventy-five with one hand here.'

What with the wind whistling past that damn open Jeep and the usual static, it was getting impossible to hear. 'Do you know who she's going to?'

'No.'

I wasn't sure I believed that, but it no longer mattered. 'I might. Can you stay on her with that Jeep?'

'I don't think she's ever seen it.' I could imagine him looking when he said, 'Moon's under right now. Always traffic on 1, even at this hour. But mainly I'm counting on distraction. She's ballistic at this point.'

He was starting to break up. 'Stay with her. I'm coming out.'

For once he didn't give me an argument. We checked car phone numbers and then I actually ran down to my car. The cleaning woman looked scared.

I went south at sixty so we were converging at a hundred and thirty-five. It was hard raising Sean, but fortunately I got to him at the very last minute, when he reported she was turning off on the waterside at a point north of Delray Beach where they've got those little towns with names like 'Briny Breezes.'

I said it was a good thing we connected because you wouldn't want to turn in there right after her. No telling when the person she was meeting, assuming she wasn't going to drown herself or commune with the sea, would arrive. So Sean and I met up the road a ways at a Texaco station where we had a nervous Coke together, then eased back down the highway, looking for another exit that would get us to the same beach. This was a lot trickier than staking out an apartment or car lot. It was after eleven-thirty; the beaches were deserted. I wished I'd called Owen or even a superior officer, but that lasted about five seconds, and then it was my case, goddammit, and my bust and there hadn't been time anyway.

SEAN

The beach was separated from a little access road by a narrow elongated copse of wind-twisted dwarf pines. Because they were close to the ground and their shapes meandered they proved good cover. We actually left our cars on the shoulder of the highway and walked down.

It was a strange night – warm, sticky, yet a little windy, too. The wind at the upper levels was obviously very strong as the clouds raced along like something was chasing them, and I guess it was. But, temperature aside, nights like that can place your heart inside a cold, tight fist. The sea was big and felt like it was reaching out to pull you in. At the same time the clothes were fastened to your body. I don't know if Frankie felt it too; we didn't say much.

There was another car parked way down the beach but so distant it was impossible to make out what it was without going down there. The moon would pop in and out occasionally, very large and by that adding to the drama being played out in the sky. We lay at the top of the beach among the pines with a good view in both directions.

A couple of times we saw someone on the sand. Two people to the north of us. Of course, going down to the beach late at night to watch the comings and goings of storms is an old Florida custom with lovers. Makes the juices run.

We were just about ready to scuttle along towards the figures when it became apparent they were moving our way, so we sank back. Everything we had was circumstantial and not worth jackshit in court, we knew that. But circumstantial evidence displayed before even the intelligent guilty can appear devastating and lead to a lot of passion and things being said that lead to other things, and sometimes even a confession.

Unfortunately, juries are so spoiled by TV they expect the smoking gun on videotape and I didn't anticipate we'd be able to deliver that. What we were counting on was scaling and then pulling down someone's wall of defenses. I've worked with less and won.

As they drew closer we could see that both were women. They moved along the surf line just out of the water's reach, but it was no idyllic nature stroll. I think they were just trying to get as far away from other humans as the sea would allow. They were in earnest, almost violent, conversation. Coming very close to us, they stopped, but the moon was absent again and it still wasn't possible to see them clearly. A dark mist created by the lunging waves wiped out even their silhouettes. I felt Frankie reach over and touch my hand but I wasn't sure what the message was. We both clutched flashlights in the other.

Suddenly, the one with short hair, wearing pants and a jacket, stopped them. She grabbed the other and aggressively kissed her on the mouth. The second woman fought, relaxed, surrendered. Light or no light, there was no doubt it was fiercely erotic. I didn't look at Frankie. They fell into an embrace. That's when she hit them with her powerful beam, and I followed with less enthusiasm, I suspect. Sylvia and Annie turned away momentarily, shielding their eyes and cursing.

Annie yelled, 'Turn that fucking thing off!' I think she knew, they both knew, that whoever we were behind that stabbing glare, we were the end of things. Sylvia recovered quickly and smiled up at me. I could imagine her as a little girl, caught out doing something horrendous and using that same smile to devastating effect.

'Aren't you clever,' she said to me, wisely ignoring Frankie. Also letting me know she was counting on me.

As we walked down to them I noticed that Frankie had her jacket open so she could get to her gun, and it reminded me that I had left my Colt in the car since it was unlicensed. They waited for us; they weren't going anywhere. Annie's expression was about as ugly as that of a spitting cobra before it strikes.

'Goddamn you, Dunn. Why did you have to stick your nose in all this? How much do they pay you for sneaking around, harassing people? That was you on the phone, I knew it was. Asshole.'

Frankie played it coolly. 'Murder in the first degree, accessory to murder, accessory to commit kidnapping, criminal conspiracy— '

'Fuck you, lady. I'm sick of you, too.'

Sylvia, like any good attorney, argued her own specious case calmly. 'Just a minute. Who conspired to do what with whom?'

I sat down heavily on an overturned dinghy. We were just starting and already I was sick of the maneuvering, the true parts of the stories as much as the lies and evasions, but mostly of all the wasted passion. Waste. That's what bothered me the most. A bunch of bored, wealthy women playing loose with what would have been desperately serious to anyone else. Capricious, without meaning . . . Jesus. At least Amelia, who I was convinced had nothing to do with the violence, had felt lousy about it.

I tried not to sigh or sound too heavy-weighted; Sylvia would take advantage of that. 'Annie, we got a lot on,' I told her. 'You'll take some work.'

'Well, thank God for small favors. Too bad you don't have any of the kidnappers.'

The moon came out for a while, painting the whole beach, which seemed like the whole world at the moment, in a luminescence that heightened expressions.

Frankie got right in their faces. With Sylvia she almost snarled, 'We've got a tape of her calling you right after we left her apartment that first time. Using the name "Blair." Pretty damn stupid, wouldn't you say?'

Sylvia began to pace; I noticed she was in her bare feet. Feet are ugly; Sylvia's weren't. Her head was down, serious, calculating. 'Look, I admit to knowing this woman socially. From a long ways back. But all it is, I came here tonight to meet her to ask her to leave my husband alone. Whatever she's done of a criminal nature, I have no idea.'

I laughed, one that sounded more like a bark, but she just gave me a taunting smile.

Annie was another matter, standing there straight up as if she was on parade, every muscle drawn tight, her fists clenched down by her sides. She was a little behind, but beginning to catch on, and she didn't like it. 'What do you mean?' she demanded of Sylvia. 'What are you saying?'

'It's what they're saying.' She made her oval eyes somehow round and hugely innocent. 'That you were involved in my husband's kidnapping. And Lord knows what else.'

'Sylvia, my God.' She was literally speechless for a moment. 'We love each other.'

Sylvia gave a flip of her hand, turning her back dramatically. 'Your taste, darling, not mine.' To Frankie and me, she added, 'I might indulge it now and then but I'm not all that "bi," frankly.'

Annie made a sudden move to reach her, grabbing her hand. Sylvia jerked it away and lit a cigarette.

'Don't do this, Syl. Please, I beg you. Whatever happens to us, we can get through it together. We'll— '

Sylvia cut her dead, speaking rapidly to me. 'I knew she had this inclination. I kissed her out of pity. But obviously I wouldn't do anything to hurt my own husband. I love James, and I know that despite his affair with her he loves me too.'

I gave her some slow, sarcastic applause. She didn't care; she was establishing the record; it didn't matter that we wouldn't believe a word of it. Besides, we might be wired.

Annie was beginning to sound stricken, breathing hard,

hand gestures quick and brittle as birds, panic edging in on the eyes. You could see her winding tighter and tighter. 'My God, how can you?' she railed at Sylvia. 'I can't fucking believe this! I can't!'

'I can,' Frankie said, disgusted.

I addressed the two of them, raising my voice because the surf seemed to have grown more powerful in the last few minutes. It could have been illusory, the swell of emotions. I wanted to know about Amelia.

'Why do you care about that?' Sylvia wondered.

'She was one of you, wasn't she?'

Annie did everything but spit. 'That cow. With all that stupid Catholic schoolgirl shit, that silly guilt. She made me sick to my stomach.'

Airily, Sylvia said, 'That's funny. You always said she had such beautiful tits.' Annie didn't know what to do; she gaped at her in horror.

In the same tone, Sylvia turned back to us. 'All right, so we fooled around a little. Big deal these days. If you told our husbands they'd be pissed because we didn't let them watch. Or maybe we did, for all you know. But you could put this in 'The Shiny Sheet' and everybody would yawn. After the Pulitzer scandal they'd find it tame. Didn't even use a trumpet.' She looked at me shyly, sucking me in involuntarily. 'Or a trombone.'

I shook my head, the way you do at an irrepressible child.

Very softly and, we should have recognized, menacingly, Annie muttered, 'You heartless bitch. You lied . . . you never cared about me at all . . .'

Sylvia ignored her. She turned, for the first time specifically to Frankie as the officer in charge. 'May I go now? Or do you have a warrant? Because as far as I can see, I'm guilty of kissing a needy woman on a beach and some other minor transgressions.'

Frankie gave her the death stare for a minute, but that

was for herself; she had nothing. Maybe Annie could be broken in the station – there was plenty to take her in on – but more likely when she calmed down she'd just ask for a lawyer and go home. Frankie broke her stare and admitted to Sylvia, 'I don't have enough to hold you. For now.' Cops always add that 'for now' because, like anybody, they hate to lose.

We would have lost, except that Sylvia for some perverse reason felt that she had to add, 'The slightest suggestion that because we played submarine it involves me in any of the crimes that have happened in our family will be met promptly with legal action. Clear?'

It was so awesomely arrogant we both, Frankie and I, looked at her with wonder.

Annie began screaming, and there was no problem in hearing her above the surf; the hysteria would have cut through steel plating. 'Goddamn you, you lying cunt. You can't fuck me over. I did everything for you. I loved you! I loved you!' The last was a truly agonizing wail carried off by a sympathetic wind.

With that she whipped out the Mauser I had seen that morning and aimed it at Sylvia. It was my fault. I should have mentioned it to Frankie, but too many things had been going down. Should Frankie have had her own gun out? You don't approach two conceivably guilty society ladies the same way you respond to a '211 in progress.'

The women did what comes naturally, even to ordinary citizens these days, throwing themselves on to the sand. In fact, I think Sylvia hit it first, always the survivor, although she did scream and that was music.

Annie capped off two rounds that I swear to this day I could hear whistling over our heads. I don't know if it was her madness, the dark or artful dodging that saved Sylvia's life, but it made you question God.

I was slightly behind the shooter, starting to rise from where I'd been sitting when the rounds went off, so, not quite upright, I put one foot back on the boat and catapulted myself at her – there wasn't any time for a run. I was practically horizontal by the time I reached out for her. I sensed even in the millisecond available that I wouldn't quite get to her the way I wanted, but I did form a fist and hit her on the back of her shoulder, blind-siding her and knocking her off her feet. The gun barrel, flung backwards, clipped my head, opening the scalp.

She gave a sob and went sprawling but rolled and scrambled back up faster than anyone I'd ever seen in hand-to-hand combat. Her physicality was astounding. And she still held the gun.

Frankie had struggled to dig hers out from under her body when she fell, but she came up with less speed and never got the pistol quite level or the safety off. Like I said, this was all in fragments of seconds; it also felt like fragments of my brain were spinning off some runaway merry-go-round inside my skull – flashes, screams, forms gyrating, plummeting, and that little gun sounding like a damned cannon.

Now Annie looked crazier than ever, with sand in her hair and on her face, her eyes rolling like a mad dog and the quivering barrel of the gun bobbing all over. First, at Frankie. I knew Frankie would never give up her own but I prayed she would be alert enough at least to hold it down by her side, and she did. Along with the head blow, the air had been knocked out of my lungs when I hit the sand, so I was no immediate threat. Annie quickly moved to where she had all three of us in her field of fire.

It was this awful puppet show for a moment, where the gun muzzle jerked from Frankie to Sylvia and back, and back again like a berserk compass. There was no telling who she'd kill; she didn't know herself.

Sylvia rose slowly to stand looking straight at her. 'Annie, please, darling . . . you don't understand.' Unfortunately, Annie understood only too well.

There were great glistening tears of rage in Annie's eyes that could be seen in the moonlight. 'You never cared about me, did you? You lied! God, how could I let you? I knew better, I lived that life myself. Until it was all taken away from me. You treat people like shit . . .'

Self-pity is the last thing you want from someone holding a loaded gun. I stood too, careful not to alarm her but determined to be positioned for another charge if it looked like we were going to die. In another spasm, a move so rapid it was a blur, she whipped the barrel of the gun around to point at her temple.

The unexpected paralyzed us all again, but only for a moment. Frankie the cop started moving slowly toward her, little miniature steps, with one hand outstretched and, given the window provided, her own gun now level and pointed.

Her voice was as soothing as a nun's. 'Mrs Robertson – Annie – give me the gun. Please. You don't want to do that. Whatever you've done . . .'

Annie's answer was to yank the gun away from her own head and point it directly into Frankie's oncoming face. Why Frankie didn't shoot her in the course of its arc I'll never know, but she seemed to sense that if anyone got shot it wouldn't be her. And she had a lot of practical reasons for wanting to see that this whole thing ended peaceably. If it had been me, I would have shot her seven times before she hit the ground. I'm glad it was Frankie.

There they were, the two of them pointing pistols into each other's eyes. Frankie's hand, when I looked, was as steady as iron, and I thought that her face in its life-or-death concentration was a thing of remarkable purity. It was beautiful. Annie's hand vibrated enough to shake loose a round. I was amazed to find that I was more scared than if it had been aimed at me.

'Give it up,' Frankie said in a much more unforgiving voice.

Annie jerked it back to her own temple, where it still trembled, steel against flesh. Frankie had a moment of confusion. She wasn't alone.

Annie asked, 'What are you going to do? Shoot me?' She laughed, but it wasn't encouraging.

'Please, listen to me . . .'

'Let her,' I said.

Frankie shouted at me without ever taking her eyes off her quarry. 'You stay out of it!'

I'll never be sure, but I always thought Annie Robertson looked at me gratefully then.

In just another of our series of mistakes, Sylvia decided to get into it and put on her nurse mask. 'Please, Annie, don't. I'll help you. I promise I'll— '

Annie screamed over her, 'Shut up!' But then a remarkable transformation came over her. She smiled slowly and in an eerily calm voice said, 'This one's for you, Syl.' She pulled the trigger and exploded brains out of the other side of her head. The body was thrust violently sideways and toppled as if blown over by a great gust of wind. Sylvia screamed and Frankie let out a cry. Annie lay still in that distinctive unreal bundle that marks any fallen corpse.

Frankie rushed to kneel over her, pleading with someone or something. 'Oh, God, she did it! Oh, Christ . . .!' She started in feeling the carotid, examining the wound, trying to get a verbal response. The only sound was the labored expiration of breath. Quickly she started CPR.

I helped Sylvia, who had dropped again at the sound of the gunshot, back up to her feet. She was sniffling.

'Is she dead?'

'Yeah.'

I moved to where Frankie was laboring frantically to bring forth signs of life. Standing over her, I said as gently as I could, 'Frankie?' and reached down to touch her shoulder.

She stopped for a second, looked up and yelled, 'Call for an ambulance, for God's sake! Do something!'

'She's gone.'

'No!' She bent over again and tried mouth-to-mouth resuscitation. That can be pretty ugly in a losing cause.

I watched, letting her play herself out, and finally leaned down to urge again that she give it up. 'C'mon, Frankie.'

She jerked away from me, gasping for air. Finally, in fragments, she spat out, 'How . . . could you say . . . "let her"?'

'It's what she wanted.'

'That's it? You didn't want me to do *any*thing?'

'Sometimes you hold their hands.'

Frankie looked down to find that that was what she was doing. When it became apparent that it was a lifeless hand, she let it slip away. Standing, pulling herself together physically and mentally, she spoke in a firmer voice. 'I'll get somebody out here!' She looked hard at Sylvia. 'You better goddamned well be here when I get back, lady,' and she stalked off up the beach and into the trees.

Sylvia, still wiping away the tears, gave me that 'Thank God she's gone' look. I moved her over to the boat and sat her down, crouching on the sand in front of her. She accepted some extra Kleenex.

Waiting for her to expend her grief, I looked around. Distant lights blinking up and down the coast but on the whole very dark, and the surf booming by now. I felt the isolation but was grateful for it. No one had heard the shots, no one had come.

I was suddenly aware that Sylvia was standing again and turned back. 'Stand still,' she ordered, and began to run her hands over my clothes.

'What the hell are you doing?'

'You want to hear from me, don't you? You might have a recording device.'

'Jesus H. Christ.' I just stood there. She knelt and ran

313

her hands up both legs and over my genitals, giving them
a little extra squeeze without the remotest indication of
frivolity. I didn't know what it meant.

'You're bleeding,' she told me, looking at my face.
'A lot.'

'It's okay.'

'It becomes you.'

Finally, satisfied, she sat again and immediately resumed
her previous attitude of distress right down to the sagging
shoulders and clasped hands. Every good deception begins
with self-deception.

'I didn't want anything like that,' she said.

'You were willing to let her dance the dance for you.'

'It *was* her all the way. I swear to God, Sean. I didn't
know until she told me the day after Jim was taken. I begged
her to let him go, but she swore it was out of her hands. I
think she realized by then she'd created a Frankenstein.'

'You didn't turn her in.'

'She said they'd kill him.'

'And you didn't want that?'

She flared convincingly. 'Of course not! What's wrong
with you?'

'Someone did. Are you trying to tell me you never even
suspected she was into something like this? Pillow talk?'

'No, absolutely.'

I didn't believe her but I waited. She lit another cigarette,
vamping while she decided exactly how much she should
tell me. Intelligent, she would understand that it had to be
most of it.

A little chuckle of dismissal announced the decision.
'Okay . . . we joked about it a couple of times. Kidnapping,
I mean. Nothing about hurting anyone. Jim was ruining all
of us financially and if he was out of the way for a while
others could step in. The publicity would guarantee that
certain facts about the company would have to be faced.
Then there was the considerable insurance on kidnapping.

We were all short of cash. But it was just a fantasy. Girls' night out, shootin' the shit. Tell you the truth, we were stoned. Except weirdo Amelia who didn't use, actually, but was throwing down the vodka like it was Evian. I'd never agree to something that crazy. You know I'm not stupid, Sean.'

'Sometimes "reckless" comes to the same thing.'

She looked up at the clouds. Increased spray or a light shower was dampening us. Sylvia murmured, 'It's all right,' to some imagined gallantry, because I had no intention of suggesting we move.

'We don't have much time. I want to know about Amelia. Your version.'

'Sweetheart, my version will be the only version. But I swear to you, she wasn't really involved. Except of course she was part of the joking around. Only she said why couldn't it be her lame husband we did dirty. And who can blame her? But she never knew Annie well enough to know she'd actually do it.'

'You did.'

She simply ignored me and plunged on. 'She must have been really spooked when she found out. From me, actually, two or three days after. Which wasn't the brightest thing I ever did. Right away, she started to suffer the creeping guilts. It seemed like she'd rediscovered this deep vein, this Sicilian thing about the wages of sin. If you ask me, all of her life everyone told her what to do, including marry my geeky brother-in-law, and when all this crap spun out of control she just couldn't handle it.'

'Did you like her?'

She shrugged. 'In the sack. As someone to sit around and trash husbands with. Or in Annie's case, all men. Not much, though. She was so different from the rest of us.'

'So Annie's the one?'

'Believe me, she went out and got that Irish thug all on her own. She told me it was only supposed to be for the ten million but he immediately decided to add a zero, so the whole thing was fucked from the beginning. I doubt these Neanderthals had any idea how much money that was, how big it would get. Greedy and stupid.'

'Why fake his death?'

'Desperation. They were improvising, they weren't getting ransom, so I guess they thought I'd be grateful if they made me a wealthy widow. Of course, Annie'd told them I was part of it to suck them in. But I never even got that picture they took, because they freaked first and let him go.' It was amazing the enthusiasm she showed for the storytelling.

This time I told her I didn't believe her. Annie wanted him dead. Unfortunately for her she chose a pretty blunt instrument. 'I think you put her up to it from the beginning. Only you never understood that while it was business with you, it was love with her. She wanted you – Jim was in the way.'

'Really? Is that what happened?'

'I think it went like this. You sent her looking for an itinerant hardboy, and she thought of the fair. The fatal flaw in Annie is, out of contempt, she has no discernment about men. Because she's willing to fuck a warthog, she gets one for the job. He's happy, he's got this classy babe wearing it down to a toothpick, and the job itself must have looked like a walk in the sun. She knew when Jim'd be coming and by what deserted route. Killing Freddo . . . well, chalk that up to the "fog of war." Nothing is predictable.

'So they got Jim and the first thing they do is screw up the ransom. Then you get on the tube with the expensive suits and say no way we pay. Nobody ever does that, so they're confused and start chewing on each other. Annie tells them, okay, the wife will pay you just to kill him. I believe you on that, it's her idea. But, anyway, these losers try to do what all losers do, have it every which way.

They're afraid to really kill him because they're discovering how big this thing is getting. And if pretending to kill him somehow doesn't pay off, then maybe not killing him will. In other words, by now they're dependent on the kindness of strangers. And by now you're the only one enjoying the game.'

She gave me a bored look and actually glanced at her watch, as if she had another appointment to ruin other lives somewhere. 'Think what you want, darling. As usual, it's irrelevant.'

'Loftus kill Amelia?'

'He'll get credit for it, but no. Annie is – was – terribly strong. That's what I found so attractive. But I was horrified when she told me just now. It was . . . so . . . out of control. I do understand dear Amelia was prepared to blab everything about us, and even things God doesn't know, to you, but changed her mind. Do you happen to know why?'

I shook my head. Didn't matter.

She looked off, trying to fathom. 'It's funny. Annie was almost proud of killing her. Doing it herself. What could I do, though? If I went to the police and she went down, she'd be sitting in some courtroom under bright lights surrounded by tabloid scum. Even if they couldn't involve me in the crimes, we'd still become the breakfast food of choice for two hundred and fifty million Americans, and that was a bit much.' She glanced at the corpse, beginning to glisten in the rain. 'I won't say I'm sorry she can't do that now. Are you finished?'

'There's your shooting of Loftus.'

She sighed and wiped the damp hair from her face. 'God. Okay, Annie called and said if we didn't pay him something he'd find a way to screw us, like write anonymous letters to the DA or something. I didn't think he was that smart. But I agreed to meet him.'

'You're telling me you were going to start paying blackmail?'

She didn't want to answer, so she simply ignored it. 'Naturally I had to take a gun because he was such a loose cannon. I was afraid of him. As it turned out, correctly.'

'He should have been afraid of you.'

She stretched languorously. 'I'm not worried now. It'll come out all right.'

'Even with your old man?'

'Even with my "old man." You'd be surprised how much he knows already.'

No I wouldn't. 'And if I should testify about what you just told me?'

'Sean, dear, Fred Flintstone could impeach your testimony. Anyway . . .' Her face coming very close to mine. '. . . you wouldn't.' She pressed her lips to my mouth, working it, moving, her tongue trying and eventually pushing past my teeth. Basically, I just let it happen. She moved back and I could see the confusion in her eyes.

We stayed close and I very gently touched her mouth with two fingers, whispering, 'Cold in there. You've got death in there, Syl.'

She slapped my face, but not very hard, without conviction. I stood and brushed off the wet sand.

Frankie reappeared, looking at us with suspicion. As well she might. 'What's happening here?'

To Sylvia I said, 'Don't upset her. She thinks the world's fixable.'

Sylvia knew exactly what I meant but it left Frankie out. She never would understand my way of dealing with the abyss, and snapped, 'You patronizing sonofabitch.'

Consistent to the end, Sylvia acted as though Frankie wasn't even there. 'What do you think, Sean? Is it?'

'Probably not,' I said, starting up the beach toward my car. 'But worth a try now and then.'

It took Frankie a moment to catch on. 'Hey, where the hell do you think you're going?' I didn't answer; I didn't know what to tell her. 'Goddammit, Dunn, I'll put your ass under arrest. Come back here!'

Without looking, I called back through the rain, 'What are you going to do? Shoot me?' Maybe it was the pain of hearing that repeated, but she gave up then.

XIX

I drove like a lunatic to Palm Beach. I don't know what I thought I was accomplishing by that but it was my unshakable mood. Thank God no cop tried to stop me; I had come to be that unsocialized. I got my pistol out of the glove compartment and stuck it under my jacket in the waistband.

Chapelle had been out earlier and was still dressed in half of a seersucker suit, watching television in the library. I just told him he was coming with me and I suppose my demeanor carried the day. I can only imagine what my face looked like. Never a lovely sight under the best of circumstances, I've been told it can appear cruel and now it had blood all over it. He could hardly miss it but he never commented on it.

Leading the way at a rapid pace from the house to the Jeep, I didn't realize I'd been mumbling until he said, 'What do you mean, it's not over? What's not over?'

I got into the car and started the engine.

Climbing in beside me, he asked, 'Is it Sylvia? Is she okay?' I was wishing Frankie was there to hear.

'That'll be the day when she isn't.'

I burned rubber taking off. It threw him back against the seat with a grunt. He got the idea and buckled up fast.

'You're being very cryptic,' he shouted as we roared down the driveway toward the gate.

I was thinking, They better have the goddamned thing open. 'That's because I don't feel like talking.'

After that he seemed to accept the idea I was on a mission and it would be best to go along for the moment. We went straight across West Palm on Okeechobee Boulevard and out the 710 into the 'Glades. When I started pulling on to increasingly small and isolated roads you could feel his anxiety grow like a living presence.

I was still pushing it, kicking up gravel and mud that banged against the windshield. After a while there wasn't a light to be seen and the only sounds were from the swamp and an occasional plane headed for the little Tamiami Airport down south. I saw a level area beside the road and hit the brakes hard, skidding in the sandy soil before yawing to a stop. Steam rose from the ground around us. For a moment we both sat there, just us and the wild animals.

'Okay, what's this about?'

I admired his self-control; by now he had to sense danger or even feel he was in the hands of a madman. It was only his inborn arrogance that was sustaining him. I'm sure no employee had ever harmed a Chapelle. Some might have given their lives for their masters, as Freddo had.

'Frankie Bodo,' I told him, looking straight into his soul. I believe I sought a sensibility there that might have spared us both.

'Ah. You like her, don't you?'

'Not the point.'

'Oh, I think it probably is.'

You could see where he was going and I would have none of it. No civilized chit-chat, no over-cocktails sharing-out of spoils between gentlemen – that was one thing I'd never been. I told him flat out, 'It's not. Frankie doesn't give a shit about me and never will. Okay?'

He grinned, insisting on his own terms. 'Just trying to be civilized.'

'Why did you have to pick her? She's got nothing to do with you people.'

'You're a little out of line here, aren't you, Sean? I think we'd better go back.'

'The only way you'd go back right now is dead. Answer the question.'

I'll give him credit, I had shocked him, but he didn't panic, didn't bluster or issue demands. He had always treated me as a serious man. And now he had bought some time.

After a while, he said, 'God, I had no idea what a thing you had for her. Syl told me you did and she's always right about matters of the heart. I should have listened. If I had I wouldn't have driven you to this point where you're so reckless. I think we should both just forget this and go home, don't you? Someday we'll laugh about it over drinks.'

Whatever showed on my face, I could tell from the way he wound down that he knew I wasn't buying it. I just sat there and stared at him, trying to figure him, his whole race, and keep my priorities in order. Killing him was on the list.

He tried smiling again but ruined it by speaking too rapidly. Chapelle was never rapid about anything and the charm pulsed away like blood from an artery. Likewise, in trying to assume a very reasonable tone, his voice caught on something and wavered. Yet he plunged gamely on.

'Look, I don't blame you for liking her. She's a good-looking young woman with a good body and a certain . . . attraction. All I ask is you be a little patient, because I like her too. I really do, and I can give her things. But it won't go on for ever, you know that— '

I hit him in the face, wrist straight, shoulder behind it, remarkably powerful considering the cramped quarters and awkward angle involved. He made a sickly sound as his head hit the side window. I had missed the nose but blood flowed from his cut cheek and stained his shirt. Amazingly, he made no attempt to struggle but took it and sat there. He was in good physical condition and no coward, so I've always believed he knew from the start what this was really about.

'Christ, I'm bleeding. What do you think you're doing? Shit!' His eyes were unfocused and he seemed groggy.

My anger was so out of hand I didn't care. Jumping out, I ran around to the other side, threw open the door and dragged him out by the collar like a recalcitrant dog. I screamed in his face, 'She's your daughter!'

His mouth gaped open and shut like a fish; I'm reasonably sure he'd never been handled this way in his life. Gasping, he managed to spit out that this was crazy, I had completely lost it . . .

'The maid you knocked up in college was her mother!'

'We paid her a lot of money. We offered to get her an abortion.' These were not smart things to say but he was beyond that. No cunning now, just instincts, and these were sick from inbreeding.

I forced him to his knees in the mud, pulled the pistol and pressed it against his forehead. At that instant I had no idea what I would do with him.

He pleaded. 'Don't! Oh, God, don't . . . please . . . Sean, no!' But I wasn't there for that kind of satisfaction.

I could feel him shaking in my hands. 'Listen to me, you degenerate sonofabitch. This time it's not going to be some fucking game where you make up the rules and change them when you want. If you ever see her again, or *ever tell her who you are*, I'll fucking kill you.' He nodded like someone having a fit, but only a gurgling sound came out of his mouth. I leaned down close to his ear and whispered, 'Nothing in the world will keep you from me.' Then I screamed, 'Do you understand me?'

I let go and looked down at him without recognizing the man I'd known all those years. He was dirty, blood-covered, whimpering as he slumped to the ground without dignity or grace.

'Yes . . . yes, I swear . . . I will . . .'

Panting, my chest heaving, I had to separate myself physically and turned my back. That helped; the rage was ratcheting down to disgust. Unwilling even to speak to him, I was addressing the black expanse of the Everglades when I said, 'You knew all the time. And you liked it.' I rubbed my face; I was tired, by God.

I never found out how Chapelle explained the damage he sustained, physically or emotionally. In the wee hours I went over to the Sheriff's station and gave them my statement. I didn't see Frankie. Owen took it and he wasn't talking much. He did tell me that Sylvia in her statement maintained that Frankie and I had saved her life from a jealous, crazed woman who had been having an affair with her husband. What else could you do but laugh?

The hurricane, as hurricanes will, didn't come in when expected but danced the gavotte over some other poor souls out in the Caribbean for a couple of days, teasing us. My boss, who's not dumb about human frailty, sensed the rottenness at the core of the solution to this case, so he wanted me out of town and away from the media. I went down to the Keys and read and fished, usually at the same time.

The storm, it was named Esperanza, had been waiting for me to get comfortable and now made another run at us. All the summer soldiers like me were emptied out of the islands in hours. The natives yawned and ordered another tequila.

Frankie, all alone on that expansive white stretch of beach, was a strange, almost eerie sight. Like one of those Boudin paintings, it gave you a feeling of unease, as if there was something you didn't know that had brought this isolation about.

Esperanza could have provided that on her own; she sat offshore pointing a finger at us, teasing us with a deceptive calm. The line of clouds on the horizon formed a sharp black line, like a hard-edged painting or an approaching tornado in the plains states. Yet walking over to where Frankie was lying face down on a blanket, I was swathed in

JAMES DAVID BUCHANAN

a pellucid sunshine, the breeze was gentle, barely touching
the cheek, rattling a few dry palms, the sky overhead its
usual innocent blue.

I don't know if she saw me coming, but I knelt beside
her and she gave no sign. I was wearing the same jeans
and sneakers as the first time we met, but she was in a very
small bikini. Not trying to be sexy – there was nothing to be
sexy about – but simply because that's what she had. I felt
her nakedness far more than she, oddly. Maybe because I
remembered Chapelle saying that she had 'a good body.'

'Hurricane out there.' She didn't say anything. 'I like
hurricanes.'

She still failed even to recognize my presence.

'You know you're out of uniform?' I never told her that
I had seen her in the red dress.

'How'd you know I was here?'

'Owen.'

She had a copy of 'The Shiny Sheet' on the blanket and
shoved it over to me without looking. When I picked it up
it was already folded back to a photo of the Chapelles at
a courthouse press conference, his arm around her. The
accompanying story said she was prepared to forgive him
for the affair and its dire consequences. As soon as the
legalities were cleared away they hoped to set off on a
tour of several continents on behalf of the World Wildlife
Fund. You didn't have to read any further than that.

'You warned me,' came from her buried head.

'Hell, I was warning myself.'

'He won't even answer my calls.'

'I'm sorry.'

She rolled over on to her back and raised herself on one
elbow, shielding her eyes from the sun. 'The Sheriff was
so relieved I couldn't make a case against her he gave me
the week off.'

'You were an embarrassment. We both are – I got sent
to the Keys for the last couple days.'

326

'My gut feels like I swallowed hot coals. I want her so bad it's killing me.'

'I know.'

'Do you?'

'I'm quitting my job.'

She sat all the way up and looked into my face. 'How come?' She sounded unconvinced.

I must have developed the thousand-yard stare at that point. I know I was absent from that beach for a while and had to struggle to pull myself back.

'A few years ago the Chapelles kept an apartment in Miami on Brickell. They like the whole Cuban-Hispanic thing down there. You know – sex, drugs and salsa. That part of it, anyway. Sylvia got into S & M with some twisted bastard, some jive-ass petty dealer, and it got pretty rough. Too much "S" and not enough "M" on his part. He hurt her. Badly. She called Jim, where he was probably doing something equally exotic— '

She waved a hand. 'Don't! Please . . .'

'I'm sorry. I have to. It's important you know.' She didn't reply and I took that as permission. 'What happened, Jim came over and killed him. Shot him.'

'Oh, my God . . .'

'Or maybe she did. We'll never know. The point is, he called someone and it worked its way down to my captain. Which is another way of saying nobody wanted to touch it. But I'd met the Chapelles so it landed on me. I was to go over and take care of it. I did.'

'How?'

'The Italians would say the victim – if you want to call him that – "he sleeps with the fishes." Biscayne Bay. It was messy.' I hesitated about telling her the rest but I'd come this far. 'He was shot in the mouth and eye. But somebody had also cut off his cock.'

I waited to see how she'd handle it. I should have known she wouldn't. Couldn't, had to turn it on me. 'God, that's so lame, Dunn. Just because your captain ordered you to do something illegal, you didn't have to do it.'

'He didn't order me, he asked me.'

'And you liked that he was polite?'

'This was the guy whose legs I'd crushed a few months before. He walks with a cane.'

'So you had to blow your whole career. Great!'

'Actually, no one ever found out. I resigned.'

She found that even more incomprehensible. Even righteous cops understand you have to get away with some things to survive.

'It just didn't feel right any more. You take an oath . . .'

'All of a sudden you got this big conscience. You worked for *them*.' Her face pushed very close to challenge me, furious; I thought she might strike out. 'And you fucked her, too, didn't you, Dunn? She always owned you. All that bullshit about how you hated them meant nothing. What a huge goddamn fake you are.'

I let her run on and when it was silent I admitted, 'I did a lot of things, Frankie.' It was my turn to look hard at her. 'You really want to hear?'

She thought it over. 'No. No, I'm a great one to talk.' Sinking back, her voice becoming slight, she told me she was sorry. 'I'm really touched you told me. I was just giving you a hard time because I feel so shitty myself.'

I realized that her eyes held tears. Suddenly she put her arms around me and hid her face between my neck and shoulder.

'Oh, Sean, I'm so ashamed.'

I hugged and rocked her. 'It's all right. That's what separates us from them.'

Holding her, I looked past her for the storm. It hadn't moved that I could tell, just hung there, hiding its purpose like a black shroud over some evil. There was only a tightening of the air, a slight whistle in the wind and the absence of birds to excite our senses. We still had time.